Curse of Seduction

Princes of Purgatory 1

Contact Information:

CRRobertson-author@hotmail.com

www.CRRobertson.com

https://geni.us/RobertsonsOtherworld
https://www.facebook.com/CRRobertsonauthor/
Publication Date: 21st June 2020
Cover Artist: EmCat Designs

Thank you so much for reading my eBook. I really hope the characters touch your soul, and make your mind wander to a different realm for a few hours. If you enjoy *Curse of Seduction*, please consider leaving a review and have a look at my other paranormal romance novels.

Books by CR Robertson

The Otherworld Chronicles:

The Gates of Hell Trilogy:

1 – Elements of Flames
2 – Elements of Dragons
3 – Elements of Fae
***
4 – Elements of Karma
5 – Elements of Light
6 – Elements of Souls
7 – Elements of Redemption

The Gaian Otherworld:

1 – Dragons of Destiny
2 – Dragons of Fate
3 – Dragons of Chaos
4- Dragons of Retribution

A Note on Language

Please note CR Robertson is from the UK.
Therefore, spellings and some turns of phrase will appear in British English.

Dedication

This book is dedicated to every little girl who dreamed of her Prince Charming, and every woman who dreamed of her Dark Prince.

***

Prologue – Two hundred years ago…

Ezekiel

We climbed to the meeting place near the top of the foreboding cliff. The trail was narrow and winding, hugging us against the rockface.

Our fathers stood in the centre of a massive chamber that had facilitated neutral talks for countless generations. The wars in the demon realms for the past hundred years had been vicious, leaving our numbers depleted. Valek, Raegel, Lycidas, and I watched our fathers from the entrance, none of us aware of why we'd been summoned here. We were the crown princes of the four main demon races found in Purgatory.

The Blood Queen Ophelia paced on a raised platform at the back of the room, her dark eyes finally finding us. "They have arrived," she said in a breathy sigh.

The massive chamber vibrated around us in pulses of energy. My eyes met Valek and we both realised at the same time why we'd been recalled from our missions.

We were a sacrifice.

Our fathers were supposed to be brokering peace accords so our people could finally live again, find lost family members. We should have known a witch as dark and powerful as Ophelia would never want peace.

We were the crown princes of our people, our magic powerful and linked to the original source of magic for our species. Vampire, Lycan, Elven, and Incubus. To save themselves, our fathers had handed us over as sacrificial lambs.

Ophelia's power slammed into my body, forcing me to my knees.

"Ezekiel," she purred, standing over me. "You have intrigued me for so long. An incubus with a conscience." She bent down until her lips pressed against my ear. I struggled, but my limbs refused to move. "I will take from each of you. Your fathers think your fates will be swift, but I intend to make you my slaves. Each of you will feed me with power until there will be no one to stand in my way."

Each of my friends struggled beside me, every one of us trying to escape whatever fate had been agreed by our sires.

"I will consume the magic of each of your lineages until I control each of your realms." She pressed her lips on the sensitive skin behind my ear. I suppressed the shiver that wanted to run down my back. I would show no weakness to this witch.

My eyes widened as her lips brushed mine, her energy infusing into me as she sealed her curse with a kiss.

***

Chapter One

Ilana

I dragged the blood-soaked T-shirt and combat trousers off my body, throwing them in the bin. Nothing would ever remove the stench of gargoyle blood from them. My unit slowly made their way through debriefing and to the showers. Bruises peppered my flesh and I cursed when I saw the one on my shoulder. It would never heal in time for the feast this evening.

Blood ran down my body and pooled at my feet when I stepped into the shower. Slowly, the water began to run clear. Exhausted, I rested my head against the wall and let the water pound down on my back. The Blood Queen was relentless, every day forging forward into our realms. We fought, but how could anyone fight against a ghost who commanded an army of the dead?

Her gargoyles weren't much better.

I've been gone from base for over a month, and in that time, the battle had been relentless. Even my vampire healing and energy had been tested to the limit. A lot of good people had been lost out there defending the borders.

I slammed my fist against the wall and refused to let the tears that wanted to fall loose. We all knew the risks, every spare soul conscripted in to fight in an endless war.

Neutralising all my emotions, I wrapped my hair and body in towels and left the shower area, dragging my weary ass to my room. Attendance at feasts was mandatory, each person dressed to show their lineage. I was a vampire – human mother, vampire father. My half-breed kind had been sneered at until the army kept being depleted and they were grateful to take anyone they could use.

The feast was in full swing when I arrived, making my way to my unit's table. We were all dressed in skin-tight black leather, the insignia on our shoulders depicting our rank.

"Something's happening," Mia whispered furiously in my ear. She grabbed my hand and nodded to a table near the top of the room. "All four dark princes are here."

My heart almost stopped in my chest, stumbling over its beat. Every woman had that one man she'd give her left fang to spend a night with. Mine was Ezekiel, Prince of the Incubi. He was sex on legs. Black hair that permanently looked like he'd rolled out of bed. Dark chocolate brown eyes that seemed to suck all the air from your lungs when they landed on you. His powerful body was designed to be worshipped at the altar of pleasure.

I'd heard the stories about his sexploits. Mia and I witnessed a woman that stumbled out of his bedchamber barely able to stand. Her bright cheeks and faraway gaze made me want to force my way through the door and lie on his bed with my legs open.

"Breathe, Ilana," Mia said, squeezing my hand.

At that moment, his dark gaze penetrated the room as Valek spoke to him. His lips tipped up in a smile that made butterflies invade my stomach. For one second, his eyes met mine and I felt the full force of that gaze landing on me. It left me utterly breathless. As if he felt my reaction, his grin widened, showing dimples, before he averted his gaze.

"If I could choose my death, it would be with that man between my legs and me screaming his name," I muttered.

Mia giggled beside me. "He's hot, but I never understood your reaction to him. It's been years and no one can send you into a flap the way he does. I would understand it if you'd been lovers, but you just worship him from afar."

She was right. No one got anywhere near the dark princes without special permission. The women at their table were exceptionally beautiful, each one specifically chosen to be there. I'd never told anyone, but I bumped into him once a hundred years ago as we were all racing into battle.

Sensations exploded through my body, setting every nerve ending on fire. I felt the pain that lived inside him, the constant craving that clawed him raw. I knew that feeling; it was the same one that dwelt in me, demanding I sink my fangs in and drink deeply from the vein.

I fought that urge every day.

The human concubines entered the room, offering themselves to anyone who needed nourishment. My fangs dropped in my mouth even though I'd drunk a bag of blood before coming to the feast. I couldn't drink from the vein no matter how hard I'd tried in the past. Father had supplied dozens of blood slaves to tempt me. The result was normally me curled on the floor screaming as my insides ignited in pain.

I was two hundred years old and he'd spent most of that time in his laboratory trying to work out what was wrong with me. Mother always smiled her enigmatic smile, saying I was a hybrid and more like her than Father. He always shook his head at her, muttering about his race being superior. She was blood-linked to him, tethered to his long life. But their love made me a hybrid, and I would never be viewed as a full vampire.

Mia selected a tall, handsome blood slave, dragging him on her seat so she could straddle his hips and dig her fangs deep into his neck. Feeding from the vein always led to sex—it was inevitable when their blood pulsed through your veins. I averted my eyes, refusing to look at the debauchery at our table. The groans and moans were more than enough.

The incubi tables slowly began to empty as they selected their concubine for the evening. The only species eating food and drinking the strongest liquor they could find were the lycans and elves. No doubt they'd join one of the orgies later, but for now, they were satisfied eating and sharing battle stories.

Taking a slow breath, I scanned the room again. My eyes were captured by a dark and brooding gaze. Ezekiel studied me, his eyes flicking to the others at my table who happily gorged themselves on the blood slaves. His right eyebrow quirked briefly in silent question and I averted my eyes.

Feasts were mandatory or I would never attend them. Every one made me feel like the freak I was. The scent of fresh blood tempted me until my fangs bit into my bottom lip. I stood abruptly, my chair clattering to the floor as I stalked from the room.

At the last second, I felt a compulsion burning into my head. I turned around to see Ezekiel watching me, his head canted slightly to the side, a puzzled look on his face. The sensation in my chest exploded in a kaleidoscope of emotions that I couldn't identify. Something about the predatory look in his eyes made my stomach tighten and the hairs on the back of my neck stand on end.

I left the room on shaky legs with a thundering heartbeat. All night those eyes haunted me until I got no sleep.

The morning came too early, and I dragged my weary body down for the latest briefing. Mia bounced, the energy of her feeding still zinging through her veins. Her lover would probably still be sleeping as his body tried to make up the blood he lost.

"Morning." She stretched. "Where did you disappear to last night?"

I shrugged. "I got a better offer than spending the night with you!"

Her grin stretched her face. "What's his name?"

"I'm not telling you. A girl needs some secrets." I winked.

I always waited until my unit was in a feeding frenzy before I left. No one ever noticed me leaving without feeding until last night. The blood bags kept an edge off my hunger, but it was always there.

"Listen up," one of our commanders shouted as he strode onto the stage. "We have new orders. Intelligence suggests The Blood Queen is at the south border of the vampire realm. She hasn't been seen for decades until last week. The dark princes have arrived to oversee the mission. They'll be assessing everyone and setting up units consisting of all species for this attack. Training starts in the lower levels in one hour. You'll be assessed on your fighting skills, as well as your ability to work with the lycans, elves, and incubi. Do me proud."

Mia and I shared an uneasy look. We always fought among our own kind. Lycans were unpredictable and just as likely to tear one of their allies' limbs off in battle as one of the enemies. The elves were haughty and didn't share well with others. The incubi were the most secretive of all the species, rarely leaving their own borders or asking for help.

I grabbed a blood bag on the way down, piercing it with my fangs.

"That must have been some session last night if you still need blood," she remarked, her lips twitching.

"You have no idea." I bounced my eyebrows suggestively. She bumped her shoulder against mine.

Every day was a struggle to hide my truth. It was easier when we were in the field, as our only food source was bags of blood.

The next several hours were gruelling. I lost count of the number of times I got hit by every type of assailant. There wasn't enough room on my body for all these bruises. An overly ambitious lycan hit me from the side, sending me spinning through the air. My nails descended and I gripped the wall, my leg arcing back to kick him in the face. He growled, his temper rising as he launched himself at me, canines bared.

I pushed off the wall with my feet to soar over his head, as his muzzle elongated.

Fuck! He was fighting his change.

That was when the lycans were at their most deadly, their saliva toxic.

His claws scraped on the concrete floor as he spun to pursue me through the elaborate training maze.

Ah shit, lycans were relentless when they set their focus on a target. I quickened my pace, but his change was complete and he was on four legs as compared to my two. We rounded a corner and I felt the warmth of his breath on my neck, his canines trying to grab me.

Everything happened in slow motion. Heat exploded in my chest, a supernova that had never combusted before. My feet ran up the wall as my body contorted back to avoid his razor-sharp teeth. Light shot from my hands, sending him whimpering back. I scrambled onward, my breathing erratic and panic blooming in me.

What the fuck just happened?

I spent the rest of the day with dread twisting my stomach, waiting for the moment when my commander would have me dragged away for interrogation.

After dinner, we all trailed into the briefing room to receive our orders. Mia bounced up and down, delighted Valek had selected her for his team. She teased me about my obsession with Ezekiel, but she hero-worshipped our vampire prince.

"Open yours," she encouraged me.

There was no doubt in my head I would be sent back to normal duties. The card inside wasn't the usual crimson of the vampire realm. It was black. My brow furrowed as I read the golden script on it.

"I'm on Ezekiel's team," I said through numb lips.

He may be my ultimate fantasy, but he was ruthless in battle, taking risks that others would never consider.

My wide eyes found Mia's.

"Wow!" she mouthed before biting her bottom lip. "Please tell me he wasn't the stud between your legs last night."

Only in my dreams. Every single erotic dream belonged to him and him alone. My cheeks flared at the image of us tangled together.

"Don't be silly!" I rolled my eyes at her.

"Then why did he choose you?" she demanded.

I should be insulted, but instead, I was terrified. Why *did* he choose me? And why were there little tremors of excitement beating against the walls of my stomach? I'd probably never see him, but the little voice that guided me in battle and kept me safe whispered in my mind that I would…

***

Chapter Two

Ezekiel

I tossed my boot across the room and kicked the other in the same direction. My head was pounding with a headache that threatened to paralyse me with its intensity.

"Finished choosing your team?" Lycidas asked from where he sat beside the fire.

"Are you sure this is going to work?" I demanded, ignoring his question. I wouldn't be here if I hadn't completed my selection. Valek and Raegel hadn't arrived, so they were probably still deliberating.

He shrugged in reply.

I selected some of the best warriors, followed by the strategists, then the unfortunates who would end up being nothing more than chew toys for Ophelia's pets. There was no way she'd let us win. Any time we got anywhere close to hurting her, she tightened her grip on one of us until she regained her strength. The last episode left me nearly comatose for almost a year.

Lycidas watched in amusement as I dragged the ceremonial jacket off and threw it on a chair. He knew I hated dressing up, preferring to be in T-shirts and jeans. Raegel always got his elf ass is a twist and insisted everything needed to be done properly.

"I'd prefer if you kept your trousers on," Lycidas remarked, his eyebrow arched.

I rolled my shoulders in my T-shirt and flipped him the finger. "I'd take them off, only I know you'd get off on it."

He gave his usual wolfish grin. Human concepts of sexuality didn't exist in the demon realms. I never understood how humans decided they could only take pleasure from one gender. I was an incubus, pleasure was pleasure. We all had preferences, but it wouldn't stop me from taking what I needed or wanted. Brunettes were my favourite, but I wouldn't kick a redhead out of my bed just because they didn't conform to a type.

Valek kicked the door open and stomped in, his expression grim. "One of your mutts ripped a limb off one of my vampires. You need to start issuing leashes for your bitches," he snarled at Lycidas, pointing at him.

His eyebrows shot up at the tone Valek used, staring at him. "Tell your vampires to run faster."

Valek lurched forward, but my grasp hauled him back.

"They were pretty vicious out there today, Lyc," I agreed. One of them had pursued that vampire girl from last night who'd caught my attention. I was going to follow them and haul him off her, but instead, I found the mutt cowering in a corner whimpering. She went straight onto my list.

Lyc's fingers trailed through his unruly hair. "It's close to the full moon. I'll need to let them loose for a few days to get rid of excess energy so they can focus."

"And my vampire?" Valek demanded.

"It's not as if I can glue the arm back on, for fuck's sake!" Lyc threw his hands up at the end of his rant.

"Glad to see we're all being calm and talking like adults," Raegel snarked. He'd crept into the room with elf stealth. I hated when they did that.

Creepy fucker.

The rest of our group all turned in unison to glare at him.

We'd spent our youth together; were closer than brothers. Then Ophelia kissed each of us and cursed us. No one else in the demon realms knew what we endured except those in this room. Each of us cursed in a different way that fed that bitch, making her stronger. We'd tried everything to break her hold on us, but nothing had worked in two hundred years. Some days I was so exhausted it was hard to keep going.

I sank into a chair when I was sure Valek wasn't going to rip Lycidas' head off.

"Any more intel?" I asked, rubbing my hands over my eyes.

"None," Raegel confirmed. "I wonder why she's surfaced after all this time?"

"To torment some other poor sod," Lycidas snarled, his canines lengthening. He'd never forgiven his father for his part in the deception that had us cursed. They hadn't shared a word since. Lycidas ruled the lycan armies while his father sat in splendid isolation on the throne.

My head leaned into the back of the chair and I stared at the ceiling. "One of my scouts said he heard rumours that magic had reawakened. Maybe she's searching for her lost witches?"

Ophelia had absorbed all the magic she found into her, draining the realms in an effort to make herself queen over all of us. It wasn't enough, hence the curse to syphon magic from our species.

"I thought she'd killed them all," Valek replied.

"Some believe a handful of them escaped, cloaking their magic and biding their time." I rubbed my temples to try and stave off my hunger headache.

"You need to eat," Raegel said softly.

We all knew what that meant. I tried to ignore the cravings until the four equinoxes when I could feed without her curse activating. "I'm fine." I waved off his concern.

"No, you're not. We're going into battle soon and we need you strong," Raegel continued. "We all become slaves to her curse every so often."

I wished that wasn't true, but Ophelia had tied each of our curses to something unique to our heritage. I nodded absently, trying not to think about the monster I'd become.

That was why the vampire female intrigued me last night. We were the only two in that room who didn't feed at the feast. I knew why I couldn't, but why didn't she partake of the blood slaves on offer? A mystery always roused my interest.

"The curse grows stronger the longer we resist feeding it," Lycidas said despondently, trailing his fingers through his unruly hair. "I feel her hold on me like a leash dragging me to heel."

"Her dishonour will be her ultimate downfall," Raegel replied, staring at the flames leaping in the fire. "I feel it in the depths of my soul. You cannot leash a wild animal and think your will alone makes it tame."

The elves lived and breathed honour. Raegel's father trusted the peace accords were real. He became a recluse after that fateful day when our fathers watched The Blood Queen curse us.

"I look forward to draining the bitch dry," Valek snarled, his fangs flashing and eyes shining silver.

"May the great demon be merciful and grant us peace from her reign," I concluded.

We all raised a glass and drank a silent toast.

***

Pleasure danced down my spine all the way to my cock that was buried deep in one of the blood slaves. Her body arched as yet another orgasm ripped through her flesh, feeding me with her pleasure. My pelvis ground against hers as I finally found my release, allowing my body to fully integrate her sexual energy as the food I needed to survive.

Her mouth opened wide and her eyes rolled back in her head. Energy fired up my cock into my body in the ultimate high an incubus experienced when they fed.

"Oh, gods," she gasped, her body spasming out of control.

I felt the moment the curse activated. The Blood Queen stole something from the woman under me. Her precious memory flashed through my mind before it was lost to her forever, giving the witch what she craved.

I should feel full and strong, but knowing I'd been the reason the woman was changed after sex with me made me feel sick. It always changed them at a fundamental level.

At first, I never realised what my curse was. Our castle retained a harem for my brothers and I to use. Each of us had our favourites we fed from. Each memory or emotion stolen from those women added to the vacant look in their eyes until they were nothing more than a breathing corpse. Now, I rarely slept with someone more than once, trying not to risk their sanity.

The only exception when I could feed without damaging the host was during the four holy equinoxes. Those were the nights when Father hosted orgies so I could eat until I was overflowing with energy.

I rolled off the woman to stare at the ceiling with unseeing eyes. I felt her confusion as her memories were altered and changed. She stared down at her body, her brow furrowed as if she was trying to work out why she was here. It wasn't the first time this had happened. It was also why I preferred to use someone in a harem and walk away straight afterward. I couldn't do that now, as I was on a military base and she was in my room.

I hauled myself off the bed and stalked into the bathroom, hoping she'd be gone when I got back. The look on their faces was always a kick to my solar plexus.

Grabbing the sides of the sink, I stared at my reflection in disgust. The man staring back at me had a haunted look in his eyes, even though his cheeks were flushed from spending the past three hours fucking the blood slave in the next room senseless.

That was a quick session for an incubus. We could keep going for several days at a time when we delved into a feeding frenzy.

The sound of the door of my suite closing made my shoulders relax. At least she hadn't waited for an explanation. I loathed when they did that and I had to use my mind-altering ability to make them go away.

My transport unit would arrive in a few hours to take my new recruits to my training unit. Each of us would teach them to fight in different terrains with alternating techniques before launching our attack on The Blood Queen.

I turned the water on and doused my face before returning to the bedroom and throwing myself on the bed. The hunger that had been clawing at me was abated, but it sat heavily in me, giving me energetic indigestion.

Sleep evaded me as I lay in the darkness of the room. I couldn't remember the last time sex left me with that languid feeling of satisfaction that made you want to fall into a bliss-induced stupor.

Instead of lying there with my troubled thoughts, I dragged my ass down to the training area and took my frustration out on a punch bag. Every kick and blow landed was directed at The Blood Queen, the need to punish her overwhelming. Feeding from sexual pleasure was the basic fundamental aspect of an incubus—after all, we were sex demons. She didn't just steal from the women I slept with, she'd stolen part of my identity.

I kicked the bag with enough force to break it from its stand and send it flying across the room. My body bowed forward and I grabbed my knees. Two hundred years she'd loomed over me like a dark shadow. I didn't think I could bear another two hundred.

It would drive me insane.

***

Chapter Three

Ilana

If dreams were monitored, I'd probably be heading straight for obedience training right now. Ever since I received that black card with his name on it, I could think of nothing else but those deep brown eyes boring into my soul at the feast.

My dreams last night left me with a physical ache between my legs that demanded I find a partner to quench. Instead, I ran until my legs could barely hold me up.

I couldn't explain my attraction to the prince of the incubus realm. There was no reason why he had the effect on me he did. All I knew was that I'd dreamt about him before I met him, only finding out his identify when he arrived at the base I was assigned to years ago. Since then, he starred as my own personal fantasy.

Grabbing my equipment bag, I flung it over my shoulder and reported to my new unit. Each dark prince was taking us to their realm for intensive training. Mia was staying here in the vampire realm with Valek. I'd never visited another demon realm before, and my stomach somersaulted at the chance or an adventure.

Ezekiel strode into the clearing as huge, black dragons flew overhead, carrying large metal crates for us to travel in. I'd never seen a dragon before, my only experience in books. For their size, they were graceful in the sky. The ground shook as a crate landed, the wings of the dragon moving the air with so much power that we were nearly blown off our feet.

I watched in fascination as a massive dragon lowered its scale-covered head for Ezekiel to rub. He muttered in its ear and the three horns on its head twisted. I've never been so jealous of a lizard in my life.

One of the incubus commanders directed us into the transport units before the heavy metal door slammed behind us. My stomach lurched as massive talons, bigger than swords, grabbed the handle above us and swung the crate into the air. I grabbed a bar to steady myself, turning terrified eyes to another vampire girl beside me.

"I hear the elves use portals," she whispered.

"That sounds preferable," I replied with a tight smile.

The beast above us shrieked into the sky and the air around us heated as it blasted fire. The fact that we were trapped in a metal cage, one that reminded me of those barbeques the humans used to cook their food over flames, made me incredibly uneasy.

Another dragon flew alongside us and I noticed Ezekiel riding on its back. The current moved his hair and he closed his eyes as if lost in a world all on his own. I wanted to visit that world and run my fingers through his hair. Something about him shouted loneliness, and it resonated deep in my belly.

Only once had I confessed my obsession to my mother. She spiralled into a panic and ranted for two hours about how I needed to stay far away from all of the demon princes. The terror in her eyes scared me more than anything in this world, even battle on the front line of a war that seemed endless.

Her reaction alone kept me from ever being in the presence of any of the demon princes, even when the opportunity arose over the years. Valek was our prince, and from time to time he would select soldiers to share his bed. I'd deliberately made myself insignificant in the crowd, unattractive and unresponsive to his call.

Ezekiel was different, and now I was flying over the demon realms to his home.

The dreams last night were more vivid and intense than normal. I'd actually felt him moving inside me, his body sliding against mine. I woke up gasping and aroused. His proximity was playing havoc with my head.

Aunt Agatha was human and taught me the ways of her people. When I was conscripted into the vampire army, she'd made me promise never to share the lessons she engrained into me. None of the other vampires used them and so they lay dormant in my memories, only coming alive when I visited home.

She'd instructed me how to view auras and how to interpret what I saw. Standing in this transport crate, I lowered my defences and stared at Ezekiel until his came into focus. Like the time I'd bumped into him long ago, he was filled with pain. Regret and longing pulsed through his aura.

He turned suddenly in my direction as if sensing my gaze. Turning my head would have brought attention to myself, so I closed my eyes and pretended to be holding onto the bar. My pulse thundered in my ears and panic rose in my chest.

What was happening? No one had sensed me before when I took a peek at their emotions.

His dragon veered off course away from the rest of the unit, leaving me feeling vulnerable. I tightened my grip on the bars and rested my head against them as the dragons took us to our new residence. Mixed feelings churned deep in my stomach and I began to feel lost and alone so far from my home.

Many of our trees and foliage were deep crimson red in the vampire realm. The incubus realm seemed to be deep purple from overhead. It was as if someone changed the colour scheme as we moved from one realm to another. The energy changed as well. A deep, pulsating seductive beat resonated through the air, sending signals to the juncture between my thighs.

I glanced around uneasily and saw the rest of the people being transported were affected as well. Men tried to discretely rub their palms over bulges in their pants and women shifted uncomfortably.

"It's the primal pulse," a tall man near the back spoke. "This realm belongs to the sex demons. The king expects all his subjects to be in a constant state of semi-arousal. It means they are always ready to feed those in need of nourishment."

My eyebrows shot up. Vampires had sex when they fed from the vein because our saliva contained enzymes that caused extreme arousal. It was an accepted part of life. A bead of sweat trickled down my back as the pulse created an ache low in my stomach. I didn't know if I could cope with this seductive beat.

A groan sounded from one of the corners, followed by a moan. Someone had obviously succumbed to the energy.

The tall man smirked. "If you're already attracted to someone, the impulse will become overwhelming. The succubae and incubi are strong in this realm because they do not refuse themselves. The orgies are legendary, especially if the princes attend."

I guessed because they were known as the dark princes or the four horsemen, I tended to forget that there were more princes in the realms than the four crown princes who led the armies. The thought of more than one Ezekiel made me a little uneasy. My attraction to him was off the scale before I got here, and this pulse made cravings worse. I was totally fucked.

"I've never been with an incubus before," the female vampire beside me replied. "Can we feed from them?"

The man shrugged. "I don't know, but I'm an incubus and am willing to experiment if you are." His eyebrows bobbed up and down suggestively.

The connection between them almost shimmered in the air and I turned away as my enhanced sense of smell picked up on their arousal. Modesty was a word that didn't exist among the vampires and clearly that extended to the incubi as well. My teammates often had sex at the dinner table, so this conversation shouldn't surprise me.

He stalked her, pressing her against the bars beside me. More and more people around me lost their inhibitions and succumbed to the tribal beat designed to stoke our libidos.

"You can join in, too." The incubus trailed a hand down my back suggestively.

I shrugged him off and he chuckled.

"Everyone gives in in the end. Sex takes the edge off the desire before it pushes you into insanity." He returned to the vampire beside me, her moan making me cringe.

I never wanted to be the way I was. There was a woman inside me who wanted to throw caution to the wind and feed and fuck like the rest of the vampires in my unit. She needed to feel desired. Something was messed up in my make-up. I couldn't feed from the vein, and every time a man touched me sexually, I froze. My body rejected any form of physical contact. Something in me was defective.

I closed my eyes and pretended that the transport unit hadn't turned into a full-blown orgy around me.

My last visit home had coincided with my aunt arriving. She'd pressed me about relationships, lamenting at the lack of great nieces and nephews for her to spoil. Something snapped and I confided about my screwed-up system.

A slow smile had curved her lips. "Sometimes fate has plans we know nothing about. Chin up, little one, your time will soon arrive."

Humans were weird with their premonitions and strange rituals involving herbs and crystals. Mum and Aunt Agatha spent hours staring at crystals they'd tossed on the ground, throwing worried looks in my direction. Father's arrival home sent them into a frenzy of tidying when they saw his frown.

“Not in front of Ilana.” He sighed, pinching the bridge of his nose. He took me outside, away from their human customs to chat about my latest war stories.

At times like this I wished they’d tell me what was wrong with me. I knew I could feel desire, my dreams about Ezekiel proved that, but my greatest fear was that he’d touch me, and I’d freeze.

***

Chapter Four

Ezekiel

Remiel stood waiting for me in the castle courtyard, his normal smirk on his face.

"What are you doing here?" I sneered, hoping he'd go away and leave me alone. The ride into our realm had made me antsy and I didn't need him here to watch me.

He shrugged. "Waiting to see the fresh meat you're bringing for training. I'm bored with our concubines."

I gritted my teeth and swallowed a retort. These were soldiers arriving, not willing slaves for him to spend all day in bed with.

"The new recruits are here to train," I eventually bit out. "I don't need the complication of your cock getting in the way. Maybe if you actually went to the front line it might cool your ardour a little."

"And turn into a frigid bitch like you? No thanks!"

My fist bunched at my side. He hadn't lived with a curse for two hundred years. The dragons came into view and he rubbed his hands in glee at the smell of sex that arrived before them. My fist connected with his jaw to send him tumbling across the courtyard. He jumped up to get in my face, but our father strode out.

"That will be enough!" he barked out. "Remiel, leave your brother alone. He is the only thing keeping that witch from our borders."

Remiel slid a furious side-look in my direction, his tensed jaw telling me he wasn't happy.

The crates landed close to us with loud bangs. The scent of arousal and sex was overpowering. I knew the energy of our realm increased arousal, but could they not have waited until they found their rooms? Our dragons were going to be as horny as hell now, and when they decided to mate, they would be unavailable to fight for weeks, if not months.

"For fuck's sake," I muttered as one of the male dragons eyed up a small female, his forked tongue licking over his bottom lip. "Get these beasts into the dragonry," I commanded their keepers. "Before we have a war on our hands."

Soldiers stumbled from the transport crates, straightening their clothes, some of them searching for clothes. I rolled my eyes as Remiel grinned.

The female vampire from the dining hall the night before emerged looking as fresh as when she wandered into the cage. She had long, deep auburn hair with streaks of gold and red through it. She walked with head lowered and eyes to the ground, trying to make herself unnoticeable. That in itself made me notice her.

Incubus read the sexual energy of their prey, and she'd managed to abstain in the carrier. That was rare for someone arriving in our realm for the first time. She'd done the same last night. Her petite figure was all womanly curves in the right places, and when she finally raised her eyes, they were vibrant green.

I started organising everyone into the groups they were going to be training in. At the last second, I substituted the little vampire with an incubus I had in my own training group. I'd felt magic earlier coming from the crate she was in. Not many people would recognise the energy signature of magic, but when The Blood Queen seared it into your soul through a grotesque kiss, then the hairs on the back of your neck stood to attention when you felt it again.

She was definitely worth watching.

Leaving my commanders to sort everyone out, I descended down the stone staircase into the private chambers under the castle. We used to live in the rooms above the castle, but due to the recent attacks, anyone of royal blood stayed down here. I hated the fact that we had to live in the bowels of our home like rats.

My hand shook as I felt the familiar tug of The Blood Queen. She was never satisfied that she'd made us bend to her will, because she still made sure we constantly felt her breathing down our necks. There were times when my father watched me with such guilt in his eyes that I couldn't bear it anymore.

Dragging my ceremonial clothes off, I stood under the shower until I no longer felt her presence. She made me feel dirty after having sex, looming over me to try and extract every piece of dominance. Long ago she'd tried to make me her lover and I'd refused. Now, I felt her touch on me everywhere I went. It wasn't a lover's caress but a violation.

Addison stood in my room when I emerged from the bathroom. My only sister in a family full of men. She was the only one in my family, apart from my father, who knew about my curse.

"You look tired." Her voice was low.

"It's been a long few days," I replied.

"You've fed." It wasn't a question.

I nodded, closing my eyes and trailing my hands through my wet hair.

"We need to find a solution to this," Addison said, touching my arm. She was an empath, someone who felt the emotions of others. She hissed and took a step back, her eyes flashing with pity.

"Addy… Please don't."

"I came to tell you that I'm leaving tomorrow," she continued as if I hadn't spoken. "I have a lead on the location of a coven of witches."

I sighed, leaning my head back to stare at the ceiling. "It's too dangerous,"

I protested.

A feral smile crept over her lips. “I’m taking Gabriel with me.”

I covered my face and groaned. “Why won’t you leave my best commander alone?”

She opened her mouth to give a wiseass reply and I held my hand up. “I’m liberal since I’m an incubus, but no brother wants to know about his sister’s sex life.”

She shrugged and fluttered her eyelashes. “A girl needs to eat.”

I made a gagging noise.

“I’ll be careful, Zek. I promise.” She stared at me this time instead of trying to touch me. “But I can’t watch this anymore. If we are to win this war, then we need to sever the cords that tie you to that bitch.”

I nodded bleakly. She was right. Every step we took forward she punished and drained us. “I’ll speak to Gabriel before you go.”

She pointed a long, bright red fingernail at me. “No big brother talks. I’m a succubus and need to feed just like everyone else in this kingdom.”

I narrowed my eyes at her, but she winked and spun before striding out of my room.

My life didn’t need any more complications. Now I had to add worrying about my sister to the equation.

***

The new recruits congregated with their commanders, men who were battle-hardened and ready to turn these fighters into warriors. I found my team in the area designated to them. Their eyes widened when I wandered in their direction.

“I hope you weren’t too uncomfortable on the journey here. Not even The

Blood Queen dares to attack the dragons. Some magic is resistant to her," I informed them, staring at each of them in turn.

My eye caught the vampire female standing on her own surrounded by sexual predators. I'd deliberately chosen my team to be mostly incubi and succubae. I could tell the way they watched her they were wondering what was so special about her. They could join the club.

"You'll be shown your accommodation and then we start training this afternoon. We don't have much time and I need to assess all your strengths and weaknesses."

I stood and watched as the soldiers flung their holdalls over their shoulders. The vampire cast a look at me under her long hair, and I felt the hairs on the back of my neck rise. She followed the others in her group, never once looking up again. There was something about her that intrigued me, more to her than any of us were supposed to see.

After a quick meeting with my commanders, I had them set up one of our fiercest battle scenarios. We needed to assess the warriors I brought here and determine a battle strategy. There was no time left for soft techniques. War stood at our boundary line, Ophelia ready to strike.

***

Chapter Five

Ilana

What the hell was wrong with lycans? I ran so fast that I was able to run along the side of the wall. I swear to the gods that someone must have doused me with female wolf pheromones, because the past few days I'd spent running from unruly wolves. Their bite hurt like a bitch, and unlike some species, my limbs wouldn't grow back if they accidently ripped them off.

Pushing off with my feet, I flipped over his head to land behind him. His claws scrabbled as he struggled to turn and face me.

I pointed a shaky finger at him. "Sit," I said, hoping the command I'd heard humans giving their tame wolves would be effective.

His muzzle wrinkled in a snarl as he prowled forward.

I didn't know why we had to face each other, the witch didn't have lycans in her army. She had something much worse, an army of enslaved souls that were no better than marching corpses she controlled from a distance. And her gargoyles, which were the bane of my favourite boots.

"You do realise that no one likes a disobedient dog?" I asked.

A low growl sounded.

We weren't allowed to use loaded weapons down here, just manual weapons like swords and daggers. An elf ran past me earlier with a bow and arrow. I created a circle with the sword in my hand, slowly moving around to evaluate my prey.

He was over seven feet of massive muscles, covered in thick, dark brown fur. It was a toss-up whether his claws or canines terrified me more. Maybe it was the murderous glare in his eyes.

"Who's a good boy?" I taunted him. "Do you need a tummy rub?"

That was the point I pushed him too far and he launched himself at me, teeth and claws exposed and ready to shred me. I ducked and the same heat I'd felt in my last training session expanded in my chest. His claws embedded in a golden shield that surrounded my body.

What in the name of the great demon was happening?

My eyes caught sight of movement to my right and black military boots came into view, stopping beside me. The wolf was dragged off and tossed against the wall as if he weighed nothing.

Slowly, my gaze came up until it met furious dark eyes.

"I think we need to talk," Ezekiel snapped. He spun and stalked away, leaving me still kneeling on the floor. "Now!" he demanded.

Pushing myself to my feet, I followed him on shaky legs. He emanated power as he strode through his castle, people stepping back to let him through. I jumped, startled when he slammed a door behind me.

"What the fuck are you?" Ezekiel stood so close to me I felt his body heat. He was bigger in real life than in my fantasies, the T-shirt he wore tight over his chest muscles. They moved as he breathed heavily, and I kept my eyes stuck to that area so I didn't have to answer his question.

His fingers gripped my chin and lifted my gaze to his. I normally had a lot of time to kill since I wasn't involved in romps with my dinner, so I read. There was always that moment when their eyes met, and her legs turned to jelly. That was the point I normally rolled my eyes. I'd obviously never stared into the right set of eyes before.

Deep brown irises that were almost black bored straight into my soul, demanding answers. My breath caught in my chest and the rest of the world fell away. No one had a right to be that devastatingly handsome. The stubble on his jaw and his messed-up hair gave him the appearance of danger.

I vaguely remembered him asking me a question, but my brain refused to remind me what it was.

His hand clamped around my throat as he pressed me against the wall. "I'm not going to ask you again."

My mouth opened and closed like a fish stranded on land. "What?" I finally managed to rasp out.

His head came dangerous close to mine and I smelt his spicy fragrance. "What are you?" he repeated.

"Vampire," I gasped.

His hand tightened. "Try again."

"Can't breathe…" My hands came up to grab his.

His lips brushed my ear as he spoke softly into it. "I know exactly how to asphyxiate someone for pleasure. You can breathe."

Heat exploded in my core at his words, and for the first time, I didn't freeze at a man's touch. I wanted to wrap my legs around his waist and cling to him. Even as he threatened me, I felt safe.

"Half human," I managed to grate out.

He moved back to stare at me, maintaining the pressure on my poor throat.

"Humans can't perform magic," he stated.

My eyes widened and I frantically tried to shake my head. His grip released and I dropped to my knees on the floor. Great, now I was eye level with his groin. The taut muscles over his stomach revealed the man didn't have a spare piece of fat. The bulge in his dark jeans made me clench my thighs together.

I felt the command of his eyes glaring down at me and I slowly lifted my head in response. His jaw tightened, his eyes furious.

"I'm half human, half vampire," I said quietly. "My father met my mother and fell in love. To keep her with him, he blood-bound her. I have no magic, I'm not even as strong as the full-blooded vampires."

His arms slowly folded over his chest. “Magic saved you from the lycan.”

“I’ve served in the vampire ranks for over a hundred years. If I had magic, Prince Valek would know.”

“You’re different,” he stated, making my muscles tighten. “You didn’t succumb to the pulse when you arrived in our realm earlier.”

I glanced away at his words. How did I tell the incubus prince that I’d never been able to let a man touch me, never mind mate me?

I shrugged and continued to study the wall. “Maybe no one attracted me.”

Ezekiel reached down and guided me to my feet with his hand on my throat, his thumb stroking over my erratic pulse.

Before I had time to think or mount a mental defence, his lips crashed against mine and the world tilted. I grabbed the front of his T-shirt to steady myself before gravity abandoned me. His lips were so soft and silken against mine as he moved them slowly to coax me. The tip of his tongue traced the line of my lips.

This was a dance I’d tried a few times with no success. I’d forced myself to try and be normal, find love. Nothing worked.

With Ezekiel, kissing was as natural as breathing. His scent and taste consumed me, even as he tipped my head slightly to take more control. Heat flared in my stomach and I finally knew what people meant when they spoke about their core growing tight and wet.

Ezekiel pulled away, his breathing ragged and his eyes shining. “How old are you?” he demanded.

My eyebrows flew up. “Two hundred. Why?”

His body caged mine against the wall. “How have you survived as a vampire for two hundred years and never had sex?”

The room collapsed around me until there was only the two of us. I wanted to look away, to find somewhere to dig a hole and bury myself to avoid the embarrassment that coursed through me. How did he know?

"It's complicated." My tongue darted across my lips and his eyes watched the action. His body canted forward toward me.

"Vampires tend to have sex when they feed," he replied.

I swallowed nervously. "I'm only half vampire."

"Meaning?"

Straightening my back, I stared defiantly into his eyes. He'd obviously deliberately kissed me to assess me sexually. I'd seen Valek bite vampires to do the same.

That pissed me off.

"Meaning that it's none of your damn business," I snapped.

"This is my castle."

"Then send me back to Prince Valek. He's never had a problem with me."

Our eyes met in a battle of wills. I may not be an experienced sexual predator, but I was a vampire and I would bow to no one.

I shoved past him. "Never mind, I'll walk until the foliage turns from purple to crimson and then I'll be back in the Dracus realm."

My fantasy crashed headfirst into reality when I realised the man and the myth were nothing alike. I made it to the door with my back straight before his hand clamped on my arm.

"Where do you think you're going?" he hissed into my ear, his body tight against my back.

His breath fanned against my cheek and I desperately wished it didn't send a shiver of awareness down my back.

"Home," I replied. "I've never had any problem in the past with my feeding habits. One day on your team, and I'm locked in a crate with delinquents with high libidos and low morals. Then I'm dragged in here and sexually molested. I think I'll go back and fight The Blood Queen alongside

Prince Valek."

"I think you misunderstand the power dynamic here. When you walked into that crate, you became mine. If I tell you to jump, you ask how high. If I tell you I need to feed, you roll onto your back and spread your legs. Understand?"

There was something dark and twisted inside me that felt a pulse of pleasure at his words. "I spread my legs for no one unless I want to," I managed to say with some semblance of calm in my tone.

His dark chuckle trickled down my back. "Believe me, if I want you on your hands and knees under me, you'll have no choice but to obey." Ezekiel pressed a kiss on my neck, and my eyes fluttered closed. "What did you mean the foliage changes between purple and crimson?"

I swallowed and forced myself to take a deep breath. "In the Dracus realm, the leaves on the trees are crimson. Flying here, I knew we'd entered the Incubus realm when the leaves turned to deep purple."

His hand left my arm, my hand still resting on the door handle.

"Stay here," he commanded, before moving me across the room to a sofa.

I stared at him wordlessly as he left the room, running his fingers through his hair in frustration. My heart desperately tried to re-establish its regular beat even as my palm covered it. No one had evoked such a reaction in me before. His every movement contained raw power, and for the first time in my long life, I'd felt vulnerable.

He returned a few minutes later with a petite woman with black hair that reflected the light. She was stunningly beautiful with bright cherry red lips and nails that matched. Her every movement was a lesson in seduction, and my body clenched as she approached me. The way she stood close to Ezekiel said they were more than friends, their body language familiar and easy. Sickness crept up the back of my throat at the thought of these two beautiful demons together.

"You've terrified the poor woman, Zek," she chastised him. "What did you do?"

My hand automatically flew to my throat and he glanced away, his jaw tensing.

She tutted. "He sometimes forgets his manners when we have guests."

"Addy," Ezekiel rumbled in protest.

She grinned at his discomfort. "What's your name?" she asked me, her vibrant blue eyes sparkling with kindness.

"Ilana."

"It's a lovely name that means tree. Not many demons have nature names."

My eyes narrowed and I cautiously shuffled back from her. It felt like this woman could look into my soul and steal my secrets.

"I'm an empath," she continued as if we were old friends catching up after a long time apart.

"Addy," Ezekiel gasped, his hand gripping her shoulder. "You don't even know her."

She gave him an impish grin and a shrug. "Something tells me that Ilana and I are going to be good friends." She turned her attention back to me. "Zek thinks you have magic in you. I've been studying magic users for some time. Can I take your hand?" She held her hand out to me.

I suppressed the childish need to sit on my hands. My mother was human and my father vampire. Magic was passed on through the witches, but Ophelia had eradicated her kind, absorbing their powers to make herself indestructible. A witch hadn't been born in over three hundred years. Rumours suggested Ophelia had enslaved a few women from her original coven, making them search for any spark of magic in the demon realms.

My eyes flicked to Ezekiel, who watched us with a guarded expression.

"I think I made a mistake taking this assignment," I said, pushing myself to my feet. "I need to return home immediately."

The woman stood in front of me, her hands up in surrender. "I promise, I only want to help." She cast a glance at Ezekiel. "You can leave us."

His eyebrows rose fractionally before his penetrating gaze moved to me. I met his eyes, strengthening my back. He may have been my biggest fantasy, but in this moment, he was an arrogant prick and a royal pain in the ass. His lips quirked as if he was amused by my reaction.

He spun on his heel and left the room without a word.

Was she his wife? Lover? Concubine?

"Zek can be a little intense, especially where magic is concerned. My name is Addison, pleased to meet you." She held her hand out and I stared at it, one eyebrow raised in silent question.

She grinned. "It was worth a try."

"Why are you interested in magic?" I asked.

She settled herself on the sofa and sighed. "Many reasons, but the primary one being that witch cursed people I love. I'd heard about a village of witches far into the elven realms, and was about to leave to find them, when Zek stopped me and brought me here to meet you."

"I have no magic," I informed her. "My mother is human, a blood slave my father fell in love with."

"Yet, Zek says you conjured a spell to protect yourself against a lycan?" she prompted.

I shook my head, unzipping the fastenings along the arms of my top to reveal my arms. A scar tracked from elbow to wrist on my right arm. "This is from a lycan who lost control in battle. He was meant to be fighting alongside me. If I was able to protect myself against lycans, do you not think I would have done it before?"

She studied my arm. "I don't know. Maybe something happened?"

I snorted. "Like what? I ate a witch?"

Her lips twitched. "Who knows?" Addison's eyes met mine. "I know you have no need to trust me, but I truly only want to help. We all want this war to end. I believe the only way to do that is through finding magic. We've thrown everything the demon realms have at her and she bats us away like bugs."

I considered her words. There was nothing to fear because I knew I possessed no magic. I didn't want her touching me in case she picked up how I felt about the dark prince since she was an empath.

Holding out my hand, I glanced away as if disinterested in what was happening even as my heart beat rapidly. Her fingers felt scorching hot against mine, heat radiating up my arm. There was a strange pressure pushing against my head, and I blinked rapidly as my vision defocused.

Her hand released mine.

"Happy?" I asked. "Now that you know I'm a vampire hybrid we can stop all this talk about magic."

"Ilana, you have a vampire half, but I'm not sure what your other half is." Her voice was soft, her eyes kind when I spun to her in surprise. "Let me get Zek. He is the only one here strong enough to protect you."

My legs no longer felt strong enough to support me, and I slumped into a chair beside the desk in front of the window. My mind spun in circles of confusion, thoughts overlapping and fighting for dominance.

"Ilana?" His deep voice swept over me and I felt tears fill my eyes. Emotion was irrational, yet I sat in a foreign land as all my carefully constructed walls crumbled around me.

"She's confused, Zek," Addison said from somewhere behind me. "Ilana means no harm, her heart is pure. Whatever is contained within her is a gift that we need to protect. I will go with Gabriel to complete my search before the camp moves on. Then I will return to help you."

"Safe travels. Tell Gabriel he'll answer to me if you are hurt."

In my dreams he'd belonged to me. It was nonsense, even I knew that, but sitting here, his words of love toward Addison cut through me like a knife.

I stood on shaky legs. "I'd like to return to my room."

I didn't look back, walking stiffly away from the lovers. I was a foolish two-hundred-year-old vampire who'd read too many romance stories, believing that my secret crush would be the love of my life. The man in my head was the product of an overactive imagination. The man who kissed me didn't live up to the fantasy.

My legs buckled when I closed my room door, my back sliding down it until my ass hit the floor. My body folded in half and my arms wrapped around my legs.

Last night I'd been so excited about coming here, dreams of Ezekiel filled my head and seduced me. The cold light of day had shattered that fantasy.

***

Chapter Six

Ezekiel

"Well?" I demanded when Addison stepped out of the room.

"I'm not sure," she replied. "She's not full vampire, but I've never felt anything like her energy before." Her gaze met mine. "You need to stop being an asshole, the girl has hearts in her eyes when she looks at you."

I rolled my eyes. It was nothing new, considering who I was. She slapped my arm and I glared at her hand.

"I mean it, Zek. I'm not talking incubus obsession."

Women wanted an incubus for the orgasms. We needed them to feed from, so they were powerful and multiple. I doubted there had ever been a time that women saw me for more than my dick.

"Fine," I muttered, my mood darkening. "What do you want me to do?"

"Protect her," Addison replied instantly. "I believe we need to find magic, and if that energy inside her is magical in origin, we are going to need her."

"Maybe she's a spy…" I hissed, my hands forming into fists.

"Or maybe she's your salvation."

The only person in my world who stood up to me was my baby sister. None of my brothers had the balls. Addison had ovaries of steel. I glared at her until her lips twitched, telling me she thought she'd won the argument.

I wanted to put my fist through the wall and walk away from this mess.

Instead, I followed Addison into the room to find Ilana staring off into space in a world of her own. She'd been so fierce earlier and now she looked vulnerable. Her kiss had affected me more than I cared to admit, and the sight of her on her knees in supplication in front of me even more.

Her green eyes were huge in her frightened face. I finally took the time to really look at her, and what I saw took my breath away. Her deep auburn curls framed her pale face. Her body was encased in a skin-tight suit the vampires preferred to fight in, which accentuated the curves I'd felt against my body earlier. Ilana's lips were still swollen from my kiss, and the faint outline of my fingers were present on her throat.

She kept watching me covertly, her eyes sending heat pulsing across my skin.

Ilana stood, her hand clutching the back of the chair as if to steady herself. "I'd like to return to my room." I watched her walk stiffly from the room, her head bowed forward. I caught the scent of fresh tears as she moved past me.

I knew I was a bastard, it was a self-protection mechanism that started the day a witch killed something inside me. For the first time, I regretted the man I'd become.

The urge to press her against me and tell her everything would be okay overwhelmed me, yet I stood with my hands at my side.

"Your reaction to magic is understandable," Addison said, her hand landing on my arm in support. "My intuition is never wrong, and it tells me you need her. Swallow your pride, Zek." She patted my arm and left me to my thoughts.

The welcoming feast meant our new recruits could meet the soldiers already stationed here. Remiel stalked the room, seeking out his prey for the evening. Ilana never came. I checked with the kitchens, and she hadn't ordered food from them.

Addison had prepared for our new guests while I was selecting them, catering to their appetites. Grabbing a bag of blood, I stomped through the castle, drowning out the voice in my head that cautioned me to be careful. I didn't have time to pamper virgins with hurt feelings.

I banged on the door of her room. A soldier needed to stay strong, and that meant eating what kept them strong. The door eventually opened a sliver and one eye cautiously peeked out. It tried to swing closed on me.

Instead of thinking, I pushed my way in, coming to a halt when I saw she was dressed in nothing more than her panties and a vest top. In my long life I'd lost count of the number of women I'd fed from, some of them highly trained sexual concubines who knew a hundred different ways to satisfy a man. Yet the sight of Ilana in her white cotton panties was among the top ten most erotic sights that instantly ignited my lust.

Cotton fucking panties.

Not lace or silk that I was used to see adorning women, and yet the simplicity sent a jolt of awareness down my back.

"What?" she demanded, folding her arms above her chest. It made the top swell of her breasts more pronounced and lifted the material of her vest higher.

I held the bag of blood up. "You missed dinner. I insist all my soldiers eat."

"I wasn't hungry."

I threw the bag in her direction. She caught it mid-air.

We stared at each other, and for unknown reasons I felt I should be apologising for an unknown sin. Addison's words still echoed in my mind. "I'm sorry."

Her eyes widening was her only response.

I dropped my head because the intensity in her expressive eyes scorched at my conscience. "I dislike magic immensely because The Blood Queen wields it to kill without thought. I felt it earlier when flying home and then I saw you surrounded in it during training." I sighed, trailing my fingers through my hair. "Can we just start over?"

Ilana bit her bottom lip, the tips of her fangs showing. I felt naked under her scrutiny.

"Nothing like this has happened to me before." Her voice was small in the dim light of her room. "Lycans have attacked me before and nothing happened. One followed me yesterday and the same heat appeared in my chest before a golden light shot from my hand."

She was trying to trust me, and I needed to meet her halfway.

I nodded. "I saw him chasing you and went to intervene when I found him whimpering on the floor and no sign of you. I thought you'd fought him—it was why I chose you for my team."

Her lips opened in a silent 'O'.

She chewed the inside of her mouth, her eyes downcast to the floor. "I'll understand if you send me home, since you thought I was something I'm not. I didn't fight that lycan, I was lucky to escape it."

My head canted to the side to study her. "Follow me," I instructed, turning toward the door.

"I'm in my panties," she protested.

"I noticed," I deadpanned. Fuck, had I noticed. My dick certainly paid attention.

I heard the sound of fabric moving behind me and smelt the scent of blood as she sucked the bag I brought. She finally appeared in leggings and a hooded top, her face flushed from her feed.

I strode from the room with her trailing behind me.

I'd spent years researching everything I could find on magic to try and break this curse. What it'd left me with was an extensive library filled with the rarest books on magic and a still unbroken curse.

"Where are we going?" Ilana jogged beside me until I finally slowed my pace.

"My library."

She stopped, meaning I had to halt and turn to face her.

"Why the library?" she asked suspiciously.

"Because not every soldier needs to have the biggest muscles to pack a punch. You're a good fighter, Ilana, but I need great warriors. If you do contain magic, that may prove to be more powerful than a thousand trained fighters."

She stared at me for what felt like ages before she gave one brief nod.

I continued our journey until I flung the doors of my library open.

***

Chapter Seven

Ilana

I hadn't been able to face leaving my room, even when the hunger pains started. There was no way I could face Ezekiel and desperately needed time to form my defence against him. When a knock sounded at my door, I thought it might be Addison again.

In a world filled with beautiful immortals who wore arrogance like a fine coat of armour, no one had ever told me they were sorry before. The fact that one of the dark princes said it to me left me speechless. He needed to protect his realm and for all he knew, I'd been sent here by the wicked witch. His humility threw cold water on my burning anger and indignation.

The fact that he brought me something to eat showed me he was trying to make amends for his earlier behaviour. It didn't change the fact that he had a beautiful lover who I could never compete with. I really needed to find a mate who could touch me.

Ezekiel can touch you...

Some days I hated that taunting voice in my head. If I closed my eyes, I could still feel the pressure of his lips on mine.

Library was too small a word for the cathedral filled with books.

"Some of the books in here are incredible old, some are the only copies left in the demon realms," Ezekiel told me. "How much do you know about the war?"

I shrugged. "Ophelia wants to rule all of Purgatory and to do that she waged war on all the demon realms located there."

Ezekiel started talking, his eyes looking back in time. "Centuries ago, Ophelia was a simple witch in a coven. The witches were the healers and potion makers, welcomed into all the demon realms. She got a taste for power and so began her journey into darkness. She killed her sister witches, bathing in their blood to absorb their power. That's where her name derives from, The Blood Queen."

Ezekiel paced the room until he braced his hip against a large window frame that overlooked a garden. "The more power she had the more she craved. The last fragments of her compassion died in her quest. She slaughtered covens of witches until the only ones who remained either escaped into the human world or bound their magic where she would never find it."

"That doesn't explain why you hate magic so much," I pointed out.

A vague approximation of a smile ghosted across his lips. "That's a much longer story for a different day." He pulled a few books of the shelves and set them on a table. "Instead of training physically, I want you to train your mind."

"But…" Ezekiel held his hand up to cut me off.

"You are a virgin in a realm filled with sexual predators. It's the ultimate prize for them to claim and I don't need the distraction, as you put earlier, of men with high libidos and low morals being led by their dicks."

My cheeks flamed, his chuckle making them burn hotter.

I jolted when his finger traced along the side of my cheek. "I can't remember the last time I saw someone blush."

"It's just hot in here," I said, trying to pretend he hadn't flustered me.

His body leaned toward mine slightly. "You shouldn't be ashamed of your reactions. Cheeks were meant for blushing, that's why spanking is so erotic."

My mouth dropped open and my eyes widened at his audacity.

Ezekiel's finger under my chin closed my mouth. "I wouldn't leave your mouth gaping open like that unless you want it filled."

I no longer had any freaking clue what I was doing. The wicked grin on his face turned salacious and my stomach tightened in response.

"Do you always say things like that?" I finally responded.

"Like what?"

"Making every conversation sexual."

I held my breath as his head lowered to mine. "Sex is the primal force of life. People can lie but in the end, everything comes down to it. The important question is—how does it affect your mind?" His voice was a caress against my throat and the sensitive skin behind my ear.

"My mind?" I squeaked.

His lips touched the lobe of my ear as he replied, "Sex involves the body, skin sliding against skin. Great sex involves controlling the mind until you can't take any more sensation. Your system overloads until you are nothing more than a writhing mass of nerve endings exploding in pleasure. That's why it's called mind-blowing."

I swallowed. I was so far from my comfort zone that I'd lost my way back to sanity. "I'll take that as a yes," I finally managed to reply.

He chuckled and stepped back, his dark eyes watching me from under his hair that had flopped forward. I suppressed the urge to smooth it back.

"I know nothing about magic," I said, lifting a book and opening the pages. "If you've read all these, can you perform the spells and incantations?"

Ezekiel shook his head. "The spellcaster needs to have that essential link to magic. Believe me, I've tried."

I settled into a chair and flicked through the pages, my body freezing into rigidity when I encountered familiar symbols.

"What is it?" Ezekiel bent over me to peer at what I was reading.

"They always told me they were human symbols," I whispered.

"Who?"

"My mother and Aunt Agatha. They said all humans used crystals and herbs for healing as they didn't have demon blood." Their lies flooded over me until I was drowning in the sea of their deception. The more I read, the worse the dread in my stomach grew. Memories of us making healing balms together in my childhood crashed into me as I read the same ingredients in the book in front of me. "They lied to me."

"With Ophelia on the rampage I don't blame them."

My eyes cut up to him and I felt his eyes boring into mine. Why did he have to be nice to me? I could steel myself against his wrath, but this quiet companionship sent my head spinning.

"They told me I was half human. For years I was less than nothing until vampire numbers dwindled drastically and they conscripted every soul available as soldiers." I buried my head in my hands. "What the hell am I?"

Ezekiel slumped into a seat beside me. "I've no idea. Whatever you are, I need to keep you hidden until we work out what this means. I promised Addison I'd keep you safe until she got home."

My back stiffened. He was being nice to be because he made a vow to his lover.

I nodded briefly and pushed myself to my feet. "I can read these books, but I don't know what good that will do since I have no practical knowledge in witchcraft."

"I'll have a storage unit put in your room with bags of blood," Ezekiel said. "Something has activated your magic since you've been attacked before without it materialising. I don't want anyone to know about this until we can figure it out."

Magic caused panic. The look on his face when we first reached his office had been enough to make my blood freeze in my veins. Thankfully, Addison had managed to calm the situation and my head was still located on my shoulders. I knew others had been automatically executed in the past when accused of witchcraft.

I chewed the inside of my mouth, my thoughts in turmoil at the events of the past day. His fingertips touched mine and my eyes moved to his.

"I won't let anyone hurt you. This is my realm and my word is law." My heart fluttered at his words. "Come here every day, and at some point I'll find you and we can try and piece this together. Addison found evidence of witches in hiding. I always doubted it, but it looks like she was right."

He stood suddenly, his tall frame looming over me. A small electric current connected us, making my body want to sway toward his. There was no explanation for my reaction to him. None of my normal awkward attempts to chat and the overwhelming sense that I needed to escape. There was a strange companionship in his silence.

The more time I spent with Ezekiel the more I was convinced he wasn't the man we all thought he was. He had layers he hid behind. I sensed them, because over the years, I became a master at hiding myself in plain sight. None of my unit ever realised I didn't feed from the vein with them.

"Can I take some of the books back to my room with me?" I asked to distract myself from the muscled chest in my eye line.

"Take what you need, and I'll grab you a few on the basics of magic."

Running my fingers over the covers, I selected the books that vibrated under my fingertips. I turned when I felt his eyes watching me, raising an eyebrow in question.

"It's just disconcerting, feeling magic, when I've avoided it for so long," he explained.

My hands slid behind my back as if I'd been caught with my hand in Aunt Agatha's cookie jar.

A small smile tipped the corner of his lips up. "Can I ask you a question?"

I shrugged and returned to searching through the books. This way I could stay in my room tomorrow and avoid Ezekiel. Hopefully Addison would return by the next day.

His heat penetrated my body as he stood behind me. "How has a two-hundred-year-old vampire never had sex? I thought feeding from the vein was intimate and erotic."

I swallowed when his hand rested on my waist and his head bowed forward, his hair teasing the side of my cheek with its soft texture.

"I can't feed from the vein. I'm only half vampire."

"I've seen half-bloods feed from the vein before."

Confusion swirled inside my troubled thoughts. That had been Father's explanation, but then they never told me my mother was a witch.

"My body rejects it," I whispered.

His hand on my waist rotated me slowly until I faced him. "Can I look inside your memories to try and help?" His breath fanned across my lips and my eyes fluttered closed.

"How?" Only one word emerged because my power of speech was limited in this vicinity to him.

"My kiss allows me to look inside a person. If you visualise a time you tried to feed, I'll be able to read the energy of it."

So that was how he knew I was a virgin from one kiss. I thought he'd guessed because I was a terrible kisser. It was wrong on so many levels because I'd wanted this man longer than I cared to admit; had fantasised about him claiming my body in every way possible.

His hand cupped my cheek to tilt my head back, his dark, fathomless eyes bored into mine. My mind went blank as my mouth opened in shock. Every nerve ending in my body was focused on his hand clasping my hair and his mouth hovering over mine. The first skim of his lips against mine sent a trickle of sensation down my spine. The second created a wisp of awareness deep in my stomach. The third made my head spin and my legs wobble.

I couldn't explain what I was feeling because I had nothing to compare it to. Ezekiel was the master of this dance and all I could do was let him lead. His tongue skimmed the juncture of my lips, coaxing and intoxicating me.

It was meant to be a simple kiss to share my memories of feeding so he could try and help me. Instead, an enchanted energy weaved between us, drawing us together in a web of seduction.

Time stood still and everything fell into insignificance except this one moment, this sensation that bound us together.

Ezekiel tugged my head back, forcing me to give him deeper access to me. Fire ignited deep in my chest, demanding that I give him everything, submit to him. He'd accused me of being a witch, but the sorcery in his lips drained my control until there was nothing left but him.

His tongue invaded my mouth as he demanded my surrender. The fragile defences I held around me lay in shattered pieces at his feet. Nothing in my dreams had prepared me for this moment. I tried to drag control back before he found the feelings I tried to hide.

Ezekiel was a force of nature, tearing everything in his path away until there was nothing left but the raw emotions between us. My back arched and my hands clutched his arms as gravity threatened to abandon me.

He eventually pulled away, fire glowing at the back of his dark eyes, his lips swollen. "What have you done to me?" he whispered, his thumb running over my lips.

I stared up at him wordlessly. There was nothing to say, I'd never experienced anything like this. His confusion echoed inside me. Something happened here tonight and neither of us could explain it.

“Is it always like that?” I muttered, my fingers touching my lips.

He shook his head, his teeth biting into the side of his bottom lip.

“Sleep, Ilana,” he whispered just as I felt his breath filling my mouth. The world faded around me. I struggled to try and stay awake, my only focus his eyes.

His power won and I fell into oblivion.

***

Chapter Eight

Ezekiel

I stared at the woman I just put into bed. Her hair was tousled, her cheeks flushed, and lips swollen from our kiss.

What the fuck had happened?

I was supposed to be looking at her memories to figure out why she couldn't feed from the vein.

She was more complicated than anyone I'd ever met before. The moment our lips met I fell under her spell and couldn't break away. She tasted unique, her scent permeating my senses until the world faded away to leave only her.

I trailed my fingers through my hair in frustration.

A fucking virgin nearly brought me to my knees in submission.

Maybe she's your salvation... Addison's words from earlier came back to taunt me.

My soul was darkened with a curse that had left innocent victims nothing more than shells of their former selves. I didn't deserve redemption for my sins. I would settle for those touched by my curse to be granted a reprieve.

My court was filled with stunningly beautiful concubines trained in pleasure, yet this woman left me feeling like a teenager trying to figure out what they should be doing. She was so innocent she wore white cotton panties. My lips twitched at the image that was engrained in my head. I didn't think a pair existed in this realm of Purgatory.

Remiel would have a fit if he knew.

That thought alone sobered me. I needed to keep her safe and hidden. The vampires may not have realised what she was, but in this realm, anyone who tasted her would know she was innocent. There was something about this tiny, ferocious vampire that ignited the possessive gene I didn't know I had.

Leaving her sleeping, I strode from the room to sort through all the training files. There was no day or night in the eternal gloom of Purgatory, only a lighter period that chased away the inky blackness that was all-encompassing.

The sirens sounded just as the sky began to taint with brightness. The screeches of Ophelia's wyverns ricocheted through the castle, bringing me to my feet in seconds. I dragged my flameproof jacket on as I stormed out of the castle, knowing Magnus would already be waiting for me outside. I raced up his tail as he took to flight, his wings propelling us into the air.

Wyverns were dragons' smaller cousins. The dragons in Purgatory had always been aligned with the incubi. Magnus had bonded with me not long after he was born. I found him lost in our forest and brought him back to the castle. He followed me in and curled up on my bed. He was too big to go inside the rooms now, but that never stopped him curling up in the entrance hall and sleeping.

His flames scorched along the back of a small green wyvern, and it curled in a ball mid-air, screeching. Flying equalled freedom, the thrill of the wind eradicating all my troubles.

A large red wyvern pulsed in the air, one of Ophelia's wraiths on its back, its black eyes studying me. If she'd wanted to attack us properly then she would have arrived in the pitch blackness with stealth. Her minion was here with a message.

I stood on Magnus' back with my arms folded, glaring at the hideous translucent form of one of her captured souls. She'd taken something beautiful and twisted it with her magic until nothing of the former soul remained. Everything she touched withered and died, her repugnant energy polluting the very air she breathed.

"Her Royal Highness requests your presence at her next grand ball." His voice echoed on the wind and scratched at my nerve endings.

"No." I'd no intention of going anywhere near the crazy bitch.

He nodded once. "She said if you decline there will consequences."

My laugh sounded maniacal even to me. "What more can she do to me? Tell The Blood Queen that the incubus toll is paid in full."

"It would not be wise to refuse my queen."

She'd taken the pleasure of feeding from me, which meant I was an incubus who lived the life of a celibate monk most of the time. Ophelia had already done her worst. I refused to reply to him, my silence speaking louder than words.

"She will not be pleased," he stated.

I shrugged. "I don't give a fuck."

He nodded and the wyvern spun and flew away.

Was that wise? Magnus' voice rippled through my mind.

"Probably not, but I'm beyond caring," I replied.

I will have my thunder increase the wards on the borders.

My head thumped and I rubbed my eyes. The walls on my carefully constructed façade were slowly crumbling.

You need to feed.

"I can't," I ground out.

You need to be strong to lead us in battle.

If only life were that simple. The stronger I became, the stronger I made Ophelia. Keeping myself constantly hungry meant that she was the same. It gave me perverse pleasure to know she had a gnawing ache inside her. She could do many things, but each of her cursed rebelled against her in our own way. She picked us specifically because she thought we would give her ultimate power. The last laugh was on her because each of us was willing to die before we gave her what she truly wanted.

Of all the stubborn incubus I could bond with, you are the worst.

I grinned at his insolent tone. Magnus and I were both anomalies among our kind. I found him wandering in the forest, lost and starving. Everyone believed I saved him, but the tiny, black scaled monster saved me in return. My connection to him was a constant thrum that calmed me when a panic attack from the curse threatened to consume me.

To shake off the encounter with the wraith, I settled myself on Magnus' back and allowed him to soar over our realm. My mind cleared itself of all the clutter from the past few days. The freedom of the sky called to me and revitalised my soul. It was in these moments that I forgot my responsibilities and troubles. They melted away until there was nothing left but the man.

My mind chose that place of peace to find Ilana. She intrigued me, her taste still lingering on my tongue and tempting me to go back to her room. Her memories revealed her previous reactions to men touching her, yet she hadn't shied away from me. Her body rejected blood from the vein the same way. Ilana was a puzzle that begged to be studied. I hadn't felt a reaction like this to a woman in decades, maybe longer.

We flew high above the mountains and I peered down. All the foliage was black in all the realms in Purgatory. Her explanation of how she knew we'd entered the incubus realm fascinated me, and that was the reason I'd sought Addison out. My sister had been my companion in researching magic for over a century, but neither of us had read anything about how witches determined which realm they were in. It could answer some of the questions about how they knew where our borders were. If they saw colour when the rest of Purgatory's inhabitants only saw black, then they could chart the realms with no difficulty.

I wondered what else she saw that we didn't. For years, Ophelia had been one step ahead of us, but perhaps fate had finally drawn a card in our favour in this never-ending game of life and death.

Addison was convinced that we needed to find magic to be able to fight Ophelia. She'd searched Purgatory for years in search of scraps of knowledge for a witch's whereabouts.

Ilana possessed magic in her touch, her hands on my chest soothing the restless beast that paced inside me. Her lips whispered in his ear as they kissed mine, calming him.

Magnus released a bellowing screech into the cool air before scorching it with his fire.

I settled on his back and finally closed my eyes, knowing he would watch over me as he patrolled our kingdom.

***

Chapter Nine

Addison

They'd been here. The scent of magic still clung inside the caves, symbols etched into the walls. My fingers trailed over them as I read their story. It was as if they knew we were coming and disappeared, constantly on the run from discovery, spending their lives in hiding.

"You need to stop blaming yourself, Addy," Gabriel said, wrapping his arm around my waist and drawing me against his solid frame.

He was my brother's closest friend. Ezekiel would kill us if he knew I'd mated without the consent of the royal council. I was a royal succubus, destined to be married to one of the princes of Purgatory to bind realms together. Instead, I fell in love with a palace guard with blue eyes and soft brown hair. Childhood enemies who discovered passion that left us raw and needy.

"I know that magic is needed to win this war. Why else would she kill every witch she finds?" I asked, resting against his strength.

"You'll find them, my love. If this girl Zek found does contain magic, then you finally have somewhere to start." He kissed the top of my head, his fingers tracing up and down my spine.

He was the only man who gave me comfort. As a horny, young succubus on her first feeding frenzy, I'd made sure he was my first lover. Who better than a palace guard sworn to protect me? I never would have guessed he would be the man I mated years later. Three days straight he'd fucked me until my hunger finally abated. Ezekiel nearly went mad, but then a succubus was allowed to choose her first lover, and instinct guided me to the man who'd helped my brother tease me. He was safety in a world full of danger.

"Trust my brother and his great hatred of magic to find a magical being in the middle of a vampire military base."

Gabriel helped me photograph the site and catalogue any items left behind. Some of the items may contain magical energy that I could syphon back home to make energy bombs that worked against Ophelia's army.

We camped for the night under the velvet darkness of our starless sky. I'd read in books that the human realm had stars that shone down, illuminating them in the darkness. Just once, I wanted to see the stars in a dark sky, witness the glory of the moon in all its phases, and feel the heat of the sun on my face.

"My next assignment is at the borders when we get back," Gabriel whispered against the top of my head. "If you need to feed, it will have to be tonight."

I'd mated Gabriel, tied my life to his, which meant he was my main source of nourishment. We could share meals at orgies, but he was the man who fed me as I fulfilled him. My rooms at the castle were private, so no one knew we spent our nights when he was home together. It had been a long time since I had sex in nature.

A shiver of fear laced with anticipation trickled down my spine.

Danger lurked around every corner as war came closer to our borders. I rolled from where I lay on Gabriel's chest until I straddled him. His hands cupped my face to draw me down to his waiting mouth. The same delicious energy that connected us from the first moment we kissed surged between us.

I spent years pretending I'd only felt that rush because it was my first feeding frenzy. We avoided each other after our initial encounter. It was only when we'd argued over something trivial years later and he kissed me to shut me up that I realised the truth. Gabriel was the only man who could leash me, dominate me, control my every reaction. He was the only man strong enough to tame me.

He bunched my skirt around my waist, and I popped the buttons on his jeans to release his hard length. He was the perfect fit, filling me with a divine perfection that made my head fall back and a silent 'O' to form on my lips. We stayed locked together, our bodies joined in the way that completed us. This was the true sanctity of sex. Gabriel's hard length filling my empty core to make me whole.

He allowed me to slide up and down, drawing him deeper as I undulated on top of him. He held my hips and watched me, his eyes never leaving my face. His intensity was one of the aspects of him I loved the most. When he was with me, I was his world.

The energy built between us, drawing us into a web that linked us. I wanted to feel his skin sliding against mine, but we were already vulnerable out here alone. I needed to feel his hot breath on my breasts as he suckled me. These stolen moments were never enough. I wanted everyone to know he was my mate, the man I'd chosen above all others.

Gabriel grabbed me, spinning me until my back hit the soft earth. His lips claimed mine in a primal kiss filled with his turbulent emotions. His hips collided with mine in a bruising attack that left me digging my nails into his shoulders to drag him closer.

There was a thin line between passion and brutality and Gabriel knew how to tread it. He always took me to the edge and left me dangling with a tantalisingly breathless feeling that I was going to fall. He'd trained in the harems and knew how to extract every drop of pleasure from my body.

Gabriel put his arms under my legs to change the angle of his movements deep inside me. My core trembled under his command. He leaned over me, his teeth trailing down my neck.

"I love you, Addy," he whispered in my ear.

I clutched him closer to me, wanting to take the weight of him.

"Gabriel." I breathed his name as if to worship him. "I love you so much."

His lips sealed over mine until the only sound was our flesh slapping against each other. Heat kindled in my core, stoked by Gabriel, our bodies moving in fluid motion. Perspiration pooled at the bottom of my back and a bead of sweat rolled down my cheek. His incubus magic trickled into me, awakening all my erogenous zones and making me moan.

The more mind-blowing my orgasm, the bigger his pleasure.

His thumb found my clit and he drew lazy circles on it. Gabriel cloaked me in his seduction and plundered my body, leaving me a heaving mass of nerve endings. This was the reason I was no longer attracted to any other man. Who would want to eat scraps when they could have a banquet?

He nearly pulled out fully before he thrusted violently into me, arching my back and making me curse. He did it again and again until I could barely take the sensation. The heat building in my stomach turned into a volcano ready to erupt. Gabriel played my body until I couldn't take any more.

"Please…" I begged in a breathless plea.

His mouth latched onto mine as he stole my words.

The volcano in my core erupted, gushing moisture. Gabriel held my hips as he lost himself in the rhythm of his dance. His cock thickened and pulsed before he exploded deep inside me, filling me with his pleasure.

This moment right here was the reason that mates could sustain each other's appetites for a lifetime. The power radiating through me was matched equally in Gabriel. We were magnets that attracted each other, the heat in our cores a golden ball of pure sexual energy generated from our love for one another. Our souls were weaved together, our bodies perfectly aligned. We gave and took, a powerful wave of energy rippling between us as we fed each other our pleasure. This was the true essence of the mating bond.

My legs trembled, goosebumps rising on my skin.

Gabriel collapsed on top of me, his weight holding me hostage.

"You need to tell them, Addy," he rasped in my ear. "I can't keep pretending not to care about you while other men sniff around you."

I kissed his neck, pulling him tighter to me, my legs clamped around his waist to hold him deep inside me. My body radiated energy from feeding, my skin sensitive to even the slight breeze that wafted over us.

"I'll talk to Ezekiel when we get home. Maybe his new distraction will keep him from killing both of us."

Gabriel chuckled against my ear. "If we're lucky, he'll let me keep my balls."

***

Chapter Ten

Ophelia, The Blood Queen

My wraith twisted on the ground, his screams echoing through my throne room.

"Did you tell him it was an order, not an invite to attend my ball?" I demanded, standing over his pathetic form.

"He wouldn't listen, my queen," he gasped, his form fading in and out.

Wraiths were created from the souls of the dead. When my soldiers died, I put what was left of them to good use. They would be forever linked to me and at my command.

I stalked to the window and glared out of it, frustrated. Ezekiel was a constant thorn in my side. There were many dark princes in Purgatory yet only one caught my attention.

Him.

Every Queen needed to produce an heir and that incubus was the one I wanted to sire my progeny. He'd refused me long ago and it still smarted. Even when I cursed him, he still rebelled against me. I drained him of his power and left him on the brink of starvation and he declined to eat. I brought war to his borders and he sent his deathly fire-breathing lizards after my troops.

Incubi were supposed to be addicted to sex, yet I lusted after the only one who seemed to wear a chastity belt.

The day I cursed the four dark princes, he resisted me the most, his lips searing against mine. Any other man in Purgatory would grovel to be my consort.

I spun away from the window and strode from my throne room to the place I conducted my darkest magic. The tapers in the hallway flickered in response to my aura, sending tingles shooting across my skin. Of all the elements, I hated fire. It was the element used most to destroy witches. My sisters who'd lived in the Earth realm had met fiery ends at the hands of the humans who set up trials because they feared them.

They should fear magic users. When I ruled Purgatory, they would be next.

The hum of magic surrounded me in my sanctuary. The scent of my herbs mingled until they formed an aroma that soothed my soul. My scrying mirror of polished obsidian hung on the wall. My long red nails drummed on the top of my worktop as I stared at it with narrowed eyes. I'd been inspired by a faerytale in a book I'd read from the human realm where the evil witch had a magic mirror on her wall. Mine didn't show me who was the fairest of them all, but it allowed me to spy on my enemies.

Many souls had been sacrificed to generate the magic used to create it. I traced my fingers over it, sensing their energies inside the black crystal.

"Show me Ezekiel," I whispered.

Colours shimmered in a rainbow over the surface, energetic ripples on a lake as it searched for him. Blackness was my reply. I frowned, my forehead wrinkling in displeasure as I tapped the side of my mirror.

"Show me Ezekiel, Dark Prince of the Incubi," I demanded.

The mirror vibrated as the souls contained within it frantically searched for the man I wanted to find. Eventually, the outline of a face appeared in the centre of the mirror.

"I'm sorry, my queen. The incubus is shrouded from us."

"What?"

I barely contained the fury that wanted to erupt and decimate everything within my castle. My mind whirled with so many scenarios that I could barely breathe. What had he done? Magic no longer existed, except where I controlled it.

It started by accident, a spell gone wrong in my coven. My sister witch was killed and I absorbed her magic. The thrilling memory of it incorporating into my own still sent my pulse racing in anticipation. I pretended to mourn with the rest of my coven, but the sense of power I received far outweighed any sense of grief.

A few years later another coven member met an untimely end, then another, until I didn't bother even hiding my thirst for power anymore. I'd discovered a way to drain another witch's magic at the time of their death.

Then my own personal witch hunt began in earnest. My sister witches tried to band together to stop me. That was when the idea of cursing the four dark princes manifested. They were the strongest of their kind, the epitome of the magic that ran in their species. Each fed me energy in their own way, allowing me to deflect the attack of my sister witches.

I contained the magic of thousands of witches, their blood running through my veins. Obviously some had survived my cull. They were the only ones who could hide my incubus from me. Where did he find them and where was he hiding them?

My tongue crept out to lick over my bottom lip at the thought of feasting on their magic.

I would direct all my troops to the incubus border. If Ezekiel would not come to me willingly, I would make sure he crawled to me on his hands and knees in surrender. The thought of his proud form bent in supplication before me sent a shot of lust through my core.

Nothing would stop me when I set my sights on something.

He was mine and nothing would keep me from possessing him.

***

Chapter Eleven

Ilana

I stared around my room in confusion. My last memory was that incredible kiss in the library, and now I was lying fully clothed on my bed, surrounded by books. I slumped back, my fingers pressed to my lips. His touch was more than I imagined it would be. He hadn't kissed me, he'd consumed me until there was nothing left but the feel and taste of him. Every synapse in my body remembered that kiss.

I groaned, covering my eyes. After our disastrous meeting in his office yesterday, I'd promised myself that I'd stay far away from Ezekiel. Especially since he had a stunningly beautiful mate.

Yet, if he'd decided to feed from me among the leather-bound books, I would have willingly let him.

"Ugh!" I muttered, still hiding behind my hands. This was ridiculous. I'd come here to fight as a vampire warrior and been demoted to a bookworm.

Worse was the fact that I could smell his scent from my hooded top and his spicy aroma made my fangs drop in hunger. My hands balled into fists as I struggled for control. The thought of feeding from the vein normally repulsed me. Breathing slowly, I stood and looked around my room. Ezekiel had left a lot of books, so many that I wouldn't need to leave my room all day. A small blood bank sat on my desk. He'd thought of everything.

Grabbing a bag of blood, I sat cross legged on the bed and opened the first book.

If you'd asked me two days ago if I contained magic, I'd have laughed in your face. Now my childhood reared up in my memories and I realised that my parents had lied to me. I wasn't half human. Those women Mum referred to as her closest friends were obviously her coven. The symbols she told me were human were actually magical and the herbs they said were for spicing our food and making tea were for spells. Each page I turned revealed truths about my past. Vague memories resurfaced of chanting and bonfires, reawakened by the truth in the books I held.

A headache threatened behind my eyes. I knew all the deceit and secrecy was to hide our kind from the psychotic bitch who was determined to rule Purgatory, but suddenly I felt lost and alone. I no longer knew who I was or what I was capable of, they'd left me weak and vulnerable in a world I knew nothing about.

I recognised the tattvas—the symbols of the five elemental forces. There was an exercise in activating them, so I decided to give it a try since there was no one here to bear witness to any disaster.

I held my left hand up in front of me, envisaging a ball of golden energy surrounding it.

"Akasha," I said, imagining the black egg that symbolised the spirit tattva.

"Vayu." The circular blue symbol of air flashed through my mind.

"Tejas." I envisaged the red triangle of the fire tattva.

"Apas." A silver crescent moon lying on its back formed in my head for the water tattva.

"Prithvi." I imagined the yellow square for the earth tattva.

The symbols danced inside the ball of golden energy surrounding my hand, bouncing along my fingertips until the illusion disappeared in a flash of light. I went to use my left hand to turn the page when I noticed the symbols on my fingertips. One for each finger on my hand. I studied my fingers, my brow creasing as I moved my hand closer and then away from my face.

What the ever-living fuck had happened?

My thumb and middle finger rubbed together and I jumped as the rug on my bed caught fire. I screamed and leapt to my feet, trying to smother the flames. Another finger touched the flames and they flared.

My eyes widened and panic set in as I dragged the rug from the bed and ran into the bathroom with it, throwing it in the bath.

I lifted my hand again. My thumb was the spirit or ether symbol. The middle finger was the red fire triangle. I rubbed them together again and the flames jumped higher in the bath. The silver crescent moon was on my index finger, and I tested a theory, rubbing my thumb and index finger together. The flames dampened down as water engulfed the rug in the bath. The symbol for earth was on my little finger and air on my ring finger. Each element seemed to be activated using my thumb.

Unconsciously, I went to run my hands down my face as I'd done so many times. At the last second I caught myself. The dark gods alone knew what sort of damage I could cause with this hand.

The rug lay destroyed in the bath. My confidence lay there with it. I was a terrible vampire who couldn't feed and now I sucked at being a witch. The irony wasn't lost on me. I returned with my hand of doom to the book I'd been reading. Settling back, I scanned the pages, learning about the elements and how to use them. Some of the explanations scratched at snippets of memories from my childhood.

Mum and her sister were constantly in the kitchen baking. It was the central hub of our home, a fire constantly burning with fragrant herbs thrown in it.

We were baking cupcakes and Aunt Agatha was explaining how important it was to put the ingredients into the batter in order.

"What would happen if you poured lots of water on a fire?" she asked.

"It would go out," I replied.

She'd smiled and nodded. "Yes, it would extinguish the fire completely and soak the earth it burned, yet if we added the same amount a little at a time then we would get smoke. How would you get the smoke out of the room, Ilana?"

"Open a window?"

"The air would clear it with a breeze," she agreed.

"How does that affect the cupcakes?" I frowned.

"Cupcakes need air to make them fluffy. The base element for them is flour from the earth, the moisture is added a bit at a time, so the batter doesn't curdle. We cook them in the heat of the fire."

"What about the spirit, Aunt Agatha?" I asked, pointing to her old tattered book filled with symbols and writing.

"The spirit is the special ingredient that you need to add to every recipe. It is the essential spark that lives inside you. You can't make cupcakes without putting a little pinch of love into the batter." She kissed her fingertips and rubbed them over the bowl as if she sprinkled her kiss into the batter. "Now you try."

I giggled, kissing my fingers the same way she had. "Like this, Aunt Agatha?"

She nodded. "Just like that, Ilana. Remember, every recipe you bake needs that special ingredient."

Father never approved of Aunt Agatha, but walking down memory lane, I realised she'd been trying to teach me bits of magic all through my life. She taught me how to make healing balms and identify herbs. All those days spent playing in the forest, she turned into classes. I'd helped in the infirmary in the vampire bases, mixing healing poultices, never appreciating what I was doing.

I scribbled notes, putting markers in some of the books at important pages. Hours trickled away as I organised the books into piles. Every so often, another flash from the past fluttered through my head.

My mum teaching me to tie knots as we said a rhyme together. Knot magic.

Aunt Agatha showing me how to make dolls from sheaths of corn. Corn dollies to bring prosperity to the land.

She demonstrated how to cut and dry herbs into bundles. Sage sticks for purification.

All the basics of magic hidden in plain sight and incorporated into nighttime stories.

"Busy day?"

I jumped at the sound of the male voice in my doorway. Ezekiel stood with his hip braced against the doorframe. His hair was damp as if he'd recently had a shower. He was dressed in his customary tight black T-shirt and jeans. I suddenly remembered I hadn't showered or brushed my hair, my focus engulfed with the contents of the books.

Running a shaky hand through my hair, I glanced around the room. "Um…"

He stepped in and closed the door. "I don't want the scent of magic permeating the castle," he explained.

I sniffed the air discretely but couldn't smell anything. Probably because I was sitting in the middle of it.

His eyes scanned the room, eyebrows raising when he saw the neat piles with markers hanging out of them. "You have been busy."

I shrugged, self-conscious that I was still sitting in the same clothes from last night. "I lost track of time…"

"That's understandable."

I stared at my hands because his presence in my room after the intensity of last night's kiss left me shy and tongue-tied. Ezekiel was around six foot two in height, but his energy seemed to take up most of the room, leaving me only the small space my body occupied on the bed.

"Thanks for leaving me food." I nodded at the unit in the corner.

He shrugged. "The castle is full of sexual predators. My brother would go crazy if he knew there was a fully grown female here who'd never had sex."

I sighed and rolled my eyes. "Could we stop with the virgin talk. The fact that I've never had sex doesn't change who I am as a person."

A small smile tugged the corner of his full lips. "You have no idea, Ilana." He took a step forward. "When an incubus or succubus reaches puberty, we enter a feeding frenzy that can last from one day to a month. That entire time we gorge ourselves on sexual energy until we become the sex demons of Purgatory."

A shiver of excitement raced up my back at his deep tone.

Ezekiel picked up a book and opened it at the marker I'd left in it.

"No one in this realm makes it past that compulsion as a virgin," he continued. "The sexual energy generated from a feeding frenzy is like nothing else you could ever experience. The succubae are insatiable, the incubi constantly hard and aroused. Some opt to stay with one partner, while others spend their time in an orgy."

"Is there a point to this story?" I asked.

His eyes met mine and my heart skipped several beats from the intensity I saw there. "Yes. Virgins are rare in this realm and some incubi would give their left testicle to have one."

I swallowed, his words surprising me. He tended to stay away from gentle descriptions, instead opting for those that shocked. "I doubt I'll be ravaged in the corridor."

"I wouldn't be so sure," he replied, setting the book down again.

I tried but failed to look away from his dark gaze. He accused me of having magic, yet he compelled me with whatever enchantment was in his eyes. I was powerless against Ezekiel. I had been from the first time I saw him so long ago. I recognised him even when I'd never met him. What I felt defied explanation. It certainly wasn't in any of the books I'd studied today. I'd been hoping it was some strange witch attraction. No such luck.

I finally dragged my gaze away to look at the piles of books. "I've sorted them into groups. If you want me to try this, then all the books in the first section have the same herbs mentioned again and again. I left a list with the books. The second section are all the crystals you might need for protection and healing, et cetera. There is another list. The next group are the different miscellaneous magical items."

"Let me guess," he interrupted. "Another list?" He bit his bottom lip in suppressed amusement.

My eyebrow arched and he dropped his head to hide his expression. The fucker was laughing at me. "There is nothing wrong with being organised," I informed him haughtily.

"And this last heap of books?" Ezekiel asked, lifting the top one.

"Those are the spells and incantations, but we need the items on the lists first."

He nodded absently, reading one of the lists. "I'll send out scouts tomorrow to start to collect them. There are crystals and other items that Addison has collected on her missions down in her storage area."

I knew I was being ridiculous, but my back tensed at the mention of Addison. My mind knew that Ezekiel wasn't mine, but my body had other ideas. A tiny little monster had taken up residence inside me and possessed green eyes and a bad attitude.

"I'll have a look and see if I recognise anything of use." I sat fiddling with my fingers, unsure if I should tell him about the symbols that were still present.

"I can take you outside if you'd like," Ezekiel said, shoving his hands into his pockets. "Since you've been shut in here all day."

My heart beat rapidly, like a bird fluttering in a cage desperate for escape. "Do I have time for a shower? I lost track of time today." I ran a self-conscious hand through my messy hair.

"Sure, I have all night. I rarely sleep."

I leapt from the bed and only remembered about the mess in the bathroom as I opened the door.

"What in the name of the gates of hell?" Ezekiel exclaimed, pushing his way past me. "What happened?" He spun to stare at me.

"Um… I accidentally set the bed on fire…"

His strong hands grabbed my arms to twist me first to the right and then to the left, his eyes scouring me. "Are you okay?"

I thought he'd be angry, instead he was concerned. That filled me with confusion and a strange giddy energy that left me breathless. Heat seeped into my flesh from his hands, tingling into my chest.

"Yeah, I just didn't expect the elements to respond to me." I held my left hand up with the symbols of the tattvas on them.

Ezekiel grabbed my hand and studied it intently, his head lowered until I felt his breath fanning across my cheek. The pad of his thumb stroked across the spirit tattva on my thumb. A shiver ran up my spine and I couldn't hide my reaction to his touch.

"What happened?" His voice was low and husky.

My eyes were glued to my small hand engulfed in his. It was a simple touch, yet there was something erotic about it. I felt tremors all the way down to the juncture between my legs.

"I was reading about the elements and there was a simple incantation in the book to summon them. I never thought anything would happen, except it did and now I'm not sure what it means…"

He lifted my hand and placed a kiss in the centre of my palm, his eyes summoning mine to ensnare them. "I'm going to organise you a new room. Somewhere that has an area for you to practice so you don't burn your bed to ashes."

I could handle the man who pinned me to the wall by my throat. I was desperately confused by the man who held my hand and stared at me with an expression I'd never seen before. I wanted to combine the two halves, for Ezekiel to push me against the wall with his hand around my throat and kiss me until I needed his oxygen to breathe.

I trembled in terror at the cascading avalanche of emotions that swept through me. Where was the rational woman who clearly worked her way through every situation? She'd obviously been left in the Drakus realm.

"You can't shower in there, the bath is filled with fire debris," Ezekiel muttered. "Pack your clothes. I'll get your books later."

I hadn't unpacked yet, only removing what I needed from my black holdall. It didn't take me long to shove the rest of my stuff in.

"Where are we going?" I asked in a loud whisper as I tried to keep up with Ezekiel. His legs were a lot longer than mine and they ate up the corridor at speed, even with my bag thrown over his shoulder.

"Somewhere more private," he snapped. Grumpy Ezekiel had made a reappearance. He seemed to blow between hot and cold, one moment smouldering with intensity, the next so icy that snowflakes threatened to descend.

My jaw snapped shut against a response and I stomped behind him, my mood rapidly matching his. I may not be pretty and eloquent, but I had feelings that he was stomping all over in his black army boots.

A small rebellion mounted inside me, demanding I return to my room and ignore him. The further we went, the more ornate the surroundings we walked through. My pace slowed as I studied the architecture and paintings on the walls.

Ezekiel stopped and swung around. “Come on,” he hissed, beckoning me forward with an exasperated wave of his arm.

“What is your problem?” I demanded, my hands landing on my hips. “Is there a bug up your ass or do you always speak to people like this?”

His jaw tensed and he quickly looked at the ceiling as if searching for divine guidance. He moved so quickly I didn’t have time to avoid him before he flipped me over his shoulder.

“This part of the castle is where the royal family lives.” His voice was barely above a whisper as his long legs moved us rapidly down the corridor. “No one should be down here but those of royal blood. It’s the best place to keep you safe, but if anyone finds you, there’ll be hell to pay. Try and behave until I get you to your new room.”

His hand on my ass wreaked havoc on my senses. My eyes were glued to his back and ass, watching his muscles move as he strode along. Since his hand was on my ass, surely it was only fair that I was allowed to touch his?

My legs wrapped around his waist, so I wasn’t dangling over his shoulder with all the pressure on my stomach, my arms slipped around his neck.

“What are you doing?” Ezekiel asked. His hand slid under my ass to support me. So much for thinking this position would be easier to handle.

“Since you decided I couldn’t walk, I thought I’d make myself comfortable,” I snarked.

“Comfortable… Right…” He shook his head and lengthened his stride.

From this position, I could look around me and take in the décor, something I couldn’t do upside down. Ezekiel flung a large, heavy wooden door open, kicking it shut with his foot when he stepped inside.

I drank in the opulence of the room we were in, the colour scheme black and red with accents of gold. I turned my head to ask Ezekiel a question when his lips locked with mine and my back crashed against the wall. All thoughts evaporated as his mouth moved against mine, my limbs tangled around him. Giving in to temptation, I trailed my hands through his hair and tugged him impossibly closer to me.

His scent intoxicated me, his taste seduced me, and his touch infused me with lust.

I finally discovered what passion was like. The push and pull of desire that demanded a sacrifice of flesh. My fangs lowered slowly in my mouth as Ezekiel devoured me.

"Fuck!" He finally dragged himself away, one hand on my hip and the other braced on the wall beside me.

I blinked until my vision cleared, leaving me staring into his eyes that were a kaleidoscope of emotions. I couldn't articulate my feelings or wants, as all of this was new to me.

Ezekiel's teeth bit into his bottom lip and he stared at the ceiling, his fingers digging into my hip. "I can't keep doing this," he muttered.

I forced his gaze to meet mine. "Do what?"

"This." His hand gestured between us. "I want you but I can't have you. There is enough tainting my soul without adding another sin to it."

"You're the first man who I've ever been able to let touch me," I whispered, the confession slipping past my lips.

"Maybe it's just because I'm an incubus and you have only been around vampires."

I shook my head. "An incubus in the transport crate tried to encourage me to enjoy the ride here, but his touch repulsed me."

His eyes fluttered closed and his body tensed. "You can't say things like that to me."

"Why?" The simple word popped out of my mouth.

His ferocious stare bored into mine. "Why? Because I am the biggest fucking predator in this entire realm. I eat little girls like you for breakfast, and toss them aside before lunch." His tone contained an anguish that lacerated my soul. His hand grabbed my throat. "You need to stay away from me because I will destroy everything good in you, leaving only confusion and misery."

His energy was so cold my skin turned to ice where he touched.

Finding courage deep in my soul, my hand covered his. "You're the only one I feel safe with."

He groaned and tried to step back from me, but my legs held tight around his waist. "I'm scared, Ezekiel. I'm not even who I thought I was. Please don't push me aside."

He glared at me as if I was his ruin, his face strained. An eternity passed as he assessed me and I laid myself open to his survey. I knew this was a defining moment, and left Ezekiel to make his own choice. He sighed. "I can't explain why, but I will not feed unless it's the equinox. Please, Ilana, you need to ensure that no matter how much we want to, that I do not feed from you unless under a sacred sky."

Raw pain laced every word and I felt his agony claw its way through me. His brute force and threatening me didn't work, but his words… They were straight from his soul, torn from him to leave him bleeding emotionally. The ice thawed and left me to bask in his heat.

I unlocked my legs and let him drop me to the floor. "Where are we?" I diverted the conversation away from my throbbing core and his hard cock that bulged under his dark jeans. Both of our breaths were unsteady, and my hand trembled as I pushed it through my hair. I didn't just want him, I needed him with an intensity that left me unsteady on my feet.

"My private suite. You'll be safe here."

My eyebrows rose as I glanced around. This was his room and he'd brought me here. "I won't wake up to an angry mate with a dagger to my neck?" I asked in a joke.

His lips twitched. "No one enters these rooms but me," he replied. "I like my own space away from the war."

I didn't press the matter of Addison. Instead, I wandered around and found his personality accentuated on the walls and the possessions that sat around on display.

"Would you not be better finding me a room with the other soldiers?" I asked softly, sensing his turbulent emotions.

His body heat scorched me as his stomach pressed against my back, his hand falling to hold my waist. His head dipped and I felt his hair mingle with mine. "I'd sleep better knowing you were close by."

Both of us felt this connection, and I was powerless to do anything about it. He'd been my ultimate fantasy for too many years to count. The man was more complex than my imaginary paramour, and that excited me more than a one-dimensional make-believe lover. His hot and cold gave him depth, both ice and flames burning in their own unique way.

My hand covered his on my hip. "What is this between us?" I whispered, gaining strength from his touch.

"I don't know, Ilana," he rasped. "I have to fight to stay away from you, your scent intoxicates me and demands I take you."

I leaned back against him. "But you can't be with me unless it's an equinox?"

I felt his head nod.

"Is it only full sex that's not allowed?" I had no clue where my brazen questions were coming from. "What about kissing or other aspects of sexual contact?"

His right hand landed on my other hip. "Are you trying to fucking kill me?" he growled.

"No," I squeaked. "Trying to understand the rules so I don't break them."

He spun me to face him, backing me one step at a time until my spine aligned with the wall and there was no escape route. "I can kiss or bring you to orgasm over and over and fucking over again with my mouth, tongue, and fingers. You can swallow my dick until I explode deep in your throat." He took a deep breath and finally met my eyes. His soul was tormented, his hunger raw, and the look in those fathomless eyes broke something in my heart. "But unless there is a sacred sky, I can't bury myself so deep inside you that you feel me etched on your soul as I feed from your nectar."

Fucking hell.

No one had ever spoken to me before the way he had. His dirty language called to a part of me that suddenly woke up and took notice. Heat gathered between my thighs and I stared at him open-mouthed.

"What did I tell you about this?" His thumb traced over my bottom lip.

A flush crept up my neck and into my cheeks.

His lips twisted in a smirk that told me he knew my reaction to him. He placed a quick kiss on my lips before spinning away to stalk across the room, leaving me in a blur of bewildered emotions.

"This is your room," he said, dropping my bag inside. "An old study down the corridor will suffice for your workroom. I'll have your books and things put in there. Take a shower and then I'll show you around outside."

When the door slammed behind him, I stood for several minutes, my brow wrinkled in confusion as to what had happened.

***

Chapter Twelve

Ezekiel

My two hands covered my face and I slid down the wall, trying to calm my erratic breathing.

What the fuck was I doing?

I never intended her to be sleeping in my suite, but as soon as I realised the danger she put herself in earlier, all reason evaporated.

I was used to lust, to passion, to sex in every way thinkable. Each of those faded into insignificance when her huge green eyes peered into mine. Compassion and a fierce urge to protect superseded other chaotic emotions, leaving me stunned by their power over me.

Remiel tended to stalk the castle, searching for any prey he could feed from, his appetite never-ending. If he even suspected Ilana's innocence, he would pursue her until he took everything she had to give and leave her a crumpled mess for someone to try and put back together again.

When she'd stopped to study the architecture, I'd felt him in the vicinity. If, for one moment, I'd known she'd wrap herself around me like that, I would have never thrown her over my shoulder. By the time we reached my room, I was hard as a rock and ready to burst.

Most women would run if I pinned them against the wall by their throat. Ilana tampered my anger with her quiet energy, taming me with her gentle touch. She made me want to forget about the curse and take her the way we both wanted.

Her lust and need were driving me in-fucking-sane.

She wore her arousal like a pheromone, and I was fast becoming addicted to her scent.

There was no way in Purgatory I could stay in here knowing she was naked, soaping up those breasts that had been pressed against me not that long ago. My control would snap and demand I help wash her back.

Her words haunted me, trying to find wiggle room in my curse, the limits of what we could do without activating it. The countless things I could do with her without feeding danced in the back of my mind, tempting me. No one had ever asked me how to find a way around it before—not even the trusted concubines who'd ended up nothing more than mindless slaves.

My fist bunched at my side and I took one breath at a time until I calmed myself. She deserved better than a broken man who daily walked on a knife edge. But I was selfish and the idea of anyone but me touching her skin sent a shudder of rage up my back to settle in my heart.

I finally peeled myself off the floor and stomped back to her room to collect everything that was there. We didn't need anyone finding any of the magic books or evidence of the fire. When I was satisfied no questions would be asked, I carried the remainder of her possessions and left them in the study I rarely used.

I smelt her fragrance of wildflowers and the sweet berries that grew high on the cliff edges. Ilana hummed as she walked around her room. To steady my nerves, I swallowed a glass of hellshine, then another, until the tremor in my hand subsided.

She emerged from her room, hair still damp and cheeks flushed from the warm water. Her bare feet padded across the floor silently. My jaw dropped as my eyes raked over her. Tight black leggings and a pink vest top that appeared to be a few sizes too small, because her breasts refused to be fully contained in it.

Ilana took my glass from my nerveless fingers and took a gulp, her widened eyes telling me it burned on the way down her throat. I watched the movement until my gaze landed on those breasts that tempted me to touch them. Her right index finger under my chin closed my mouth.

"Careful," she chided me. "You never know what someone will put in there."

Our gazes met and held in a wordless war.

"You're playing with fire," I warned in a low voice.

Her little fangs showed when she grinned. "But the anticipation only makes the burn that much more exquisite." She drank the rest of my drink. "I'll go grab my shoes," she said, handing me back the glass. The leggings hugged her ass, making me bite the inside of my mouth.

She was going to kill me, or make my balls explode.

***

Ilana wanted me to show her what made my realm unique. I grinned as I led her through the castle. What made us special was also one of my greatest passions.

Magnus lay curled in a ball, his snout resting on his tail as he lazily watched the world go by. His ears twitched when he heard my footsteps and his double eyelids blinked over his amber elliptical eyes. His nostrils flared as he analysed the woman beside me.

He looked ferocious and was the biggest dragon in our thunder, but he was completely loyal to me.

"Magnus, this is Ilana," I introduced them.

He snorted and a little firebolt shot out of his nostril.

"Behave," I warned. Today was the day he decided to be a dick. My dragon was as temperamental as the weather and today was damp and drizzling with a forecast of asshole.

He blinked at me and returned his stare to Ilana.

She contains a lot of magic in one so small.

I nodded in reply, already knowing she possessed magic. Magnus was able to detect it since he was created from that very element. It was the reason Ophelia couldn't harm dragons—they'd descended from a higher magical source than witches did.

"Can I touch him?" Ilana asked, her eyes wide with excitement.

Magnus' ears twitched.

"Yeah, he likes when you rub behind his ears."

"Like a dog?" Ilana rubbed behind one of his ears with both of her hands even as he snarled at her reference to the four-legged furry animals on the Earth realm.

I am NOT a pet! His voice roared in my head in indignation.

"Who's a good boy?" I grinned, tickling behind his other ear.

He growled and my lips spread wider.

"His scales are so warm and soft. He's the most beautiful beast I've ever seen," Ilana cooed in his ear, her hands travelling down his neck.

A noise that sounded suspiciously like a purr emanated from his chest. The fucker was enjoying her attention. I narrowed my eyes at him.

Magnus' head tilted to the side to allow Ilana to reach further, his three horns twisting in pleasure. Tendrils of smoke curled from his nostrils into the air and the barbed tip of his tail tapped the ground in happiness.

"This is the only realm in Purgatory where dragons live," I told Ilana with pride. I loved the freedom of the air, flying high over all my problems with Magnus.

"Do they not like the other realms?" she asked.

Magnus' eyes fluttered closed and the tip of his forked tongue rattled between his teeth as she ran her hand up and down his horn.

I readjusted myself and bit the inside of my mouth. Her actions were innocent, yet my dick stood to attention as her hand glided over Magnus' horn.

Fucking fires of hell. She was going to be the death of me. Could a man die from frustration? Right at this moment it certainly felt like it.

"There you are!"

I groaned at the sound of my younger brother. My other brothers were all out on missions, but Remiel rarely left the comfort of the castle.

He prowled into the dragonry like he owned the place. Every dragon here was loyal to only one person. Me.

"What do you want, Remiel?" I asked, folding my arms across my chest.

His eyes zeroed in on Ilana grooming Magnus, his jaw tightening as he watched her hand moving.

"Remiel?" I repeated.

He blinked and cut his attention to me.

"What do you want?" I asked again.

"Who is she?" He deflected and answered his own question. "I haven't seen her around."

"And you won't," I snapped. He needed to leave now. My control was finely balanced, and he could be the factor that made it fracture.

He took a step toward her and Ilana finally noticed my brother. A predatory light lit at the back of his eyes, and a smile curled his lips. "I'm pleased to meet you. I'm Prince Remiel. And you are?"

None of his damned business.

Ilana's gaze met mine for a moment before she focused on Remiel. "Ilana."

His attention zeroed in on her, his eyes roving over her body. "You must be new here. I insist you join me for dinner later as my guest."

A flush crept up her cheeks and I could almost hear him salivating at her reaction. “I’m sorry, I promised Ezekiel to join him this evening.”

“You can’t spend all night with him,” Remiel said, confusion in his tone. No one ever dared refuse his charm.

A secretive smile crossed her lips. “That was definitely the plan.”

If she’d slapped my face, I couldn’t have been more shocked. I knew the innocence behind her remark because she was staying in my apartment, but the way she said it definitely made it sound like she was my mistress.

Remiel’s dark gaze swung to me in accusation. I shrugged and raised an eyebrow, refusing to comment.

My brother never backed down from a challenge. “Tomorrow night then?” His smile would have made most women swoon.

“Sorry.” Ilana smiled, tucking herself behind Magnus. “I’ll be spending that with Ezekiel as well.”

No one ever wanted to spend time with me. Normally, women wanted the notoriety of being with a prince, or an incubus, or both. Ilana had yet to ask for anything from me, even after I’d tried to scare her. The fact that she didn’t swoon at Remiel’s charm was impressive. He was pushing serious pheromones in her direction.

“You really should get to know all the incubus princes,” he coaxed, sending another wave of sexual hormones in her direction and placing his hand on her arm in suggestion.

Her body froze and she took a step back from him.

Magnus snorted and a firebolt nearly collided with Remiel. My dragon had no great love for my brother. Ilana giggled and smoothed her hand on his scaled head. I swear he was smiling for her. What sort of magic did she weave that had males losing their head around her?

“Were you not about to take me for a ride, Ezekiel?” Ilana asked, watching me from under her hair.

I knew I had a dirty mind—hell, all men did. It didn't matter if you were a sex demon or not, sex was never far from people's thoughts. I would love to take her for a ride in more ways than one, but I refused to let Ophelia feed from her.

I pushed past Remiel and curved a protective arm around her waist, tugging her against my hip. Her body moulded to mine without hesitation. The muscles of my back tightened as her arm slid around me in reply.

Remiel's eyes narrowed. "When did you take a serious lover? I thought you'd sworn off relationships?"

"Things change," I snapped, my tone daring him to pursue the matter. "Is there something you needed before we take Magnus out?"

"It'll keep," he sulked.

I knew he'd be waiting for me with a thousand questions when we got back. He'd go through all the records of the people I brought back yesterday in my absence. I'd already removed Ilana's file and put it in my room. He would find no trace of her.

I tightened my arm and lifted Ilana onto Magnus' back, walking up his wing to settle behind her.

"Hold on," I whispered in her ear, wrapping my arms around her. There was no chance of her falling off, but she didn't know that. Remiel's jaw tightened as he stared at my hand splayed on her stomach. Father really needed to deal with his appetites. Our world was filled with deviants, but my brother pushed every boundary, crossing lines whenever possible.

Ilana screamed in delight as Magnus propelled us into the air, her head settling against my shoulder. I chuckled, revelling in her emotions. I didn't realise how much I missed companionship until this moment. Every day I spent drowning under the weight of a curse that seemed to affect every aspect of my life. Ophelia loomed over me like a dark shadow that sucked all the joy out of my life.

I drank in Ilana's emotions of experiencing the thrill of flying for the first time. Some of the weight that stopped me breathing properly lifted from my shoulders. I felt the man I'd been two hundred years ago. I preferred him to the shell I'd become.

"Oh, my dark goddess!" Ilana shouted, her arms opening so the wind would beat against her. Ilana's childish innocence and enjoyment was infectious, burrowing under my skin and making me smile.

Magnus puffed his approval under her. My grumpy dragon who hated the world had accepted this small woman a few seconds after meeting her.

I laughed, closing my eyes and letting the air push against us as Magnus coasted in the currents.

"What is the green realm over there?" Ilana pointed toward the Elven lands.

"You do realise the rest of us see just black foliage everywhere?" I said into her ear.

She turned around to stare at me, startled. "Really?"

I nodded. "When you said about the colour yesterday, I knew you were different."

Her eyes widened.

"That's the Elven Realm," I told her. "Raegel built his towns and villages in the trees."

Her gaze returned to the other realm. "I thought everyone saw the leaves as crimson back home."

I shook my head, my hands grasping her tighter. "Only you."

She scanned the world below her, seeing it with new wonder. She pointed to an area between the incubus and elf realm. "What's that?" Ilana shouted over the noise of wind.

I shrugged. “Just part of the border.”

“It’s the only place that is black.”

Every single muscle in my body tensed and I focused on the area she pointed at. “Magnus…”

On my way.

He moved his right wing down to allow us to change direction and swoop toward the area.

“Can you sense anything?” I asked. Dread curdled in my stomach and sent fiery acid up my throat. We all knew Ophelia had camps set up throughout Purgatory, but none of us had managed to find them. They drained magic to strengthen her.

“Like what?” Ilana turned to stare at me with worried eyes.

I bit my bottom lip, chewing to stretch the skin as I debated what to say. Her wide eyes beckoned me to tell her the truth. “Ophelia has magical camps set up all through Purgatory that none of us have been able to find. What if you can find them because they are different colours to those with witch blood?”

Her gaze returned to the area she identified. “It feels cold even in the heat, like it is absorbing everything around it. The trees there grow in isolation from those in the network around them. Fear pulses in waves from the area.”

Magnus flew over it as if we were just out for one of our border patrols. I mentally catalogued the area, already picking out the soldiers I was going to send in to investigate. This was the first possible lead we had on one of her bases.

I didn’t know how I managed to find her, but Ilana seemed to be the answer to a prayer I’d uttered too long ago to remember.

I like her. You need to be nice to her and keep Remiel away.

As always, Magnus was able to read my mind.

***

Chapter Thirteen

Ilana

I knew the moment Ezekiel's mind focused on the threat of Ophelia. He still held me against him, but he was far away, commanding his troops.

I leaned forward, rubbing my hands over the neck of the giant dragon. They'd terrified me a few days ago, yet today I felt exhilarated to be in the air. Magnus ground his teeth together and arched his neck for me to scratch further up.

When we landed, Ezekiel escorted me to my room, his hand on the small of my back, his mind still thousands of miles away.

"I need to speak to my commanders," he said when we got to the room, pacing with excess energy.

"You need to be careful, Ezekiel. That place is cold and desolate, draining the goodness and life from everything around it."

Ezekiel nodded absently, chewing the inside of his mouth. He tended to do that when debating what to say, as if he was practicing the conversation before having it.

"It'll take a few days to plan and I need Gabriel back. He's escorting Addison in her search." He sighed and I wondered if he was worried about his lover with another man.

Remiel's words from earlier flitted through my head. *"When did you take a serious lover? I thought you'd sworn off relationships?"* If that was true, then what did that make Addison?

He trailed his fingers through his already messy hair. "I put all your books in the study with the storage unit for your blood. I need to speak to my commanders tonight, so they can start to strategize. Do not leave this room."

His dark eyes bored into mine, the weight of his worry settling on me.

"Don't worry, I'll avoid Remiel." I knew that was who he was talking about, as his body language had been shouting earlier when his brother tried to seduce me. His facial features resembled Ezekiel in the way siblings tended to be similar, but everything else was different. He'd touched me earlier, and my revulsion at being touched appeared again. So much for worrying about being attracted by Ezekiel's brothers. It was becoming clearer every day his touch was the only one my body responded to.

"Are my feelings about him that obvious?"

I pinched my finger and thumb together in front of me. "A little bit. Go plan your war and leave me to my books."

He laughed as I pushed him toward the door.

A smile formed on my lips as I watched him go. He was nothing like I expected, and that made me fall for the man harder than I fell for the fantasy.

Ignoring my turbulent emotions, I organised the study until it felt like it belonged to me. Mia would scream and bounce up and down if she knew I was living in the apartment of my fantasy lover. She'd be snooping everywhere, trying to find out every secret he possessed.

I was happy to discover every aspect of Ezekiel as he revealed himself to me.

***

Three days I'd lived in his apartment. I'd woken up the day after my dragon ride to find the study filled with all the ingredients from my lists, and extra books sitting on the desk. I was beginning to think Ezekiel never slept.

I began with the basics and what I knew, creating the healing balms I made in my youth with Mum and Aunt Agatha. Jars appeared for me to fill as we fell into a pattern of me leaving lists and Ezekiel fulfilling them. Eventually, I took over most of the office with all my books and apparatus.

Every day, the manipulation of the elements into the basic spells and potions became easier, more fluid, as if my soul recognised the steps of the intricate dance. My favourite part of the day was when Ezekiel arrived. His easy smile calmed me, and he listened to me prattle on, throwing in suggestions since he'd read all the books several times. We became relaxed in each other's company.

He hadn't touched or kissed me from that day we flew on his dragon and I struggled with my complicated feelings, trying to figure out why I missed something I'd never known before. I didn't make friends easily, and in a few short days, he'd managed to find out more about me than even Mia knew.

Night four I woke to the sound of a male voice shouting. I scampered out of bed, thinking we were under attack. With my vampire stealth I crept across the main living area, following the voice. I found Ezekiel thrashing on his bed, covered in sweat. He shouted in his sleep, his face twisted in rage.

Climbing onto his bed, I shook his shoulder, trying to waken him.

His agitation increased. "Let me go or I'll fucking kill you." His voice was filled with hate toward the person polluting his dreams.

"Ezekiel," I coaxed. "You need to wake up."

"Let me go, Ophelia. Lift your curse and just let me go." His voice broke and my heart fractured in my chest.

A curse. Ophelia had cursed Ezekiel.

I can't explain why, but I will not feed unless it's the equinox. Please, Ilana, you need to ensure that no matter how much we want to, that I do not feed from you unless under a sacred sky.

His words echoed in my head and I mentally flicked through the books I'd read. The cursed could not reveal what had happened to them. Their family and friends never knew unless they guessed, or the curse was lifted.

My loathing of Ophelia increased. How many others had she cursed in her search for ultimate power?

"Ezekiel." I shook his shoulder harder. He whimpered as if I'd hurt him. The look on his face tore into my heart and made me bleed emotional tears.

Straddling his waist, I grasped his arms, shaking him with my full strength. She couldn't reach him when he was awake, but I felt her connection to him like a low, electrical current over my skin. Her vile energy touching what didn't belong to her. No wonder he never slept.

Without thinking, I placed my left hand with the tattvas on it in the centre of Ezekiel's chest and concentrated. His body bowed under mine before his eyes flashed open. There was no recognition there, just confusion. Ezekiel's hand grabbed my throat before he rolled me under him, his weight holding me hostage. My eyes bulged at the pressure on my throat.

He was somewhere between nightmare and reality. This wasn't the hold he'd used before; this one intended to kill his prey. The more I struggled, the less oxygen I had. I relaxed my body, trying to preserve what precious air was left in my body. My hand clasped his wrist, my eyes pleading.

Ezekiel blinked, awareness slowly returning to him. My vision got fuzzy and darkened, my hands losing their grip.

"Ilana?" A voice sounded in the distance.

"Ilana!" A shout followed by warmth surrounding me.

"Fuck!" More heat flooded into me, this time pulsing deep in my core, making me want to moan in pleasure.

"Don't you fucking dare die on me." Consciousness returned and with it a need that erupted. A heartbeat pounded between my legs and lust snaked up my spine.

Ezekiel loomed over me, his dark eyes almost black as he watched me with concern.

"Thank the great demon. I thought you were…" I cut him off when I dragged his mouth to mine. Whatever he did to revive me meant I was burning up with desire. His rigid body melted until he pressed me into the mattress, our lips locked together in combat. I cried out as his hand fisted in my hair, his tongue invading my mouth. I gave everything he demanded, matching him until we were wrapped around each other.

This wasn't like his other kisses. There was no sensual exploring. It was hot and dirty and made me want to bite him to taste his blood. My fingers combed through his hair to hold him in place. My legs snaked around his waist until our bodies were fully aligned. I never truly understood the fascination with kissing until meeting Ezekiel. He made me burn with an all-consuming need that demanded a sacrifice of flesh and blood.

Sweat pooled at the bottom of my back as my internal heating exploded.

Ezekiel dragged his lips off mine, his breath ragged. "We can't…" He gasped.

His reluctance had to do with the curse, because the hard flesh pressed between my legs definitely said he wanted to.

I lay panting under him, my body aroused in a way it had never experienced before.

"Why are you in my room?" he asked softly.

"I heard shouting, you were having a bad dream," I croaked, rubbing my bruised throat.

His face tightened. "What was I saying?"

I shook my head. His secrets were his to keep. "I couldn't make it out. When I tried to wake you…" I let my voice drift off, he knew the rest.

It was his eyes that spoke to my soul. They contained his horror that he attacked me, his hatred of what he'd become, and concern for me. I'd spent years in the vampire army, suffered my fair share of injuries, and never once had anyone ever looked at me the way he did. It was as if he could feel my pain.

"I know we can't have sex, Ezekiel, but you could hold me." My voice pleaded. He'd awakened a beast inside me and it paced with barely controlled lust.

His fingers stroked the side of my face, trailing down to trace over my throbbing throat. "I had to heal you with my breath, that's why you feel so aroused."

My eyes widened. How did he know I was turned on?

The corner of his lips turned up in a vague smile. "I'm an incubus, we feed off sexual pleasure. We can sense arousal just like vampires can scent blood in the air."

My mouth opened in a silent 'O'.

So slowly, I stared vulnerably into his eyes, his head lowering until our eyelashes touched and his lips gently pressed against mine. "I'm sorry," he muttered, giving me delicate kisses. With every swipe of his lips across mine, I yielded to him, powerless to resist. His kiss deepened until there was just the two of us in a cocoon.

Time became irrelevant as I clung to him helplessly. Kissing said more than our words ever could, it told us how we were both feeling with honesty. Every day he demolished another of my defences until I lay bare and exposed to him.

My arms wrapped around his torso, and I lost myself to the sensation of just being with him. His kisses dragged down my neck, healing with every light caress. Ezekiel's fingers found my left breast as his mouth found my right. My flimsy vest top ripped down the front to grant him access.

I'd never been touched like this. An invisible cord connected my nipple to that pulsating need between my legs. Every tug of my nipple with his fingers and teeth made me pant with desire. It was too much and not enough, my back arching up to demand he suck harder, torture my nipples more in the search of pleasure.

"Ezekiel… I need…" I didn't know what the fuck I needed. All I knew was that he was the only one who could give it to me.

His body crawled over mine until he spoke against my lips. "What do you need?"

You, I need you.

My fangs peeked from under my top lip and my eyes jolted open when he pricked his finger on one. A bead of blood formed on his fingertip. I wanted to demand to know what he thought he was doing, but my eyes rolled back in my head when he allowed the drop to land on my tongue. His taste exploded across my taste buds, my vision lightening as I stared up at him.

"You need to feed to heal the damage to your throat," Ezekiel whispered against my lips.

I shook my head, my eyes wide with fear. I'd never been able to feed from the vein before.

"Trust me," he said before kissing me with an intensity that set fire to the blood pumping through my veins. He lifted me until I straddled his hips as he sat back on his knees, never once breaking the connection between our mouths. His tongue probed the roof of my mouth, stroking along mine as he fucked my mouth with his.

He broke away, his eyes meeting mine. "Trust me, Ilana. You can feed from me."

Ezekiel guided my mouth to his neck. The strange part in all of this was that I did trust him when I'd never trusted anyone else before. The tips of my fangs traced along the artery, feeling the pulse vibrate under them. His hand fisted in my hair as he held me against him.

I closed my eyes and gave up the fight, my fangs piercing his skin. He stiffened slightly before relaxing. My mouth filled with his blood as I sucked deeply, allowing him to fill me with his vitality. My body wrapped around him as I fed like a vampire for the first time. His emotions crashed into me and I felt him inside me through his blood. His thoughts, his emotions, his physical need to be inside me.

Finally, I managed to pull myself away and lick his wounds. We stared at each other, breathing hard. I couldn't deny the connection between us, there was something that defied description. His blood pumped through me, healing me and awakening a soul-destroying need deep in my core.

Without a word, Ezekiel pushed me onto my back, his body covering mine. His lips journeyed from my lips, to my breasts, to my belly button. My system was in overload from his blood and this unquenchable lust.

I tried to buck up when my panties ripped and his breath fanned between my legs. No one had ever touched there before, not even the medics on our base.

My body spasmed as his mouth and tongue moved in an obscene kiss that made my legs widen and my breath catch. My fingers latched into his hair as he devoured me, his finger penetrating me to rub a place that made my eyes cross.

What. The. Fuck.

It was my body and I never knew that place existed. I'd brought myself to climax a few times by rubbing my clit when I woke from a particularly erotic dream and I was on the edge. His breath stimulated my clit when he blew on my exposed skin.

I was on fire, the need to erupt like a volcano gathering in my core.

He didn't stop, his mouth, tongue, and finger on a quest to unravel me completely.

Perspiration covered my skin, passion laced my senses, and pressure built steadily deep in my womb. One suck of my clit was all it took to send me hurtling headlong into the strongest orgasm of my life. My legs stiffened and widened, my head fell back, and my fingers tightened in his hair as pleasure exploded from my womb to radiate through me.

Ezekiel climbed up my body, pressing soft kisses on his journey.

"Feel better?" he asked, his lips teasing mine.

His erection dug into my stomach and it killed me that after giving so much he received so little in return. My fingers tentatively touched his hard flesh. His eyes closed and his top teeth bit into his bottom lip.

I'd never tried this before, never touched a man. My movements were hesitant, my strokes clumsy. Ezekiel groaned and my eyes flashed to his face. His dark gaze held mine, giving me the courage to push him onto his back.

"I'm sorry," I mumbled. "I've never done this before…"

His fingers lifted my chin until we stared at each other. "You don't need to, Ilana. Honestly, the need will pass."

I shook my head. We may not be able to have sex, but I could ensure he found pleasure after what he'd given me. His blood still pounded inside me, connecting us at a fundamental level.

"I want to."

His eyes never left mine as I straddled his legs, my hands wrapping around his hard length. I started slowly, finding a rhythm, watching his reactions to what I was doing. His head fell back onto the pillow as he gave control to me. I was surprised how something so ferociously hard was soft to the touch. My fingers explored, tracing the thick, bulging vein, finding a sensitive area at the base between his shaft and his balls.

He groaned when I massaged him, using my palm to rotate around his testicles.

"Fuck, what are you doing to me?" he gasped.

I had no idea. Literally none. Instinct alone guided my actions.

His hips bucked against me when I ran my tongue from base to tip.

"Fuck," Ezekiel hissed.

I stopped, my body freezing. His eyes flew open.

"I'm sorry, I didn't mean to hurt you." My words melded together, my cheeks flaring in embarrassment.

He pushed himself up, his hands grasping my face. "It wasn't pain I felt. You have no idea what your touch does to me." He kissed me, returning my hand to his stiff cock, his hand guiding mine up and down.

I returned to my previous task and he flopped back on the bed. I alternated between my hands and mouth, using the small motions of his hips to teach me what he liked. I'd watched Mia giving thousands of blow jobs as she fed from the vein on her blood slaves' cocks. Stealing a few tips from her, my fangs descended, and I traced the tip of them along his vein.

Looking up, I saw his dark gaze watching me. My fangs sank into his vein and his eyes rolled back before his head slumped into the pillow.

"Fuck me." Ezekiel gasped, his hands fisting the sheets on either side of him.

I used his blood as a lubricant to take him deeper into my mouth, feeding from him even as I sought to bring him pleasure.

"Ilana…" His voice held a warning I chose not to heed.

The taste of his blood roared through me in a cacophony of flavours, his pleasure adding to mine as we were joined through a blood link.

His cock grew bigger and pulsed before it exploded.

I never thought I would have the ability to make a man climax, considering that every time one touched me I turned to stone.

“Did I do it right?” I asked, crawling up his body to lie on top of him.

A smile ghosted across his lips. “Yeah, you did it right.”

I grinned up at him and something passed between us, a private moment that no one would ever be able to touch or destroy.

He tugged me up and settled me beside him, his arms holding me securely.

I snuggled closer and closed my eyes.

As much as I tried, I couldn’t shake the fact that I felt like I finally found where I belonged.

***

Chapter Fourteen

Ezekiel

I lay staring at the ceiling in shock. I'd lived around four hundred years, had fed from countless women, and didn't think I'd come so hard in all my life.

Her questing fingers and tentative touches still echoed on my dick. It was the closest I'd come to feeding without sex. I felt her energy infusing into me and giving me strength. None of what was happening made sense anymore.

She'd come in here because I was caught in one of Ophelia's night-time attacks. No one had broken through them before. They happened to all the cursed princes from time to time when she wanted to prove her power over us.

My fingers created patterns on Ilana's skin while my mind got lost in thoughts. I couldn't risk her. Several times I nearly lost control and sunk into her welcoming warmth. What was worse was that I knew she'd never stop me. Ilana would accept me and I would destroy her, taking her piece by piece until there was nothing left of the beautiful, intelligent woman currently lying in my arms.

"You're thinking too hard," her voice said from where she lay on my chest.

"I have a lot to think about," I replied.

She pushed herself up to stare down at me. "Stop, Ezekiel, just stop."

My brow furrowed.

"You're trying to work out how to let me down gently because you don't want to hurt me." She sighed. "Your blood links us."

I neutralised my expression. That was not something I'd ever heard before. "Is that normal?"

"How the fuck should I know?"

Her curse made my eyebrows fly up.

Her hand landed on my chest. "You need to stop worrying. My mum always told me not to argue with Fate when she had a plan. You're the first man who can touch me or feed me. There has to be a reason why."

I stared at her, unsure what I was supposed to say. How did you tell a virgin who wore white cotton panties that she'd given me something I'd never experienced before? That she nourished me without feeding me?

I sensed her guilt at what we'd shared. She wanted me but there was something eating away at her even as she clung to me. Acid rose at the back of my throat at the thought of her regretting being in my bed.

"Please don't send me away." Her plea nearly crippled me.

I didn't know if I could send her away even if I wanted to. She'd crawled under my skin and infected me with a fever in my blood that I could no longer contain. Ilana would either be my salvation or ruination.

"You need to sleep," I said, tugging her beside me again because those green eyes saw too much. "It's not every day you have your first feed."

"It's been a night of firsts…" she whispered.

I already knew that. The fact that I was the first man she allowed between her legs made me heady with desire. The violence that thrummed inside me at the thought of any other man touching her terrified me. I may only be able to fuck her four times a year, but Ilana was mine and there was no way I was letting anyone else near her.

***

For the next three nights, every time I closed my eyes, Ophelia was waiting for me. She was furious I'd refused her invitation to her ball. Her vengeance was to try and drain me until I needed a feeding frenzy to replenish my energy.

Yet every night when my body was held in paralysis by her magic, Ilana crawled into my bed and broke her hold on me. Occasionally she fed from me, other times she just tucked herself in beside me. She made me want to be a better man to protect her.

Feeding made Ilana crave a sexual release, her body open and willing for me. Yet when we lay together afterwards, her guilt and regret stabbed me in the heart. Was there someone she loved back home but couldn't touch? Did she only crawl into my bed because she finally found someone to feed from but didn't want to be with me?

I'd spent years being nothing more than a sexual conquest for women. They wanted orgasms from an incubus but not the man behind them. They giggled and whispered, trying to attract my attention. Remiel was more than happy to drag them into his bed and kick them out in the morning. Raegel refused to let him back into the elven realm after he found him fucking one of his elven warriors up the ass while jacking him off. My brother was going to get himself killed because of his dick. He didn't care what the orifice was as long as he could penetrate it.

Addison and Gabriel finally returned with magical items, but the witches had fled before they reached them. Relief settled on me that they were home safe. She was the rock I clung to when my curse tried to eat me from the inside. My sister was intrigued when I filled her in on Ilana's abilities. She planned to work with her the next day.

Even though he was tired, Gabriel spent hours in our latest strategy session about Ophelia's possible base on our border. He immediately took over, ordering new land maps, and demanding the dragons fly tomorrow so new close-range images could be obtained. We'd fought this war together so long that he was my right hand.

When I wandered into my room to go to bed, Ilana was already asleep in a ball in the centre of the bed. I closed my eyes and blew out a sigh, unsure if it was of relief or frustration. I crawled in beside her, and she automatically snuggled against my heat. No matter where she started in the bed, she always ended up using my chest as her own personal pillow.

No dreams came that night, no Ophelia, just blissful rest.

***

The banging on my door woke me, and I stumbled wearily to open it. Addison and Gabriel stood gaping at me.

"What?" I demanded.

"Were you still asleep?" Addison glared at me standing in my black boxers. "You never sleep."

"Everyone sleeps sometimes," I muttered, stretching as I turned away from them so they could enter.

I felt Ilana enter the room, my body accustomed to her since she slept beside me every night. My own personal dreamcatcher who kept Ophelia away.

Addison and Gabriel's attention swung to her and I bit back a groan.

"Is Ilana staying here?" Addison demanded.

Ilana's body froze and her eyes widened as they darted to me.

"It's the safest place for her to practice her magic." I evaded her real question. My sister wanted to know if I was sleeping with Ilana. I was, but it really was just sleeping.

"She could practice in my rooms in the dungeons," Addison snapped.

"Look." Ilana stepped forward with her hands out in front of her. "I know that Ezekiel is your lover or husband or whatever, but honestly he's just been helping me with my magic."

My eyes nearly bulged out of my head at her words. Lover?

Gabriel choked back a snort and Addison stared at Ilana as if she was completely mad.

"Ezekiel is my brother," Addison said in stunned disbelief.

"Oh, thank the dark goddess." Ilana slumped against the wall.

A slow smile curved my lips as I finally understood why she felt so guilty about the pleasure we gave each other. Ilana thought I belonged to Addison and didn't want anyone to be hurt.

She was too good for me.

Addison stared at her and then me and then back to Ilana.

"Why is she sleeping in your bed?" Addison demanded. I went to deny it, but she held her hand up to stop the lie before I told it. "You're both in your underwear, for fuck's sake."

I couldn't stop my eyes from running over Ilana. Her panties and vest top did little to hide her voluptuous curves. Her hair was tousled from sleep and her body held that languid 'I've been fucked last night' look that made my dick twitch. Addison was right, we looked like we were living together.

"What exactly are you two doing here?" I deflected the topic.

Addison folded her arms and glared at me. "I was going to help Ilana with her magic and Gabriel was about to go on a reconnaissance mission. I couldn't find Ilana and he was helping me search. It never occurred to me to look in your bed."

"Give me a second to get ready and I'll be right with you," I said to Gabriel.

I grabbed Ilana's hand on the way into my bedroom, slamming the door behind us, knowing it would drive Addison mad.

My lips crashed against Ilana's before she could ask me one of her constant questions. Her arms wrapped around my neck to drag me closer, her legs trying to climb me to wrap around my waist.

"Is that why I kept sensing your guilt and regret?" I asked against her lips.

She nodded, her huge green eyes staring at me.

I ran our interactions with Addison through my head, realising I never told Ilana who she was. She'd spent the rest of her time in my apartment. "We'll talk about this when I get back." I kissed her again, wishing it was an equinox because she was driving me crazy. "Stay here while I'm gone."

She nodded, tugging my head down again. I lost myself in her until someone banged at my bedroom door.

"Seriously, Zek?" Addison shouted. "I would say get a room, but…"

I rolled my eyes. "Do you have siblings?" I asked Ilana.

She shook her head, giggling.

"Consider yourself lucky," I muttered, glaring at the door when it banged again.

Just to annoy Addison, I pulled Ilana under the shower with me. We'd fully explored each other's bodies, stopping ourselves before we engaged in full sex. Several times, I'd slipped just inside her hot sheath, tormenting myself with the feel of her.

My hands glided over her body with the lubrication of soap, our bodies moving together without any awkwardness. Ilana washed my back and scrubbed shampoo in my hair and I returned the gesture. This level of intimacy was new for both of us. In the past, I fed in the harems or on bases, but my room was private. Ilana's scent was all over it, mixed with mine. It was the tiny things, like her hair ties on the bedroom floor that made whatever this was real.

Addison and Gabriel broke apart from their shared embrace at my window when we walked out of my room. I wondered when they were ever going to tell me they were mated. My best friend and my sister. Our parents would go mad as they'd planned her marriage from before she could walk. Personally, I didn't care. Being cursed for two hundred years gave you a different perspective on life.

I pointed at my sister. "No prying, Addison. I mean it. You're here to help Ilana with magical matters, not pry into my private life."

Gabriel chuckled. "Good luck with that."

I pulled my fireproof coat on and winked at Ilana before leaving with Gabriel.

The fact that she blushed made a grin spread across my face.

***

Chapter Fifteen

Ilana

Addison barely waited until the door closed before her eyes met mine. She studied me as if she expected to find something different from the last time we met.

I stared at her in return.

"Are you okay?" she asked hesitantly.

I nodded, confused by her reactions. "Yeah. Ezekiel's been looking after me. He's set up a magic room in his study." I wanted to change the subject because everything between us was new and precious. It needed time to nurture and grow. I knew there was some form of curse and that Ezekiel was doing his best to protect me. For now, that was enough. I would figure the rest out in time.

"I'd love to see what you've achieved." Addison took a step toward the study and stopped. "If you'd like me to."

"I've been waiting for you to return. I just need to change."

Ezekiel had given me a pair of his training bottoms to put on and they were huge on me. I quickly pulled on leggings and a baggy top, my skin still tingling from where he touched me in the shower.

There wasn't a part of my skin he hadn't caressed over the past few nights. He showed me what he liked on his body until I felt confident touching him. Step by step, he led me in this strange new dance. His kisses intoxicated me, his blood made me mad with desire, and his body made mine feel safe.

A few weeks ago, if someone had told me I'd be sleeping beside him every night, I'd have laughed at them. Now I was drinking his blood and sharing a shower with him. I wasn't sure what to make of how far my life had changed.

Addison sat at the desk in the study examining all the jars and books. Her brows were furrowed and her lips pressed together in a thin line.

"Is everything okay?" I asked from the doorway.

"You did all this in a few days?"

A sad smile crossed my lips. "When I was reading the books, I realised that my childhood cookery and bakery classes weren't really that at all. It was my Aunt Agatha's way of teaching me witchcraft. Her camping trips incorporated finding herbs and preparing them under moonlight in the Earth realm. The books list the magical properties that imbues them with. At the time, I thought it was for flavouring dinner. The healing potions I'd made before under the disguise of soaps and shampoos."

Addison's eyes showed her compassion. "You were a witch in all but name."

I nodded.

"I'm sorry about my reaction earlier." She glanced away as if to gather her thoughts. "I'm protective of Ezekiel, his life has been difficult. He deserves to be happy, but too many hurdles stand in his way."

I didn't pry, Ezekiel would help me piece his story together.

"I was going to try a few incantations today if you want to help me," I said, moving the topic away from her brother.

She nodded eagerly in reply.

We spent hours working through different spells in the books, summoning items, levitating objects, manipulating the elements. It was more enjoyable with someone there to help. Ezekiel was right; he and Addison had a vast wealth of knowledge when it came to magic, but no practical experience.

Addison sampled some of the different potions in the jars, spreading them on her skin to sense them. Slowly, we became friends, sharing stories. I'd had to hide so much from Mia, but here, a different Ilana had evolved. I was able to look at the images from the witches' campsites and fill in gaps for Addison from what I remembered in my childhood.

My abilities grew stronger as Addison deliberately tested me, pushing me out of my comfort zone.

The screeches came first, making Addison stiffen and glance up at the ceiling.

The castle shook around us, dislodging dust to fall from high hiding places.

Shouts echoed outside Ezekiel's window in the living area, but Addison dragged me back when I went to look out.

"She never normally attacks, but I think you've been blocking her getting to Ezekiel," Addison said.

My brow wrinkled in confusion.

"He looked more his old self, relaxed and alive. Ophelia will never tolerate that."

My eyes swung to the window. Even though we were far under the castle, someone had created a courtyard and a garden, giving it the appearance of being a room in a castle tower. Now I understood why we were underground.

Rage coursed through me at the thought of her deliberately harming Ezekiel. Anger burned hot in my veins and combusted in my chest. Magic was a gift that she had twisted into a horrible curse. Ophelia was an abomination who belonged in Hell, not Purgatory.

"Gather all your healing balms and potions," Addison whispered urgently. "When her wyverns have finished, they'll leave devastation."

"The dragons…" I started.

"Are all out on patrol with Zek and Gabriel. She's been watching and biding her time."

"Maybe I can help. I have magic."

Addison laughed. "You have basic magic while she has accumulated the power of generations of witches. We need more than just you to stop her. We need to find every witch still alive in Purgatory and form a coven strong enough to stand against The Blood Queen."

I finally understood Addison's search. It wasn't just for magic, she wanted to make an army.

The screeches and screams died down, the hairs on the back of my neck standing to attention. Addison and I made our way through the castle until we found the devastation. Bodies lay strewn in the hallway, blood running along the floor in rivers.

A wraith hovered over a young female, sucking her life energy from her still form.

Heat built in my chest as I stared at the child being murdered. Power trickled into my hands, activating the tattvas there. My thumb stroked against the middle finger on my left hand before flames burst from my hands, incinerating the wraith.

He shrieked, trying to twist from my hold, but I held him captive until elemental fire consumed him in a bright explosion.

Addison gasped, her hand clutching my arm.

My eyes searched the room. Every wraith I found suffered the same fate as the first until none remained. I fell to my knees beside the girl, my medical training kicking in.

One after another, Addison and I helped the medics try to piece the victims of the attack back together again. We used my healing balms to glue flesh back together again, tinctures to relieve pain.

A screech from the corridor leading to the soldiers' room echoed into the hall. Addison and I shared a worried look before making our way toward it. A red wyvern flapped its wings, seeking a route out, but one of its claws was caught on a chandelier as it hung upside down.

Avoiding its wings, I crept under it, sensing the animal's distress and panic. I stroked its head and whispered soothing words in its ear. The scales felt warm and soft under my fingers. "Shush," I whispered. "No one is going to hurt you."

I'd seen Ophelia's wraiths riding on them, but a captive beast could not choose its owner. Tracing my hands over the scales, I searched for injuries. One of the bones in a wing felt broken with the violence it had tried to free itself with. Aunt Agatha spent most of her spare time healing sick animals and I spent a lot of my free time with her as a child. I used the same cooing voice and tone with the wyvern until it stopped struggling.

"I need something to hold its wing and a tincture for pain," I instructed Addison. The sound of her footsteps got fainter as she scurried away.

There were a few lacerations to its skin, but my fingers stopped at a strange bulge where her wing met her body. I ducked under to examine it. There was a foreign black semi-circle attached to the wyvern. Her feet tried to reach the object, but it was just out of reach. My finger traced over it, and magic pulsed up my arm, trying to lull me into obedience.

Ophelia.

She'd put this on the wyvern to make it obey her.

The wyvern gave a low moan and nodded at it again. She didn't want to be controlled.

All I possessed was intuition because there was nothing like this in the books I'd read so far. My thumb had the Akasha tattva for spirit depicted as a black egg shape. It looked the same as the object on the wyvern. Gently, I rubbed my thumb over the foreign item until it vibrated under my touch.

Addison returned, and I held my finger to my lips and nodded at the black orb. Who knew what Ophelia was capable of? Her eyes widened as she stepped closer. She motioned for me to wait a moment while she dashed off. When she returned she held a jar.

I caressed the object again while concentrating, setting the intention that this animal find peace from the tyranny it lived under. Freedom was a basic right to every being. Ophelia stole that every time she ensnared a soul.

The wyvern rested her head on my shoulder, her breathing erratic. Addison stroked her wing, her face pinched as she experienced the pain of the wyvern through her empathic abilities.

After several minutes, the hard black crystal began to move as my magic combated the magic contained inside it. It pulsed and slowly twisted until it fell into my hand. I quickly dropped it into the jar and Addison screwed the lid into place.

Our eyes met in a united revulsion of what Ophelia did to everything she touched.

I returned my attention to healing the wyvern. We needed to free it from the chandelier, but it was too high for either of us to reach.

"I could try and climb up the wall," I said dubiously. Normally I could run up walls and cling to them in a battle situation. The corridor was long enough to build up speed.

The poor creature slumped against my shoulder, the pain relief taking effect.

"What the fuck is going on?" Ezekiel stormed toward us, his face tight with fury. "Step back from the wyvern." He held a blaster gun.

"No!" I wrapped my arms around its neck.

Gabriel charged down the corridor. "Thank fuck, no one had seen you." He stared at Addison in relief.

Ezekiel's gaze locked with mine. "Those things kill at Ophelia's command."

I pointed to the jar on the floor. "She's controlling them with those."

He didn't drop his blaster's aim once even as he approached and picked up the jar, rattling it to examine the contents.

"Please, Ezekiel, we need to free her," I pleaded. "She's in pain and needs to heal."

He moved his stare from me to the wyvern, his jaw tense as he studied her.

"Fine," he snapped, pushing the blaster in the back of his black jeans. "You are going to be the fucking death of me."

A grin tugged the corner of my lips.

Between them, Ezekiel and Gabriel dragged the chandelier apart until they released the wyvern.

"Mother will be pissed," Ezekiel muttered, surveying the unsalvageable chandelier on the floor.

The wyvern lay limp and exhausted. Addison and I worked rapidly to stabilise the broken wing with splints before gluing the wounds together with some of my ointments.

"What are we supposed to do with it?" Gabriel lifted his chin in the direction of the injured wyvern.

Ezekiel glared at me for several moments. I begged him with my eyes to save the life of the poor creature that rested its head on my lap. We battled with each other in a wordless argument. The muscle at the side of his jaw tightened and I knew I'd won when he groaned and rolled his eyes.

"She can stay in my old room until she feels better," I tentatively suggested. "No one will see her."

I knew if anyone saw a wyvern, they'd shoot her on sight since Ophelia owned them.

“That’s not a bad idea,” Addison added in support.

Ezekiel and Gabriel shared a look that said they thought we’d lost control of our faculties. Without a word, they lifted the big beast between them and Ezekiel moved in the direction of my old room. Addison squeezed my hand in excitement of our small victory.

They deposited her on the bed, and Addison and I moved her body to make her comfortable. Gabriel moved the furniture against the wall to try and make the room wyvern safe.

Exhausted, I wandered into the bathroom to wash the blood off my hands and try and revitalise myself by splashing water on my face. When I finally glanced up, my hands braced on the sink, Ezekiel’s eyes met mine in the mirror.

“Thank you,” I whispered. There was no doubt in my head that no one else would have helped save the wyvern except him.

His hands landed on my hips to drag me back against the heat of his hard body. His voice sent shivers down my spine. “I thought you were dead when I returned and found you gone. Then someone said they’d seen you and Addison in the hall, helping the medics. I recognised your jars on the floor.”

“We couldn’t stand by and do nothing,” I whispered, my gaze never leaving his in the mirror.

“Then I find you with a huge beast lying on top of you.” His eyes fluttered closed for a few seconds. “You are going to give me a fucking heart attack.”

I turned in his arms until our bodies aligned against each other. “I couldn’t watch it suffer when I could help.”

His fingers tilted my chin back until there was nowhere for me to hide. His proximity made me weak at the knees, and each day made my feelings for him increase. “You were meant to stay in my apartment. You would have been safe during an attack."

"That's not who I am," I argued.

His fury pulsed against my skin even as he dominated my body with his. "I need to know you're safe when I'm not here."

My hands cupped his face. "I was safe."

He groaned before his lips found mine. The weight of guilt at being with him had lifted from me and I let him consume me. His fear for me was an aphrodisiac to my soul, telling me without words that I meant something to him.

When we broke apart, I smiled shyly. "Thank you for saving the wyvern."

He leaned down to whisper in my ear, "When I get to the apartment tonight, I want you naked on your knees. Then you can thank me."

Colour bloomed in my cheeks and my eyes flashed up to his. Lust swirled in his depths and ignited a fire deep in my belly. The image of me on my knees in submission before him gave me shivers of anticipation.

Every night he managed to make me squirm and scream in abandon. His touch was my greatest addiction but my ultimate strength. He made me finally feel comfortable in my skin.

"I think I can do that." I stood on my tiptoes to press my lips against his to seal my promise.

***

Chapter Sixteen

Ezekiel

I'd nearly gone out of my mind when we returned to find Ophelia had attacked. It was my fault since she hadn't been able to torture my sleep for the past few nights. I no longer felt like I was walking around in a trance. Ilana had given me a reprieve with her presence in my bed.

Gabriel and I had stormed through the castle to my apartment, thinking Ilana and Addison would be behind the door that would keep them safe.

Were they there?

No, they'd decided to go and play doctors with wraiths and wyverns still lurking about the place.

I'd never felt so helpless in my life. I struggled over whether I should hug her or punish her when I finally found her with a seven-foot wyvern collapsed on top of her. She was driving me insane.

The Incubus Council all sat around the large oval table when I stalked into the room. Some of my brothers were present, recalled after the attack on the castle. Remiel sat beside our father, staring at the table.

"Where the hell where you?" I demanded.

His shoulders stiffened and his gaze finally met mine in rebellion. "I was busy."

The brother closest in age to me, Jethro, snorted and rolled his eyes.

"Addison was up there in the middle of it helping the medics." My voice rose with every word. Gabriel looked like he wanted to crawl over the table and send my brother to the medics right now. His panic matched mine when we discovered the women missing from my apartment. "She could have been taken or killed."

He slouched in his chair. "She should have stayed below ground," he muttered.

"You need to grow the fuck up," Jethro snarled at Remiel. "We've all had enough of you being the coward who hides behind women's panties."

"Zek's only pissed his woman was up there with Addison," he retaliated.

All eyes moved to me. Ilana, to this point, had been my secret and I would have preferred to keep it that way. "And?" I brushed off his snide comment as if it was old news. "Do you want every woman in this castle to fight on your behalf? Both of those women have bigger balls than you do when it comes to a fight!"

"You were the last dark prince remaining in this castle," Jethro stated. "The protection of the people fell to you. I've already checked. You were in the harem. Again." His tone was more lethal than a sword, his words hanging in the air with venom dripping from them.

Jethro was a warrior. He kept his own harem separate from the main one in the castle. His women were his alone to feed from and protect. If I disliked Remiel, then he downright despised him.

"Father, tell them to leave me alone," Remiel whined, reverting to being the youngest son.

Our father sighed and pinched the bridge of his nose. "It's time you grew up and protected this realm as your brothers do."

Remiel deflated beside him. War was on our doorstep and every one of us needed to fight. That included my youngest brother.

"What are the totals?" Jethro asked, his tone sombre.

I shook my head and dropped into my seat beside Gabriel. "My new recruits were here and managed to force them back, but there were civilians killed. Women going about their daily business and kids playing in the great hall. All the dragons were out on patrol."

Ophelia had not been so brazen in a long time.

"The medics were praising the healing ointments that Addison's friend supplied," Jethro said, his gaze boring into me. He wanted to know about Ilana.

"They've been studying old manuscripts and books to find cures for wyvern and wraith attacks," Gabriel intervened.

Jethro leaned back in his chair until I finally gave him my attention. "Spit it out, Jet."

"How do you have a lover living in the castle that no one has met? Who is she? Where is she staying?" He continued to stare at me.

"Ilana lives in my apartment because that's where she belongs. My private life is no one's concern but mine," I snapped.

Remiel smirked since the attention had diverted away from him. "He took her on a dragon ride the other day."

Jethro's eyebrows rose fractionally. I never let anyone ride Magnus except me. It was an unwritten law.

Taking a deep breath, I brought the full weight of my power to descend on everyone around the table. I hadn't been strong enough in a long time to make this many yield to my will. Ilana's presence gave me that strength. She nourished me without me having to feed. She allowed me to rest from Ophelia's reach.

"We are here to discuss the attack on the castle, not to discuss my woman. Do I make myself clear?" I glared at each of them until they lowered their eyes. "Gabriel, bring us up to speed on everything that's happened today."

I sat fuming while listening to the list of dead and injured. Our reconnaissance mission earlier had confirmed it was a hidden base for Ophelia. Her wyverns and wraiths were already out, we just didn't know they were at our castle because we'd come the other way to make it look as if we weren't targeting the area.

The bitch had been camping out on our land, draining life from our realm. It had taken all my willpower not to make Magnus burn the entire area to the ground.

Jethro's scowl grew deeper when he heard about the base, his temper rising until it practically vibrated through the air.

"I will recall my full ground unit," Jethro said, his fingers steepled under his chin. "We will need to surround them with stealth until they have no means of escape."

"The equinox is in three days," Father interrupted. "It would ensure everyone is fully fed and ready to fight."

He always hosted his famous orgies on the equinox because he knew the restrictions of my curse. He was there when she brought me to my knees and ripped my free will from my chest.

Jethro nodded. "It will give me time to get my unit in place."

"I've ordered the kitchen to prepare a banquet for tonight," Father continued. "We need to show the witch that we will not cower to her attack. I expect everyone in attendance." His eyes met mine and I read the message there. He expected Ilana to be there for everyone to see.

Fuck!

I zoned out of the discussions about security. Gabriel and I worked so closely together that he knew my thoughts on strategies. We were leaving the room when I caught Gabriel by the arm. He stared at me in confusion.

"Don't think I'm going to be thrown to the wolves with Ilana. If I have to sit there with her beside me, do you not think it's time you let the realm know you've mated with Addison?"

His eyes widened and his mouth dropped open.

"You didn't think I knew?" I asked in disbelief. "You only ever smell of her and her of you. I thought you were going to demolish the castle earlier when she was missing."

His expression froze. "You're not going to try and kill me?"

"Father was going to give a succubus to an elf. We both know that was never going to work. They're too full of honour and rules to be able to satisfy a succubus."

Gabriel released a breath. "I've been going crazy thinking of ways to tell you."

"She chose you as her first lover. Addy has had the hots for you since she was little. I may not like to think of my little sister having sex with my closest friend, but I'm not stupid or blind. Fuck's sake, Gab." I rolled my eyes at him, taunting him as I stomped past. "Don't hurt her or I'll pin your balls to the wall in the dining hall."

There was no doubt in my mind that Gabriel would protect my sister with the last beat of his heart. It was the only reason I didn't lose my shit when I worked out why the two of them always arrived exactly two minutes apart, why their eyes always managed to find each other in a crowded room, and why she always took him with her when she was off hunting witches.

Remiel was lurking outside my apartment as I walked down the corridor. My stomach clenched in anger. He'd only just found out she was there, and here he was.

"Remiel." I stopped in front of my door, folding my arms across my chest. "Have you forgotten where your apartment is?"

"No. I was just wondering what you're hiding. There is no way you're letting anyone live with you. We all know that is bullshit."

"Piss off." I sneered and turned my back on him.

The fucker pushed past me into my apartment when I opened the door. He slid to a halt when he saw Ilana wandering out of my room in nothing more than a towel. She rubbed her washed hair with another towel, the motion of her hands above her head making the towel around her dip precariously.

"Is that you, Ezekiel?" she said. "I'm not quite naked yet, but you're back early."

Ilana came to a stop, her eyes trailing from two sets of boots to Remiel and me standing there.

Nothing in the world would wipe the grin off my face at the image of her. Her teeth bit into her bottom lip as our gazes locked.

"Sorry, babe. Remiel burst in. He doesn't believe you live here with me." I brought her up to speed while walking toward her. Fuck, she looked amazing and smelt even better.

Her laugh washed over me. "Where does he think I live?"

I pushed her damp hair behind her ears. "No idea. Where do you think she lives, Remmy?" I deliberately used the name he despised in his youth.

"You never bring lovers home with you. No one is allowed in your sacred space but you. What was I supposed to think?" His face was almost purple with rage.

I slid my arms around her waist as I stood behind Ilana, propping my chin on top of her head. "Now you've seen her, you can piss off."

"She should be in the harem. She's not bound to you," he insisted. The fucker only wanted her there so he could try and seduce her.

Ilana's hands gripped mine at her waist.

"Ilana is going nowhere. I'd advise you back off before I lose my temper." Too long I'd had to curb my nature because I didn't have the strength of my birthright because of the curse. I let a trickle of power loose and watched him struggle against me. I was the firstborn of our father, superior to him in power and strength.

He blanched and took a step back. "I'll see you both at dinner later." He sneered at us before storming out and slamming the door.

"Are we going somewhere for dinner?" Ilana queried.

I groaned and released her. "It's a long story with Remiel meddling in the middle of it. Father expects everyone at dinner tonight. That includes you. Remiel made it sound like I was deliberately hiding you away."

"You have been hiding me away." Her green eyes watched me pacing the room.

"To keep you safe."

"Will I be safe tonight?" Her soft words were a kick to my solar plexus.

I wanted to grab her and leave on Magnus and find somewhere that all our differences and problems no longer mattered. I trailed my fingers through my hair. "I have no idea. Virginity is prized because your first lover imprints themselves on you. If anyone works out what you are in that room, every incubus with a dick will be knocking my door down."

I couldn't do anything about that for another few days…

She stepped up against me. "How will they know?" Her voice was low and husky.

I swallowed the lust that was creeping up my throat. "Your scent, your reactions, that blush that steals over your cheeks when I look at you…"

Her lips ghosted over mine when she reached up, her hands braced on my hips to steady herself. "Then make me smell like you, keep me close so you control my actions, pollute my mind with your filthy words until they no longer shock me."

I stared at her while my mouth went dry.

My eyes dropped when her hands opened the front of the towel and it dropped to the floor. She sank to her knees at my feet and peered up at me. "I believe this was what you demanded when you got home."

I was lost. There was no way I was winning the war against this woman.

She destroyed every piece of my sanity until there was nothing left but her image engrained in my mind.

Her fingers went to the front of my jeans and I closed my eyes.

If this was the descent into insanity, then I was willing to throw myself off the cliff into her waiting arms.

***

Chapter Seventeen

Ilana

Addison had delivered a dress for me to wear this evening. The delicate red lace made the inner girl in me squeal in delight.

After a quick shower, Ezekiel had dedicated himself to ensuring I was covered in his scent. His body fluid dried on my flesh in patterns denoting his passion. When I first arrived and he said anything sexual to me, I blushed. Now my thighs tightened, and I wanted him to finally own me. I knew there were reasons he couldn't but that didn't stop the want inside me.

I'd pulled my panties on when he walked into the room, buttoning his black shirt. He stopped and stared at me before his lips twitched. He opened a drawer and pulled out a pair of red silk panties and threw them toward me. "To go with the dress."

My brow furrowed as I looked at my white cotton panties. "I'm not wearing another woman's panties."

He rolled his eyes and stalked toward me. "I ordered them for you. Everything in here is new and for you."

My cheeks flamed.

Ezekiel put his hand on my waist and drew me against him. "If you blush tonight, I'm going to have to do something to divert their attention."

"Such as?" I arced an eyebrow.

He growled against my ear. "Putting you on the table and eating you for dinner."

My mouth fell open and he grinned before kissing me.

"No one will see your panties but me, but you'll feel different in silk and lace. It'll give you confidence, make you feel seductive, allow you to let me dominate you since that's what they'll expect."

His words went straight to my womb that pulsed erratically in my lower tummy.

His rough, strong hands pushed my panties down my legs to pool at my feet. "Try them on."

I was a fighter and had never ever considered getting sexy underwear. Ezekiel knelt in front of me and held them for me to step into. His fingers traced along my legs as he pulled them up. "Perfect," he breathed, pressing his lips to my throat.

His eyes bored into mine and I felt his true power seeping into me, giving me confidence. "Don't leave my side and follow my lead. If at any time you feel uncomfortable or out of your depth slip the word red into the conversation."

I breathed deeply and nodded. He lifted the dress and helped me zip up the back. My hair fell in waves down my back. I'd left it down so I could hide my face behind it if I lowered my head.

"Ready?" Ezekiel asked, holding his hand out to me.

I was so far out of my comfort zone that my skin felt too tight and my nerves danced under my flesh. His black trousers and button-down shirt made him look dark and dangerous.

"Addy and Gabriel will be there, stop worrying," he instructed, pressing a kiss to the side of my mouth.

Straightening my spine, I met his dark gaze and nodded.

A breath-taking smile crossed his lips as he led me out the door.

The room was filled with laughter and people chatting. The smell of food hung in the air, tempting me. I could eat normal food as well as blood, it just didn't give me the same type of nourishment.

Ezekiel's hand engulfed mine as he strode through the great hall, never once stopping, no matter how many pairs of eyes turned in our direction. He reached the table at the top of the hall and pulled out the seat beside Addison for me to sit in, before seating himself beside me.

Vulnerability snaked through my veins at the assessing gazes that landed on me. Ezekiel's hand landed on my leg under the table and he squeezed to reassure me even as he spoke to his father. His energy infused into me, giving me strength.

"This must be the woman I'd heard about earlier today who was healing people in the hallway." A serious man with dark hair, beard, and eyes stared at me as he spoke.

"Ilana was with me when we heard the attack," Addison replied. "We didn't know what else to do, so we helped as best we could." She smiled innocently.

"Jethro," Ezekiel said from beside me. "This is Ilana. Ilana, this is my brother Jethro."

I smiled politely even as he glared at me. My hand nervously gripped Ezekiel's under the table.

"What is she?" he demanded.

"Don't be rude," Ezekiel snapped. "I've already had Remiel barging into my apartment, terrifying Ilana as she stood in nothing but a towel. I won't tolerate any more today."

His father chuckled. "She's a rare beauty, Zek. They tend to mess with men's heads."

"My only concern is which head," Jethro retorted dryly.

Remiel stalked through the room wearing his foul temper like a cloak. He scraped his chair out and threw himself into it like a petulant child, scowling at me.

"Father," he started, and my back tensed. "I've just been to the harem. The law states that anyone not bound or in the army must reside there."

Ezekiel tensed beside me, his hand on my leg tightening.

"What exactly is Ilana's role here?" Remiel queried with a shit-eating grin on his face.

I knew Ezekiel had removed my military file so I could work on my magic in private.

"What exactly do you mean by bound?" I asked, ignoring his previous question.

"It means that you feed exclusively from each other," Remiel replied with a devious glint in his eye. "In the harem, anyone can feed from you. But when you're bound, then no one else can touch you."

I smiled. "That's simple then. I'm bound to Ezekiel, he's the only one able to feed me." It was the truth. "I'm a vampire, and by your terms, when we are bound to someone, anyone else's blood makes us sick. I can guarantee you if I tried to feed from anyone else at this table, I would be physically ill."

Remiel moved his attention to Ezekiel. "And you, big brother?"

He shrugged. "As you pointed out earlier, I've never let a woman sleep in my bed before. Do I look like I've been slumming it in the harem?"

His insult hit its mark. Remiel stiffened and a vicious glean entered his eyes.

"Drop it, Remiel," their father instructed. "His scent is all over her and all I smell on Zek is Ilana. They've obviously been feeding on each other. We have more important things to worry about than your brother's love life."

I breathed a sigh of relief when our meal started to arrive. After the banquet, blood slaves entered the hall to cater to other appetites. Full vampires needed blood regularly and the incubi in the military didn't have access to the harems. Blood scented the air as it always did at this point in the meal and my fangs lowered unconsciously.

Remiel grabbed a young blood slave and seated her on his knee as he openly groped her. I wasn't a prude, but something about the way he watched me as he did it made my skin crawl.

"You don't normally sit at the family table," Jethro remarked to Gabriel, who sat at the other side of Addison.

"Gabriel is mated to Addison," Ezekiel remarked casually. "His place is at her side."

Silence echoed around the table and the attention moved from me to the woman at my side.

"Who gave them permission to mate?" Ezekiel's father demanded.

Ezekiel tossed the remainder of his drink down his throat. "I did as her eldest brother. Gabriel is dedicated and loyal. In war we need to keep all our assets safe, and Addison is secure with Gabriel at her side."

"I had agreed a marriage for her," the king hissed.

"With an elf," Ezekiel agreed. "We all know that an elf could never nourish a succubus. I'll speak to Raegel about it."

None of the family wanted to make a scene, yet their faces said this conversation wasn't over. It certainly explained why Gabriel was always with Addison.

Remiel returned to groping his blood slave and Jethro chatted to the male beside him.

"How are you holding up?" Ezekiel whispered in my ear, his breath fanning my neck.

I turned to look at him and our noses touched. His thumb traced my bottom lip before sliding under my top lip to caress my fang. "Hungry?" he asked.

I hadn't fed today, the worry about tonight had made my appetite vanish.

Ezekiel spun to face me and tugged me onto his lap, his hands arranging my dress so I could straddle his hips. The splits at the side now made perfect sense. He spoke against my ear. "Bite me, Ilana. Nothing will convince them that we're bonded more than you feeding from me."

My legs tightened against him. I kissed up his neck until I reached his ear. "And the fact that I'll be aroused?" I asked.

His lips twitched. "I think I can handle that."

Fuck it. I was tired of trying to be good. I'd never fed in public before. If I was going to do it, I may as well feed from my fantasy man.

My fangs punctured into his neck and he groaned, his hands grabbing my hips to steady me. His taste exploded on my tongue and trickled down my throat. My fingers combed through his hair to anchor myself.

I felt Ezekiel hardening under me. For once, I wanted to be free, to be like every other vampire who was feeding and fucking. His lips captured mine as I licked his wound, his tongue pillaging the recesses of my mouth. My heart skipped a beat as he unbuttoned his trousers and slid his zip down. Was he seriously going to have sex with me in front of an entire room full of people? And why did that arouse me like nothing before?

He slid my silk panties to the side and let his cock slid between my nether lips. It gave the illusion of sex without the penetration. I felt eyes watching us, yet I didn't need to act. I buried myself against his strength and let him control my body. His hips moved against mine and I lost myself in the sensation of his thrusts. My fangs pierced his skin again to inject another dose of eroticism into his blood.

I moaned softly as his cock pressed delicious friction on my clit, angling my hips to give him better access. His lips traced down the plunging neckline of my dress until they found my breasts and he suckled my nipple through the lace. The rub of the fabric on my sensitive skin made my eyes roll back in pleasure.

"Ezekiel," I moaned, my back arching.

"Give it to me," he gasped against my flesh.

The pressure in my womb built into an inferno until I exploded against him. He released a few strokes after me, his seed spurting against my ass.

As I slowly came back into the awareness of my body, and my eyes finally opened, I realised every person in the room was watching us. I should have felt embarrassed, but I didn't. This was every fantasy I'd had coming to life.

Ezekiel's father chuckled. "It's been a long time since you enthralled an entire room, my son."

I had no idea what that meant, but my eyes locked with Ezekiel's as his lips twitched into a smirk. Lust still swirled in his eyes, but everything had changed. He'd claimed me in front of everyone in the castle, putting a layer of protection over me.

No one would ever dare put a finger on me since they all knew I belonged to the dark prince. My heart fluttered erratically even as he pulled me against him.

I was beyond lost. He owned my heart completely and I'd willingly handed it to him.

***

Chapter Eighteen

Ezekiel

I'd planned to attend the dinner and leave as soon as possible. Remiel and Jethro had pissed me off, but when I felt her fangs against my thumb I couldn't resist.

Banquets in the past consisted of me feeding from whoever I wanted, their bodies lying across the table as I gorged myself. I hadn't fed like that since the curse. Tonight, for the first time in two hundred years, I felt some of my old powers re-emerging. My shoulders tightened at that familiar tug of magic that had lain dormant for too long.

Remiel's eyes had feasted on Ilana as she came apart in my arms. No one would ever know I hadn't fully fed from her. Our sessions gave me enough pleasure to take the constant edge off my hunger. My uninterrupted sleep brought clarity to my thoughts.

Ilana was mine, she just didn't realise it yet.

My hands drew her back against my chest when we arrived back in my apartment. It was our apartment now, her belongings invading more and more of the space every day.

"You okay?" I asked against her neck.

She nodded. "I've never fed in public before," she whispered.

My body tensed. "Are you embarrassed?"

"No, I just never thought I would do something so intimate… with you."

My brow creased. "Why not with me?"

She sighed and walked away from me. "Just forget it."

I grabbed her chin and forced to look at me. "Why not with me?"

Her eyes moved to the side to avoid me and my hand moved to her throat.

I knew it turned her on, I'd smelt her arousal the last time. Asphyxia when administered by the correct hand could bring ultimate pleasure.

I waited until she finally gave in and stared at me. "You've been my ultimate fantasy for years. Even the mention of your name set my panties on fire."

My eyebrows raised at the image.

"I've lost count of the number of times my friend Mia threatened to accidentally push me into your path. It's embarrassing." She covered her face with her hands.

"I don't think I've ever been someone's fantasy before," I confessed.

She rolled her eyes at me.

"Honestly." I pressed her against the wall, my hand still around her throat. Her arousal scented the air. "Women tend to want an incubus' dick because we'll bring them multiple orgasms. They tend not to care about the man operating it. I've been a fantasy because of my species, not because of me."

"I never cared you were an incubus. I bumped into you in a corridor years ago when alarms sounded, and we were all racing into battle. That was the start of my fantasy."

My thumb stroked over her pulse. "The equinox is in three days and I'm going to show you exactly what experiencing a fantasy means."

Her pulse leapt under my thumb. Ilana arched her throat and curved one leg around my waist. "Do you promise?"

She was going to kill me. I would end up dying from ecstasy in three days' time.

"You won't be able to walk when I'm finished," I threatened against her lips.

"I better not," she retaliated before her lips met mine.

How did I go from hating anything to do with magic to wanting a witch more than my next breath?

I thought I'd pushed her too far earlier, but she gave herself over to me and let me control her. Every eye in that room watched her writhe in my arms. Our energy had commanded their attention, making them mad with desire. I could guarantee there wasn't an incubus or succubus not feeding right now.

My little witch finally slept draped over me. The familiar sensation of Ophelia caressing my mind never appeared while she touched me. The only time I'd been able to sleep before her arrival in my bed had been on Magnus since his magic protected me from her.

For the first time in two hundred years, I finally gave in to hope. Ilana eased the symptoms of the curse, making me feel like the man I'd been before Ophelia kissed me. It didn't matter what she asked of me, I would give it to her. Hell, there was a wyvern sleeping in a guest room in the castle because she'd stared at me with those huge green eyes.

I dragged her closer to me and closed my eyes, a future emerging instead of despair.

Would the pieces of me that were left be enough to keep her at my side, or would she become repelled by the limitations of my cursed existence? I had to know, because I was falling deeper under her spell every day.

The man I'd been before the curse would never have accepted a vampire as a mate. He would have dragged Addison kicking and screaming to her marriage bed because solidifying power was the most important goal in our realm.

The man I'd become had learnt compassion. I knew the value of friendship, that real power came not from possessions but being possessed by the right person.

Remiel's behaviour disgusted me because he represented the man I'd been before the curse. I'd been the biggest man whore in our realm, feeding from entire harems in a night. The thirst for supremacy sent me on a quest to find more exotic partners to feed from, different species to test who gave the greatest rush of power through my veins.

Shame settled heavily on my conscience.

I was no longer that man, but the woman sleeping in my arms made me want to be the best man I could be.

She gave me her trust without thinking.

She wrapped me in a layer of protection every night.

She took a broken man and pieced him back together again.

Ilana was more than anyone saw.

She was the light that guided me from the darkness.

She was my mate.

***

Chapter Nineteen

Ophelia

No matter how hard I tried, I couldn't reach Ezekiel. At night, I used to find him in his dreams, claim his body the way I wanted to do when he was awake. I sensed his struggle, but in that place before waking, he belonged to me.

Five nights he'd disappeared. Was he spending more time with that dragon of his? Had he finally realised that my magic could not penetrate the mental shield of a dragon? Or had one of the meddlesome witches who had evaded my capture stumbled upon my curse?

Frustrated on the night of the full moon, I turned my attention to the lycan. I drew his curse closer to me, feasting on his wild energy as the wolf transformation gripped him. My bloodlust coursed through his veins as I forced him to slaughter to appease my hunger.

I sent my wraiths and wyverns to search for Ezekiel. He wasn't in the castle. I still felt the throbbing pain of several of my wraiths being slaughtered. No one had ever achieved that before. Each of them were tied to me by etheric cords. If I concentrated, I could see through their eyes, manipulating their form that was stuck somewhere between a soul and a body. Next time I sent them out, I would be watching to observe what was happening out there.

I stood in front of my mirror. "Show me Ezekiel."

Energy rippled across the gleaming black obsidian, yet nothing materialised.

"Show me Lycidas."

The image of the broken werewolf appeared, his skin still healing from the night of the full moon, his soul shattered at the acts I forced him to commit.

A dark smile crossed my face. One day I would have Ezekiel lying at my feet like that, begging me to take his pain away.

I wandered to the dead tree in the corner of the room. My crow, Badb Catha, sat on a branch, watching me with beady black eyes.

"Be my eyes, my darling. Find and watch Ezekiel," I cooed, stroking her feathers. Her head tilted to allow me to reach that delicate spot under her head. "He is ours."

Her beak nibbled along my finger in affection.

I could be generous to those who pleased me. Ezekiel needed to learn that. He could rule at my side, given everything his heart desired. Instead he opposed me, refused to eat, and now disappeared from my sight.

I missed touching him at night. Over the years, I had mastered astral travel to enjoy pleasure. He resisted me at first until I drained him enough to plunder his mind and his astral body. It had been enough to satisfy me, but now I'd been denied, anger coursed through my core.

I would have to seek out pleasure from another. Maybe that elf whose pride would be his ultimate downfall.

Badb Catha shook herself and preened her long flight feathers. She screeched and stomped around before she flew from the window to search the demon realms. Nothing would stop my beloved pet from seeking Ezekiel out.

When she found him, I would pay him a personal visit.

***

Chapter Twenty

Ilana

The red wyvern bounced up and down on her back legs, her wings flapping. She appeared ferocious, but in reality, she was playing. The moment the black crystal had been removed from her skin she became a different beast.

Addison and I spent our free time with her, training her. We'd moved her down to the rooms Addison had allocated to her in the dungeon, far from the prying eyes and ears of the rest of the castle.

I sensed her magic, it amplified mine. Ophelia had been very clever enslaving them to give her access to more magic. She'd killed and engulfed the powers of her fellow witches. Then she moved to the dark princes, and now we'd found proof of her syphoning energy from the demon realms.

The more I read on curses, the more I was convinced all four of the dark princes were afflicted. None of them were the men described in the history books. Something happened around two hundred years ago that changed them drastically.

I threw another egg for Izzy to catch. She jumped up to snatch it and chomped happily on it. She still couldn't fly with her injury, but she flapped her wings to test them. Addison laughed and threw a piece of meat.

We concentrated on the next stage of my training, and even Izzy the wyvern decided she was a critic and nudged me with her nose when she wanted me to do something differently. In fairness, her guidance was always correct.

Addison and I practiced the entire day, my skills increasing, until I was exhausted and collapsed into a chair beside her.

"How can Zek feed from you without affecting you?" Addison asked.

My back tensed but I kept my answer vague. "What do you mean?"

"I assume you know about his condition?"

I nodded. "I'm aware of Ophelia's curse." It was the truth, but Ezekiel hadn't told me, I'd figured it out myself.

"When he feeds, Ophelia removes something from that person, a memory or an emotion. Every time he feeds another piece of them is stolen until they are no longer who they once were. He refuses to visit the harems because his favourites became mindless, nothing more than living flesh."

I shivered at her description.

"What's different about the equinoxes?" I asked.

"For reasons unknown, Ophelia can't touch him during them. He can feed freely."

That certainly explained why we were on a countdown to the summer solstice. Ezekiel wouldn't touch me unless he knew I was safe. Another piece of my heart attached itself to him.

"So how can he feed from you without altering you? Is it your witch blood?" Addison stared at me as if she was trying to see inside my DNA.

I didn't want to tell her that technically, the only one of us who had been feeding was me. Ezekiel was too much of a gentleman to fully take me. It wouldn't have taken any coaxing on his part, I would willing have given myself to him.

"I honestly don't know," I replied.

"I haven't seen him use the amount of power he released last night since before the curse. It was like looking at the old Zek again."

My head canted to the side to study her. "What power?"

She looked at me as if I had spoken in a foreign language. "At dinner, every person in that room was captivated by both of you. There wasn't a pair of dry panties in the place, male or female. Zek used to be able to send the entire court into a frenzy of lust that descended into weeklong orgies. Poor Gabriel was dragged back to our room last night to be ravished."

I wasn't aware of the effect of our passion last night.

"So, you and Gabriel…" I steered the conversation away from my fledgling relationship.

A smile turned her lips up. "Yeah, I thought Zek would freak out. I never would have guessed he would have been the one to cover up our indiscretion."

My eyebrows rose in question.

"We never asked permission to mate. Technically, Father or Zek could have forced us to separate. By saying he sanctioned it, he gave us his blessing and ensured Father couldn't force me to marry an elf prince."

"My friend Mia says elves hide a lot of passion behind that cold exterior." I winked at her.

Addison laughed. "I doubt they can match the passion of an incubus."

"I'll ask Mia next time I see her, she has experience of all the realms."

Izzy pressed her head under my hand for me to stroke her. Wyverns appeared to be affectionate creatures with intelligence and the enthusiasm to learn. Ophelia had made people fear them.

The fingers of my left hand tingled as my tattva marks traced over her skin. She purred in contentment.

"What are we going to do with her?" I asked Addison.

"Considering Zek saved her because you stared at him with your big green eyes, I'm sure he'll let you keep her. After all, his word is law in this castle."

My back straightened. "I doubt he saved her for me," I grumbled.

Addison laughed. "You have no idea, do you?"

I blinked once as I stared at her. My knowledge of men and relationships was zero.

"My brother is dragonshit crazy about you. No woman has ever been allowed into his apartment, never mind allowed to sleep in his bed. I thought he was going to rip both Remiel and Jethro's heads off last night because they dared to feel desire for you. Zek is a dangerous enemy, but to those he loves, he is the fiercest protector."

I wanted to argue with her that he didn't care about me, that I was only there so he could hide me from the rest of the castle. Yet, he'd walked into that room with me last night holding my hand to give me strength. Everyone knew I lived in the castle now, so there was no need for me to hide in his apartment any longer.

The thought made me feel sick and want to cry. I didn't want to leave him.

"He put me in his apartment to hide me before anyone discovered I was using magic."

Addison chuckled. "Keep telling yourself that, Ilana. You might start believing it."

I wandered outside for some fresh air before going back to the apartment when I saw Remiel approaching me. Suppressing a groan, I turned to walk away.

"Ilana," he called.

I froze, my body tensing before I slowly moved to face him. "Remiel."

"I was beginning to wonder if you weren't allowed to leave Zek's room."

I glared at him and didn't reply.

"You still owe me dinner." He produced a smile that would make most women weak in the knees.

"I'm not hungry," I replied. "And I don't recollect owing you anything."

His smile wavered and fell into a scowl. "I am a prince of this realm. If I tell you I need to eat, you ask me how I want your body served to me to feast from."

My spine stiffened. "The only man who feeds from me is Ezekiel."

"My brother has no problem sharing with his siblings."

Nausea churned in my stomach and acid crept up the back of my throat. My chin lifted to meet his gaze. "I think he would have a problem. Maybe you should ask him first."

His boyish smile returned. "We don't need to bother Zek with minor details. We're both adults and allowed to enjoy each other's flesh. I don't mind if you take a bite."

"No thanks," I replied, spinning and walking to get away for him.

The only problem was I spun too far and was walking outside and would have to pass him again if I reoriented myself. My feet moved faster to get away from him, but his footsteps echoed mine. His hand grasped my arm and he swung me into a dark doorway.

"I have no problem chasing, vampire, but if you make me work for my dinner, I can't guarantee your delicate skin won't be marked." His finger trailed from my throat to between my breasts. I struggled to break his hold, but he was stronger than I gave him credit for. His touch burned against my flesh, making me suppress a whimper of pain.

This was why I never let anyone touch me.

"I can give you pleasure or I can merely take my own. The choice is yours, because I don't need to feed right now, but I am curious about what you have between your legs that has captivated my eldest brother."

"Get your hands off me," I gritted out between clenched teeth.

He pressed his body tightly against mine, his erection rubbing against my stomach. "My brother might be pissed, but we're family and blood will always win an argument." His lips crashed against mine, his tongue demanding entry.

I instinctively bit his tongue as it invaded my mouth. His head jolted back and blood trickled down his chin. Pain exploded at the left side of my face as he backhanded me in retaliation, my neck cracking as it whipped around.

I screamed and struggled, but his strength was greater than mine. I finally realised what people referred to as the incubus thrall when my limbs became sluggish as his eyes bored into mine. Without thinking my training kicked in and my knee rose quickly to between his legs in a last attempt to escape.

He collapsed onto his knees, his watery eyes glaring up at me. "You fucking bitch. You'll pay for that," he snarled.

I stumbled to get away, his hand catching my leg and making me fall hard to the ground. My shoulder took the full brunt of my fall, releasing a resounding crack accompanied by horrendous pain.

I kicked him in the face and ran, not knowing where I was heading. Anywhere away from the psychopath with an endless libido. I heard his footsteps. Panic bloomed in my chest because I couldn't use my greatest weapon against him—my magic.

I skidded around the corner and found myself face to face with a large black dragon. He blinked once and lifted his wing. Without a second thought, I dived under it and it enveloped me in its safety. I held my arm as pain thrummed down into my fingers.

"Where the hell did she go?" I heard Remiel shout. "Which direction did she go, I know she came in here."

The skin of the dragon vibrated as it growled at him.

"I hate you big lizards," Remiel replied. "Zek should have you all chained up instead of letting you roam free."

Another growl followed and the heat that rippled beside me reminded me of Magnus blowing fireballs.

"Fucking lizards!" Remiel shouted before his footsteps moved away.

I didn't move, instead, hiding under the dragon's wing. I knew it was Magnus, and in my head, I believed he came because he felt my terror. His wing moved over me as if to soothe me. I clung to him, refusing to leave the safety of my hiding place.

Minutes or hours passed but finally his wing lifted and my eyes moved from black boots on the ground, to combat trousers, to a tight black T-shirt stretched over powerful abdominal muscles. Ezekiel's eyes blazed with fury.

"I'll fucking kill him," he snarled, his gaze roaming over my shaking form.

I flung myself into his arms without thinking, my body trembling as I burrowed against his heat. "How did you know I was here?"

His hands combed through my hair until he tilted my head back to examine me. "Magnus summoned me."

I had no idea what that meant, so I stared at him without words.

"Are you okay?" His thumb traced over my bruised lips.

Tears sprung to my eyes and I swallowed a sob. His eyes darkened until they were almost black.

"Thanks, Magnus. I'll look after her from here."

The huge dragon nudged me with his nose, and I rubbed his horn. "Thank you," I whispered, kissing his snout.

I didn't want to walk through the castle in case we bumped into Remiel. My greatest fear was that he was telling the truth and Ezekiel would give me to his brothers when he no longer wanted me. His hand grasped mine and I squeaked in pain. He studied me for several seconds before he grabbed my other hand. His stride never faltered as he stalked through the castle with the grace of an apex predator.

It wasn't until the apartment door closed that his façade crumbled. He tugged me against his strength, sharing it with me.

“I can feel your torment,” he said into my hair.

“I can’t bear the touch of a man. It makes me burn with pain,” I confessed.

He leaned back to study me. “Yet, I can touch you.” His fingers traced over my throbbing cheek. My eyes fluttered closed at his healing touch.

“You’ve seen my memories. You are the only one who I can feed from, the only one who can touch me.”

A strange emotion that I couldn’t identify flickered in the back of his eyes. Was it pride or possession? How could you tell when you had nothing to compare it to?

“Let me look at your arm,” Ezekiel said, his hand moving to my shoulder. I whimpered as he tried to manipulate my arm from my T-shirt. Ezekiel ripped my top, exposing my swollen shoulder that was already changing colour. His jaw tightening was his only reaction, his fingers tracing over the injury. “Take a deep breath,” he ordered me.

I had just gasped a lungful of air when he twisted my arm and a sickening pop resounded. Tears sprung to my eyes and Ezekiel wrapped me in his arms, his chin on top of my head. His comfort brought fresh tears to my eyes, and I clung to him with my one good arm.

“Stay here,” he spoke into my hair.

I watched as he stormed from the room, his aura a dark pulsating mass. My T-shirt was missing an arm, but I followed him to the door and watched as he prowled down the corridor. I slowly moved behind him, terrified he was going to do something he’d regret. He didn’t knock the door he stopped at—he kicked it open and stalked inside.

A door opposite opened and Addison appeared, Gabriel following her. Her eyes found mine and took in my appearance. She pushed Gabriel toward the door Ezekiel kicked in and came to me, her hand gripping my strong one.

Shouts echoed down the hall accompanied by the sound of smashing furniture.

"Is that Remiel's room?" I asked.

Addison nodded.

"He'll kill him," I whispered, moving toward the noises.

"Remiel needs to learn not to touch what doesn't belong to him," Addison replied.

We crept to the doorway. Ezekiel had Remiel pinned against the wall with his hand around his throat, his other hand pummelling him. Gabriel was desperately trying to separate the two of them.

"She's been fucking teasing me since she arrived," Remiel gasped.

Ezekiel flung him across the room and stalked toward him.

"Princes of this realm are allowed to fuck any unmated females," he taunted Ezekiel, who dragged him up by the hair and kicked him in the stomach.

"I am fucking sick cleaning up your messes. Raegel barely speaks to me after you violated his elf commander," Ezekiel shouted in his face.

"He enjoyed it!" Remiel protested.

"You fucking used your power on him. The man had no interest in your dick up his ass!"

Addison and I shared a worried look.

"Keep you fucking hands and dick away from Ilana or I will ensure you lose your ability to feed. Permanently." Ezekiel loomed over him like the harbinger of doom and destruction.

"She's a cock tease…"

Ezekiel's power leaked out, levitating Remiel and sending him crashing against the wall.

"What's going on?" King Maximus pushed past Addison and me. Neither of us had seen him approaching.

"I'm teaching the spoilt brat of the family some manners," Ezekiel snapped.

"You can't assault your brother." Maximus put himself between his elder and youngest sons.

"I can if he touched my mate."

Maximus' eyes cut in my direction, widening when he took in my appearance. "Remiel," he groaned. "Ezekiel made his feelings clear last night at dinner."

"She approached me," he whined.

Ezekiel nearly knocked his father on the floor to get to Remiel. He dragged him onto his feet by his throat. "I don't fucking think so." He sneered into his face. "Final warning, brother. You so much as breathe near her and I will cut your delinquent dick off and shove it down your throat. Understand?" He tossed him onto the floor without waiting for an answer.

His eyes met mine as he stomped to the door, finally realising Addison and I stood there. Without stopping, his arm circled under my ass and lifted me to carry me with him.

I didn't utter a word, shock pulsed from my core from him calling me his mate. My good arm slipped around his shoulder and I pressed a kiss against his neck. His arm tightened around me.

He slammed the apartment door closed and stood with his back to it.

"Thank you," I whispered.

His furious gaze met mine. "My brother assaulted and tried to rape you and you're thanking me?" he asked in disbelief.

"You believed in me without even asking what happened." My voice emerged small and wobbly.

"I know what Remiel is, I just helped to hide him from the rest of the world. I won't let him hurt you."

I kissed him, my heart beating erratically in my chest. He'd beaten his brother half to death because he dared to touch me. Actions spoke louder than words, and his were crystal clear.

Ezekiel laid me on the bed, staring down at me as he pulled his T-shirt over his head. "You need to feed to heal," he said as I watched him.

"I wish I could feed you," I whispered.

He crawled over me. "You'll be feeding me in two nights."

My insides tightened and I bit my bottom lip to stop myself from whimpering in need. His cheek rubbed against mine, tickling me as he hadn't shaved today. I wanted the intervening days to disappear. I needed to feel Ezekiel inside and outside me. A powerful cord bound us together, tightening every day until we were intricately wrapped around each other energetically.

"Feed," he commanded, bringing my mouth to his neck.

My tongue traced his artery, the beat of his heart thrumming along the tip, tempting me.

His touch soothed where Remiel had damaged. He gave when Remiel took; he healed my soul as well as my body.

My fangs sank into his artery and he groaned, one hand wrapping in my hair and the other grasping my waist. "I love the feel of you taking my blood."

I lapped at the wound on his neck, savouring every drop of his flavour. Nothing tasted like Ezekiel. He reminded me of the chocolate Aunt Agatha bought me when she took me to the Earth realm, dark and delicious with a decadence that should be savoured. I dragged his lips to mine, my inner temperature soaring with the flush of his blood pumping inside me.

His blood healed every injury Remiel inflicted on me, knitting flesh together, eradicating bruises.

"You have no idea how much I want you," Ezekiel muttered against my lips.

A breathless laugh escaped my lips. "I think I might."

"I feel like I'm dying right now…" His lips continued drugging me with long, slow kisses.

Darkness cocooned us in our own personal bubble. One item at a time, our clothes disappeared between caresses. We knew each other's bodies intimately, had spent hours committing every pleasure zone to memory. My spine arched up as his lips and hands explored my breasts. His stubble added friction to my aching skin.

He tugged my nipples between his teeth and that delicious pain made me moan with pleasure. Ezekiel created a duality in me, teaching me that pain and pleasure were two halves of the one whole. My fingers combed through his hair, holding him against me even as my legs widened to wrap around his waist.

"I need you, Ezekiel…" I moaned as he kissed down my stomach, his dark eyes locked with mine.

"You have me." His tongue made me squirm and pant, but I wanted so much more.

I needed him.

My arms stretched above my head as I grasped the metal railings of the headboard.

"I need to feel you inside me, please…" I begged. "You don't need to feed, but I'll explode if you don't."

He braced himself on his arms. "You don't know what you're asking."

I grabbed his face between my hands. "I know about the curse, I worked it out in pieces. You need to ejaculate in me to feed. I just need you to fill the void inside me, even for a few moments."

Ezekiel gave a strangled cry as his lips descended on mine. I was addicted to the taste of him, intoxicated by his energy.

Tentatively the tip of his erection rubbed my entrance. My vampire feeding frenzy made me need him like my next breath. Inch by agonising inch, he pressed his hard flesh inside me. I'd had fantasies, thousands of them with Ezekiel in the starring role, yet none came close to the sensation of him stretching and filling me.

Divine pressure built in my core as he kept pushing forward, his hands at my thighs spreading my legs wider to grant him access. My back arched as he filled me, the pressure too much, bordering on painful. I panted, my eyes staring blindly above me as I tried to accommodate his length and width. No one ever told you about the discomfort and unbearable stretching sensation.

Finally, our bodies lay intertwined, Ezekiel lodged deep inside me. My muscles finally relaxed as I wrapped one leg around his waist.

His mouth moved over mine in kisses so deep they touched my soul. Our fingers threaded through each other's as he pressed my hands on either side of my head.

"I need you so much," he muttered against my lips. I knew he'd go no further, he'd never let Ophelia take anything from me, no matter how much both of us wanted this.

Instead, we lost ourselves in the passion of his kisses, perspiration coated our skin even as our hair became damp. This was as close as we dared go, even now we taunted the curse with our inability to stay away from each other.

"Only two nights," I said into his mouth.

His forehead rested on mine, his breathing ragged. "I don't know if I can cope."

His pelvis rocked against mine and my eyes rolled back in my head.

"Fuck!" he dragged himself out of me and threw himself on his back, his arm covering his eyes.

I'd pushed him too far. His agony tore through me in waves that felt like lashes on my skin. My core was empty and aching for his touch. I crawled over him, lifting his arm so I could stare into his eyes.

"We'll cope together. Two nights and then you can have me each and every way you can think of."

I kissed down his body as his gaze bored into me with an intensity that made me legs tremble. I eased his pain with my fingers and mouth, making his hips buck against me. His groans coaxed me onward until his body slumped onto the bed.

***

The banging at the door made me moan and tighten my hold on Ezekiel. Whoever needed him could go away. He was currently in use as my pillow.

"What the fuck?" he groaned, rubbing his hands over his eyes.

"Open up!" Gabriel's voice sounded muffled. "Ophelia's in the air and at our borders."

"Fuck!" Ezekiel exclaimed, dragging himself out of bed.

I dressed in leggings and a vest top as he tugged black jeans and a T-shirt on, followed by his heavy boots.

"Maybe I should find my fighting gear…" I said, watching him. I was trained as a warrior.

"No." He stood, pulling me against him. "You stay here with Addison."

"I can…"

His lips landing on mine cut off my words, his hands gripping my arms. "Stay here," he said against my lips, his forehead resting on mine.

Addison and Gabriel stood outside his door.

"She's pissed," Gabriel said in way of a briefing, Ezekiel falling into step beside him as he dragged his flameproof black jacket on.

"When is she not? She picks now, just before the equinox. It can't be a coincidence," Ezekiel snapped.

Addison wrapped her arm through mine as we followed them.

Fear made my legs tremble and my heart beat in rapid time. I'd walked into battle countless times and never experienced these feelings. My friends had stood at my side and I'd watched as many of them were slaughtered by The Blood Queen over the years, yet today was different.

Ezekiel strode through the castle with an air of invincibility, but we all knew that wasn't true. Our species were immortal but that didn't mean we couldn't be killed. My hand gripped Addison's as we both braced ourselves to watch Ezekiel and Gabriel go to war.

In the entrance hall, the commanders handed out weapons. Ezekiel strapped blasters to his legs and waist. His eyes met mine and his lips twitched in a semblance of a smile to try and comfort me.

"Everyone, load up!" Gabriel shouted and troops shuffled outside to the waiting dragons.

My feet moved by themselves until I stood toe to toe with Ezekiel. "Be careful"

He tucked my unruly hair behind my ear. "This isn't my first battle."

"It's your first with me standing here." That brought a faint smile to his mouth.

I straightened his jacket and held the front of it. "If there are wyverns, aim for the crystals below their wings. It will break Ophelia's hold over them and weaken her troops in the air."

He nodded, his hands dragging my hips against his. "Stay with Addison in my room. Open the door for no one except me or Gabriel. Understand?"

"Come home to me," I whispered, tugging him down to kiss him. His lips were brutal claiming mine, our emotions tethering us together.

He squeezed me once before turning and prowling out of the castle. I watched as he ran up Magnus' tail even as the large dragon flapped his wings and took to the air.

My heart stopped for several beats before it lodged in my throat. Realisation sunk into my soul that he'd just taken my heart with him, because somewhere in the past week, I'd fallen for him completely. Not the fantasy, or the youthful crush, but the complicated man.

"This is the worse bit," Addison said, linking arms with me again as her eyes tracked her mate.

I nodded, still stunned by my realisation.

"At least no one will doubt your status here with Ezekiel gone," she continued absently.

I stared at her in confusion, my brow wrinkled.

"He beat Remiel half to death last night for touching you," she explained. "But the two of you looked like we interrupted Zek mid feed this morning, and the temperature rose in here about twenty degrees when you said goodbye."

Before him, I would have been embarrassed anyone saw me showing emotion, but the tear that fell down my cheek refused to stay hidden in my eye. My heart fractured into a million pieces at the thought of him hurt.

"Let's get you back to your apartment," Addison said, trying to lead me away.

Remiel stood glaring at both of us, hatred seeping from him in waves. He should be out there risking his life. I wanted to shout at him to get out there and protect his brother, but someone that selfish would never understand sacrifice.

“We need to get Izzy,” I said so low no one would hear except Addison.

“Why?”

I shrugged. “I don’t know, I just feel we need to keep her close.”

Addison didn’t argue. We slipped away to the dungeons and brought her back while everyone’s attention was diverted.

While we sat shell-shocked in the living area, Izzy clung happily to the window frame, chattering away to herself.

I’d never felt so helpless in my life.

***

Chapter Twenty-One

Ezekiel

The wind pounded against my body as Magnus manoeuvred us high in the sky. Ophelia's wyverns ridden by wraiths hung above our border. The elves were already in their trees, their arrows trying to take our enemy down. Their tree magic would ensnare enemies in the forests, but the incubi were the sky fighters.

The dragons held our battle wagons in their talons. They dropped some in the forests with our ground troops, the others were filled with soldiers armed with weapons. Little could penetrate the crates, so our soldiers were relatively safe in the air.

Gabriel had spread the information about the crystals on the wyverns and our sharp shooters would already be taking aim.

"Ezekiel," Ophelia purred from her carriage held aloft by four wyverns. "There you are, I thought you were avoiding me. I haven't heard from you in such a long time."

"I didn't realise I had to check in with you," I retaliated. The way she looked at me made my skin crawl with revulsion. She hadn't been able to infiltrate my dreams since Ilana slept beside me. Ophelia used her magic to violate me in dreams until the thought of sex became repulsive.

Her eyes narrowed into slits. I knew she was attracted to me—every incubus could sense when a potential meal was available. It didn't mean we had to consume it. Ophelia would cause a severe case of food poisoning—and not the type that would result in vomiting.

"You are mine until I release you," she snarled, her top lip curling.

Magnus's wingtips moved slowly to keep us static. "Those were not the terms," I reminded her. "Get off my land before blood is spilt."

I sensed her mindless soldiers creeping through our forest.

She regarded me, her hands coming to rest on her hips. "I will never stop until Purgatory is mine."

"Magnus…" My voice emerged as nothing more than a breath. We'd planned for the moment she was in our sights. He was more than a dragon, he was connected to me in a way I'd never expected. Our thoughts and emotions synced in battle.

His body vibrated under me seconds before fire erupted from his mouth. She obviously never thought I would bring the fight directly to her. Part of the agreement was that none of the four princes that she'd cursed could land a killing blow on her. Technically Magnus was not covered in her devious plotting for Purgatory domination.

She screamed, her wyverns lurching away in panic as Magnus' flames licked over them in an obscene caress.

"Kill them!" Ophelia shouted and her wraiths pulled the reins on the wyverns to force them toward us.

Magnus had his sights fixed on Ophelia, batting off the wyverns who dared to come too close. The other dragons released fire to keep them back as my soldiers fired from beneath them. I took aim as Magnus navigated us through the battle. Time and time again, I fired at the black crystals. I'd never noticed them before, but when I finally knew where to look, they were obvious.

Wraiths tumbled to the ground as freed wyverns bucked them from their backs. They flew rapidly away from the fighting, their instincts guiding them to safety in the mountains. Seeing their success, my troops focused on stopping the air assault by removing the creatures that allowed Ophelia to fight in the air. My ground troops awaited the wraiths with our latest weapons.

I saw Raegel standing on top of the tallest tree on the border. Directing Magnus down, I waved him onto my dragon's back.

"Aim for the crystals under the wyvern's wings," I instructed him.

He didn't ask why, he took aim with his bow and arrow and hit his mark over and over with his spooky accuracy. Sigils marked his arrows, infusing elven magic into the primitive weapons made of wood from their magical trees.

Our new weapons Gabriel had developed were more effective against the wraiths, their bodies exploding with the force of the electrical blast. He'd combined magic syphoned from some of the magical objects Addison and him collected.

Now Ilana was with us, she could help incorporate magic into our fight. The memory of her brought an ache to my heart. I'd flown into battle over a thousand times, but never like this morning. Her image engrained into my mind as she stood with her heart and emotions in her eyes. I wanted to stay and protect her, yet the greatest way to achieve that was me standing here facing Ophelia where she would never sense the magic of another witch.

Raegel and I stood back to back, our focus set on our enemy. I didn't know where Ophelia went, but I had no doubt she'd ran from Magnus' fire. His initial flames had hit her, I was convinced of it. Her scream of pain had been real, and I knew I was twisted because it sent a flutter of pleasure through me.

Time became irrelevant as we clashed with the enemy on our borders. Hours passed as we stemmed the tide of her never-ending evil souls.

A horn sounded far in the distance and the remaining wyverns and wraiths retreated from the battle.

Raegel and I faced each other, our haggard expressions saying more than words.

"You fought well, brother." Raegel gripped my arm below my elbow and I returned his gesture in a show of solid brotherhood.

"As did you," I replied. "She's getting bolder."

"My new recruits train daily in preparation. I did not expect her to come to our borders." He slung his bow over his shoulder.

"I've been blocking her," I admitted in a low voice.

His eyebrows rose marginally. "That may explain it."

"I think she killed the other witches not just to steal their powers, but because their touch can block her."

He didn't reply, we were too exposed here for truths to be revealed. Raegel nodded as he contemplated my words.

"We need a meeting soon with the others to discuss this further." He scanned me in the way elves did as they assessed your strengths and weaknesses, his head tilting to the side. "You have changed since I last saw you. You are stronger, more your old self."

I felt like the old Ezekiel, the man who wielded power without thought of having to conserve energy due to my strict diet. Ilana made me stronger.

"We'll discuss it another time," I replied cryptically.

"I see your younger brother still does not fight with the rest of the realms." Raegel hated Remiel. It was an emotion that was fast spreading.

I sighed, my fists bunching at my sides. "He is recovering from injuries," I ground out.

Raegel never missed anything. His dark green eyes flickered down to my hands before he read my aura. "You have always been a good man. Your protection of his wickedness was always destined to end. Family loyalty can only stretch so far before it breaks."

I nodded stiffly, my eyes gazing into the distance in case Ophelia tried to return to our borders. "I'd always hoped he would change. I now know he never will. I'm sorry."

I'd pretended his transgressions with the elf commander were nothing more than two adults succumbing to pleasure. He never survived the humiliation of cheating on his partner, dying in battle not long after. Raegel always believed he ensured he never returned home because his conscience was weighed down by guilt. I'd never apologised before, but suddenly I could no longer defend my youngest brother.

"Thank you. He was a good man." Raegel's voice was nothing more than a whisper.

We'd barely spoken to each other since the incident and now I felt the layers that separated us peel away. The four dark princes of Purgatory had been closer than brothers in the past. We were the chosen ones who would ensure peace between our realms, and that started with the rulers.

"We need to talk," I said, thinking of the base between our borders. "Meet me in our old rendezvous point in two hours."

Our realms lay side by side, and my youth was spent climbing rock faces with Raegel as we pushed our bodies in training. It broke something inside me when my father forced me to uphold Remiel's actions.

I'd been a dick to Raegel because I knew I was wrong defending my brother. Jethro and I had been typical incubi in our youth, fucking our way through orgies, feeding until we couldn't take any more. Never once had I used my incubus thrall on them. That was an unwritten law between us. It didn't force people, just lowered their inhibition and allowed them to do what they really desired. The elf had been attracted to Remiel, but he'd wanted to be loyal to his mate.

"I need to check on my people and then I'll find you," Raegel replied. "There seems much that we need to discuss."

He leapt from Magnus' back and dove into the trees, grabbing a branch to swing himself into a tree. He was far too elegant compared to the rough and ready personas of the others Ophelia had cursed. Throughout our trials, Raegel had remained calm and in control.

I envied him that.

My control was seriously close to breaking. Last night I wanted to put the curse to the back of my head and just be with Ilana. The sensation of her heat surrounding me made me groan and rub my face with my hands. She consumed my every spare thought. It was only because I felt her eyes on me as I punished Remiel that I stopped before I ripped him apart with my bare hands for touching her. The only bruises on her delicate flesh should be from me when we lost ourselves in passion.

I needed to be a better man if I deserved to be with Ilana.

Gabriel barked orders at our troops, taking command the way he always did. Over the past two hundred years I'd offloaded so many of my responsibilities. I really needed to learn to govern again. Fuck, I didn't even know the name of my soldiers anymore. Nameless men died in our war and shame crept up my spine at that realisation. Every one of them should have a name and a place of honour in our home.

Are we going to the mountains? Magnus asked in my head. He'd heard my conversation with Raegel.

"Yeah, we need to face Ophelia together or she'll kill us all," I replied, settling myself on his back.

She makes you the man you once were.

I didn't know whether to laugh or cry, our situation so desperate because we could only really be together four days a year. The remainder of the time, she'd have to watch me feed from other women because I would never risk her.

The thought of sharing her with another man made me incandescent with rage. There was no way she wouldn't feel the same way. Addison was right when she said Ilana looked at me with romantic hearts in her eyes at the start. Somewhere in the middle of it all, that had changed and her actual heart was in her eyes when she stared at me. I felt the full blast of her feelings for me before I left her in the hallway with Addison. I couldn't bring myself to look back or I would have ended up on my knees at her feet.

If I was a good man, I'd walk away and save her.

There was very little good left in me. What remained was nourished by Ilana's light. It would wither and die without her beside me. It was damn near dead when she first crawled into my bed that night to save me from the nightmare I was trapped in.

Magic evolves and creates cures for curses. Trust in her, I can sense her power.

"I can't risk destroying her," I groaned, my head falling against one of his horns.

Sometimes you need to let the old crumble and die to allow the new to grow.

I gave up trying to understand my dragon and closed my eyes.

My problems would still be there later.

***

Chapter Twenty-Two

Ilana

Addison and I had sat for several hours saying nothing, staring off into the distance as our hearts pounded in our chests. Eventually, I grabbed a few books on magic and curled up in the corner of the sofa.

Izzy crept over to lie beside me, her head leaning on my leg. I turned the pages of the book while stroking her head.

The next book I lifted was all about magical beasts. Staring at Izzy, I flicked to near the back where the 'W' creatures would be. I scanned the pages while Addison paced the room. There was nothing I could do to ease her anguish of not knowing what was happening. Fear tiptoed up my spine, paralysing me when I envisaged Ezekiel hurt or dying.

Wyverns were the familiar to those of witch blood. They didn't amplify powers, but helped the witch they served control and focus them. The witch and the familiar needed to bond for them to work as a team. The wyvern was able to lend the witch magical energy to boost the strength of a spell.

"Is that what she was doing to you?" I asked, scratching behind her ears. "Was Ophelia stealing your gifts?"

Izzy whimpered and rubbed her snout against my arm.

I thought of Mum and my Aunt Agatha. They'd spent their entire lives helping others, hiding in plain sight while still trying to ensure the next generation learnt magical skills they might never use. Every day I realised how much they'd infused into me through bakery classes and gardening lessons. I'd been wielding magic without ever knowing.

Another wave of panic rolled over me and I bent forward to brace my hands against my knees. Addison stared at me with a peculiar expression on her face. Izzy nudged me with her snout.

"I'm fine. Sometimes I can sense what Ezekiel's feeling."

Addison sat on the coffee table in front of me. "Can you focus and get a clearer picture of what's happening?" she asked, her hands clasped in front of her so tightly that her knuckles were white.

I shook my head, my eyes meeting hers sadly. "I don't know how."

Izzy's claw tapped the page I'd been reading. Both Addison and I turned our attention to the book. There was a spell to link a witch with their familiar.

Addison stared at Izzy. "You could try it…"

"What if she doesn't want to be linked to me?"

"Izzy seems to be the one suggesting it," Addison pointed out.

We both looked at the wyvern at the same time and Izzy blinked at us.

"Fine." I sighed. "I'll try. Are you okay with this?" I asked the red wyvern staring at me. Her head dipped in acknowledgement.

I centred myself and held the book in my right hand, placing my left on Izzy's head. The words looked foreign but their pronunciation slipped from my tongue with ease. Images flashed through my mind of Izzy's past, the cruel way Ophelia had ensnared and enslaved her. I continued to chant, the tattvas on my fingers burning with an intensity that made me suppress a shudder.

Magic crawled under my skin and permeated the flesh under it. Izzy's eyes blazed golden before a flash of light sent me hurtling across the room to land with a splat against the wall.

I felt Izzy deep inside me, her emotions.

She stood and shook herself until a beautiful woman with long flowing red hair replaced the large red lizard. Addison and I shared a worried look. The book didn't mention anything like this.

She bowed to me. "Thank you for releasing me."

My mouth opened and closed several times with no reply.

"Ophelia enslaved us, since a witch can only bond with one familiar."

Now I was bonded with her and she wasn't the big red lizard I believed her to be.

"You do not need to fear me. I cannot hurt you any more than you can harm me." She sat beside me. "The battle continues. There is death and injury on both sides." Her eyes took on a faraway gaze that saw more than the four walls of this room. "Elves and incubi fight side by side. The black dragon has burned The Blood Queen. She hides behind a wall of her slaves, feeding from them to heal herself."

Addison's hand gripped mine. "Can you see my mate, Gabriel?"

"He fights in the air."

I didn't want to say the words that were stuck in my throat. Ophelia had come here for Ezekiel because I had stopped her from feeding from him.

"Your mate stands beside the elf prince. They fight together as they have done since childhood."

My fingers tightened on Addison's. I didn't debate the use of the word mate, because I knew in my heart there was no one else in any realm I would ever want to be with but Ezekiel.

Izzy blinked several times before turning her bright golden gaze to us.

"Is this your normal form?" I asked. She was ethereally beautiful, her magic cloaking her in a golden aura, her scales blending to form a tight catsuit-type outfit.

"No." She shook her head. "My kind learned to shape-shift long ago to hide. I cannot talk in my natural form and you both required answers about the men you love."

I felt Addison's heated gaze boring into me, but I refused to look at her. The person who deserved to know how I felt first was Ezekiel, not his sister.

"Thank you for releasing me from her servitude. Bonding with me as your familiar means she will never be able to enslave me again." Her hand rested on a pendant at her throat. She raised her eyes when I focused on it. "My mate gave it to me long ago. The Blood Queen forced him to join her army by hurting me."

I shuffled forward and grabbed her hands. "We will try to find him. Ezekiel promised he would try to free the wyverns instead of killing them."

Izzy swallowed, her gaze set on the window beyond me. "I do not know if he is still alive. She uses the male wyverns differently to the females. Her greed for power is nothing compared to the lust she craves. That is why she wants your mate to impregnate her. No being has been strong enough to gift her with a child, and she believes that the crown prince of the incubi would be."

Nausea rolled inside me at the thought of her and Ezekiel together.

Izzy wandered to sit on the window ledge, lost in her own thoughts, sometimes giving us updates on the battle.

"How do you know what is going on out there?" Addison asked her, intrigued by new knowledge on magic.

"As the incubus frees my kind I can see through their eyes," she answered cryptically.

Addison stared at me and I shrugged.

I left the two of them in the living area and wandered into my old room. Most of my belongings migrated with me into Ezekiel's room as I invaded his space. One day I found my stuff in a wardrobe he'd cleared, his version of accepting me into his life without question.

Lifting my old kit bag, I emptied the remaining contents on the floor, searching for the wooden box that had been stuffed in the bottom at the last minute before I left my old life. Aunt Agatha had given it to me when I was recruited into the vampire academy to begin my warrior training. It was only to be opened when I felt the time was right. In over a century, it had never felt right.

Today was the day that it called to me.

I carried it into the other room where Addison and Izzy sat in silence. Quietly, I placed the box on the table and everyone turned to stare at it.

"What's in the box?" Addison enquired.

I shrugged. "No idea. Aunt Agatha gave it to me years ago with instructions to open it when the time was right."

Addison's eyes swivelled from the box to me. "Is the time right?"

"I rarely think about it, leaving it in the bottom drawer of my room. I wasn't going to bring it with me on this mission since the rest of my stuff is still in my room back in Dracus." We all stared at the plain wooden box with apprehension. I wasn't sure if I expected it to spring open or explode. Nothing would surprise me anymore. "I still don't know why I lifted it."

"Everything slots into place when you find your fated mate," Izzy announced, returning to her vigil at the window.

Honestly, I didn't know how to reply to that, so I distracted myself by lifting the box to examine it. There were no doors or lids to open it, no seals or indentations for my nail to try and lever it open.

Exasperated, I flung myself back on the sofa and glared at it in frustration. Maybe it was just a box to give me a link to back home.

"Concentrate and do whatever makes your fingertips glow," Addison instructed, her brows drawn down as she studied the mysterious box.

I strummed my fingers together, activating the tattvas on the tips and touched the box. Both Addison and I leaned forward in unison to stare at it. Bright sigils flashed across the surface, witch symbols from the books I'd been reading—the secret language of my people. The box twisted until it opened along a seam across the middle that hadn't been there before.

A piece of paper sat on top of a velvet pouch. Lifting the letter, I opened it with trembling fingers.

My dearest niece,

This box would only have opened if you've found your magic. Your mother and I buried your gifts deep inside you until you found the man I saw in a vision after you were born. The dark prince who will protect you from a world that is no longer safe for our kind to walk in.

Remember my lessons, for every one of them connect you with the ancient powers of our bloodline. Each family of witches have unique abilities. When Ophelia gained a thirst for power, our visionaries saw that she would stop at nothing to harvest every scrap of magic in Purgatory. Four families went into hiding, burying our magic where she would never find it. We taught you in secret, knowing you were the chosen one in our family.

You carry our hopes for a better world inside you, and we love you with all our hearts.

Don't be afraid to let yourself love, Ilana, because that truly is the greatest magic of all.

Your Aunt Agatha.

I lifted the pouch, which felt heavier than the box had been. Inside were crystals etched with symbols.

"You belong to the divination witches." Izzy watched me from the window ledge. "The stones are for you to find your path."

The clear quartz stones vibrated in my hands as I poured them out of the pouch, each one humming with a different frequency. Instinctively, I threw them onto the table, my gaze running hungrily over them and the patterns they formed.

"Ophelia is injured," I said, my mind far away in a fog. My finger raced over one of the stones. "They are taking her to safety even now."

"Gabriel?" Addison gasped.

"Is on the ground organising soldiers to face the wraiths as they invade."

"Ezekiel?"

My heart stopped for two beats at the mention of his name. The image of him standing on Magnus' back with his hair moving in the breeze fluttered through my head. He held blasters that he aimed at the wraiths, the elf at his side firing arrows at the crystals under the wyvern's wings.

"In the air, fighting to free the oppressed."

"Will they win?" Addison gripped my hands, her eyes boring into mine.

"This war has no winners. Only death surrounds it until the magic bearers awake their fate."

Pain lanced through me and my head nearly exploded with the energy surge that hit it.

Izzy was beside me in a few seconds, throwing a blanket over me. Her hands gripped my arms until I felt them turn into talons as her magic fused with mine. Cool energy rippled over me until I was numb, devoid of all feelings and emotions.

The world went black.

Slowly pushing myself up, I groaned, my hand tentatively touching my head. "What happened?"

Addison helped me up, her face a mask of concern, her eyes scanning me. "Ophelia or one of her captive witches sensed your magic and turned their evil eye toward you. Luckily Izzy knew what was happening and covered you so they couldn't see through your eyes. She melded her magic with you to suppress all your thoughts and emotions. You've been passed out for a few hours."

The world tilted and swam around me for a few seconds. I held my head before it tried to fall off my shoulders.

"You need to rest." Addison was in full bossy mode.

I shook my head and looked at the table. The crystals were all safely back in their pouch.

"You need to cast a protection circle before you scry," Izzy admonished me.

Yeah, I remembered reading that in one of the books, but I never planned to do anything but see what was in the velvet pouch.

"Any sign of Ezekiel or Gabriel?" I asked.

Addison shook her head, her lips pursed, and eyes filled with terror.

"I need a drink," I muttered, pushing myself onto shaky legs.

The water was so cold, it burned my dry throat on the way down. My thoughts were shattered into pieces that refused to fit together. The box would only open when I found the dark prince destined to protect me? Did that mean I belonged with Ezekiel? Was that why I could only feed from him, that he was the only man who could touch me without hurting me? Too many questions danced inside my sore head without answers.

My fingers gripped the kitchen counter as my vision swam again. I needed Ezekiel here. His energy always calmed and centred me.

I remembered Aunt Agatha's lessons, but none of them were about fighting an evil queen. They pertained to potion making and controlling the elements. I didn't know how any of that fit together.

As soon as Ezekiel got home, I was going to visit my mother and aunt.

Scrap that. Summer solstice was one day away. When Ezekiel got home, he was going to make sure he lived up to my ultimate fantasy lover. Then we were going to see my parents.

***

Chapter Twenty-Three

Ezekiel

Raegel climbed into the cave barely out of breath. His brown with green eyes studied the cave we hadn't set foot in for over two hundred years, before his gaze rested on me. He didn't waste words and at times barely spoke. He waited for me to tell him whatever it was he needed to know.

"One of the vampires I selected for my unit has magical abilities," I shared with him. For Raegel to help me, he needed as much information as possible.

His eyebrows rose, but that was his only reaction.

"Her touch prevents Ophelia from reaching me in dream state. For the past week, I've slept without her violating touch. She hasn't been able to drain me or activate the curse."

The muscles in Raegel's jaw bunched, his brow furrowing. "Do you think she can break the curse?"

I shrugged because I had no idea. The curse affected each of us in various ways. Mine was through feeding, the others were controlled by Ophelia through different desires. She held our balls in her grimy hands, gripped them in a punishing grasp when we displeased her.

"All I know is when Ilana touches me then Ophelia can't."

His eyes bored into my mine with an intensity that felt like he was trying to find answers without words. "How did you discover this?"

"I saw a magical shield surround her when a Lycan attacked, so I pulled her from training. Addison convinced me to hide her so she could study her magic—I told you all, she's been tracking magic users for years. Long story short, she heard me having a nightmare as Ophelia was mind raping me and when she touched me to wake me up, she broke the connection."

Raegel folded his arms across his chest, making the tattoos on his biceps bulge with menace. He leaned against the cave wall and sighed. "This is either a blessing or a curse."

I waited for him to elaborate.

"It is a blessing because Ophelia cannot reach you when she is with you. It is a curse because it brought her to your border."

"About that…" I took a deep breath, because Raegel would not be happy. "Ilana sees our realms in different coloured foliage."

His head canted to the side and his brow wrinkled in confusion.

"The vampire realm had crimson leaves, mine purple, and your realm is green. She identified an area of blackness between our border. We've been studying the anomaly for a few days to determine what it is."

Raegel pushed himself off the wall, his pointed ears flaring back against his head.

"Ophelia has a base that lies on the border between our two kingdoms. She's using it to hide herself in the void area and syphon energy from our realms."

Murderous rage flooded Raegel's dark changeable eyes. He was always so calm and collected until something flicked his switch and activated the crazed psychotic murderer. He definitely looked like that switch was short-circuiting right now.

"I fucking hate that bitch." He sneered, his fangs sliding down.

"We both do," I agreed, rubbing my hands over my face. "Look, we're going to raid the base the day after the solstice." There was no need to spell out that I was going to feed first to go in with full strength. We all needed to bring our best game to the fight.

"I will have my warriors ready. You will need to show me the location." The tips of his ears twitched, displaying his anger.

I nodded. "Raegel, Addison may be right. We need to find any missing witches to stop Ophelia. We stand against her, but she comes back stronger. Every time we think we've hurt or weakened her, she punishes us until she brings us to our knees in submission. Ilana's touch stops her connection through the curse. What if witches in our army can stop her permanently?"

His eyes narrowed, his brow furrowing in concentration. "You say she was in the vampire army?"

"Yeah. She was unaware she descended from magic."

His fingers tapped his bicep as he lost himself in contemplation. "Then surely Valek would have noticed this magic?" He remained silent for a moment. "What changed that she discovered it?"

"I've no idea," I confessed. "Maybe the lycan attack?"

"Or maybe you," he suggested.

I chewed the inside of my mouth. "You think she sensed my curse?"

He shook his head. "My grandmamma always believed there was that one special person out there that the Great Spirit designed specifically for you. Sometimes it took many lifetimes to find that soul, but eventually you do. Maybe her magic activated to save you."

Shit. I never contemplated that her magic only emerged when our eyes had met at that banquet. When she'd met my gaze, she'd held me captive with those bright green eyes. I'd felt her loss when she left the hall. I put it down to hunger and exhaustion. "What makes you think that?" I asked, my thoughts in confusion.

"You have changed since we last met and it hasn't even been a month. A man only changes that much in such a short time when another influences him. I need to meet her. If I read her energy signature, I should be able to identify other spell casters."

Elven magic was different to that used by incubi. He saw the fabric of the world, the lifeforce that surrounded us and lived in the trees and plants. An elf never killed without reason, and even then, that death touched their soul. The elaborate tattoo on his back had a tally for every life he'd taken. He wore each death on his skin in memorandum of the souls he'd dispatched to Hell.

I felt her touch, the hairs on the back of my neck standing to attention and my skin raising in goosebumps at the violation.

"Raeg…" I choked out as my knees gave way.

This was Ophelia's retaliation for my attack. Her claws dug deep into my soul as she took possession of me.

I felt Raegel grasp me to haul me up. "I have you, my brother. Stay strong."

Magnus was waiting outside the cave. His worry rolled over me, his voice garbled in my head. The world swam in and out of focus as I began to drown in unwanted sensation.

Her hands touched me, her lips traced a path down my skin. Revulsion curled deep in my stomach and my body shivered. I didn't want this. My hands dug into Magnus' back as I tried to sever her connection with me, but she'd latched onto me hard.

Even Magnus' magic wasn't strong enough to detach her ethereal form from me as she feasted on my soul.

My energy seeped from me until I could barely feel my fingers and toes.

I tried to hold onto Raegel as he knelt beside me, knowing he'd try and break her connection to ease my pain. Each of us would do anything to keep the others safe from Ophelia. I'd felt their pity in the past. They knew she targeted me more than them because of her perverse obsession with me.

My body convulsed and I lost my battle to stay awake. In dream state she forced me to bend to her will, my body nothing more than a slave to her whims. I hadn't looked at or touched another woman since Ilana wandered into my life. Holding her while she slept, I'd promised myself that she would be enough to sustain me. That I wouldn't share my body with anyone else while she was in my life. She made me want to be a better man, a man who deserved the love I witnessed in her eyes.

Oh gods, Ilana. I'm sorry…

***

Chapter Twenty-Four

Ilana

"Something's wrong with Ezekiel," I stated, my feet already on the floor and heading for the door.

"Ilana, wait." Addison tried to pull me back. "Zek said to stay here. Any injured incubi coming back will feed on whoever they can to heal themselves."

I didn't care. There was a magnetic force in my chest that pulled me from the room and through the castle. Addison jogged beside me, trying to convince me to turn back. I couldn't even if I wanted to. The pressure in my chest intensified until my feet started running.

The hall contained the injured arriving back from battle. I sensed Magnus' form in the distance as nothing more than a black dot in the dark sky. My hair moved as he landed, his huge body ploughing through those standing about the hallway.

My stomach plummeted at the image on his back.

Ezekiel was slumped over the shoulder of the Elven Prince Raegel. His arms hung low and the elf held him firmly with his arm around his legs.

"Where is his mate?" he demanded as he stormed down Magnus' wing.

I stepped forward without thinking, my focus set on the man hanging without any sign of life. Grasping his head in my hands, I brought his face up to study.

His skin was pale and clammy, his mouth hanging open. The vitality and charisma that defined him was absent. My heart squeezed painfully in my chest.

"Ophelia is trying to drain him," Raegel's voice whispered urgently against my ear. “You need to stop her.”

My eyes met his for several seconds. I nodded. “Follow me.”

His subjects didn’t need to see Ezekiel like this. Raegel strode behind me as I led the way to our apartment. Terror rippled up and down my spine and paralysed my thoughts. The thought of him vulnerable made fury rise from the depths of my soul to radiate through me.

Something inside me snapped when I watched Raegel carrying him into our bedroom. Ezekiel’s face was too pale against his black hair, his expression vacant, chest barely moving. She’d done this deliberately.

Izzy’s words reverberated deep in my core that Ophelia wanted him to breed with her. I knew she haunted his dreams, I’d caught some of the images when I touched him. She taunted him every night with her power over him until it changed him at a fundamental level. He barely fed, never slept. He was a ghost of the man he should have been.

Yet, that man was the one who took possession of my heart. Not the arrogant prince, but the broken man who wanted to protect me, even at the detriment to himself.

“I’ll look after him, thank you,” I said, my eyes never moving from Ezekiel on the bed.

The room door closed and I heard voices outside, but right now the only person who needed my attention was Ezekiel.

I crawled over his body until my mouth hovered over his.

When I’d connected with the scrying crystals earlier, they had added a layer to my memories. For the first time, my childhood incorporated magical colour. I saw my mother and aunt working with auras, when before, I only remembered their hands sweeping through the air. A badly injured man had been brought to my aunt for healing. I thought she had been smelling his mouth to determine if he’d been poisoned. Now my memories showed her breathing golden energy into his mouth.

"Come back to me, Ezekiel," I whispered against his mouth.

I quietened all my doubts and fears and let instinct alone guide me. I took a deep breath, letting it settle in my lungs as a golden ball of energy pulsed deep in my chest, infusing through the air. Pressing my lips against his, I filled him with that golden energy.

I had no idea how long I stayed there, pushing healing into him, but I only stopped when I felt his lips twitch against mine. Then I kissed him until he finally responded, even though his eyes were closed.

My gaze flickered to the clock beside the bed. It was almost midnight.

I threw his boots across the room and dragged his jeans down his legs. Undressing your lover was supposed to be sexy. That wasn't the case when they were six-foot two of hard muscles lying unconscious on the bed. I didn't even try with his T-shirt, slicing up the front of it with a dagger from his knife collection on the wall.

Please let this work, I silently pleaded.

My energy infusion had brought him round, but what Ezekiel needed was to feed. I almost felt like a pervert climbing over him and taking his limp dick in my hand. I blew golden breath over the surface of it until it twitched in my hand.

"Forgive me, Ezekiel," I muttered before bringing my head down to the hardening flesh in my hands.

***

Ezekiel

Golden energy surrounded me, heating me in the cold darkness.

Ophelia's claws were peeled from me one finger at a time until she no longer drained my energy.

"Come back to me, Ezekiel," a voice whispered in the darkness, tempting me to swim back to consciousness.

But the darkness allowed me to rest, the heat made me sleepy.

Soft lips caressed mine. The same lips that tempted me daily. I knew their taste and texture because from the first moment they'd met mine, they felt like they'd been made for mine alone to kiss.

They slowly tempted me from the darkness.

"Forgive me, Ezekiel," the disjointed voice whispered.

Heat blossomed in my core, and my eyes rolled back in my head. My dick pulsed with a heartbeat all its own, and I fisted the sheet as the wet warmth of those lips and mouth moved over it.

Fuck!

My eyes opened and fought to focus, even as my dick told me to relax as he had his fun. I bit my lip to stop the groan that wanted to emerge. My gaze travelled down my body until it found the form of Ilana crouched over me, my dick in her mouth and her tiny hands wrapped around it.

What a fucking sight to wake up to. My heart beat rapidly and my stomach muscles tightened.

"Not that I'm complaining, but what the fuck is happening?" I rasped, my back arching as she gasped and sucked me deeper into her heat.

Her eyes met mine and locked. A flush travelled over her breasts to flood her cheeks. "You were injured and Raegel brought you back." Her eyes dipped to my dick still pulsing in her hands. They finally crept up to meet mine. "Happy summer solstice."

Seriously?

We'd made it to the equinox?

My dick thumped to attention and I closed my eyes for a few seconds to centre myself and stop myself from throwing Ilana on her back and burying myself deep inside her.

Fuck good intentions, they never tasted the same as the road to sin and debauchery.

I didn't know what she saw on my face, but Ilana's cute little fangs bit into her bottom lip, her eyes wide. My libido kicked into action as a salacious grin spread my lips.

"Get naked," I demanded. "Now!"

She jumped slightly before her shaky hands went to the front of her top.

"Never mind." I reached down and ripped it down the front. "I always like to open my own presents."

***

Ilana

I thought he'd hate me for touching him the way Ophelia had, without his permission.

The intense heat in those dark eyes ripped those thoughts from my head and left them a burning heap of ash on the floor.

"By the way." His lips hovered over mine. "Best wake-up ever."

His mouth teased mine with tiny kisses peppered across them, his tongue skimming over my bottom lip. I'd spent nearly two days sick with worry, my imagination torturing me. Then I felt his panic and pain as Ophelia plunged her twisted curse deep into his heart. I'd never been so afraid in my life. I reached up and grabbed his hair, crushing my lips against his as I willingly gave myself up to the sensation of him.

Ezekiel chuckled. "Miss me?"

"You've no idea," I muttered.

He kissed me with his entire heart on display, his emotions fusing into me. There were no barriers left between us, there was only us laid bare before each other.

Ezekiel gently moved me on the bed until my head rested on the pillow. He shifted, settling himself between my legs before kneeling back to study me, his teeth biting into the corner of his lips.

He shook his head, a smirk appearing on his kiss swollen mouth. "I don't know what I did to deserve you, but after today, I'm never giving you up."

Ezekiel lifted my left leg, pressing a kiss to the side of my ankle.

His dark eyes never left mine while he pressed soft kisses up the inside of my leg as he slid it over his shoulder. My head fell back at the sensation of his breath against my core.

"Eyes on me, baby. I want to feast on your reactions."

My head snapped up.

There was a place deep in the forests where I grew up that black butterflies lived. Their wings were delicate on your skin as they fluttered past you. An entire flock of them felt like they invaded my stomach, their wings beating inside me in anticipation.

My mouth dropped open as I watch his tongue skim over the flesh that pulsed between my legs. There was a predatory gaze deep in his eyes, the look that told the prey just to give up because they would never escape. It was the most erotic experience of my life. Normally I closed my eyes and let him bring me to climax, I'd missed the full experience.

"Gods, I can't, Ezekiel." Everything was too much after my heightened emotions from earlier.

"Did no one ever tell you that you needed to prepare your feast before consuming it?" His tongue slid between my folds and I shivered. I'd seen enough people having sex, even incubi at some of the feasts. None of them had ever done this. He devoured me, his eyes never leaving mine, watching as I bit my lips, grabbed the sheets, my hips bucking under his hands. Perspiration coated my skin as I tossed and arched.

He was going to kill me. The pressure built into a crescendo deep in my core, destroying everything in its path of fire and destruction, leaving only pleasure behind. His tongue should have a hazard warning stamped on it. It was a weapon of mass seduction and me his willing victim.

I screamed because I couldn't keep my emotions contained anymore. They erupted in a volcano of pleasure that swept through me with an intensity that left me lying there panting and unable to move.

Ezekiel crawled over me, his gaze still locked on mine. "You sure about this?" he asked, suddenly serious. "Your first partner is a big thing in my world."

My hand cupped his face. "You're already my first, considering we lost that battle the other night."

His eyebrow twitched and his lips curved in a familiar smirk.

"You better make good on your promise and fuck me until I can't stand," I whispered, our lips nearly touching. "You've kept me waiting long enough."

We crashed together, his mouth searching mine, his erection pushing into me inch by exquisite inch. My legs widened to allow him to fully seat his length deep in my core. His fingers intertwined through mine as he pressed them into the bed on either side of my body.

"Fuck!" he gasped when we were fully joined, and I felt his hard dick throbbing inside me, his pelvis grinding against mine.

I lay open and vulnerable beneath him, pinned to the bed with his hands, mouth, and massive dick. Ezekiel had defeated every barrier I'd erected around myself, tearing every one of them to pieces. His mouth left me breathless, his tongue leisurely exploring my mouth, running along the back of my fangs.

Ancient tribes used to tie virgins to sacrificial rocks for the gods to claim. I imagined myself lying here as an offering to Ezekiel. I couldn't move with his heavy body holding me captive in his embrace, chained to him by emotions instead of metal and rope.

Slowly his hips moved as he pulled his length out until only the tip remained. He plunged back inside, and I moaned into his mouth. We'd never made it this far before and I craved to share everything with Ezekiel. Over and over he retreated and advanced until I was a writhing mass of nerve endings on the precipice of a new discovery.

In my head he'd take me hard and fast. The opposite was true. He tortured me by keeping me floating somewhere between consciousness and the heavens. Ezekiel pressed his forehead to mine as we gasped for breath. I never imagined this divine friction of him thrusting in and out of me. Mia's stories didn't do this justice.

My body moved with his, my legs wound around his body as I rode this storm with Ezekiel. He angled his hips up and ground his pelvis hard into mine. My neck arched and my fangs fully descended. He did it again and the monster that lived deep inside me crept to the surface. I didn't need to feed, but right now I *wanted* to.

My fangs penetrated his artery at the same time he surged deep into me.

"Fuck, baby, suck me dry." Ezekiel gasped, his hands landing on my hips to hold me as he changed rhythm from slow to fast, gentle to vicious.

Bright lights detonated behind my eyes and every one of those nerve endings that had been zinging in anticipation exploded in a supernova of pleasure. My entire body arched as my muscles spasmed in pleasure before I collapsed in a languid heap.

"Mind if I finish?" Ezekiel kissed my neck. I lay there stunned as he moved over me, his thrusts elongating my orgasm until the flesh between my legs was so sensitive that I wanted to weep in pleasured pain.

His cock stabbed into my core in deep plunges that left me clinging to him. Ezekiel buried himself completely, his back arched and mouth open. He was more beautiful than ever before as he spilled himself inside me.

Heat ignited in my womb to feed him, my entire body spasming in a different type of orgasm. I screamed, my legs locking above his ass to pull him harder into me, trying to fuse us together forever in this mind-altering sensation.

Ezekiel collapsed on top of me, his hair wet against my shoulder.

No words would form in my head. I didn't know what to expect, but this wasn't it. He blew me apart and held me together with his arms tight around me. Ezekiel went to pull out of me, but I clung to him.

His laugh vibrated on the skin at my neck. "I'm not finished with you, baby. Promise."

I just needed a moment to pull myself together, so I buried my head into his shoulder, suddenly shy.

Ezekiel pushed himself onto his hands, his cock still embedded in me. His finger traced the side of my face. "You okay?"

I still couldn't speak, just nodded.

"That was just the appetiser, Ilana. By the time midnight arrives again, you'll not be able to walk for a week."

"I can't walk now," I snarked, my voice finally returning.

He kissed me and my arms snaked around his neck.

"Now before I have to drag myself out of this bed for an hour to debrief after Ophelia's invasion, get that gorgeous ass in the air. I want you on your hands and knees."

My core convulsed around him and a grin twisted his lips. He knew what he did to me.

"Can't move," I breathed, arching my body under his.

Ezekiel narrowed his eyes at me in warning before he pulled out, leaving me empty. He rolled me onto my stomach and lifted my hips up before burying himself to the hilt in me.

"Oh, my gods!" I muttered into the mattress.

He leaned over and whispered in my ear, "Nah, just an incubus prince." His breath behind my ear making me shudder.

Naïvely, I thought sex was sex—stick it in and out, and voila! An orgasm. Nope, at this angle he massaged the front wall of my core. He felt bigger and oh-so deeper. I whimpered, my hands grabbing the metal railings of his headboard because I was about to fall off the edge of Purgatory straight into Hell.

"Ezekiel, please," I begged. I didn't even know what I was pleading for. All I knew was that whatever it was, he was the only one who could give me it.

His strong hands roamed my body, tweaking my nipples, rubbing over my clit. Just as I focused on one sensation, he'd moved to give me another. My body was an instrument that he played like the finest musician, elucidating mewls and moans to accompany his grunts and groans.

My hips pushed back as he plunged forward, our bodies rocking against each other.

Ezekiel's hands moved from where they dug into my hips until they were braced on either side of me. His body covered mine and I felt tiny under his massive frame. His movements were smaller now, his length lodged deep in me, the friction rubbing that spot that made me bite my lip and close my eyes.

I threw my head back until it rested in his shoulder, his cheek resting against mine.

"Is it always like this?" I gasped.

"No, baby. Normally it's just sex. This is something different." Ezekiel wrapped his hand around my hair, pulling my head back so his lips could find mine.

My heart crumbled with his words. I knew he spoke the truth, because his emotions cascaded through me. Every day our connection got stronger, our lives intertwining around each other the same way our bodies were now.

Life before Ezekiel now seemed cold and dark, a place barren of emotions. He brought heat from his passion, warming with his desire.

My body trembled, my legs barely able to hold me up. Ezekiel rotated his hips and I fell into the pleasure abyss, drowning in sensation. Two deep thrusts and he followed me.

We collapsed onto our sides on the bed, his hand grasping mine, his chin rested on top of mine. I wasn't sure what had happened, but somewhere in the middle of this, I had handed my heart to Ezekiel. There was no doubt in my mind that I loved him.

***

Chapter Twenty-Five

Addison

"Will he be okay?" Gabriel stared at the door Raegel just closed.

"I've seen him worse after one of Ophelia's attacks," Raegel replied, dropping wearily into a chair.

"He was fine when he flew from the battle," Gabriel insisted. "What the fuck happened?"

Raegel glared at me for a few seconds before his head canted back and he pinched the bridge of his nose.

I took Gabriel's hand and led him to another sofa. He continued to watch Raegel warily as if the elf was going to murder us all. His reputation was well earned when he lost control. I had no doubt it was linked to his curse.

Struggling to find where to start, I stared at our joined hands instead of his face. "Two hundred years ago, Father, along with the other kings, brokered a peace with Ophelia. They told her to name her price and they would grant it so our realms could find peace after the slaughter on all sides."

I took a deep breath, my gaze flickering to Raegel. He held himself static, displaying no emotion. "She wanted the firstborn sons of each of the realms. The magic of their race ran through their veins and she craved their power. Ezekiel and the others arrived to find themselves sacrifices."

Gabriel gasped, his hands tightening around mine. I met his eyes and he shook his head slowly. "They wouldn't…" he said softly.

"They did. She cursed each of the four dark princes to feed her appetites. Each curse is different, designed to empower her. I only know Ezekiel's because I found him collapsed years ago and saw the truth through my empathy. They are bound never to speak of it. She obviously never knew about my gifts."

"Zek…" He looked to the closed door into Ezekiel's room.

"When he feeds, Ophelia steals something from his partner. A memory, a feeling, a connection to a person or place. Something special to that person. It alters them."

"Ilana…" He tried to stand, his protective instincts kicking in.

"She's fine. He can feed without repercussion on the four equinoxes." We all stared at the clock on the wall that had just passed midnight.

Gabriel covered his face with his hands. "The girls in the harem," he groaned.

"That's how he learned what his curse was. She never told any of them what she'd done to them."

Raegel made a choking sound. He stood abruptly and went to stare out the window where Izzy sat in her wyvern form. My heart broke for the proud elf.

"And tonight?" Gabriel demanded.

"Tonight," Raegel answered. "She was pissed because Ilana's touch stopped her reaching him. She drained him in punishment. Every fucking night, that psychopathic witch fornicated with him, raping him in his sleep. I would love nothing more than to kill her…" his voice trailed off.

Gabriel opened his mouth to speak but I shook my head.

"They can't. None of them can strike against her directly," I told him.

"Poor bastards," Gabriel muttered.

"Thanks," Raegel replied with heavy sarcasm.

Muffled noises came from Ezekiel's room. I relaxed, knowing that Ilana had brought him back from the edge. His energy had been almost depleted, his breathing shallow when they arrived home earlier.

"What can we do?" Gabriel asked. "Surely there is a way to break the curse?"

Raegel spun, his eyes filled with anger and desperation. "Do you think we haven't tried? That we've spent the past two hundred years enjoying her tormenting us?" He took several deep breaths to try and control his anger. "That woman in there is the first time Ezekiel has had a reprieve in all those years. Her touch stops the violation of his soul. The rest of us can only dream of such a reprieve."

Silence engulfed us, shattered by Ilana's scream. A woman only released that sound when she'd surrendered herself to complete possession and passion.

"I need a walk," Raegel muttered, his fist clenched at his side.

He always held himself with such power and control that his body was taut and rigid. When that control snapped, there wasn't anywhere in Purgatory that he wouldn't be able to track you to enact his revenge. For a long time, I'd suspected his anger was part of his curse. He never let me close enough to touch him and find out.

"Why don't we go to our apartment and have a drink?" I suggested. "Gabriel managed to buy a few bottles of whiskey from the Earth realm."

Raegel nodded, following us from the room as the noises behind Ezekiel's door escalated.

He'd be well fed tonight.

***

Chapter Twenty-Six

Ophelia

I hollered in frustration when my connection with Ezekiel was severed abruptly.

He needed to understand that I didn't want to hurt him, but I couldn't let his behaviour earlier go unpunished. I craved him with an intensity that made my insides tighten with wanton need.

I stormed through my castle, the walls vibrating in response to my rage.

That incubus would be mine if I had to tear the incubus realm apart.

My wyverns flew out of my way as I strode through the courtyard. Dozens were missing and I couldn't sense them. Had they developed stronger weapons that killed my pets? My nails scraped the insides of my hands at the thought of what my visit to find Ezekiel had cost me.

He'd stood defiantly in front of me on that black beast, the most magnificent sight I'd witnessed in an age. Unfortunately, I'd learned a long time ago that love spells never ended well for witches. The partner became a mindless drone as their freewill leached away. I wanted Ezekiel to come to me willingly, to impregnate me with his child.

My coven sat in a room specifically designed to hold them. Their magic worked in here, but their souls were tethered to me in servitude. Their loved ones lay in stasis chambers so I could access their magic.

I glared at them, demanding to know what happened out there and where my precious pets were.

"Our Queen." My sister sank to her knees at my feet. Aurelia was a weakness of mine. She was not a powerful witch, but she was my blood relative, a reminder of the girl I'd once been. "We felt the flare of magic earlier."

My spine straightened. "Where?" I demanded.

She shook her head. "It was brief and then suppressed."

"A dragon?"

"No, it was another witch."

Surely he wouldn't have given himself to another witch when he made his feelings about our kind so clear in the past? My inability to touch Ezekiel in his sleep flashed through my head again.

"Was it in the incubus realm?" I had to know. Hatred burned deep in my soul toward any woman who touched him. It was the reason I incorporated that delicious twist in his curse. No woman would keep coming near him if he removed a piece of her with every feeding. Those who did would be nothing more than mindless slaves.

"We do not know, sister. Maybe a witch child has been born?"

I considered her words. It was possible. I knew there were rogue witches still on the loose out there. They had hidden their magic, but perhaps at the moment of birth, magic flared before being bound.

"Let me know if you sense it again," I snapped. My gaze roamed over the remains of my coven. We'd been strong, but I found a way of making myself stronger. Invincible. "What about my wyverns?"

"We have tried to connect with their crystals, but they no longer touch living flesh." Magenta was the crystal expert of the coven. She'd designed the crystals that controlled my wyverns. "I suspect the wyverns are dead."

Annoyance curled inside my stomach and permeated through me. They were my pets and those elves and incubi had killed them. I'd always disliked elves. They were too noble, always judging and looking down their regal noses at people. They refused to mate outside their own race, the only exception being a royal alliance to strengthen bonds between realms. The resulting match was rarely happy.

My wyverns hadn't bred in centuries, no matter how much I encouraged them. I carefully selected males and females, enchanted them to have sex under the energy of the full moon in the Earth realm. We may not see the moon in the dim light of Purgatory, but we felt the influence of it.

I'd even managed to trick some of the male wyverns into their human form, tying them with charmed chains to my bed to ensure they wouldn't turn back before I finished with them. Never once had they managed to impregnate me. My magic was too strong for them.

No, the only man strong enough to breed with me was Ezekiel.

He would yield to me, even if I had to drain him night after night until he lost his mind.

I trekked to my magical haven at the top of my tower. I opened my grimoire, my fingers caressing the pages. It contained every spell and incantation I'd hunted down in Purgatory. The secrets of our people. I turned the pages slowly to savour the scent of magic as it emerged from the words.

The section at the back had been added by me. It contained a note of every witch I had killed, and the powers I'd stolen from her. My own personal record of my journey. It started as penitence and emerged as a genealogy of our people. There were gaps, lineages that had escaped my witch hunt. Were they breeding out there, sparking new magic into existence?

They'd evaded me by suppressing their magic. I needed to devise a spell to find them because the power of their blood would make me unstoppable. I would finally rule Purgatory and join it to the Earth realm. Then I would walk in the sun and bask in the moon, and enslave all the souls there as well.

***

Chapter Twenty-Seven

Ezekiel

I couldn't get enough of her.

Ilana was different to every woman I'd every fed from, her energy revitalising me in a way I'd never experience before. Was it because she contained magic or was it because of my feelings for her?

"We need to get up," I said, tucking her messy curls behind her ear as she lay over my chest.

"Can't stand," she murmured, her hand smoothing over my right pectoral muscle.

I grinned at her reaction.

Two weeks ago, she'd never properly kissed a man.

A week ago, she'd never had a man touch her sexually.

Now she lay sated on top of me, the evidence of what we did drying on her skin.

I rolled her over and settled between her legs. "We either get up for an hour to sort out the Ophelia problem or I'm going to have to fuck you again."

Her eyes widened before they ran down my body.

Yeah, I was wide awake and ready to go again. After all, I was a sex demon.

"Is he not tired or broken yet?" she wondered, her finger touching the tip of my dick.

I hissed between my teeth. "Definitely not tired," I grated out. I'd already had her four times and my energy levels were through the roof. Interspecies couldn't breed in Purgatory or her sexy vampire ass would be knocked up right now.

Her big green eyes met mine. "Once more and that's it for a few hours before my vagina runs away." She stretched her luscious body. "And we need to shower before you go anywhere. I have semen leaking out of me and drying in places that I'm clueless about how it got there."

I kissed her shoulder. "We could do both at once," I suggested.

Her brow wrinkled in confusion.

"Shower sex, baby," I informed her. It never failed to amaze me how this woman had lived this long and knew so little about sex. "It's okay," I smirked against her lips. "You're in safe hands."

I dragged her up and walked her backward to the bathroom playfully. She bit her lip and gave me a huge eye stare which just turned me on even more. She giggled when I grabbed her and pulled her under the water with me. Ilana was addictive and I was fast becoming an addict.

Addison and Gabriel hide their amusement, but Raegel frowned at Ilana and me. Our shower had taken longer than I anticipated because every time I soaped the sexy minx up, she moaned and aroused me again.

I'd fed so much I felt like a kid on Halloween night after eating too much candy.

"How am I supposed to read her energy when you've contaminated it with yours?" he demanded.

Contaminated? That was harsh, even for him. "Hey, man, I was nearly drained."

He sighed and glared at me. "Gabriel showed me the area where Ophelia's base is located. I will go there and examine it before we strike tomorrow."

"Are you not staying for the feast?" Addison asked.

Raegel took a step back as if she struck him. Our feasts normally descended into orgies. There was no way he would be involved in that. Raegel held himself above all vices and sins. I doubted he'd even consider participating in sex outside marriage anymore.

"I'll walk you out." I opened the door and he gracefully strode through it. "Be back in a few minutes," I told Ilana, pressing a quick kiss on her swollen lips.

Raegel and I walked toward the castle entrance. "Thanks for getting me back to Ilana in time," I said.

He nodded solemnly. "I felt Ophelia's connection with you break when Ilana touched you. It was remarkable."

She certainly was.

"Be careful, Raegel. That base is heavily guarded with wraiths."

A small smile turned the corners of his mouth up. "It is the equinox. One of the few days she cannot sense us. Technically, a wraith is already dead, so their demise will not burden my soul."

I rolled my eyes at him. "Yeah, well, have fun out there."

A wolfish gleam entered his eyes that would have better suited Lycidas. "I will be back when the equinox ends."

We clasped our hands just below each other's elbows, granting the other strength and support. "Stay safe."

He nodded and strode out of the castle. I watched as he jumped off the end of the cliff face and into the forests beneath. One of these days he was going to go splat instead of managing to grab a tree on the way down.

Magnus lay curled in the entrance hall, people squeezing past him as they prepared the feast for tonight. It was a paradox because I doubted there would be much physical food consumed.

"Hey." I scrubbed behind his ear.

He blinked, revealing his elliptical amber iris. *She saved you.*

"Yeah, she did. I have no idea what to do anymore," I admitted, rubbing behind my neck.

Ilana affected me more than I dared admit. She tasted different to anything I'd tried before, and I'd fed from just about every species that lived in Purgatory. Jethro and I had gone through a wild phase of feeding frenzies. Ilana made them all pale in comparison.

Waking up from the nightmare of Ophelia to find Ilana with my dick in her mouth. That was an image I was never going to forget.

Several of my commanders stopped me with updates from the battle. Most of them gave me strange looks until I realised this was the first time I'd been at full strength for a long time. Ilana didn't just feed me, she nourished my soul.

She was studying the maps of the area of Ophelia's base with Addison and Gabriel when I returned over an hour later. I knew from the pitying look on Gabriel's face that Addison had told him about the curse.

"Seriously, Addy?" I demanded, my arms folding over my chest. "I don't need anyone's pity!"

Gabriel glanced away guiltily.

My sister sprung to her feet, her temper rising. "You arrived half dead over the shoulder of Raegel. What did you want me to say? That you're tired?"

My anger rose to meet hers as we glared at each other.

"Enough!" Ilana stood between us. "The time for secrets is past. We need to focus on the future, and that includes breaking this curse once and for all."

My eyes cut to her. "Ilana," I growled in warning. "We've tried and she hurts innocent people in retaliation."

"Ezekiel." She pressed her hands to my chest, her head canted back so she could peer up at me. "Curses are living magic. When they are created, the witch involved must put a reversion clause into it."

My brow furrowed. I'd never heard any of this before, even in all the books I owned.

"Curses were designed to make people see the error of their ways," she explained, her hands slowly pushing under my folded arms to relax my stance. "There had to be a chance at redemption incorporated into them."

Addison gasped, understanding hitting her at the same time as it landed on me.

"It can be broken?" I asked.

Ilana nodded. "Over time, curses were used by evil witches to try and get their own way, but the basis behind them remains the same."

"How?" Addison demanded. "How do we break it?"

"That's my job." Ilana smiled up at me. "I need to find what Ophelia mixed into it."

"I don't want you getting hurt," I said, pushing her riot of messy curls behind her ear. She didn't have time to dry it after our prolonged shower. I loved it when she left it natural.

"Why do you think you can break it?" Addison asked, studying Ilana. "I've read every book I can find on magic, searched Purgatory for witches for decades. You've only just found that you contain magic."

"Exactly." Ilana grinned up at me, her eyes locking with mine. "I was thinking about this while Ezekiel was facing Ophelia. I was born after the curse. Nature tends to create the cure to a poison. What if magic generated a key to break her hold over Ezekiel? Her hold over him is severed when I touch him. She was only able to drain him because he was out there, and I was in here."

"It's possible," Addison conceded, pacing as she contemplated the situation. "There could be other witches out there that could sever her connection to the others…"

My eyes never left Ilana's. She wanted to save me and that sent a kick into my solar plexus. I didn't deserve someone as pure and beautiful as her. Ophelia would break her to punish me.

"Stop," she whispered. "You would do the same to save me. This is no longer your fight, Ezekiel, it belongs to all of us in this room. Let us help you," she pleaded. "You can't do this alone anymore."

Alone…

The realisation hit me at how alone I had actually been for all these years, even before the curse. Women had wanted me because I was crown prince and an incubus. Men sucked up to me for a position in the court. When the curse hit, no one except Addison realised that I was different.

No one had cared.

"If we work together, then we can stop her." Ilana turned and reached her hand out to Addison, who grasped it in return. "We've been making so much progress that I need to share with you about how Ophelia is gaining power. Every wyvern you released weakened her, every wraith you send to the spirit realms drained her. Let us help you, Ezekiel." Her eyes were huge and so green that I lost myself in her gaze for several seconds.

"Please, Zek," Addison whispered. "I can't watch you in pain anymore. I want my brother back."

Gabriel grasped my shoulder. "I wish I'd known sooner. I would have fucking blown her head off her shoulders. This ends now, Zek. No more keeping her away from our borders. That bitch needs eradicated from Purgatory and sent to the depths of Hell."

I stared at each of them wordlessly.

Ilana drew my attention back to her. "For us to have a future, we need to get rid of the past."

For her alone I would agree to anything.

I would walk into Hell for Ilana.

If that was what it took to get rid of Ophelia, that was what I'd do.

I nodded slowly and the people around me moved closer until I was engulfed in a group hug.

***

Chapter Twenty-Eight

Ilana

Ezekiel flicked through reports, his focus fixed on the latest dragon reports from Ophelia's base. Raegel had been a busy elf.

"What do people normally wear to these feasts?" I studied my limited wardrobe. I only had fighting clothes and training outfits with me. I lifted the dress I'd worn to dinner. Would anyone notice it was the same one?

"Mostly people are naked," he replied nonchalantly.

My body froze and back stiffened. "I'm sorry. What?"

He chewed the side of his mouth as he held a map in his hands. "Huh?" Ezekiel looked up in confusion when I stood in front of him with my hands on my hips.

"Why are people going to a feast naked?" I demanded.

A lazy grin spread across his full lips. "Because it's a feast and we're incubi." He winked at me.

I scowled and took a step back, shaking my head. "No way."

His eyebrows lifted slightly before he stood to tower over me. His hands gripped my hips and he hauled me against his hard body. "I like you naked."

"And I like you naked on your back while I have my wicked way with you," I replied, running my hands over his bare chest since he was wearing nothing but low-riding jeans. "But that does not mean I want every woman with a pulse to see you like that."

His characteristic smirk appeared at my possessive tone.

"Would you like Remiel to see me like that?" I enquired, kissing the centre of his chest. I knew my arrow hit the mark when his hands tightened on my hips and a low growl emerged.

"I'll arrange a dress for you," he informed me. "No one gets to see what's mine."

Mine… I really liked the sound of that.

We were over halfway through the equinox and Ezekiel had fed from me over a dozen times. His energy levels were through the roof. I'd never seen him so relaxed and confident. Although… my vagina was not used to this level of sexercise. She nearly ran away before he coaxed her into submission last time. I had no idea how we were going to cope tonight.

Tonight. The very thought of attending an incubus orgy filled me with dread and excitement in equal measure.

"What if someone else tries to feed from me?" I asked, tucking my head under his chin. I wasn't the innocent vampire who'd arrived here, but that didn't mean I could face the touch of another man.

Ezekiel's fingers gripped my chin and he tilted my head back until my attention was fully on him. "No one will ever touch you but me. Understand?"

I blinked, my gaze locked with his as his head slowly lowered to mine.

"Do you understand?" he repeated against my lips.

"And you?" I couldn't help myself. If I belonged to him, then surely, he should belong to me.

"I'm all yours, baby. I'll try to fight this curse and live only on what you give me every equinox, but there may be times that Ophelia attacks and I need to feed."

"Then you feed from me," I insisted.

His eyes fluttered closed, his nose rubbing slowly against mine. "I can't let her take parts of you, Ilana. Please don't ask me to do that."

It was a problem for another day. Instead, I gave in to temptation and nibbled his lips. The tips of our tongues touched each other, and I opened to his exploration. Ezekiel's hand wrapped around my hair to angle my head. I pushed his chest until he fell back onto the sofa, taking me with him.

I grinned against his lips as my legs straddled his hips. We lost ourselves in our kiss. Nothing else mattered but each other, our hands and mouths in lazy exploration. We had one day before our lives were once again monitored and controlled by a crazy witch.

Ezekiel's hands had just crept under my vest top when a female voice sounded behind us.

"Mistress, you need to come with me. The other wyverns have arrived to join you." Izzy stood in human form, her hands clasped in front of her.

"What the fuck?" Ezekiel was on his feet in two seconds, pushing me behind him. I felt power radiating from him in dark magnetic waves.

I jumped between him and Izzy. "Ezekiel, this is Izzy, my wyvern. She's one of the issues we need to discuss."

His eyes swung between me and the stunning woman with bright red hair. My stomach twisted in a knot of apprehension. Everyone in this world seemed to be more beautiful than me.

"She had been sitting on the window ledge as a giant lizard all morning," he said in disbelief.

"Um, yeah, she has two forms. She can't talk in her wyvern form," I uttered in explanation.

"I am not a lizard. We descend from the same magic as dragons." Izzy brought her deep blue eyes up in disdain. "Calling me a lizard is rude."

Ezekiel stared at her open-mouthed. I put my fingers under his chin and closed it, quirking an eyebrow at his questioning expression.

His lips twitched in response.

"We'll put this on our discussion list for tomorrow," I said before turning my attention to Izzy. "What wyverns have arrived?"

"Those released. Come, you must follow me."

Ezekiel dragged a hooded jacket on and I stuck my feet into shoes. We followed her through the castle, ignoring the curious stares we encountered along the way. Magnus had the wyverns all herded together, his watchful eye on them.

"They have no home, Mistress. They came here because they sensed my bond with you."

I stared at the dozens of wyverns in a variety of colours. My gaze moved to Ezekiel. This was his realm and it had just been invaded by magical creatures in search of a witch.

"Is there room in the dragonry for them, Magnus?" Ezekiel asked, wrapping his arms around my waist and tugging me in front of him to rest his chin on top of my head. My hands grasped his.

The big dragon eyed the wyverns and nodded his head once.

"Get them food and water for the night and we'll sort them out in the morning," Ezekiel continued. He moved his attention to Izzy. "Do they need anything else?"

"No." She shook her head. "They just need sanctuary from The Blood Queen."

"Can they change form like you?" I asked.

Izzy nodded.

"We could get them a room in the castle?" I tilted my head to look at Ezekiel in question.

"We can after tonight. This is the equinox and there is a feast planned. I would prefer that we keep any new residents until tomorrow."

My mouth opened in an 'O' of understanding. Anything walking around the castle tonight was officially on the menu. Ezekiel's lips skimmed my ear. "Need something to put in that mouth, baby?"

My eyes widened and I snapped my mouth closed even as his smirk appeared. "Maybe I do," I snarked, earning a quick rise of his right eyebrow.

"Mistress, I will stay with them tonight. We are bonded and our connection will bring them peace." Izzy walked among the other wyverns, stroking their heads.

I felt their terror pulsing in waves. How long had they endured as Ophelia's slaves? They were the familiars of witches, and I sensed the difference it made to my magic, being connected to Izzy. Following her example, I walked among them, running my fingers with the tattvas on them over their rough skin.

A small black wyvern sat huddled at the edge, eyes wide and wild. I knelt beside it and it crouched low as if I would strike it. I noticed the injury on its side where the crystal had been ripped away. The golden energy I'd shared with Ezekiel earlier vibrated inside me, and I touched the injury with the fingers of my left hand, while sending golden healing energy to the scared creature.

It let out a tiny squeak and hid its head under its uninjured wing.

Ezekiel lifted it and headed to the dragonry. "Come on, let's get you settled for the night." Its eyes peered at me from over his shoulder. The bleeding had stopped by the time we'd gotten into the huge area reserved for the dragons.

It reminded me of a massive stable, but with perches and huge windows they could fly out through. Ezekiel led them to an area near the back.

"Not many people go beyond the first section. The dragons are territorial, and they only allow a few of us they trust back here," he explained.

Some sank into the heaps of straw, exhausted. Others formed groups and curled around each other.

"They feel safe here, far from Ophelia's watchful gaze," Izzy said, appearing beside me. “The dragon’s magic will help keep them hidden from her coven.”

“She has a coven?” Ezekiel asked, still petting the distressed black wyvern.

Izzy nodded. “She has a coven bound into a magical circle in her castle.”

Ezekiel trailed a hand through his already messy hair. “We’ll need to sit down and discuss this with Addison tomorrow.”

“They have come to serve at your side, Mistress,” Izzy stated. “You are the only other witch in Purgatory.”

“I’m not the only one,” I muttered, thinking of my mum and aunt. They had a lot of explaining to do. We needed to add them to our list. Ezekiel studied me but didn’t probe me on the matter.

Magnus nudged Ezekiel. “The feast is almost ready,” Ezekiel said. “We need to go.”

I knew as crown prince he had to be there. His father ensured the feasts coincided with the equinoxes so Ezekiel could feed fully.

I left the wyverns in Izzy’s capable hands. My life was slowly spiralling out of control.

“We’ll need to warn your mother about Ophelia,” Ezekiel said in a low voice as we made our way through the castle. “If she has an active coven, they could be searching for magic and yours has recently activated.”

He was right and it made my heart leap that he knew what I meant in the dragonry. I threaded my fingers through his and leaned against his arm.

Addison was waiting for us in our room, the living area a cacophony of colours. “I brought dresses and accessories,” she declared.

Ezekiel shook his head in amusement and pushed me toward her. “Enjoy. Addy always wanted a little sister to boss around.”

He disappeared into one of the other rooms with Gabriel and a bottle of whiskey.

Addison waged war on my appearance and hair. I found the easiest way was not to argue with her as she chose and discarded outfits. Eventually she deemed me ready for the feast. She'd managed to transform herself during the process.

I felt awkward in the frivolous clothes, unused to anything like this. My wardrobe consisted of warrior or training apparel. Addison ordered her maids to take the other new outfits away before she dragged Gabriel out of his meeting to get ready.

Ezekiel emerged a few minutes later and all the preparation was worth the smouldering expression that appeared in his eyes. The tip of his tongue swept along his bottom lip before he bit down on it.

"We're not going any-fucking-where. I think we'll just stay here." He advanced toward me with a predatory gaze that made me take an involuntary step back. "You look good enough to eat."

"Have you not eaten enough today?" I asked innocently.

"Apparently not," he replied, running his heated gaze over the areas of exposed skin.

My outfit consisted of elaborate ribbons crossed over my body. Silk panels covered my breasts, ass, and lady bits. Little was left to the imagination, just enough to keep me decent. Addison had declared red and black 'my colours'.

My hair was a mass of curls twisted on top of my head to cascade over my shoulders. Her expertise with make-up made me look sultry and wanton. I didn't recognise the woman in the mirror.

"You need to get ready," I reminded him.

He shook his head again, his eyes roving over me in a heated embrace that made goosebumps rise on my skin. "You are driving me fucking insane," he muttered before striding into our room.

Ezekiel emerged a few minutes later in dark jeans, a black button-down shirt, and his normal boots. His hair was damp, but tamed. He smelt divine and I just wanted to push him back into our room and spend the rest of this glorious day together.

"Ready?" he asked, quirking an eyebrow in my direction. A dark smile appeared as he watched me practically salivating over him.

"How long do we need to stay?" I asked, pushing him against the wall.

His grin was feral, his eyes filled with desire. "Not long. Why?"

"Because there aren't many hours left in today."

He lifted me by the waist in a fluid motion, pinning me to the wall. His lips skimmed up my throat. "Don't worry, baby. I plan to make good use of the time left." His mouth hovered over mine, nothing more than a breath away. "Stay close to me. If anyone even looks at you twice, there may be blood shed tonight."

Ezekiel plundered my mouth until we were both breathless. My legs wobbled when he lowered me to the floor. My fingers clasped his forearms to steady myself.

He lifted my hand in his and led me to the banquet hall. Every eye turned in our direction. My skin prickled with unease as the image of me being led like a sacrifice to the altar at the top of the room flashed through my head. The sex demons in the room were all on edge on this one of the major nights in their yearly calendar.

Addison rolled her eyes at us. "Could you not leave her alone for two minutes? Her make-up was perfect when I left."

Ezekiel flashed her a smirk and wrapped his arm around my waist. "Nope," he retorted cheekily.

Silver trays of food were already arriving at the tables. Vampires and incubi preferred blood and sex, but could eat food as well—there just wasn't the same nutritional value to it. Delicate pastries filled with fruits and creams. Succulent meat steaming on platters. Roasted puddings doused in alcohol and set alight. The banquet was like nothing I'd seen before.

Ezekiel plucked a small pastry from a tray and held it to my lips, grinning. I opened my mouth and he popped it in, wiping the excess cream from my bottom lip with his thumb. The taste exploded on my tongue in a rhapsody of flavours.

"Good?" he asked. "They've always been my favourite."

The entire hall filled with people fell away until there was nothing left but the two of us. I lifted one to his lips and he bit the edge of his lip, teasing me.

"Open your mouth, Ezekiel." I leaned forward to whisper in his ear, "I promise to put something good in it." I winked and he engulfed the pastry and my fingers, running his tongue along my flesh as if he was tasting me as well.

Addison coughed to bring us back to whatever the king was saying. I didn't pay attention as my gaze moved through the banquet hall. Ezekiel's hand on my thigh kept me grounded and safe, even under the predatory watch of all the sex demons ready to feast on flesh.

Noise erupted when the king sat down and the feast began. This was the part that had my stomach in knots. There were orgies on the bases I'd lived on, but I always slipped away before they got heated. I had no point of reference, no idea what was expected from me. Already, some of participants were indulging themselves in more than what was available on the tables.

"When the meal is finished, the great hall is opened to everyone," Addison leaned over to explain. "The blood concubines have already laid it out like the harems with full floor bedding. All the room doors must be left open tonight, except the royal quarters, so everyone is available to feed and be fed on."

I would have been available for anyone who wanted to take me tonight. The only thing saving me from that fate was the man beside me. My body stiffened and Ezekiel increased the pressure of his hand on my leg, telling me to relax.

Remiel arrived, sulking into his chair, his expression filled with loathing for everyone there. There came a point in the life of every bad boy when they had to get their shit together or they became an eternal petulant child. There was nothing sexy about a grown man throwing a temper tantrum.

Our table was filled with delicate fancies unique to this realm. I'd spent most of my childhood eating solid food, including morsels Aunt Agatha brought back from the human realm. Some of the little desserts tasted suspiciously like chocolate. Addison and I chatted and ate, ignoring what went on around us. Ezekiel laughed with his brother Jethro, who was accompanied by his first wife.

"So, I've been reading up on tradition in the library," Remiel stated to no one in particular. I did my best to ignore him even as his words sent trails of horror rippling up my spine. "It is custom that the youngest child of the king can chose whoever he wants as his partner at an equinox feast."

Silence descended around our table.

"He can choose any unmated partner," the king clarified, his dark gaze fixed on his youngest son as if to warn him from going any further.

Remiel nodded once, his lips pursed in concentration. "Since the food is almost finished, and the festivities are about to begin, then it's time for me to make my choice." His eyes scanned the room, but I knew deep in my stomach what he was about to do.

My fingers laced through Ezekiel's and his tightened on mine in response.

He lazily turned back to us and his eyes landed on me. What was his problem? I was nothing special. Any other woman in this room would have gladly opened her legs for him. A dark smile spread over his lips. "Well, since you're so close, why don't I see what has my big brother tied in knots?"

Every muscle in my body froze, every nerve ending shouted in protest, and every eye at the table moved to look at me. The blood drained from my face and I dared not to look at anywhere but the table.

Ezekiel lifted our joined hands to his lips, pressing a kiss to my inner wrist. "Choose another," he said, his voice dark and threatening.

"But tonight I get to choose," he whined, determination in his expression. "And I choose Ilana."

Ezekiel straightened, his aura dark and pulsating, his true strength on display. "You are allowed to select a partner for the night from any *unmated* female in the court. Ilana is not unmated."

I tried not to show any reaction.

Remiel bit out a laugh. "You aren't mated. She hasn't been here long enough."

"Have you fed from anyone else in the past month, Ilana?" His voice was a soft caress in this turbulent atmosphere.

"No." I shook my head. "Only you."

"She can't feed from you, she's not a succubus," Remiel pointed out.

"True," Ezekiel conceded. "But she's a vampire and I have the marks on my body to prove she's fed from me repeatedly."

"The law means mating between incubus and succubus," Remiel hissed, his aura flaring.

"It doesn't say that," Ezekiel casually replied.

Remiel cast a desperate look to his father, who glanced away.

"In fact, our laws state that if an interloper deliberately tries to feed from a mated female without the consent of her mate, then they are subject to the full punishment of the court."

Remiel's eyes narrowed. "You wouldn't dare," he snarled.

Ezekiel's power flared and every person in the room was forced to their knees, including Remiel. The only people exempt were those seated at the table with us. This was what people feared when they spoke of the dark incubus prince. Ezekiel stood slowly, his movements threatening. He was the apex predator in the room, and my heart twisted in my chest as I watched him.

"Remiel, I sentence you to the punishment of this court. You will be taken from here and your body forfeited for the evening to whoever wishes to avail of it. You will take no pleasure or feed while enslaved."

Enslaved.

Addison gasped, her hand covering her mouth. I knew from her reaction that it had been a long time since this punishment had been given.

Remiel finally struggled to his feet, knocking a chair back until it hit the floor and he faced Ezekiel.

"You were warned," his father said. "We do not follow the old traditions for a reason."

"I'll fucking kill her," Remiel hissed, reaching over the table to grab me by the throat.

The full weight of Ezekiel's power pulsed around him until finger by finger, his hand was peeled off my throat with invisible fingers. He stumbled a few paces back under the influence of Ezekiel, dropping to his knees. Terror filled his eyes. He'd spent two hundred years thinking Ezekiel was weak. Today he was proved wrong.

"Take him out of here!" Ezekiel commanded some of the guards at the side of our table with a chin jerk.

He was dark and powerful with the essence of masculinity pulsing from every fibre of his body. My heart beat double time at the sight. He was a feral god of olden times, hellbent on tyranny and destruction. He drew everyone's attention with his magnetic personality. My panties caught on fire at the sight and my fangs dug into my bottom lip.

"What will happen to him?" I whispered to Addison.

"Others will be able to feed from him, and he'll be left aroused but unable to reach fulfilment. I've heard it's incredibly frustrating." She cast a quick look at Ezekiel. "He shouldn't have pushed Zek. He's actually been easy on him considering the insult Remiel just gave you."

"That doesn't sound too bad," I agreed.

Ezekiel sat beside me, his hand tracing up my leg, his breath fanning the sensitive shell of my ear. "Imagine being completely aroused and on the precipice of an orgasm, yet it is denied to you again and again and again. You feel it deep in your core, your body screaming for release, but it never comes, even as each person with you cries their pleasure."

I shivered.

"It's even worse for an incubus. We crave pleasure, both the giving and receiving. Remiel will be tormented for hours without any possibility of feeding."

I turned to Ezekiel, our faces so close together that our eyelashes kissed, the tips of our noses rubbing against each other, our lips hovering close to each other. "Am I your mate?" I whispered for only him to hear.

"In more ways that you can know."

Butterflies invaded my stomach and took flight through my body, raising goosebumps on my flesh.

"What happens now?"

His lips twitched, giving me a tease of a kiss. "Now we can either go back to our room or we go to the great hall. Either way will end with the same result."

"Which is?" I arched my eyebrow.

"Me fucking you into submission."

A slow smile spread across my lips. "I've never been to an orgy before," I admitted. "What's the difference?"

He sucked my bottom lip, his hands sliding up my legs to fasten themselves at my waist. "It's all about energy. At an incubus orgy the air vibrates with the culmination of everyone feeding at once. A primal force of nature."

My heart thudded at his explanation, sending the pounding to my ears and fingertips. My life had been spent hiding, but Ezekiel made me bold and brave. "Show me," I whispered into his mouth.

Desire blazed deep in his eyes, excitement peeking through. Many of the diners had already disappeared from the banquet area. Gabriel led a giggling Addison down the side of the room, stopping every so often to kiss her.

"Are you sure?" Ezekiel stared so deeply into my eyes, I was sure he could read my thoughts.

"As long as I'm with you, I'm sure."

His hands lifted me under my ass and my legs wrapped around his waist. I refused to focus on anything but Ezekiel. Our lips teased each other, nipping and sucking until I wanted to taste his tongue deep in my mouth. My fingers threaded through his hair to hold me in position.

Ezekiel carried me from the room as if I weighed nothing. There was nothing I wouldn't do for him. In the time I'd been here, he had lain waste to my barren life and rebuilt it with him firmly in the centre.

"Who do you belong to?" Ezekiel said the words against my ear.

I shivered, my legs gripping him harder. "You, Ezekiel, only you."

"That's right, baby. Now and forever."

I gasped, but his lips fastened against mine, stealing every word I would have spoken.

Once upon a time, I thought orgies were nothing more than basic sexual urges being met, animals rutting together in the search for a quick release. What met us in the great hall was nothing like I expected. It was like an orchestra playing a symphony. Every note adding to the melody that filled the room. Bodies moved to an unheard rhythm, passion building step by step in the air.

Ezekiel walked us to an area in the centre of the room, where there were raised beds. I clung to him, nerves fluttering in my belly.

"Relax," he said, his lips trailing down my throat. "No one will touch you but me."

Remiel was strapped to a St. Andrew's cross, his wrists and ankles held in place with leather straps. A succubus fed from him, her lips wrapped around his cock as his hips jerked, his face was screwed up in pleasured agony.

"He deserved worse." Ezekiel followed my line of vision. "I could have given him the same fate as that elf who'd wandered into his path a few decades ago."

My brow wrinkled in confusion, but his fingers on my chin brought my attention back to him. He gently placed me on the bed and crawled over me. "Trust me," Ezekiel muttered as he pressed kisses in between the elaborate ribbons that covered me. I trusted him with my life, I'd already given him everything else.

He lifted a long back ribbon and tied it over my eyes, removing my sense of sight. "Just feel me," he whispered beside my ear. His lips moved over my flesh in kisses that kindled my fire everywhere they travelled. His hair that flopped over his eyes left tantalising trails that made me shiver.

Ezekiel sucked my nipples through the thin material that covered my breasts, keeping his promise that no one would see me but him. My back arched as his fingers slid under the material between my thighs. The lack of sight made the sensations stronger. The moans of pleasure around me added an element of excitement that I'd never contemplated before. His touch ignited my desire.

Ezekiel kissed the inside of my wrist and I felt smooth fabric wrapping around it. I tensed, but he moved over me, his lips teasing mine. "Relax, baby."

I allowed him to tie my wrists together, my ability to touch him gone. He was making me submit to him a piece at a time, every sense taken until only he was left. My arms were pulled over my head when he attached the other end of the tie to the top of the bed.

"Fuck, Ilana, you have no idea what you look like." Ezekiel kissed me so deeply that my soul united with his, my legs widening to let him rest in the curve of my body. His hands slid from my wrists, down my arms, and along my sides to rest on my hips. "I don't think I've ever wanted anyone as much as I need you."

I lost myself to the sensation of his touch. His fingers mapped the contours of my flesh, his mouth took control of pulsating need between my legs. I lost count of the number of orgasms Ezekiel sent hurtling through my core to make my womb explode in ecstasy. He fed from my pleasure, and he was about to dine on an entire banquet of exquisite climaxes that left me breathless and panting.

"Roll over, baby." His hands on my hips moved me onto my knees. My hands were stretched in front of me and I rested my head on my tied wrists, my elbows on the bed. Soft material tied my ankles in position, my legs spread wide as I rested on my elbows and knees, vulnerable.

"Ezekiel," I moaned, either in protest or question as his touch had left me.

"I'm right here." He crawled over me, and I felt skin sliding against skin, his clothes gone.

"I…" I had passed my normal comfort zone a long time ago.

His body covered mine in a cloak of flesh. "You are fucking beautiful," he whispered in my ear. "A goddess."

"I feel like a sacrifice," I replied, my back arching and my head fitting between his neck and shoulder.

"Would you sacrifice yourself to me?" Ezekiel kissed the pulse at my neck.

"I already have," I gasped as his hardness rubbed between my legs.

His chuckle sent tendrils of pleasure shooting from my neck to my core.

He moved the delicate fabric between my legs aside and pushed himself inside me with a torturously slow pace from behind. My lower back arched and my mouth fell open. Every nerve ending in my body was focused on that slide of his hard erection. I couldn't move, my body held in place with bindings of finest silk.

"Open yourself to sensation, Ilana. All around you, bodies move to the ancient beat of desire. Feel the movement of their bodies, take the energy deep inside you."

In my mind's eye I saw undulating bodies as people surrendered to their deepest desires. My skin prickled with their pleasure.

"Smell the scent of sex as it infuses in the air, created from arousal as dicks move in and out of their partners."

His filthy words did something to me, and my core clenched around his hard length buried in me. The unique smell of sex made my nipples hard and my own arousal grow. I could almost taste it on the tip of my tongue.

"Listen to the smack of skin against skin, the moans of submission, the grunts of domination."

Holy fuck, what was he doing to me? I tried to buck my hips against his, need nearly crippling me. The sounds washed over me, and I imagined Ezekiel harnessing the energy of every man in that room. The arousal of every woman sinking into me. They were there only to add to our pleasure.

His hands possessively caressed my skin. "You are mine, Ilana. Now and always. Remember that."

Without warning he drew back suddenly and slammed into me, forcing my body forward as I grunted in surprise. There was nowhere for me to go, my body prisoner under his as he took me with a punishing rhythm. The darkness that swirled inside me welcomed him, craved him, wanted him. I let the shackles that had held me back all my life fall from me and the soft ribbons he bound me with tie me to him instead.

I gave Ezekiel something I'd never given anyone before—full control over me. It liberated me in a way I'd never experienced. He elevated our bodies moving from sex to a transcendental state. Pressure built deep in my core, the culmination of multiple orgasms building into a crescendo. By eliminating my sight and ability to touch, Ezekiel ensured that I focused only on the pleasure he gave me.

Everything was too much, the friction between my legs bordering on pain. Over and over he plunged until I couldn't bear it anymore. I moaned, biting my lip, my head pushing into my wrists as his hips crashed powerfully against mine. I needed to move, to touch him, to alleviate the pressure that was going to explode.

"Ezekiel," I moaned in desperation.

His hands moved from my waist to trace over me until he grasped my wrists. He thrust upward, jolting me off my knees again and again and again. That delicious area along my front wall bore the brunt of this sensual assault until I wanted to scream. His fingers laced through mine and I knew he was feeling everything I was, his body in tune with mine.

"Oh fuck," I gasped as he rotated his hips.

It was too much.

My mouth opened and my head tilted back.

I screamed as a tsunami of pleasure swept through my body in a massive wave from my head to my core. His dick pulsed deep inside me as he fed from me, our bodies writhing together in ecstasy.

My body collapsed forward as my limbs turned to jelly.

"What the fuck have you done to me?" Ezekiel panted, his body pressed against mine.

I couldn't answer because I didn't know.

All I knew was that he owned me now. Every piece of me.

***

Chapter Twenty-Nine

Ezekiel

Ilana was quiet when we got back to our apartment. I chewed the inside of my mouth, worried I'd pushed her too far. I was a sex demon, but she'd wandered into my life a shy virgin.

In the great hall, I'd never fed like that with anyone. The residue of it still throbbed inside me, nourishing me. She'd responded, but maybe retrospectively, Ilana was regretting attending with me.

She wandered around, pulling clips from her hair and frowning as she removed the ribbons of her outfit. I didn't know how I was going to last three months until I could feed from her again. She intrigued and captivated me every single day, ensnaring me more and more under her spell. I had a colony of fucking wyverns in my dragonry because she'd looked at me with those huge, pleading eyes.

I grabbed her wrist as she walked past me, drawing her in front of where I sat. Her body was rigid as I peered up at her. "I've hurt you," I said. There was no other explanation for her behaviour. I'd felt her pleasure earlier, knew what she wanted, but regret was a bitter taste that came after the sweet.

"No." She cast her eyes to the ceiling. "I…"

"Talk to me," I coaxed, my thumb tracing the erratic pulse at her wrist.

She took a deep breath as if she was warring with herself. Finally, those huge green eyes came down to meet mine. My heart flipped in my chest.

"I love you, Ezekiel." She rushed the words out as if she was terrified of saying them or what would happen when she did. "It doesn't mean that you have to feel the same or that you need to tie yourself to me…"

That was exactly what she wanted. When a woman told you what you didn't have to do after a declaration like that, it meant that was what her deepest desire was.

I tugged her hips forward, staring up at her as she put her hands on my shoulders to steady herself. "Why does that scare you?" I asked.

"What scares me?"

A brief smile touched my lips. "Saying that you love me?" She avoided my eyes and her body swayed back unconsciously. "Do you think I would have claimed you in front of my family if I didn't feel the same?"

I lost the battle against my feelings for Ilana the first night she crawled into my bed to save me from the clutches of Ophelia. She'd held my heart in her tiny hands from that night.

Her shocked eyes met and locked with mine, searching for confirmation that my words were true. I slowly stood and hauled her body to mine. "How can you doubt that I love you?" I asked in disbelief, tipping her face up with my fingers under her chin.

"I…" Her forehead creased in concentration and she swallowed.

"Then let me make it clear. I'm in love with you, completely and utterly head over heels and losing my mind crazy about you."

Her teeth bit into her lip and a tear trickled down her cheek. I dashed it away with my thumb. "Is there anything else troubling you?" I asked, as my head descended to hers.

"No." She shook her head.

My lips captured hers and my hands lifted her under her ass.

The equinox was nearly over, and I wanted to spend the rest of the day just with her. There was no one here but both of us in our own private cocoon. We took our time exploring each other, muttering words of love and devotion.

As we approached midnight, Ilana sheathed me in her warmth, riding me slowly, lost in sensation. She was glorious, her breasts bouncing as she undulated on top of me.

I knew without any doubt in my head that I wanted to spend every day for the rest of my life with this woman beside me. I was prepared to do whatever it took to ensure I survived the curse to do just that.

Pleasure danced down my spine as my balls tightened. Her hands grasped my shoulders and mine her hips as she took us to heaven one more time before midnight.

***

Our troops stood ready beside the dragons at the front of the castle. Raegel filled in the aspects of the base from what he'd observed from his ground surveillance. All our knowledge so far had been from dragons pretending to be patrolling the borders.

He'd gone on a hunting spree against Ophelia's wraiths, dispatching several dozen directly to Hell. Now he was visibly relaxed and almost smiling. Almost. Even by elf standards Raegel was tense, the tips of his ears always on high alert.

I'd left Ilana sleeping, exhausted from yesterday. Her hair was a glorious riot of curls around her face, her skin still bearing some of the marks from my fingers where I'd gripped her. I no longer wanted to fight this war. All I'd wanted to do was wrap my arms around her and go back to sleep.

Instead I stood here, organising my soldiers. Gabriel already had troops on the ground, heading toward the border. Elves were hidden using tree magic on their side, surrounding the base. The dragons would seal off any escape into the skies.

Raegel had been intrigued by the wyverns when I took him to the dragonry earlier. He'd freed quite a few of them, so I thought he deserved to see the difference he made to their lives. The small black wyvern padded over to me and nudged me with its snout until I rubbed behind its ears.

"Their magic is strong. I can see why Ophelia enslaved them," Raegel commented. "What are you going to do with them?"

"No idea." I sighed and raked my fingers through my hair. "They arrived because Ilana is here. One problem at a time, Raegel. Today we eliminate Ophelia's base, tomorrow we start the search for magical answers."

He nodded his agreement. "My archers know to aim for the crystals under their wings. I've carved a special rune on their arrows that should alleviate pain to the wyverns."

My commanders organised the last-minute details, Gabriel and Jethro overseeing them.

Raegel grasped my arm as he always did when he greeted you or said goodbye. "Stay safe, my brother. Today we start a new stage of our journey that will free us from her."

"May the dark gods be with you," I replied, slapping him on the back. He disappeared into the crowd.

On my way back to my apartment, I popped into the main hall. Remiel still hung from the cross near the back. Father had insisted he be left there to stop him feeding for a few days. His behaviour had become too decadent, even for an incubus prince, his appetite too extreme. His aura was strong, he was just pissed at being denied his orgy, like an insolent child who always got his own way being scolded. I left him, hoping he'd learnt his lesson.

Ilana stretched and smiled as I crawled over her.

"Good morning," I muttered against her luscious lips.

Her arms wrapped around me to drag me against her soft, warm flesh. "Why are you out of bed?"

"Raegel and I have been planning a war," I informed her, trailing kisses down her neck.

Her body froze and head jerked back. "No way, Ezekiel. You're going nowhere without me."

"Too late." I pressed a hard kiss on her lips to stop her speaking. "We leave in a few minutes."

She struggled to get up. I pinned her wrists above her head and shook my head at her. There was no fucking way I would let her anywhere near Ophelia. One look would tell her how I felt about Ilana, and that would make her public enemy number one. I wouldn't put her at risk.

"I'll be back soon. The troops are already in place, they left first thing this morning. I only came back to say goodbye."

The sadness of the world crept into her eyes as they filled with tears.

"I'll be back soon, and we'll sort out the wyverns and discuss the role magic will take in this fight." I kissed her again until she went languid in my arms.

I tried to get up and leave, but Ilana gripped me, rolling me over until she pinned me down with arms and legs. "You better return with not so much as a scrape on you," she warned, her eyes filled with fire. "Do you understand?"

A slow grin spread over my lips. I loved the fact that she was possessive, claiming me. "Yeah, I understand. Fuck, you're hot." I broke free from her hands and grabbed her face to kiss her without restraint, our lips and tongues warring against each other. "Don't leave this room," I said against her mouth before giving her one more hard kiss.

She sat with her legs tucked to her chest, watching as I grabbed my jacket. "So, I just sit here and worry?" Ilana pouted.

"You could sleep," I said, zipping my jacket up.

She rolled her eyes. "I'm trained as a warrior. You picked me to be on your team."

"I'd rather you be in my bed," I retaliated.

"I'm a fully-grown woman." She folded her arms over her chest, making her breasts bulge over the top.

"Believe me, I noticed." I quirked an eyebrow and she blushed. She knew it turned me the fuck on when she did that. "Listen." I sat beside her on the bed. "Magic seems to be the next part of this journey. Get ready, and when I come back, why don't we visit your home and see what your mum and this Aunt Agatha of yours have to say?"

I pressed my forehead to hers and blinked a few times. Our eyelashes tangling together always made her smile.

"You're trying to distract me," she moaned.

"Is it working?"

She rolled her eyes, which made them twist more.

I grabbed a kiss and stood up, ready to leave.

"Wait." Ilana stumbled out of bed, trying to unravel herself from the sheets. She padded to the office with all her magical stuff lying around in it, dragging one of my T-shirts over her head.

"Here." She held out a black stone.

I raised an eyebrow in question.

"I played around with the magic in the stone on Izzy and created my own version. Keep it against your skin. It may contain enough of my energy to block her from draining you when I'm not with you."

I seized Ilana and spun her around until she squealed, before capturing her against the wall. "You are fucking amazing," I said into her mouth before kissing her again. Her fingers combed into my hair as she responded with everything she had.

I finally stepped away, sucking my bottom lip in between my teeth. "Be ready when I get back."

I didn't look back because I wouldn't leave if I did.

The first dragons carrying troops were already gone when I arrived back. Gabriel gave me a quizzical look, grinning when he studied me.

Asshole.

We took off to join the rest of our men and the elves at the base.

***

The base was well hidden below the treeline, a thin layer of magic making it blend in. It could have been here for years and not one of us had noticed it. We'd been so busy defending the borders between us and the outer realms where Ophelia ruled, that we'd forgotten about the borders between our own realms.

Once this issue was dealt with, we'd be all over the entire expanse of our borders.

Magnus hovered above it like a harbinger of doom and destruction, his focus set on the area of darkness between the incubus and elven realms.

Raegel gave his battle cry and pandemonium let loose.

I cracked my neck to the side and summoned my power from my solar plexus. For the first time in too long, I was full and ready to fight. Ilana's power ran through my veins, nourishing me like never before.

The first wraith that tried to escape on a wyvern disintegrated under the full weight of my power lashing out at him in a pulse of black energy. I focused on the wyvern and hit it with a blast of energy under the wing. It spiralled toward the ground before shaking itself and returning to the sky.

Its eyes locked on Magnus for a few seconds before it took off toward our castle.

“Something I need to know?” I shouted over the scream of the winds buffering us.

Izzy taught me how to talk to them last night.

“I guess we were all busy last night.”

His dark chuckle rippled under my feet. I didn’t think he would have caught my last muttered comment.

Our ground troops flushed wraiths out into the waiting arms of the elves on the ground and us in the air. Power thrummed down into my fingers as again and again I dispatched her evil wraiths. This was why Ophelia wanted me weak. No other incubus prince could wield this ability. Not even my father had mastered it.

I unleashed blast after blast of dark magic, losing myself in the dance of the battle. Magnus directed me through our connection, his flames herding the wraiths into my attack. It was definitely better than having to use the weapons I’d resorted to in recent years.

I’d hung the black crystal Ilana gave me in a cage around my neck. It heated on my flesh and I knew that Ophelia was trying to drain me to stop my attack.

“Fuck you,” I muttered and annihilated another wraith from existence. I was tired of being her bitch, a weak impersonation of who I was born to be. I would rather go to meet my ancestors than stay under her rule anymore.

A black crow hovered close to us, its beady eye directly on me.

“Magnus,” I said, all my attention moving to the bird. There was no doubt in my mind it belonged to Ophelia. I hit it with a wave of dark power at the same time Magnus released a stream of fire. It squawked and struggled, trying to break away. The magic it contained must have been immense for it to withstand an attack from both of us.

“Bring that fucking bird down,” I shouted to anyone who was listening.

Magnus' wing sloped down and I fought to keep my balance. Raegel had landed beside me. He aimed an arrow directly at the bird at the same time I hit it with another blast. That bird should be roasted. The arrow hit it and it hurtled through the air impaled on it.

A wraith grabbed the bird and flew away on a wyvern.

"Fuck!" I screamed into the sky.

"What was it?" Raegel asked, his hand on my shoulder.

"I think it was her familiar."

Raegel whistled and a flock of huge hawks flew from the trees below to pursue the wraith with the crow. "I don't know if they'll reach it in time, but they'll certainly see where they go."

I nodded. It was better than nothing. "The base?"

"Cleared."

Magnus took us down so we could disembark. Raegel and I stomped through the base that sat between our realms for too long. Acid churned in my stomach when I saw the images they had of all the members of the royal court from both realms. They'd been here quite a while.

Raegel snarled, his fangs showing when he saw images of his younger sister.

Gabriel arrived, whistling low at the intelligence inside the base.

"Get this place cleared and blow it up," I instructed. "I want to know what they know about us."

"What are you going to do with all this?" Raegel demanded. There was as much information in here about the elves as about the incubi.

"Gabriel, all this goes to my private offices until Raegel and I have been through it." I raised an eyebrow at Raegel and he gave me a level stare that said he didn't object.

He called his second in command to help Gabriel strip everything from this place. Ophelia could send reinforcements any minute.

I took Raegel's arm and led him outside. "I'm going away for a few days. I need to find out how witches can help us. Ilana is going to take me to where her mother and aunt live."

"Is that wise?" he asked.

"We're running out of options. I'll take Addison and Gabriel with us. Addy has been researching magic for years."

"And Gabriel?" he asked with a significant stare.

"I guess you realise they're mated?"

He nodded.

I blew a breath out through my teeth. "I didn't know, Raegel. Did you really want to mate with my sister?"

"No, but that's not the point."

"I'm sorry. I was going to tell you when things weren't so hectic."

"Your sister terrifies me," he admitted.

I grinned at the look on his face. Most women would terrify him. Raegel was a fighter, not a lover. Making him mate with Addison would have been an interesting experiment. My sister would have broken through that aloof exterior until he was nothing more than a man with sexual needs. Inside every man was a deviant waiting to emerge with his dick in his hand.

"Gabriel seems happy enough with her brand of dominance," I responded.

Raegel said nothing, but his eyebrows lifted slightly.

Addison was strong-willed with a voracious sexual appetite. Gabriel had to be stronger than her to make her submit to him as a mate. My second in command must have testicles of steel.

We kept watch as boxes were loaded into our transport carriers and flown away by dragons. Gabriel set the explosives, his face grim as he walked out. Something was wrong, but now was not the time to ask.

He cleared the area and as we flew back to the castle. Ophelia's base detonated into a fireball, destroying everything inside.

***

Chapter Thirty

Ilana

Izzy arrived a few hours ago, sensing me trying to weave crystal magic. Everything I did was based on childhood memories and instinct. Giving Ezekiel that crystal had been spur of the moment. I had no idea if it would work, but after sensing the spell on the crystal attached to Izzy, I reverse-engineered it and adapted it for him.

The elements, quite literally at my fingertips, infused into the coloured stones, manipulating the energy to my desire.

"You're getting stronger," Izzy observed, lifting a crystal to sense the energy in it.

"Your being here helps," I replied. "How are the other wyverns?"

"Lost. They are unsure what to do and are terrified of The Blood Queen finding them."

I sighed and set down the crystal I was working on. "Ezekiel is taking me home. I'll speak to my mum. I thought they were human blood slaves, now I realise they are a coven. Perhaps they could give them a home?"

Izzy perked up at the suggestion. "We spend our lives seeking our witch."

"How did you know you were meant to be my familiar?" My head canted to the side in question. Poor Izzy really didn't have a choice, I was the only witch here.

"If we were not destined to bond, then it would never have happened. What were the chances of me getting caught in that chandelier and you finding me before one of the guards?" I'd never thought of it that way. "The Blood Queen killed so many witches that many of my kind will never find their guardian."

We fell into an easy silence while I worked with the crystals laid out on the table in front of me. Each crystal felt different when I lifted it, almost as if it had its own personality and wanted to talk to me.

"You have an affinity with stones," Izzy commented.

"I've always loved them, even as a child," I shared. "Aunt Agatha helped me make lots of pendants. I left them at home when I joined the vampire academy."

Suddenly, I wanted to touch those crystals again, to sense what I poured into them in my childhood innocence.

"Ilana?" Ezekiel's voice boomed through the apartment.

I was on my feet and moving toward him without thinking, launching myself at him.

He laughed and caught me mid-air, my legs settling around his hips. "Miss me?"

"You've no idea." I grinned and wrapped him in a huge hug.

"I didn't get a welcome like that," Gabriel grumbled to Addison behind us. I heard the sound of her slapping him and his chuckle.

"Everything okay?" I asked against Ezekiel's neck.

"Yeah, base destroyed. Ophelia will be pissed."

I heard another slap and turned to find Gabriel gaping at Izzy standing in her human form. Yes, my wyvern really was that smoking hot.

"What?" Gabriel demanded. "I thought Zek was starting a harem."

"I have my hands full with one woman, thanks," Ezekiel retorted and squeezed me. "We're going now while Ophelia's attention is diverted. Did you pack for us?"

I nodded. "Yeah. Just let me grab the crystals I was working on."

He dropped me gently until my feet hit the floor. "Go quickly." He pushed me and returned his attention to Gabriel. "Can we risk taking dragons?"

"Maybe Raegel can open a portal to the Dracus realm?" I called out from the study as I placed the crystals in a velvet pouch, putting them in a small travel bag with some other items I'd packed.

"That's not a bad idea," Gabriel said. "I'll go check if he's still here."

I glanced up to find Ezekiel watching me with his arms folded over his broad chest.

"What?" I asked, smiling at his intense stare.

He lifted my hand and kissed my palm. "I felt your crystal heat when she reached out to me."

"Did it stop her?" My heart beat double time at the thought of her trying to drain him so soon after the equinox.

He nodded, tugging my body to him. "I don't deserve you," he whispered, his gaze filled with fire and desire.

"And yet you have me."

His lips twitched before he kissed the tip of my nose, releasing me. "Is this everything?"

I nodded.

"Let's go." He grabbed the bags and headed to the door, my hand grasped in his.

Addison gave Izzy a cloak so she could walk through the castle undetected. She could change into her wyvern form when we got outside. No one needed to know any of our secrets yet.

Raegel's dark gaze ran over all of us, his stance stiff. I saw the curse pulsing deep in his chest, demanding release. Whatever Ophelia had done to him, it was different to Ezekiel. He held the index and middle finger from his right hand out, creating a circle in front of him. The energy expanded until a golden circle the height of Ezekiel appeared.

"Go quickly," he urged. "Normally, I can hide my magic in nature."

We all stepped through rapidly, even as the curse pulsed stronger in him. Ophelia would punish him for this. My eyes met his and he shook his head in silence. He would bear this pain to help us.

Valek met us on the other side, his bright blue eyes assessing our group.

"We don't have time to explain," Ezekiel said as we strode through the vampire military base. "Raegel will arrive later to bring you up to speed."

"Is there a reason you're dragging one of my vampires along with you?" Valek asked, his gaze on our joined hands.

"She's not your vampire anymore," Ezekiel muttered, his fingers tightening on mine.

Valek gave me a raised eyebrow stare but a slow grin formed on his lips, showing his fangs.

"We need a fleet transport," Gabriel interrupted. "Nothing that will draw Ophelia's attention."

"Follow me." Valek took charge, shouting orders.

In no time, a transport unit was waiting for us in the departure area. Gabriel slid in, flicking switches and putting a head unit on. Normally, when I went home, I used the local portals and my feet. This all seemed a little extreme.

Ezekiel packed our equipment in. As I was about to step onto the transport unit, Valek grabbed my arm and pulled me back. "Are you okay?" His eyes were filled with concern. "If he tries to feed from you…"

I stepped back. "I know about the curses," I said simply.

His thrummed deep in his solar plexus, ready to be activated any time Ophelia wanted.

"For fuck's sake, Valek. Get your hands off my mate." Ezekiel removed his hand from my arm and pushed me onto the unit.

Valek stood with his mouth open in astonishment.

"You should really close that," I told him. "You never know what someone will put in it."

Valek snapped his mouth closed and narrowed his eyes at Ezekiel. "You're a bad influence on my vampire." He pointed at us and Ezekiel laughed, flicking him a middle finger salute.

The door closed and Ezekiel tugged my back against his chest. "You are going to be the death of me," he muttered into my hair.

I grinned and closed my eyes, absorbing his strength.

***

Chapter Thirty-One

Ilana

"Mum!" I protested as she hugged me until my eyes bulged. "It hasn't been that long since I was home."

She pushed me back and gave me the disapproving look that only a mother could muster for her wayward child. Aunt Agatha flung the door open and entered like a force of nature.

"There she is!" She opened her arms and I stepped into them. I always had two mums—the stern one who gave birth to me and the fun aunt who taught me how to be naughty. "Welcome home, little one," she whispered into my hair.

Her attention diverted to the people staring at us. Mum moved beside her, and Aunt Agatha tried to push me behind her.

I moved around the back of both of them and took my place beside Ezekiel, threading my fingers through his. Their gaze dropped to our hands.

"Mum, Aunt Agatha, this is Ezekiel," I introduced them, unsure how I was supposed to do this as I'd never brought a boy home with me. "This is his sister Addison and her mate Gabriel. Izzy," I called, and she stuck her head around the door. "This is my wyvern, Izzy."

"Well fuck a duck," Aunt Agatha stated, her hands coming to rest on her hips. "I guess you figured out you're a witch."

A shy smile tugged my lips. "Thanks for all the bakery and cooking lessons."

She pressed her lips together to prevent a smile as Mum stared at her. "You taught her about magic?" Mum demanded. "I said she was never to know."

Aunt Agatha shrugged. “I taught her about herbs and cooking. If she learnt about magic through that, it’s not my fault she’s too clever for her own good.” Her eyes ran from Ezekiel’s toes to his head and back again. “He’s much more handsome than I saw in my visions. Is he as powerful as I predicted?”

I felt Ezekiel stiffen beside me and I couldn’t believe it when my incubus’ cheeks blazed red. I waved my hand in front of me. “So-so.”

Addison burst out laughing at Ezekiel’s expression.

“You know, there are herbs for stamina,” Aunt Agatha informed him seriously.

Ezekiel’s cheeks deepened and he nearly choked. “I’m good, thanks. Your niece can attest to that since she could hardly stand this morning.”

It was Mum’s turn to splutter her protest.

“He tries hard,” I whispered to my aunt in conspiracy. “His enthusiasm makes up for…” I squealed as Ezekiel lifted me over his shoulder and went to stride from the room until I erupted in fits of giggles. Aunt Agatha always had this effect on me. She had an effervescent personality that spread joy everywhere she went. Ezekiel dropped me to my feet as if I was contagious.

“Fine,” I gasped. “He’s sex on legs with endurance that never wains.”

“He does look like a fine specimen,” Aunt Agatha agreed, her head canting to the side to study him.

“For fuck’s sake!” Ezekiel exploded. “You do realise that I’m more than just my dick?”

“He’s right, he has abdominal muscles that…”

Ezekiel cut me off with his hand over my mouth. “It’s very nice to meet both of you,” he interjected.

I licked his fingers and he glared at me. My fangs lowered to nip his flesh. His eyes narrowed in warning even as I licked the tiny drop of blood that escaped. His hand disappeared from in front of my mouth.

"Mum." I turned serious. "We need your help."

She slowly turned to face me.

"Ophelia cursed Ezekiel and the other princes of Purgatory. She drains them to make herself stronger. They've been facing her while we hide in plain sight. Our wyverns were enslaved to give her power. We can't stand by and do nothing anymore. This is my fight now because Ezekiel is my mate."

Mum's hand grasped the kitchen counter for support, her face pale. "Agatha always said this day would come. I refused to believe it, forbidding her to teach you magic, letting you think you were a vampire-human hybrid. But magic has had the last laugh. My daughter, the heir of our realm, found her magic and activated it without us."

"Heir?" I asked, my forehead crumpled in confusion.

"The outer realms were once known as the magical realm. The other witches hid us in this pocket realm so Ophelia could never reach us. If she took our magic, she would be unstoppable. You are my daughter, and therefore the heir."

Aunt Agatha went to support Mum, her arm snaking around her waist. "Our mother was Queen Amelia. She died to create this safe-haven. She was the greatest visionary the magic realm ever knew, and she predicted the reign of darkness. Her last gift was to place a curse on Ophelia that she never knew existed. She would never have the one man she truly wanted, because his love belonged to someone else. He was the key that would one day open the lock to magic."

Her eyes cut to Ezekiel, who was staring at both of them as if they'd spontaneously started speaking a foreign language.

She continued. "Only my coven knew. I inherited mother's gift of sight and saw him the day you were born. She had him bound before her with three other men. The moment she cursed him, she activated her own curse. A life without love is a lonely place."

Ezekiel staggered back a step, Addison and Gabriel moving behind him. His eyes met mine and my heart sunk. He was cursed because of me.

"No," Mum said, grabbing both my hands. "His curse has nothing to do with you. It was inevitable from the day he was first born in his realm. Ophelia wanted a link to the magic of the realms, that is why she demanded the crown prince from each. She cursed all of them to feed her need for power, not just one."

She wrapped her arms around me and glared at her visitors. "She would always have cursed you, My mother gave you a chance at redemption."

Ezekiel straightened to his full height, his back rigid. "I don't give a fuck about curses and traditions. If what you said is true, you've just painted the biggest fucking target in Purgatory on my mate's back. If that psychotic witch realises that Ilana is the missing piece for her to seize ultimate power, she'll hunt her with everything she has until she kills her."

His eyes were fierce and protective, his aura pulsing with his turbulent emotions. He opened his arms and I flung myself into the safety of his embrace. His chin rested on my head and his dark aura surrounded me until calm flooded my system.

"I need to summon your father, he's been keeping watch over you for years, waiting for any sign of magic." Mum stroked my hair as she walked past.

"I'll make tea," Aunt Agatha chirped happily.

"My magic only activated when Ezekiel finally noticed me a few weeks ago," I said to Aunt Agatha as she moved around the kitchen.

"When I noticed you?" Ezekiel asked, leaning back to look down at me.

I avoided his gaze, embarrassment stealing my words.

Aunt Agatha chuckled. "My niece had quite the crush on you for years. What was it you told Mia?" she mused.

"You wouldn't," I threatened her.

An evil pixie grin tipped her lips up. "Oh, yes. That if you could choose your death, it would be with that man between your legs as you screamed his name."

If my face got any redder it would explode.

Gabriel snorted.

Addison coughed.

But Ezekiel… When I finally found the courage to peek up, ferocious heat radiated from those dark chocolate brown eyes. My panties caught on fire and my core burned in response.

"Just think," Aunt Agatha continued. "If you'd got your head out of your ass decades ago, this would have all been sorted."

"Aunt Agatha!" I scolded her.

"What?" She gave me the bug-eyed stare. "I'm just saying you did your part and he dropped the ball. Tea's ready, you can all sit down."

"Is she always like this?" Ezekiel whispered.

I nodded, grinning. I loved Aunt Agatha. She filled my childhood with fun and adventure, taking me to the Earth realm with her a few times without Mum and Dad knowing. She trained me, knowing the day would come when I'd need my magic.

Aunt Agatha snapped her fingers and plates flew from the shelf to the table, and a cake levitated into the centre. She carried the teapot to the table and settled herself.

"Oh." She snapped her fingers again, cups and saucers followed her command. She winked at me the way she always did in my childhood.

Mum and Dad arrived to find us having tea and cake, Ezekiel on his second slice.

"Could it not have been the elf?" Dad demanded, raking his hands down his face. "She had to fall for the incubus?"

Ezekiel and Gabriel shared a look that said they'd heard these sort of objections before.

"Dad!" I hissed. "He's sitting right here!"

"One day, if you have children, you'll understand," he stated as if that excused his behaviour. "I'll take mine with extra sugar, Agatha."

I glanced at Izzy, who greedily ate some leaves Aunt Agatha found. Apparently, they only grow here, and wyverns loved them.

"Ezekiel rescued quite a few wyverns from Ophelia. They need to find a home," I said, nonchalantly.

Mum's cup clattered against her saucer. "I'm sorry, what did you say?"

Ezekiel intervened. "Ilana worked out that Ophelia had put crystals on the wyverns to control them. She removed Izzy's and told us to do the same with any we encountered, instead of killing them. There are around fifty of them with my dragons."

"We thought when Ophelia enslaved them, they couldn't be saved," Mum replied. "All those familiars out there without a guardian."

Ezekiel shrugged. "They seem fine. Magnus has taken it upon himself to look after them."

"Magnus?" Aunt Agatha enquired.

"My dragon."

Her eyebrows rose, but she didn't respond.

"Can you help with the curses?" I asked. It was what we were here for.

"We can try," Mum replied. "But each curse is unique and depends on the original intent of the person who cast it. Sometimes what they say and what their heart means are different entities. We'll have a look at the problem in the morning."

Dad tried to show Ezekiel to a guest room until I dragged him into my old bedroom with a pointed stare at Dad. It wasn't as if we were going to do anything. The equinox was over, and I'd been well and truly debauched.

Ezekiel grinned as he threw himself on my bed with his arms folded behind his head. "At least you didn't die last night with me between your legs and you screaming my name."

I threw a pillow at him that he easily caught. "So embarrassing," I muttered. "I can't believe Aunt Agatha sometimes. She's supposed to be my friend."

"So, how long has this 'crush' lasted?" he asked in amusement.

"Ugh!" I threw my hands up in despair, facing him with a stern expression. "Every woman has that one man that she lusts over and who plays the hero in her fantasies. Mia had the hots for Valek and I lusted rather unsuccessfully after you."

I dragged my jeans down to change for bed. His hands on my hips made me stop while bent over, my breath catching.

"I'd say you were successful in your lusting. No woman has ever slept in my bed before you."

I straightened and rested on his chest. "I can't believe she told you that," I grumped.

His arms slid around my waist to tug me closer. "It's cute."

"A woman doesn't want to be cute. She wants to be sexy, seductive, and irresistible." I pouted when he spun me slowly around to face him.

"You definitely tick every one of those boxes." His eyes dipped to where my fangs dug into my bottom lip. "Hungry?"

"I forgot to eat today, and someone used a lot of my energy yesterday."

"I think I can fix that for you." Ezekiel hauled his black T-shirt over his head.

"Dad probably has some blood bags downstairs," I protested. "I can't feed from you in my parents' house."

His hands on my hips walked me backward, a step at a time until my legs hit the bed. "There is no way you're drinking from a bag when I'm right here." He pressed a delicious soft kiss on my lips. "No one will know you fed if you don't scream my name."

"I always scream your name." I sighed.

"I know." He sucked my bottom lip into his mouth. "I've heard you."

I gave up when he nudged me to fall onto the bed, crawling over me to present his neck to me. My fangs traced the artery and Ezekiel shivered. Clinging to him, I sank my fangs in, sucking his blood into my mouth. Today he tasted of pure power and seduction. Yesterday had returned him to the man he was destined to be. I could see why Ophelia wanted him.

"Mine," I hissed against his neck.

"Only yours," he agreed, holding my head in place.

Heady erotic pleasure pumped through me as I fed. I rubbed my core hungrily against his hard length.

"Easy, baby. I'll make sure you're fed properly. Relax."

When I'd gorged myself on his blood, Ezekiel took care of my other hunger, his hand over my mouth as I tried to scream him name.

I fell asleep draped over him as he drew patterns on my back.

***

Chapter Thirty-Two

Ilana

Ezekiel and Gabriel chatted to Dad about all the information he'd gathered over the years. He'd been studying the war from the point of view of the witches. Something no one had considered before. Instead of defending borders, he'd been analysing her types of attack in each realm, the magic employed, and what deterred her.

Addison sat happily talking to other coven members about what she'd found in her searches for magic over the years. They were eager to hear about any witches still alive in Purgatory, if any of the other families in hiding were safe. The symbology helped them identify covens evading Ophelia.

Mum and Aunt Agatha took me to the still room they worked magic in. I remembered helping Aunt Agatha tie herb bundles in it as a child. She used pretty ribbons and tiny bells that I loved to play with. The memories trickled back, only this time I recollected the herbs' aura and the magical energy in the ribbons. When Ezekiel had ripped my magical blindfold off, all my perceptions had changed. My world that had once been grey was filled with colour.

They guided me through basic spells, Mum giving me smiles of encouragement. Aunt Agatha pushed me to perform more complicated spells, each one building on the knowledge she'd given me as a child. Basic magical defence came next, followed by some offensive incantations. There wasn't nearly enough time to fit an entire lifetime of knowledge into a few days.

The family grimoire rested on the table before Mum. She stared at it, her fingers caressing the cover. "This was your inheritance. You were born the vessel to wield our magic," she said, her shoulders slumping. "I failed you. I thought if you never knew about magic that you'd be safe." Her eyes rose to meet mine. "Now destiny has intervened, and you stand in the front line against the greatest threat to our kind."

Aunt Agatha grabbed her left hand, her knuckles white from the grip she had on Mum's hand. "Stop, Angelica. Ilana is smart and talented. She activated her tattvas by herself. Maybe magic doesn't need to be defined and controlled. Perhaps it needs to be wielded by instinct and compassion."

I didn't know what to say or do. Instead, I placed my hand over their joined hands. "Fighting Ophelia will only make her more determined. We need to break each of the curses," I said. "She created them for a reason and has gotten steadily stronger since their inception."

"She has a point," Aunt Agatha replied.

"I was born not long after Ezekiel was cursed," I continued. "You saw him as my destiny, Aunt Agatha. That's not a coincidence."

"No," Mum responded thoughtfully. "It's not."

"Maybe Ilana is the key to breaking the curse," Aunt Agatha mused. "Do you know what his curse entails?"

I took a deep breath, knowing they weren't going to like my answer. "When he feeds, Ophelia takes something from the person—a memory, a feeling, an emotion—until piece by piece, she takes that person."

Suddenly their hands weren't under mine anymore, they were clutching mine. "He's fed from you," Mum stated instead of asked.

I nodded. "On the equinox. Her curse is latent on those days."

"Oh, thank the goddess," Aunt Agatha said, gripping her chest.

"But now Ezekiel is expected to starve until the next equinox," I pointed out.

"Or feed from another," Mum replied, staring off in contemplation.

"That is not an option." My tone was final. Ezekiel would not be feeding from anyone else. If he did, Ophelia won.

"Ilana could take him to the Earth realm. Magic is different there, her curse may not reach across the divide," Aunt Agatha pondered.

"I need to go alone to the sacred grove and consult the crystals," Mum replied.

"I tried that but didn't know what they meant." I sighed, thinking of my limited experience.

"What?" Mum exploded. "You used scrying crystals out there?" She pointed at the door and I glanced toward it as if there were monsters lurking on the other side.

"I opened the box Aunt Agatha gave me."

My aunt rubbed her hands over her face. "Maybe not my best idea."

"What if Ophelia sensed your magic?" Mum demanded. "What if she attacked you?"

"And what if I died on the battlefield because I never knew I had magic?" I asked in a quiet voice. "What if I hadn't met Ezekiel and my magic hadn't protected me when the lycan attacked that day?"

Mum glared at me.

"Life is full of ifs and buts. I can't change the past, so teach me what to do in the future," I retaliated. "Show me how to protect the people I love, because the best I could do for Ezekiel was to try and adapt the magic she used in the crystals to control the wyverns."

"Angelica, go and scry. Ilana and I will look at her crystals. Now is not the time to panic and lash out at each other," Aunt Agatha intervened.

Mum stood stiffly. "I only want what's best for her."

Aunt Agatha rose to face Mum, her hand landing on her shoulder. "Then we need to teach her as much about our craft as possible in the short time we have. You are the Queen of what remains of the free witches and cannot leave this pocket realm. I will return with Ilana and continue her training. If need be, I will stand against Ophelia."

"No, Agatha, I can't let you sacrifice yourself."

My aunt sighed. "We both know that it was always my destiny to return one day. It has finally arrived."

The two sisters stared at each other in silent conversation. Palpitations nearly crippled me because there was such pain in their eyes that I dreaded to know what they'd seen. Mum squeezed her eyes closed and nodded, leaving without a word.

Aunt Agatha wrapped me in a too-tight hug. "Everything she does is to keep you safe," she whispered against my head.

There were times I felt closer to my aunt that my mum. Both had been integral parts of my life, but now I saw that Mum had to put her role as leader first. Aunt Agatha spoiled me, lavishing the love and affection on me that I craved. Mum protected me as only a mother could, putting my needs ahead of her wants.

"Bring me your crystals and all the pendants you made with me when you were little. Let's see what we can achieve with a little hocus pocus." She released me and pushed me to the door.

Addison joined us, intrigued by the use of crystals in magic. She couldn't cast, but that didn't stop her learning as much as she could. Aunt Agatha made her several pendants for different areas of Addison's life, including fertility.

I lifted a pendant made from an orb with patterns of the deepest greens and blues. It vibrated in my hand.

"We made that together so you could visit the Earth realm with me," Aunt Agatha said, glancing up from the spell she was weaving on a crystal for Izzy. "It's Azurite. You picked it because you said it looked like the pictures of Earth."

"How did it take me to the Earth realm?"

Aunt Agatha smiled. "The same way all spells are created. With a pinch of magic, a sprinkle of love, and a lot of intent." She touched the tip of her finger to the crystal. "When you dedicate a crystal to a particular purpose, then holding it and visualising that intent is enough to make it activate."

She showed Addison and me how to create a small magical box that only we could open. It fit dozens of crystals and objects, even though it was small enough to fit in our pocket.

"It means you can take them everywhere with you." She winked at our expressions.

Finally, she made me fetch Ezekiel. He stared at my aunt as if she was going to bite him. He was the biggest sexual predator in the room, but never once had I witnessed him using that power. He shied away from overtly sexual advances in some of the banquets I'd witness him attend in the past, discreetly passing aggressive females to one of the incubi with him. As we talked in the darkness of night, he'd confessed to hating being objectified as an incubus instead of a man. Ezekiel was more than anyone ever saw. I was ashamed to admit he was more than I ever saw. The man was better than the fantasy in every way.

Aunt Agatha examined the black crystal he wore around his neck. "It's interesting you chose an Apache tear for him." She held it between her thumb and forefinger. "Your magic is strong in this. You said it heated when Ophelia tried to connect with you?"

Ezekiel nodded.

"Hmmm. Your magic is fighting Ophelia for Ezekiel." Aunt Agatha touched the crystal with the tip of her finger. "I would never have thought of infusing a crystal with this type of energy."

"I have no idea what type of energy I placed in the crystal. I was trying to work out what Ophelia used in the wyvern's crystals," I replied, hunting through some of the other crystals I'd worked with as a child.

"Can I see the crystal she used on Izzy?" Aunt Agatha enquired, her posture tense.

Addison rummaged through one of the bags we'd brought and handed the jar to my aunt.

Aunt Agatha's lip twitched. "It was clever to put it in a jar, removing it from any elemental stimulus." She shook the jar, her eyes narrowed in concentration. "Magenta," she whispered. "I thought she was dead."

Ezekiel stared at me and I shrugged.

"Who's Magenta?" Addison asked.

"A witch I knew a long time ago," Aunt Agatha replied. "She was the strongest witch ever known to control crystals. She wasn't in Ophelia's coven, but if she's alive and working for her, it could shed an entirely new light on The Blood Queen."

"How?" Ezekiel demanded.

Aunt Agatha stared at him for several seconds as if analysing him. "Ophelia murdered her original coven, one member at a time, feasting on their magic. A witch's magic is unique, bequeathed at the time of their birth and returned to the great goddess when they die. Ophelia found a way to intercept it at the moment of death. Magenta belonged to a family connected with the earth element. They specialised in crystalline magic. She would never had joined Ophelia willingly. It may indicate that she's formed a coven from powerful witches, enslaving them somehow to do her bidding."

"There's a tower in her castle that no one is allowed to enter," Izzy said from the window ledge. "The wyverns aren't even allowed to fly over it. Only The Blood Queen enters or leaves it. The scent of magic is constant from that tower."

Ezekiel and Gabriel gawped at Izzy. They obviously never thought to ask her about her previous home.

"Can you describe it?" Aunt Agatha asked.

Izzy walked toward the table and lifted a clear quartz. She held it to her lips and whispered in the wyvern language she sometimes used to mutter to herself. Her hand changed form and her talons crushed the crystal. She blew it into the air and a shimmering image formed. A castle with five towers in the shape of a pentagram.

"That is the tower that no one is allowed near." She pointed to the top point of the pentagram, her finger moving to the next tower clockwise on the castle. "The Blood Queen lives in that tower, the wyverns and the wraiths in these bottom towers."

"And the last tower?" I asked, a shiver of fear creeping from my stomach through my body.

"That is the tower she uses to torture her enemies," Izzy replied quietly. "Men enter but they never leave."

Five towers to protect a central castle. "What's in the castle?" I asked.

Izzy shrugged. "Nothing. She uses it to host balls and house her elaborate collections. It is cold and beautiful, a museum dedicated to her greatest triumphs."

Aunt Agatha paced around the image hovering above the table. "That isn't a museum, it's a mausoleum." She crumbled a stick of cinnamon in her hands and sprinkled it onto the hologram. Fine particles of cinnamon dust congregated in focused areas in the castle.

"Fuck!" Ezekiel exclaimed.

I turned to him, raising an eyebrow in question. He trailed his fingers through his hair and continued to stare at the castle's image.

"Dragons descend from an ancient race," Ezekiel said in a shaky voice. "The progenitor species was savage, slaughtering everything in their path. The dragons formed an alliance with the incubus realm. We used our power to lull them into a slumber, the dragons dragging them to the gates of hell and throwing them into the abyss. The war was bloody and brutal, with great losses on both sides. Purgatory was supposed to be free of the draconians."

I studied the image and finally identified the outline of a massive body under the castle, the shape similar to a dragon sleeping.

"Where the fuck did she get a draconian?" Gabriel demanded. "I doubt she built her castle there by chance."

"I'd suggest she's utilising the magic contained in it," Aunt Agatha said, sprinkling crushed lavender onto the image. The area Izzy said was forbidden to enter highlighted. "Witch magic," she confirmed to those of us sitting around the table. There was an area high in the tower and another down at the base.

"Why the two areas?" Addison asked, her brow furrowed in concentration.

"The willing and the unwilling," Aunt Agatha retorted. "Knowing Ophelia, she's making those witches cast for her by keeping someone they love."

The web of deception became more and more entangled every day. In the beginning, I thought it would be as simple as killing The Blood Queen. Now, there was much more at stake, lives at risk.

"What are we supposed to do?" I asked my aunt.

She smiled and stroked my hair back as she did when I was a child. "Your mother will be home soon, and her meditation with crystals is always enlightening. The coven is preparing a celebration to welcome you home. Put everything else out of your head for the moment." Her lips smiled, but the expression in her eyes remained bleak.

Uneasiness twisted deep inside me until it gnawed at me. I pretended to laugh and enjoy the revelry with everyone else, but I'd changed at a fundamental level when I saw that castle. It pulsed with darkness in our twilight world. The image of blood trickling down the walls of the towers played in the back of my mind. Smoke and fire bellowed in rage.

"Hey." Ezekiel settled himself behind me on the grassy incline where I watched everyone, his long legs sliding down on either side of mine. "What's going on in your head?"

I shook my head in fake denial.

"You do realise I can sense your emotions since we fed from each other?" His words echoed along the delicate flesh of my throat.

"Just my overactive imagination," I replied. "It used to happen all the time when I was a child. None of my visions ever came true."

"That you know of," he responded. "After all, you never knew you were a witch."

I didn't reply, just grabbed his hands at my waist and held on for dear life. I'd seen all four dark princes at her castle with their armies, so many dead and bleeding. My eyes fluttered closed and I focused on my breathing.

No one needed to know what was in my vision. I would do everything in my power to stop it.

***

Chapter Thirty-Three

Agatha

My family were descended from the first witches in Purgatory. Throughout human history there had been witch trials that resulted in the deaths of innocent women. They believed the deaths would appease gods who had created disease and suffering. My ancestor reached Purgatory, and instead of going to Hell or bargaining their way to the higher realms, they stayed and made a home.

She'd been a powerful visionary, and one spell at a time, made a niche for herself and the generations that came after her. We claimed the outer realms where wild magic was first born, harnessing it to create a home. The pocket realm we currently resided in was created by our mother centuries ago when she foresaw Ophelia rising to power.

That was the trouble with visions – they tended to come true no matter how much you tried to prevent them. I'd witnessed my fate a long time ago and it was finally here. I didn't know whether to be excited or terrified.

"Are you sure, Agatha?" Angelica watched me carefully from over the top of her mug.

I shrugged. "You cannot leave, and who else would protect Ilana the way either of us would? She will run headfirst into trouble to save his life. We've both seen the future, we know there is only this one slim chance to break the curse. Even at this stage it may not work."

"A sacrifice has to be given. It is the basis behind breaking any curse." Angelica set her mug down to rub her temples. "I thought if she couldn't perform magic this day would fall to another."

"We both know that is not how the universe works, sister," I replied. "The only way to try and circumvent it is to keep the future as close to the original vision as possible and substitute one element at the final second."

A life for a life. The balance would be maintained.

Our mother had sacrificed herself so we would live, and so the circle of life and death continued.

"What of our childhood vision of your mate?" Angelica asked softly.

I laughed. "If he hasn't found me in all this time he's lost or dead."

"Or perhaps he should have asked for directions, but his pride got in the way," Angelica snorted.

I rolled my eyes at her and refused to reply.

Too many years ago to remember all the details, we had been using crystals to scry under our mother's watchful eye. I'd predicted she would meet and marry a vampire. At the time Angelica had wrinkled her nose at my suggestion. Ilana was the living proof of that prediction. In the same session, Angelica had foreseen me marrying a strong dark stranger who would destroy everything in his path to find and protect me. *Yeah, that had worked out fantastically well*, I thought sarcastically. There was definitely no prince coming to sweep me off my feet the way Ezekiel had done with Ilana.

I wearily got up and went to pack what I needed for the journey. This had been my home for so long that I wasn't sure I'd fit into the wider world of Purgatory anymore.

There had been no great love of my life, Ilana the surrogate child I never had.

I would willing give my life to keep her safe.

***

Chapter Thirty-Four

Ezekiel

Raegel had already summoned the other princes to convene a meeting, Valek returning with us. He stared at Ilana as if he could summon her magic from her by the force of his will. I glared at him until he glanced away, but a few minutes later he was back to watching her.

"She never had magic before," Valek muttered in explanation when I slapped the back of his head on my way past to speak to Gabriel, who piloted our transport vessel.

He turned his staring to Agatha.

"If you don't want to be a frog, I'd look somewhere else, vampire," Agatha snapped at him. She was my favourite out of all Ilana's family, taking no shit from anyone.

I covered my grin when he hissed at her a few minutes after she zapped him.

"Your niece is one of my vampires," he taunted her.

Her eyebrow arched. "My niece is next in line to the witch throne and mated to the incubus. Your claim means nothing, bloodsucker."

They fell into an uneasy silence with Valek shooting her death glares every so often, and Agatha examining her nails.

I was grateful to finally disembark from his transport unit back at our castle. Raegel and Lycidas waited for us in my meeting room. It was locked against anyone else but me getting in. I'd given Raegel the key before I left as Ophelia's files had been stored there.

All eyes turned to the additional witch. Lycidas snarled and Raegel's eyes narrowed.

Agatha planted her hands on her hips and stared them all down. "I'm here to help my niece. I don't care what your curse is, and I'll help if I can, but my one reason for being here is Ilana."

Raegel's eyebrows sprung up at her abrupt speech. He was used to people speaking to him with the respect befitting his position. He eyed her as he would a rabid animal about to strike and bite him.

I brought them up to speed with all the information we had and how Ilana's touch broke Ophelia's connection with me.

"What about her?" Lycidas nodded at Agatha. "What does her touch do?"

I was about to warn him, when with a flick of her wrist, a white fluffy poodle sat where the lycan had a few moments before. He barked, but it was a high-pitched squeaky sound. The room descended into silence.

"Aunt Agatha," Ilana chided her.

Agatha's lip twitched and my fondness for her increased. She wasn't a woman who hid behind others, she was a badass psycho who'd left her safe home to help us. We needed someone like her against Ophelia.

"He asked, I merely demonstrated." She smirked. "Sit!" she commanded when he jumped off the seat to growl in front of her.

"She zapped me earlier," Valek moaned to Raegel as he sat far from Agatha.

Raegel's head canted to the side to study the feisty witch. She glared back at him, her fingers curled at her sides.

"You definitely picked the sane one as your mate," Raegel commented before returning his attention to the paperwork on the table

Agatha's gasp of annoyance filled the air and I saw the flare of magic around her fingertips.

"Witch, if you zap me or turn me into a pet, I will not hesitate to punish you." Raegel met her furious gaze in silent combat.

Ilana's hand slipped into mine and she moved marginally behind me as if the shit was about to hit the fan.

"Can we all stop comparing dick sizes?" I asked.

"I don't have a dick," Agatha snarked. "The elf is the biggest dick in the room, ears not included in his height."

Raegel's eyes deepened to nearly black, his fangs slowly descending.

"Enough!" I dragged a chair out and slumped into it, dragging Ilana onto my knee. "Any idea what we're going to do?"

"I doubt you have time to talk about it," Agatha retorted. "Ophelia is here."

"What?" Valek shrieked.

We were all on our feet in an instant, Agatha waving her hand over Lycidas to turn him back into a man.

"She would have sensed me the moment I stepped foot out of the pocket realm." Agatha stared at Ilana and said to me, "Keep her hidden. She doesn't need to know there is more than one witch here."

Screams sounded from outside and my heart sunk to my feet. We moved as a united front, all of us following the sound of chaos.

Ophelia stood surrounded by wraiths in the entrance hall, her gaze wild with fury.

"Ophelia." Agatha nodded at her, carefully folding her arms across her chest.

The Blood Queen's eyes gleamed with malice. "I thought all your family was dead."

"We're all very much alive. Thank you for your concern."

Her eyes swivelled in my direction and I stood in defiance with the men she'd cursed. "Ezekiel," she purred. "Is this why I can't reach you at night?"

A shudder threatened to race down my back, but I refused to show her that she intimidated me. Her gaze roamed over me in violation and I straightened my back.

"You do realise if you have to rape him while he sleeps, it means he doesn't want you?" Agatha asked, deliberately stepping between Ophelia and me. She knew Ilana would do something reckless to save me.

"You will pay for that," Ophelia hissed.

"Someone should have put you in your place long ago," Agatha retaliated before hitting her in the centre of her chest with a blast strong enough to make Ophelia stumble back several paces.

A noise that made every hair on the back of my neck stand to attention filled the air. I realised it was coming from Ophelia—a strange wailing that made my molars grind together.

Power coalesced around Ophelia and the light felt like it was being sucked out of the room along with the air we needed to breathe. Whatever was about to happen scared the shit out of me, even as Ilana found me, her arms snaking around my waist. Ophelia's eyes narrowed on the gesture and her lip curled in distaste.

Agatha followed her gaze and I saw her lips move as a pulsating dark shadow shot toward us.

Ilana and I fell though darkness until we landed on a hard floor in a room bathed in light.

"Where the fuck are we?" I demanded.

Ilana blinked several times. "This is Aunt Agatha's home in the Earth realm."

Fuck!

***

Chapter Thirty-Five

Raegel

The crazy witch had a death wish. She stood fearlessly before The Blood Queen, taunting her with her bravery.

"Where is he?" Ophelia took a threatening step forward.

Agatha had teleported Ezekiel and Ilana away the moment Ophelia's eyes had landed on her niece. Her magic was wild and powerful, untamed like the woman who wielded it.

"Where you can't find him," she sassily replied.

"I'll kill you for this," Ophelia hissed.

Agatha clapped her hands together, rubbing them while chanting in a language I didn't understand. The crystals fell from the bodies of the wyverns in close proximity. Power echoed around us in throbbing waves, making me want to drop to my knees in supplication.

Ophelia's eyes widened as a portal opened behind her. With a flick of her wrists, Agatha forced her through, closing it by slamming her hands together.

I saw Agatha's knees give way and stepped forward to catch her trembling body. She'd temporarily forced our enemy back but had injured herself in the process. Her tiny hands clutched the front of my shirt.

Addison rushed forward to fuss over the witch, but I easily swung her into my arms.

"Show me to your guest suite," I said urgently as a crowd developed to stare at us.

Gabriel took charge, dismissing them to hunt down the wraiths left behind, while Addison quietly showed me to the guest rooms within the royal wing of the castle. Lycidas and Valek followed. She had a tongue on her, but the witch had saved all of us because none of us could lift a finger against Ophelia.

Placing her on the bed, I stood over her tiny, unconscious frame. "I'll stay with her," I informed Addison, stopping her with a look when she tried to protest.

There was something about this witch that spoke to my soul like the wind rustling through the leaves in my forests. The little voice that guided me in battle told me to protect her. I didn't understand it, but I'd never ignored the voice before.

Addison ushered Valek and Lycidas into the other bedrooms in the suite. There were normally at least six in these apartments. I stayed to watch over the witch, studying her magic. She was strong and powerful, her gifts strumming under the surface of her skin in a steady rhythm.

Ilana's essence had been influenced by Ezekiel's when I saw her on the equinox after he'd fed from her. Agatha's was pure witch energy. In many ways, it was similar to elven vitality. Magic was found in nature and we lived and thrived in nature, harnessing the full extent of the powers of the elements.

She'd depleted her vibrancy fighting Ophelia. When she arrived, her power pulsed in steady waves that made me lose focus because it demanded my attention. Her green eyes bored deep into my soul. Her sass tested my temper, making me want to warm her ass with my hand. She was a conundrum that I couldn't decipher, even as I stared at her still form.

"How is she?" Addison stepped into the room and grasped the end of the bed to watch Agatha.

Father had decided the succubus was to be my bride, solidifying our realms. She was pretty in a sex demon fashion but had never been to my taste. I'd witnessed her prowess in the past, and never once had she piqued my interest. Not that I'd ever admit it, but I'd been relieved to find she'd mated with the incubus Gabriel.

"The same," I replied in a clipped tone that conveyed I didn't want to chat.

"Do you know where Zek is?" Her voice was small and quiet.

"The witch sent him through a portal to save her niece from the attention of The Blood Queen."

"Do you know where?"

My eyes flicked to her in annoyance. This was why I could never have her as a mate, the constant twittering in the background would drive me mad. "It felt like the Earth realm."

Addison opened her mouth to speak again and I narrowed my eyes in warning. She glanced away for several seconds before returning my gaze. "Are you annoyed with me?"

My eyebrows lifted fractionally. "About?"

She sighed and shrugged slightly. "I always thought you would be the elf I was promised to in marriage."

"I was."

She chewed her bottom lip. "Are you annoyed I mated Gabriel?"

I stared at her until she cast her eyes to the floor. "To be annoyed I would have had to care first."

Her gasp and expression should have made me feel guilty. It didn't.

People believed me to be heartless, unfeeling. The opposite was true. I tried not to let myself feel, because if I did then I would be lost in a world of sensation that I couldn't control. I'd never felt anything for Addison, and the thought of bedding her after our marriage did nothing to arouse me. She was better off with the incubus.

"Do you have to be so nasty?" she demanded, straightening her shoulders.

There was nothing to say to that, so I returned to keeping vigil over the witch. Eventually, Addison left and my body relaxed again.

Agatha muttered something and I leaned forward to catch the words. Her body started to convulse, and I leaned over to hold her down before she hurt herself. A deep, protective urge pulsed deep inside me, overriding the neutrality I cloaked myself in. Her body shook against mine. I felt heat travelling through my veins where our flesh touched.

Her eyes eventually opened, and I was lost.

***

Chapter Thirty-Six

Ilana

Aunt Agatha had sent us to the Earth realm. This was the home she used to bring me to when I was a child. The gardens still contained the herbs she harvested that grew under sun and moonlight.

Ezekiel stomped about for a few hours, searching for a way back, convinced Ophelia was rampaging through his castle. Eventually, he'd succumbed to sitting staring out a window at daylight. It hurt his eyes at first, but now it held him transfixed. The rainbow makers in the windows fascinated him.

Purgatory was eternal dusk. Earth contained the full range of light and dark.

I couldn't wait to show him the stars at night-time.

I wondered why Aunt Agatha had spent so much time telling me about this house when she'd be teaching me magic with Mum back home. She must have known all along she was going to send me back here. Nothing much had changed since I was last here, the village still small and the inhabitants welcoming to the family who lived in the old house that was barely ever used.

The cupboard under the stairs had an enchantment placed on it to give the person opening it whatever they needed. Clothing was our first priority, followed by cash for groceries.

Magic barely existed in this realm. This house was built over a nexus and imbued with the blood and powers of the witches who came before me. My fangs didn't descend when I was hungry, and for the first time, I experienced the hunger that humans felt, my stomach rumbling. The same happened to

Ezekiel, his incubus abilities dormant in his body. On the third day, I woke to him kissing and caressing me, my body on fire with lust and desire. We'd succumbed before when I fed from him, but this time was different. This was purely about our feelings for each other.

"Do you think her curse can reach us here?" Ezekiel asked, pressing soft kisses from my neck to between my breasts.

I arched under him, begging for him to tease my nipples. Instead, he continued his teasing on my too-sensitive skin. I growled, tightening my knees at his waist and rolling him onto his back. I pinned his arms beside his head on the bed. Passion flared in his chocolate brown eyes, his flesh hardening under mine.

"I really hope not," I muttered, leaning down to kiss him. "I love your mouth and hands, but they never reach the same depths." I wiggled my hips over his, grinding down on him and making him groan.

"I miss your fangs," Ezekiel whispered between deep kisses, his tongue probing one of my canines.

Abruptly I stopped, sitting up to peer down at him. "Does that mean if you're not an incubus here in the Earth realm that you'll be a terrible lover?"

I was teasing, but Ezekiel stared at me in abject horror. His expression sharpened and his eyes narrowed when a giggle escaped me. I screeched when he grabbed me and flung me onto the bed, his long, hard body covering mine.

"I guess I'll just have to work a little harder then." His lips slammed into mine, stealing my breath and thoughts.

I was caught in a web of seduction that enveloped me, dragging me further and further under its control. Our bodies knew each other, yet it felt like this was our first time. I no longer sensed our connection through his blood pulsing in my veins. It was a deeper emotional bond born from our mutual experiences that had brought us to this point.

"You intoxicate me in every realm," Ezekiel muttered, his lips moving on a divine path down my stomach.

Only the fine threads of the web that supported us held me together; otherwise, the sensations from his lips would tear me apart.

"I can't wait any more," I gasped, my nails digging into him as another wave of pleasure exploded from my core.

"Fuck!" Ezekiel exclaimed. His body covered mine, the head of his cock probing my entrance. "What about the curse?"

"Can you control it?"

His brow wrinkled in pained confusion.

I grabbed his face in my hands. "Concentrate on what to take from me if you sense it activating. Something I can live without." Before he could reply, I dragged his head down to mine, widening my legs in invitation.

His tongue and cock surged into me at the same time, filling me with his essence. We lost ourselves in the moment, writhing together, communicating with our bodies. Nothing mattered but this moment, our connection. We were both sacrificing ourselves at the altar of flesh and desire. Moans and groans were our vows, undulating bodies our promise to each other.

We both knew when the moment came that the curse should have activated. Ezekiel pulsed deep in my core, my legs wrapped around him in mindless pleasure. His heat spread deep into my womb and he slumped on me.

"She can't reach me here," he said with relief.

I rolled him onto his back to stare into his face. "I don't care about Ophelia or her curse. In the middle of this crazy adventure, I fell head-over-heels helplessly in love with you. Not the incubus, or the prince, but the man who strives every day to be the best version of himself."

His eyes widened even as I kissed him to cover the twinge of embarrassment. My words left me open and vulnerable, even though I'd told him that I loved him already. Raw emotion laced every single word I'd spoken.

Ezekiel grabbed my hips and brought me onto my back on the bed, his length still lodged inside me. "I fell for you the day I walked into your room and saw you in a pair of cotton panties. Every day I find another reason to love you, even though I don't deserve you. I love you, Ilana, and no matter what happens, you alone carry my heart."

A tear escaped from my eye to slip down my cheek. Ezekiel wiped it away with his thumb.

Please, I thought. *Please let us survive this.*

***

Our days fell into a pattern of me tending the garden while Ezekiel fulfilled the tasks that the house found for him. One day we found ladders and a new roof tile, another a new pane of glass for the sunroom. When people arrived, the house took the opportunity to have someone tend to its needs.

We enjoyed long walks along the beach or into the forest, made love under the light of the moon, and every day fell deeper in love with each other. We'd given up hiding our feelings. This was the only man I wanted to spend my life with, and I was no longer afraid to admit it.

One week slipped into another and then another, until almost a month had passed. Ezekiel's pale skin turned golden under the warmth of the sun, his sunglasses adding an air of mystery to him.

No matter what realm he lived in, women stared at him with desire in their eyes. He never noticed them, his affection only ever for me, making me feel special.

If we never returned to Purgatory, we could be happy here. As much as I was ashamed to admit it, the longer we spent in our own bubble, the longer I wanted to remain here. Far from the reach of Ophelia and the war that had tormented our people for centuries.

Our peace vanished the day my mother appeared in the kitchen. We were sitting eating breakfast in the sunshine when a portal opened and she walked through.

"It's time to return, Ilana. Agatha has held Ophelia back for as long as she could. You need to return." Sadness filled her eyes when she looked at us.

Ezekiel stood slowly, reluctance and acceptance in his stance. We knew this day would come, we just never knew when. Now that it was here, I wanted to hide in our room like a child with the door closed against the monsters.

I pushed myself to my feet. "What's happening?"

"Ophelia is standing at the incubus borders. She demands Ezekiel or she'll lay waste to their lands." Mum's eyes moved to Ezekiel. "Sometimes the greatest sacrifice brings the highest rewards. Remember that when all hope is lost, and you are surrounded by darkness."

I wanted to demand she explain what she meant, to scream that he was mine to protect.

Yet, all that disappeared when his eyes met mine. He would save me first. I knew that with every fibre of my being. He would die to ensure I lived.

"Life is not worth it without you by my side," I told him in a low voice.

He nodded, a sad smile tugging his lips.

We'd spent the past month getting to know each other until he was an integral part of my life. He was no longer my lover, but someone who knew more about me than anyone else. Ezekiel was my mate, the only man I could ever love.

Our hands joined and not a word more was spoken between us. We entered another portal Mum opened for us as she watched with tear-filled eyes. Ezekiel and I didn't need to communicate; we'd said everything we needed in the last month. Each of us knew how the other felt.

The dim light of Purgatory disorientated me. I'd lived my entire life here, but a month in the sun left me squinting to try and get my bearings. I heard the roar of the dragons, the wail of the wraiths. My heart plummeted in my chest, Ezekiel's fingers tightening around mine. Our powers reactivated when we arrived back in Purgatory, my vampire strength returning and my fangs lowering.

Ezekiel spun, hauling me against his strength. "No matter what happens, I love you, Ilana." His lips bruised mine with his intensity, then he was gone. Magnus appeared from nowhere to carry him away on his back.

"Izzy!" I screamed. There was no way he was going into battle alone.

My wyvern appeared a few minutes later. "I need to reach Ezekiel." She lowered her body for me to climb onto her back, rising quickly into the air. The feeling of dread unfurled in my stomach, even as we reached the border.

Dragons flanked the length of the treetops and the elves held bows and arrows in the branches below them. Ophelia stood on her carriage, a terrifying sight as she held Addison's limp form by the neck. Ezekiel stood on Magnus' back, his stance defiant and filled with suppressed rage.

"Oh, please, gods no," I muttered. "Can we get wyverns below her in case she drops Addison?" I asked Izzy.

Her head bobbed up and down and I sensed wyverns moving into position.

"Tell them to form a pentagram below them," I said into Izzy's ear. It was the most powerful magical symbol I knew.

An idea floated through my mind. "Can you speak to them directly?" I asked Izzy and her head bobbed again. "Bite me." I thrust my arm under her snout at the same time I sunk my fangs into her. Izzy's emotions and thoughts flashed into my head, and I felt a connection to the other wyverns when she bit my arm.

I need you to help me… Then I outlined my impromptu plan.

"Ezekiel," Ophelia purred. "I couldn't feel you anymore. None of the others would tell me where you disappeared to when Agatha intervened." She glanced down and raised her eyes in a flirtatious manner. "I thought you'd left me."

His back straightened, arms folding across his chest. "I was never with you in the first place, witch. Release my sister. Your fight is with me."

The other princes arrived to take their place beside Ezekiel, a unique power pulsing between them. How had I never seen it before? It was the reason Ophelia wanted them—they had a bond that united them, something unique and priceless.

"Where's my aunt?" I asked Izzy.

The elf took her to recuperate in his realm when you left. He said their magic was similar to hers and she would be safe there.

Surely it would have been easier to return her to Mum? I didn't have time to worry about it now, my full attention back on Ezekiel since I knew my aunt was safe.

"Choose, incubus," Ophelia snarled. "I had to take your sister for you to show yourself to me. Submit to me or watch her die."

A cold hand squeezed my heart. Ezekiel would never risk Addison. I felt his conflicting emotions echo through me and watched as his shoulders slumped as he made his decision.

Now! I mentally commanded the wyverns.

Some swooped from their hiding positions above us, dragging Addison from Ophelia's clutches as I hit her with the full impact of all my tattvas activating together. All we had was the element of surprise, because she was significantly more powerful than me.

I sent a prayer to fate and her sister destiny that the love they'd instigated that drew Ezekiel and I together would be enough to get us through today.

***

Chapter Thirty-Seven

Ezekiel

Wyverns flooded the area. A pulsating ball of electrical energy hit Ophelia in the centre of the chest, making her release Addison for a split second. I watched a huge blue wyvern grab my sister and move in the direction of the castle. Ilana was here somewhere close by—I felt her and knew she was taking the choice out of my hands. She would never let me sacrifice myself.

I didn't know whether to be proud or terrified at the thought of her this near to Ophelia. If we got out of this alive, I was tying her to my bed and leaving her there. The rails and bedposts were there for a reason, and it wasn't for decoration.

Raegel's elves launched an attack from the treetops beneath me, and all the dragons released fire together. Ophelia was pissed, the façade of beauty slipping until there was nothing left but the evil that lurked under the surface. I felt Ilana's pendant heating on my chest as Ophelia tried to drain my power.

Lycidas howled as she forced him to his knees, his wolf struggling to get out at her command. Valek's fangs descended and his eyes turned a glowing red. Raegel's eyes flooded with black, his fangs descended, and his ears flared back. She was activating all our curses at once.

There were innocent people here.

Fuck!

I projected a rippling wave of power toward her wyverns because the curse meant I could not directly strike against her. They screeched, upsetting her platform, their wings frantically flapping.

Izzy flew alongside Magnus and I closed my eyes for a brief second to search for divine intervention to help with my stubborn mate. There wasn't any, so I stared at her.

"Get on Magnus," I commanded. "At least I'll know where you are."

She was definitely getting tied to the bed in future. I didn't care if her sexy little vampire ass got her white cotton panties in a twist. For my sanity, I needed to know she was safe.

Ophelia's gaze zeroed in on Ilana and Izzy on Magnus' back. It didn't take a genius, never mind a jealous rejected woman, to realise that Ilana and I were together. Our body language shouted it to anyone who looked at us.

"You could only belong to Angelica," Ophelia said to Ilana, her tone flat and dead. "No wonder Agatha sent you away from me. Your mother and I did not part on the best of terms."

Ilana straightened her back and slid her arm around my waist. "This is the only chance I'll give you to walk away, Ophelia. You claimed a crown that doesn't belong on your head. The witches have grown stronger and are ready to enter this fight. My mother will take what rightfully belongs to her."

My arm crept around Ilana, anchoring her beside me. United we were stronger. I no longer cared who saw my feelings for this woman, she'd broken down every barrier I'd created to protect myself following the curse.

"Ezekiel is promised to me," Ophelia snapped. "We belong together, just as this crown belongs to me."

I sensed the magic culminating in Ilana before the crown exploded on Ophelia's head. She desperately summoned the elements to quench the flames, ending up a sodden mess with wild eyes filled with hate.

"That crown belonged to my family. I will never tolerate a bitch like you wearing it." Ilana took a step forward. "Ezekiel is mine, now and always. Your curse means nothing. It shows the pathetic excuse for a woman you are, creeping into his dreams to take what he refuses to give."

With every word Ilana spoke, a haunted, wailing echoed through

Purgatory, sending shivers across my skin and goosebumps to rise. Ophelia's face distorted, her nails lengthening into claws. Her aura expanded around her as the screaming increased in volume.

I'd lived a long time and there were not many things in Purgatory that stunned me or rendered me speechless. The sight of the dozens of flying creatures heading in our direction was definitely now on that list. They consisted of the head and torso of women. Their legs, lower abdomen, arms, and wings belonged to a bird. Crows.

Harpies belonged in Hell, not Purgatory.

"They're what remains of the witches she devoured the powers from," Ilana whispered beside me, her hand clasping the back of my jeans.

"Ideas?" I asked, real panic coiling through my system like a snake ready to strike.

"Kill the witch, live happily ever after," Ilana deadpanned.

"Seriously?"

"Yeah." She grinned. "I think you'd be good at a happy ever after."

Lycidas lost his fight against the transformation Ophelia forced on him and his howl rang out through the forest below us.

"Someone dart that fucking wolf!" Raegel shouted, swinging from the trees to the ground.

The first harpy swooped low to us with her talons outstretched. Ilana strummed her thumb along her fingers, the tips glowing. She flicked her fingers toward the harpy, and she exploded. That death signalled our descent into hell, with a flock of the winged enemies surrounding us.

The dragons released streams of fire that sent them pummelling to the ground into the waiting arms of the elves.

Together, Ilana and I destroyed harpy after harpy, fighting them back.

Ilana rubbed her hands together, her focus set on Ophelia as I used waves of dark power to eliminate our winged enemies. Their bodies crumpled and disintegrated when hit with the full force of my incubus energy. Wyverns arrived to surround us, their large jaws snapping at the harpies, tearing off limbs or heads.

Chaos reigned as smoke distorted my vision and the heat became unbearable.

Ophelia launched something in Ilana's direction, and I dived in front of her, taking the impact. Pain exploded in my stomach even as my legs gave way under me. I saw panic flash across her distorted face as sound silenced around me.

Ilana dropped to her knees beside me, her face my only focus.

A metallic taste tainted my taste buds as blood bubbled from my mouth.

Ilana shouted but I couldn't hear anything. A golden energy surrounded me as she tried to plug my injury with her hands. I fell onto Magnus' back, the vibrations of his breathing soothing me and coaxing me to sleep. Ilana's hands grabbed my face, her lips meeting mine as she poured heat into me.

My body went numb, the pain evaporating in the blissful nothingness. All that remained were Ilana's lips on mine, infusing me with heat. I wanted to react, but even my lips no longer responded.

I blinked a few times when I realised I was viewing the scene from high above, watching Ilana straddling my immobile form. Her hands were bathed in golden light as she infused healing into my abdomen, while she breathed her essence into my mouth. Tears ran down her beautiful face.

Ophelia screamed, her arms outstretched toward me as Magnus flew away. Whatever she'd done was designed to kill. Her intended victim had been Ilana, only I saw her attack first. She screeched again, her hands tugging at her hair, her eyes filled with horror.

Ilana slammed her fists against my chest and my vision flickered in and out of focus. She did it again and pain ricocheted through me.

"Don't you dare fucking leave me, Ezekiel," Ilana shouted in my face, moving her lips to mine as she breathed more of that heavenly taste into my mouth. Her fingers dug into my stomach, hurting yet soothing the pain and burning there at the same time.

I gasped as she tore something from my abdomen. I'd never experienced pain like it before. My body arched and that blissful numbness disappeared to be replaced by agony that exploded from my core and radiated out.

Magnus skidded into the dragonry, his breath forming a mist that surrounded us and kept everyone else out.

"Ilana, please," I begged her. She needed to let me go. There was too much damage for me to heal without feeding.

"No!" Her eyes met mine in determination. "You promised me forever."

Forever was a long time when you were dying right now.

"I'm not feeding from you," I whispered, closing my eyes.

Her energy infusion had brought me back to consciousness, but I felt the extent of my internal injuries. She needed to let me go.

I tried to push her hands away as she used a dagger to shred my clothes.

Ilana grabbed my face, her eyes wild, tears cascading down her face. "You will fucking feed from me and direct what is taken by the curse. Understand?"

We'd discussed this in the Earth realm. When I concentrated, I could allow the curse to take certain memories from a person. I shook my head, pleading with her. This was the last thing I wanted to do. I was too weak to control what memories were stolen from her.

Ilana's fangs dug into me, sending erotic energy through my flesh and arousing my dick. Fuck!

Her body covered mine, sheathing me. Ophelia would know that someone was trying to feed me right now and she'd consume everything from them to punish me. I felt the tug of my organs and flesh knitting together, my body using the last of my incubus power to heal me so it could feed.

"Ilana, baby, please I can't let you do this. Every memory makes you who you are." I was desperate. My body wanted her while my soul was fracturing into pieces deep in my chest. They pierced my emotions making them bleed fear and lust at the same time.

"I will never watch you die if I can save you. I love you, Ezekiel. I knew the risks in loving you, staying with you." Her body rose and fell over mine and I bit my lip to stop the groan that wanted to escape. "Whatever happens, she can never steal our love."

I screamed my release and watched her eyes intently. They glistened with confusion, containing an indefinable frailty in their depths. Something shattered within Ilana, piece by jagged piece that ripped deep into her soul and stole something precious. No one needed to tell me, because the panic that entered her eyes and the way she grasped me trembling revealed the truth.

Me.

I was the memory removed from Ilana. She was right, love couldn't be removed, but if she didn't know who I was what did it matter?

My body healed, but my heart lay in shreds.

Two hundred years living with a curse that tormented me every day, but Ophelia never broke me. Today she succeeded. I watched the woman I love forget me, a frown forming on her face, confusion flooding her eyes.

"Sleep," I said, blowing energy into her mouth.

I couldn't watch any more.

All I had left was vengeance. I would find a way to kill Ophelia and then I would walk straight into Hell and hand my soul to the devil.

***

Chapter Thirty-Eight

Ilana

I stretched, my body loose and languid, the erotic dream still on the edge of my consciousness. A man with black hair and eyes so dark they were almost black. Every night he found his way into my dreams, loving me.

Dragging my ass out of bed, I wandered down to find Mum in the kitchen.

"Hey, any sign of Aunt Agatha?" I asked, dropping myself into a chair and yawning.

"No, she's still away gathering herbs." Mum smiled, placing a mug of tea in front of me. Tea was apparently the cure for everything.

I'd been injured in battle, unconscious for days. Dad had insisted I come home to recover. Prince Valek agreed without argument, telling him to look after me. The battle must have been horrendous because Valek kept looking at me as if I was a dead woman walking.

I was starting to get cabin fever being under house arrest for a month. There were no physical injuries on my body, but every day I fought a terrible exhaustion that threatened to pull me under its spell.

Apparently, the tea was supposed to help. Dad brought blood bags home, but they made me vomit. Something was wrong with me, but I didn't know what. Maybe The Blood Queen had been experimenting with new toxins that killed you slowly?

Mum set a plate on the counter in front of me, all my childhood favourites on it. My stomach rolled and I raced for the toilet again. At this rate, I was going to starve to death. Her cool hands held my hair back and felt my forehead.

"Your dad is bringing a new blood home for you to try," Mum said in a low tone. When I looked up, her eyes were filled with tears. She shook her head at my questioning gaze. "We're all just worried about you, Ilana."

She settled me with my head on her knee, singing to me and stroking my hair like she did when I was a child until I fell asleep.

***

"Drink, little one." Dad sat beside me, holding a cup in his hand. He helped me up and placed it to my lips.

I braced myself for the nausea and revulsion, but nothing came. A sweet taste rippled over my tongue as it trickled down my throat. It was dark and seductive, reminding me of something that I couldn't put my finger on.

"What is it?" I asked.

Dad gave me a tight smile. "A rare blood that we had in the laboratory. Try and drink a little more, Ilana."

I finished the glass, feeling the exhaustion and pain leave my system. My eyes fluttered closed again even as his lips kissed my forehead.

Day by day the new blood made me stronger until I insisted on returning to the base. The way Mum and Dad kept constant vigil over me terrified me. The feeling that something was being kept from me grew stronger every day.

"Ilana!" Mia shouted, waving at me. She grabbed me in a hug, her arms squeezing me. "I've been so worried about you after that attack. Valek said we weren't allowed to contact you when you were healing."

My brow furrowed. What the hell was going on?

I listened to Mia's constant chatter. Everything was the same and yet different. It was hard to explain, but my life felt slightly out of focus. I overheard snippets of conversations that implied I'd been to the incubus realm, yet I had no recollection of that. Valek kept me out of frontline duties. I never remembered speaking to him before, but he seemed to go out of his way to be nice to me and ask me how I was feeling.

"What's up, Ilana?" Dad asked, looking up from his microscope. I'd decided to visit the one man who never lied to me.

"Something's not right," I replied, lifting random items in his laboratory to study them.

"In what way?"

I sighed and plunked myself into a wooden chair. "Was I in the incubus realm?" He stared at me for several seconds. "I heard someone mention I was injured there. They tend to whisper when they think I'm not listening."

Dad pinched the bridge of his nose. "You were caught in an attack there. You were hit with a blast from Ophelia at the same time as a power ripple from an incubus. It affected your memory."

My eyebrows flew up. That would explain some of my problems.

Dad continued, "None of us know what the long-term effects will be, Ilana. You need to give yourself time. When our medics got to you in the forest you were barely breathing."

I nodded, contemplating this new information. My issue was that no one ever told me anything about what was wrong with me until I discovered something and asked about it. I listened to him talking about the newest experiments they were working on for a while, making my escape when his assistant arrived.

"Hey, we're all heading to the banquet later." Mia linked her arm into mine. "Come with us, you need to get out of your room."

I hated banquets and feasts. It meant I had to pretend to feed or discretely leave when the others were high with feeding frenzy. A brief image of a man pulling me to his neck and telling me to drink hovered on the edge of my memories. Weird, I'd never drunk from the vein. It made me sick.

My room had always been my sanctuary, but now it felt cold and lonely—

empty, even though it was filled with my possessions. Maybe I should change the colour scheme. Black and red felt comforting.

The people and the noise in the dining hall were the same, yet my head felt like a revolving kaleidoscope. Noise surrounded me, the people at my table moving in and out of focus. Nausea settled deep in my stomach at the thought of trying to eat anything.

Mia bounced with excitement beside. "Oh, my goddess, look who's here! Get ready for your fill of your favourite eye candy."

I scanned the room, confused by her reaction.

"Ezekiel," she said, looking at me as if I'd grown another head. My brow creased in confusion. "The incubus prince that you've lusted after for-fucking-ever."

She nudged me and I stared at the top table. Lycidas and Raegel were there along with Prince Valek. Another man sat between Raegel and Valek. Jet black hair and dark eyes set in a sinfully gorgeous face. Looking at him made a headache pound in my temple. His eyes bored into me and pressure built in my chest until I thought I'd explode.

The room swam around me and sweat broke on my brow.

Pain burst through my head and the world went black.

***

"How are you feeling?" Dad peered down at me, concern written in every line of his face.

"Tired and sick," I replied, closing my eyes against the intensity in his. I'd insisted in returning here because my skin no longer fit at home. Now it felt too small for me here as well. After a while, I heard him moving away.

"She's sleeping," he told someone over to my left.

“What the fuck is wrong with her?” a male voice demanded. “You told me the blood was making her better.”

Something about that voice made me want to curl up beside it, let it tell me there was nothing for me to worry about. It was unknown but familiar at the same time, soothing me with its baritone.

“It was. I have no idea what happened tonight,” Dad said so quickly it melded into one sentence. He was nervous—something my dad never was.

“Doctor?” the deep voice spoke again. “Can you explain Ilana fainting?”

There was a discreet cough. “Usually I’d run a blood profile. Pregnancy can sometimes cause exhaustion and fainting.”

I almost laughed out loud. I was a virgin so zero chance of being pregnant.

“Interspecies can’t breed in Purgatory,” the deep voice snapped.

Say what? I almost sat up in indignation. Did I finally have sex and didn’t remember it?

“Maybe I should take her home and see if Angelica can do something? Agatha is still in the elven realm but maybe if the two of them work together they may be able to help,” Dad suggested.

Why was Aunt Agatha in the elven realm? I didn’t just have a bit of memory loss from an accident. I had a huge chunk missing from my brain.

A woman broke into the conversation. “Ophelia took too much from her. Zek was too intricately woven into her life. Maybe it was his proximity tonight that made her collapse?”

Who the hell was Zek and why would being close to him make me faint? Had I had sex with him? My head started to throb again as I desperately tried to remember.

People were lying to me, even my dad. I needed to get away from here and sort out my troubled thoughts.

Footsteps started to leave the room, but I nearly jumped out of my skin when soft lips pressed against my forehead. "Stay safe, baby." Fingers trailed down the side of my face.

I listened to the sound of his retreating footsteps. It was the same deep voice that was talking to my dad earlier. Those lips and fingers sent tidal waves through me, deep emotions that I'd never experienced before. By the time I opened my eyes, he was gone.

What the fuck was going on?

When I was sure there was no one about, I slid my shoes on and took off. I needed time to think. I desperately needed time to remember. There was a waterfall I used to sit and think at about a mile from the base. The Blood Queen never attacked this far into the realm.

The noise of the water soothed me, and I sat cross-legged, staring into the inky depths. It was the same as my mind, dark and hiding too many secrets for me to fathom. Time slipped past while I contemplated everything I heard.

Eventually I noticed a pair of eyes in the water watching me. I jolted, trying to scrabble back away from whatever creature was lurking there. Some of the wildlife wasn't very friendly in these forests. A red wyvern scampered out of the water, terrifying me. Did The Blood Queen have her lizards hiding in our realms to spy on us?

"Please, I didn't mean to scare you." A woman appeared where the wyvern had been. She had vibrant red hair and her scales formed a catsuit over her body.

That had me on my feet in a second, magic twirling around my fingers.

I stopped.

Magic?

What the fuck?

My eyes darted between the woman, wyvern, whatever and the glowing symbols on my left hand. Little sparks flew from them.

"Let me explain, Ilana." The female approached me with her hands out to show me she meant no harm.

Izzy. Her name appeared in my head. Another image of her sitting with her head on my lap. My knees buckled and I found myself on the ground.

"You're my familiar," I whispered.

She nodded.

"Why didn't I remember you?"

She glanced to the side as if debating with herself.

"You are my familiar, no one else's. Tell me." Maybe my life would start to make sense.

"Ophelia stole some of your memories."

My mouth opened and closed several times, but no words came out. Izzy sat beside me in silence. Her presence brought snippets of memories with Izzy in them, but there was another woman who featured in them as well.

"Who's the beautiful woman practicing magic with us?" I asked.

"Addison, she's a succubus."

More cracks formed in my head, leaving gaps and partial memories because they stopped when someone else entered them.

"Which memories did she take?" I eventually asked.

"Mistress, I swore that I would not trouble you. You were never meant to see me, but I sensed your distress. We are joined and I couldn't bear for you to suffer alone."

I fixed her with a steely glare. She glanced away with pain in her eyes.

"Is that why I've been feeling so tired and sick?" I asked. "Ophelia taking my memories?"

"The baby is draining you, it needs its father's blood," she said matter-of-factly.

If she'd slapped me across the face, I couldn't have been more shocked.

Baby?

I looked down at my stomach, pulling my top up. My brow furrowed. I didn't look any different. What the hell had happened and why couldn't I remember?

"I can't be having a baby," I muttered in a dark tone. "You need to have sex to get pregnant."

"From the noises the two of you used to make, I would suggest that you definitely had sex. Multiple times."

I folded my arms and stared at her. "Tell me everything. Right now."

She sulked but eventually shared our story.

Ezekiel? The incubus prince? I guessed I knew who *Zek* was now.

"The blood that Dad found for me to drink?" I already knew the answer but asked anyway.

"Ezekiel's," she confirmed. That was obviously why I started to feel better.

"What am I supposed to do?" I asked, covering my head with my hands.

"Nothing. Your memories are gone, and every day Ezekiel mourns your loss. For both your sakes you need to pretend you don't know anything."

"And our baby?" I demanded.

"I don't know, mistress. Your father will probably continue to provide you with your mate's blood for the duration of the pregnancy."

"And what are you going to do?"

She shrugged and stared at her feet. "I could stay in your room. At least then I would be close to you to ease your symptoms."

Izzy was right. Being with her did alleviate some of my symptoms. I gave her a long coat to pull on and guided her through the back passages into the base, collapsing against my door when we finally reached my room. "This is the second time I've sneaked you into my room."

She nodded.

That evening, nightmares paralysed me. Images of harpies attacking me tormented me. Then the dreams changed and became erotic.

“Trust me.” His lips traced the length of my spine. A black silken scarf covered my eyes. It felt so real, every movement within and on my body. A foreign emotion filled my chest.

Love.

I loved him and stealing my memories couldn’t change that.

A flutter in my lower belly woke me, my hand spanning my flat stomach.

Our child. A magical baby that was half me and half Ezekiel. Ophelia could steal my memories, but she couldn’t change the fact that there was something of Ezekiel inside me. More fluttering and I gasped, jolting upright as pain sliced through me. My head pounded and hands grasped my sheets.

“Mistress.” Izzy loomed over me, her hands covering mine. “Breathe, mistress. I can feel the magic of the child. Just breathe.”

The ribbons of suppression fluttered free, releasing me from the taint of Ophelia’s curse, even as my memories cascaded back into my head.

“Ezekiel,” I murmured before I passed out on Izzy.

***

Chapter Thirty-Nine

Ezekiel

"Find her," I snarled at the terrified vampire.

"You need to stop scaring my baby vamps," Valek grumbled.

"You do realise she's under your care?" I demanded, fury racing through my veins like poison. Ilana had looked tiny earlier in the medical bay. It took every piece of my willpower not to lift her and take her home with me.

I kicked a chair across the room before collapsing into another. Ophelia hadn't just taken Ilana's memories, she ripped my heart out and sent it with her. I hadn't slept, hadn't fed, and everything in my body was running on virtually nothing. The only thing keeping me sane was the crystal hanging around my neck.

"You could pretend to meet her and start from the beginning…" Lycidas suggested.

I scowled at him. "She collapsed tonight because her brain and body couldn't cope with my presence."

"Agatha said you need to trust her and Angelica. This was the only way," Raegel repeated the same shit I'd been listening to for the past month or so.

The only way for what? And why did he still have her aunt in his realm?

I growled at him.

"Do I look like I know what that woman is talking about?" Raegel demanded. "That witch has me terrified half the time, sending me off on missions to get her herbs for her conjuring."

He didn't look terrified. That strange gleam entered his eyes every time he talked about her. If I didn't know any better… "You like her," I said in shock.

The tips of his ears burned red.

Valek and I shared a look, his lips twitching.

"This is your fault." Raegel pointed at me as if I had brought ruination to his realm.

My eyebrow arched. "Me? How?"

"You arrived back with her. Now she has taken over my home and makes demands," he spluttered.

A slow grin turned the corner of my mouth up. "What type of demands?"

Raegel glared at me, refusing to answer.

Interesting.

I'd spent so much time wallowing in my own misery I'd missed this development.

He got up and stormed out of the room.

"What's got his elf panties in a twist?" Lycidas asked.

I grinned and shook my head. Maybe my ultra-tense elf friend had finally found his mate. Agatha petrified me, but maybe Raegel needed a dominating hand to guide him.

A small knock sounded at the door. Valek swung it open and the girl I'd seen with Ilana stood there.

"Ah, Mia, come in." Valek beckoned her inside. "Thank you for coming. Ilana has gone missing from the medical bay and I wanted to know if there was anywhere she'd go if she was feeling a little vulnerable?"

Her eyes rapidly scanned the room. "Is Ilana okay?" Her gaze fell on me for several seconds.

"She's still unwell from her illness," Valek replied, placing his hand on her arm. This was his realm, his coven. His touch to her would be something similar to an incubus thrall.

Mia blinked rapidly. "No, Ilana mostly keeps herself private. She sometimes walks in the forest to clear her head."

I was through the door in an instant, barking orders to my men. Every one of them knew her. If she was out there, they'd find her. And when they did, I was taking her home.

***

"Did no one think to check her room?" Valek asked, exasperation tingeing his tone. "Fuck's sake!"

Apparently, Ilana was fast asleep in bed when they found her. She wasn't in her room last night. I'd already checked and spent the entire night prowling Valek's base and forest. My nerves were just barely holding my shit together.

"The equinox is next week," Raegel informed me, reading my aura.

"I'm not hungry," I snapped.

His ear twitched and mouth tightened in response.

"Sorry," I muttered. "It's being this close to her without being able to touch her or talk to her."

He nodded silently.

I never realised how much I'd appreciated being able to share my thoughts with Ilana. My world had been quiet and lonely. For a brief time, it was filled with love and colour. Now… Now it was a shattered mess.

My day was filled with the commanders who plotted and debated while I sat deep in thought. Every so often Gabriel kicked me under the table, and I nodded in agreement as if I'd been following the conversation. I'd no idea what the fuck they were talking about. Gabriel was there as my right hand. He wasn't just a commander in my army, he was family now that he was mated to my sister.

Valek had arranged another evening feast. I wished he hadn't. His specially selected blood concubines for the high-ranking officials table kept touching me and trying to sit on my lap. My skin crawled in revulsion, even though hunger snaked in my belly.

I saw Ilana and Mia enter the hall arm in arm. Valek had instructed Mia that she was Ilana's unofficial guardian. Her eyes briefly met mine before her head ducked and heat burned in her cheeks. I missed the innocent Ilana who blushed at sexual innuendos. The fact that she flushed now told me she didn't remember any of those moments that constantly replayed in my head, tormenting my soul.

Mia chatted animatedly, dragging Ilana into her conversation. The blood concubines arrived for the general vampire populace. True to form, Mia grabbed a tall, muscular male, her fangs already down in excitement. Ilana stared around the room. This was the point she normally tried to escape so that no one would notice her lack of feeding.

Tonight, Mia snagged her a meal who was walking past, tugging him down for Ilana. I sat forward in my seat and watched in abject horror as Ilana cast a furtive glance around before climbing on his knee, her knees hugging his waist. Her fangs flashed and his body tensed before he relaxed, placing his hands on her hips.

Fuck!

I couldn't watch this anymore. When Ophelia removed me from Ilana's mind, it obviously unlocked what held her back from feeding. I doubted she needed my blood donations anymore.

"Are you ready to feed, Prince Ezekiel?" The blood concubine had masses of blonde curly hair that covered her breasts because her only clothing was black lace panties.

"Sure," I replied, throwing her over my shoulder and moving toward the door. If I stayed here a moment longer, that male under my mate would be impaled on the wall. The need to kill him pulsed deep in my chest stronger than a heartbeat.

The pain clawing inside me had to end. There were plenty of brothers to take my place as crown prince. I just wanted to find peace.

***

Chapter Forty

Ilana

My mouth dropped open when Ezekiel strode from the room with the half-naked woman over his shoulder. I remembered the time he carried me like that. The male blood concubine with me was under a spell, my thumb pressed against his pulse to control him. There was no way I could or would feed from him, but Izzy and I had agreed that I needed to pretend I was still influenced by Ophelia's curse.

I dragged the blood concubine from the dining hall toward my room. At the door, I stared into his eyes. "Go to your room and sleep." I released a little golden energy through my breath to command him. He walked away in a daze.

I closed my door and slid down the back of it, my hand covering my tummy. Tears sprung from my eyes, trailing down my face.

Izzy watched me from the bed. She still hadn't found her mate among the released wyverns. Both of us sat in silence with our hearts breaking.

Finding my resolve and wiping the tears from my eyes, I stood on shaky legs. "We need help. Can you find Addison?" I asked Izzy.

She nodded.

I opened the window of my room. "Is it easier to find her in your wyvern form?"

A woman walked across the room, and a small dragon creature flew through the window. I braced my hip against the window frame and lost myself in the memories that had been stolen from me for over a month.

Izzy landed beside me around ten minutes later, her snout rubbing against my arm. A quick tap sounded on my door a few minutes after that. Addison stood there with her eyes wide, quickly stepping in when I opened the door. She studied me apprehensively.

"I remember everything," I said simply.

"Oh, thank the dark goddess," she uttered, dragging me into a bone-crunching hug. "How?"

I took her hand and placed it against my abdomen. Her eyes met mine in understanding.

"I don't think our baby approved of me not remembering their father."

"We need to go to Ezekiel…" She turned to the door.

"No." I took a deep breath. "We have one opportunity to break the curse Ophelia has over Ezekiel. A few days won't hurt."

Addison slowly faced me. "What do you mean?"

"I only remembered after I ran away from the medical unit. Izzy found me in the forest and my memories of her returned, and then you reappeared. I only remember Ezekiel because there is a piece of him inside me." My hand rested protectively over my stomach again. "Ophelia doesn't know that I remember. The baby is part of the cure. We just need to figure everything out and put our plan into action."

Addison sat on the side of my bed. "He's barely holding on."

"He fed earlier," I replied, hurt tainting my tone. It was unreasonable but I couldn't help myself. Watching him leave that room nearly ripped my heart out.

"He hasn't fed since you left." Her eyes met mine. "Everything he does is a charade. Gabriel was trying to stop him from killing the blood concubine you fed from this evening. Valek's going to be pissed about his furniture."

I took a deep breath and closed my eyes. "I held him static with my magic. I can't feed from anyone except Ezekiel. The baby needs his blood."

Addison's eyes widened in understanding. "Both of you need your heads banged together."

"I need to speak to Aunt Agatha. She'll know what to do."

Addison rolled her eyes. "Good luck with getting her away from the elf. I swear he gets more protective of her every day. Behind every rigid repressed man is a sexual deviant waiting to escape. Your aunt won't know what hit her when that elf finally gives in to his base instincts."

No one wanted to think about their family members involved in sexual escapades, so I gave Addison the grossed-out stare to stop her.

"I keep forgetting you're not a succubus," she retaliated sadly. "I always wanted a sister."

I sat beside her and took her hand. "We are sisters, Addison. Now we need to band together to work out how to save Ezekiel."

Several hours later, she returned to Gabriel with the promise of trying to keep Ezekiel from going insane. Ophelia had spies everywhere, I was convinced of it. If we revealed our hand, she'd strike. Our baby was a secret that she never saw coming because an incubus and a vampire could never breed in Purgatory, but our baby was conceived in the Earth realm.

Ezekiel still had the pendant I made him. It would keep her from touching him in his dreams. Addison said it was the only thing keeping him on the right side of sane.

I fell asleep curled around Izzy.

***

Chapter Forty-One

Ezekiel

"We need Agatha here to help. Her knowledge is invaluable," Addison argued.

Raegel gave her a filthy glare. "No. She's safe where she is."

"Addison's right. We all agreed magic is important in this fight. Angelica can't leave the pocket realm and Ilana can no longer help us. Agatha must return." Gabriel leaned across the table to get in Raegel's face.

I'd finally drunk myself in a stupor last night after leaving the blood concubine in the corridor and going home alone. The images of Ilana having sex haunted me. Gabriel had stopped me from tearing her door off the hinges and killing the bastard for touching her. She was entitled to a life away from my curse.

"Just bring the fucking witch back, Raegel!" I snapped. "She can stay in your room if it makes you happy."

He turned his glare in my direction.

I trailed my fingers through my hair in exasperation. My temper was so short it was about to become non-existent. "Seriously?" I demanded, returning his stare. "If Ophelia even guesses that Agatha may be your mate and is the one fucking chance to break her curse, she will destroy half your realm to find her. I should know." My voice broke and I turned away so no one would witness the pain that coursed through me.

"She is not my mate," Raegel ground out in exasperation. "Fine. But she is not to be allowed into the meal area. No one knows where she is, and I want it to remain that way."

"I don't care if you keep her cuffed to your bed, Raegel. If Addison needs her here, then we all have to work together."

Everyone filed out, leaving only Gabriel and Addison. My body slumped and I closed my eyes. Every day got a little bit harder to keep going. I was starving, my energy levels so low it took enormous effort to stand. And now I had to witness the love of my life with other men.

"We need to talk." Gabriel's tone said I didn't want to hear whatever it was.

I jerked my chin in reply for him to continue.

He slid a folder across the table to me. I stared at it before looking at him.

"Read it," he replied.

I lifted the folder and slowly flicked through it. Page by page, my blood boiled higher until I was ready to explode. "The fucking bastard. I'll kill him! Where did this come from?"

Gabriel rubbed his hands down his face. "It was in Ophelia's base. I hid it in my jacket before anyone else saw it when we were packing everything up. Then things got crazy and you disappeared to the Earth realm, then Ilana…" His voice trailed off.

My eyes met Addison's. She was pale, her face pinched with the knowledge in that folder.

"Suggestions?" I asked her. Addison had a better strategic mind than most of my commanders. It was a travesty succubae were kept safely at home and not allowed to fight.

"Valek is having a masquerade ball for the equinox next week. His sister Isodora will be in attendance to select her mate for the upcoming year. I suggest we invite some of our brothers. It's always advantageous to have family close by." Her hand landed on Gabriel's shoulder and his hand clasped hers in return.

"It means you can feed as well before confronting him," Addison continued.

I shook my head. “Could you feed if you knew Gabriel was out there but couldn’t remember you?”

“Ilana wouldn’t want this,” Addison interjected. “She loved you, Zek. If there is even a chance we can break the curse you need to be strong enough.”

She was right. I knew it deep inside where all truths hide. Yet, I still couldn’t do it. My dick had never objected to pleasure for centuries. Not until a feisty little vampire sauntered into my world and turned it upside down. Now he wasn’t interested in anyone but her.

I didn’t bother answering, because what was the point?

***

“Have you been hiding from me?” Isodora giggled, trailing her finger down my arm. She’d arrived for the equinox feast in two days.

My jaw clenched and I suppressed the full body shudder that wanted to emerge. Valek’s sister should have been born a succubus. The woman was a sexual predator with a ferocious appetite. Every year she selected another unfortunate male to drag off to her castle deep in the heart of the vampire realm. I couldn’t remember the last time one was seen after she’d ensnared him. In my head, I imagined her castle with a huge spider’s web throughout it, and her conquests hanging in those strange little graveyards spiders have at the side of their web.

I really needed to eat something.

“Who would hide from you, Isodora?” I asked. “You barely leave you castle to grace us with your presence.”

She grinned and batted her eyelashes at me. I’d lost count of the number of times she tried to get me to her castle over the years. I obviously needed to change my cologne because all I seemed to attract were psychotic females with stalker tendencies. Ophelia and Isodora were the prime examples.

"You know you have an open invitation to my castle," she purred.

Holy fuckballs. I glared at Valek for help. He blinked and began to chat to Lycidas. He was as terrified of his sister as the rest of us. At least he was exempt from her sexual advances. I would never forget the day we encountered her with Raegel pinned against the wall, panic in his eyes, and his ears flat against the side of his head.

"Prince Valek, you requested to speak to me?" Ilana stood at our table and my dead heart decided it could beat after all.

She didn't react to my presence, so that first day when she fainted must have been due to something else. Addison insisted I had to keep donating blood. I'd tried to argue that she seemed to be feeding every night, but no one ever won an argument against my sister.

Valek smiled and the hairs on my neck stood to attention. "Ilana, yes, we have additional dignitaries arriving over the next few days. Since you are not on active duties in the field, I wanted you to liaise with my master of ceremonies and help him organise the needs of our guests. Addison specifically requested your assistance."

Ilana's green eyes cast around our table until they fell on Addison.

"I bumped into Ilana the other day and I know she still has difficulties after the attack, but we caught up and she would be perfect to help me with organising my outfits and hair," Addison explained. She'd never needed help with her hair and outfits before—in fact, she'd been the one to help Ilana with hers.

My eyes narrowed at my sister. She gave me her best innocent stare.

Isodora pawed my arm again and I felt the weight of Ilana's gaze landing on the gesture. For a split second our eyes met, and fire burned in her depths.

“I’ll report for duty in the morning and let them know what Addison needs.” Ilana gave a slight bow and walked away.

Something was going on and I was definitely out of the loop. Gabriel’s and Addison’s heads were together in private conversation, and the feeling that they were keeping secrets from me churned inside me in irritation.

My eyes wandered the room until they found Ilana again. She chatted to Mia, but her gaze met mine as if she felt me watching her. There was no timid virgin or mindless victim staring back at me. Power pulsed through me with a kick to my solar plexus. Those eyes belonged to my lover who’d stood against Ophelia and saved my life twice.

I didn’t know what the fuck was going on, but Addison better have some answers when I knocked on her door.

***

Chapter Forty-Two

Ophelia

None of them had attended my ball, yet the vampire organised one for the next equinox and didn't invite me.

Whatever the witch had done, I still couldn't see Ezekiel in my mirror or visit him in his dreams. She was back with the vampire prince, living her life like he didn't exist. I knew she was trying to feed him after he took the attack destined for her. So I took something precious from her. I snatched the man she loved, erasing him from her memories.

Her memories never arrived for me to feast on, probably because she was part witch. I didn't care, though. She was out of his life and my sources reported he was weak and vulnerable. My heart soared with excitement at the possibility he would come to me, begging for pity.

Ezekiel was broken and miserable, but I would take him anyway. That was the true essence of love and he would eventually learn that what he felt for the halfling was nothing more than infatuation.

I'd kicked my lover out of bed early this morning to carry out my latest task. He had a certain boyish charm, although he tended to be a little petulant. What he lacked in ability he made up for in enthusiasm. There was nothing worse than a man who was selfish in bed, thinking only of himself and his enjoyment. He was sufficient to scratch an itch, but nowhere near powerful enough to fulfil me.

Only Ezekiel could do that.

I released my beloved crow to fly over the vampire realm, to seek information for me. She was one of the few beings in my world I trusted, her soul directly connected to mine.

It would take time, but my witches were still trying to create another crown for me after the halfling destroyed the one I tore from the head of my enemy a long time ago. The witch's crown was forged from the original nexus of magic. Only a descendant from that line could destroy it, meaning she came from Angelica's lineage.

A smirk crossed my lips at the punishment I inflicted on her.

It was one thing to watch someone you loved suffer. It was a totally different agony to see the one you love and not even know it was them. Every time she was near him, her soul would twist and she would never know why.

My curses were designed to extract the maximum misery from my victims. Every emotion contained an energy signature and misery tasted delicious. I wasn't one of the goody witches who loved to meddle and help. No, I gained power from the darker emotions. The more miserable my four princes were, the stronger I became. The deadly sins were a perversion of basic necessities of life, and in Purgatory, their energy was key to my power.

Using the basic building blocks of our world against the princes was inspired from a curse that one of the original witches cast a long time ago. She manipulated the fabric of Purgatory to increase her power. I'd found her grimoire on my travels.

I might not be able to find Ezekiel in my scrying mirror, but I felt the misery deep in his soul. He was in emotional agony from his little witch being taken from him. When he fell low enough, he would beg me to make it stop and then he would be mine.

I would be waiting with open arms.

***

Chapter Forty-Three

Ilana

I knew something was wrong by the expression on Addison's face. Ezekiel lounged in her room, his long legs stretched in front of him while he studied the ceiling. Her eyes screamed a warning to me. My heart sunk because I hadn't been able to hide all my emotions last night. In fairness, when I saw Isodora pawing all over Ezekiel, I had to fight the urge not to peel her perfectly manicured nails off his arm and trail her over the table by her immaculate hair. I'd heard tales of what she did to the males she took. Mia's brother lived in isolation, now broken by the experience.

Addison and I locked our gazes, her hand squeezing mine, giving me the strength to neutralise my expression. I entered her suite with my clipboard in front of me as armour.

"Princess Addison, I have the list of incubi arriving from your kingdom for the feast tomorrow. Do you wish to discuss their feeding requirements?" My voice stayed even through willpower alone.

"Thank you, Ilana. This is my brother Ezekiel."

I fought to keep my body relaxed and expression neutral. "Prince Ezekiel." I dipped my head as per custom. "I hope you're enjoying your stay in the Drakus realm." Then I turned my full attention back to Addison as if the love of my life wasn't sitting there staring at me.

I wanted to throw myself into his arms, to reassure him everything was going to be okay. More than anything, I needed to tell him that we were going to be parents, that the proof of our love was currently growing inside me. Instead, I began to discuss rooms and seating plans with Addison as she told me where everyone was to sit to avoid petty squabbles.

I deliberately put Remiel beside Isodora in the hope she'd take him away to her castle of debauchery and break him as he had done to so many others.

Throughout our meeting, Ezekiel never took his eyes off me. They bored into my soul, seeking answers to questions I couldn't answer.

Aunt Agatha arrived late last night. Raegel had insisted she was staying with him 'for her protection'. Ordering my aunt to do something never worked and I was deep in her hug within minutes of her arrival. My entire story came tumbling out the same way I shared everything with her as a child. She'd always been my closest confidant.

She immediately dispatched Izzy to organise the wyverns to surround the base to stabilise our magic.

Ezekiel looked exhausted, his hair messy as if he was constantly tugging at it. I wanted to go and smooth it, hold his head against my stomach the way I used to in the Earth realm. This close to him I could smell the masculine, earthy scent with a hint of spice that he emanated. A surge of emotion threatened to choke me because it used to comfort me. Now I lay awake every night because I was alone and miserable.

"Is there anything else?" I asked Addison.

My resolve diminished with every minute spent in this room.

Addison shook her head. "No, I'll see you later to help me prepare for the festivities."

I turned to leave the room and was caught in the full blast of Ezekiel's hypnotising gaze. Butterflies beat in my chest and my breath caught. Addison stepped between us, ushering me from the room.

"Addy, we need to talk," I heard Ezekiel say as the door closed.

***

The dragons arrived with the guests from the incubi realm. Magnus bumped me with his snout and I discretely stroked the side of his face while everyone else was distracted. His nostrils flared and lowered to the level of my abdomen.

"Please," I whispered. "We have a plan. He can't know yet."

There was nothing that Ezekiel and I hadn't discussed in our time together. His connection to Magnus was one of them since he'd saved me from Remiel. Speaking of the devil, he stood watching me with a predatory gaze while biting into his bottom lip. My stomach rolled in disgust.

The big black dragon spun as if he was preparing to take to the air, his tail flicking Remiel to send him landing on his ass. He blinked one big amber eye at me as if in conspiracy and flew off.

"You need to train that fucking lizard!" Remiel shouted at Ezekiel, dragging himself from the ground.

"Why?" Ezekiel demanded. "He's the best dragon in our thunder."

"He hates me." Remiel sneered, his top lip lifting in disgust.

"How's that my problem?" Ezekiel countered. "Fuck up, Remmy, you're embarrassing yourself."

I kept my face neutral even though I'd spent time with all the people arriving. Jethro stared at me intently, studying me for a reaction. I acted the same as the other vampires welcoming our guests.

We led the way through the compound deep into the mountain. The vampire castles were located far into the Drakus realm, close to the centre of Purgatory. Ophelia would have to make her way through most of this realm before she got to them. The compound was secure against most creatures, including dragons. Valek took the security of his people very seriously. When the shields went over the entrances, there was no way to get in unless you wanted to demolish a mountain.

The outer areas were a basic military structure, but the further in we journeyed, the more elaborate the decorations. The suites were opulent, the communal meeting areas spacious and filled with luxurious furnishings to allow everyone to relax and enjoy their downtime.

"Miss me, sweetheart?" Remiel managed to catch up with me and paced beside me.

I watched him from the corner of my eye. "I'm sorry, Prince Remiel, but I don't believe we've met before."

Most of our encounters had Ezekiel present. A wide grin spread over his lips.

"My mistake. I insist you are my guest this evening." His hand grabbed my elbow to tug me toward him.

"I'm busy this evening," I replied, desperately resisting the urge to smack his hand away. The man was a dick.

"And tomorrow?" His voice lowered and I felt him pushing seductive incubus energy in my direction.

I stopped to stare at him, a fake smile touching my lips. "I look forward to it."

His smug smile soured my stomach. I moved on before I vomited on his shoes.

Ezekiel pushed past us, shoving Remiel out of the way. Remiel gave a dark chuckle, enjoying Ezekiel's obvious distress. Jethro strode between us to follow his elder brother, slapping Remiel across the back of the head on the way past. I felt like hugging him.

Addison saved me from Remiel by lacing her arm through mine and walking between us. My nerves were frazzled with all the pretending after being sick for over a month. My head felt fuzzy since I hadn't eaten all day. Addison's grip on my arm tightened as her empathy tuned into my feelings.

"Stay here," she instructed, settling me into a chair in her room. "Make sure no one comes in," she said to Gabriel as she left.

I gave Gabriel a sad smile. He was generally quiet, and I'd never really chatted to him before.

"You doing okay?" he asked.

I shook my head and sunk further into the chair. "Nope. Remiel being here doesn't help." I'd noticed he had no great love for his brother-in-law.

"He's always been a dick. Most men grow out of the phase when they become adults. Remiel just languishes there."

"How's Ezekiel?" I knew Addison was shielding me from the worst of it. I'd seen myself that he was barely holding his shit together.

Gabriel sighed. "Zek is my oldest friend. He's not good, if we're being honest. He hasn't eaten since the day you left, and he's not sleeping. If this continues, there won't be much left to save from the curse."

I chewed the inside of my cheek.

"Incubus can go mad if they're hungry for too long," he continued. "He's not far off that stage now."

I nodded.

Aunt Agatha and I had spent a few hours earlier practicing enchantments and creating barrier spells to activate on the equinox. Ezekiel only needed to hang on for another day.

"We're trying," I said in a quiet voice. "If only my memories had returned sooner…"

"They're back now." He stopped me going any further. "That's all that matters."

I closed my eyes and leaned my head back, exhaustion washing over me.

"I'll keep Remiel away from you tonight. Zek can sort him out tomorrow when you and Addy put whatever hairbrained plan you have into action."

"Thanks." At least that was one less thing for me to worry about tonight.

The door opened and Addison hurried in and said to Gabriel, "You need to go to Zek. Jethro's trying to restrain him."

Fuck! I was on my feet in an instant.

She shook her head, her eyes distressed.

"I need to go to him, Addison."

"We've come this far. In a few hours, the equinox will be here and Ophelia won't be able to touch him for twenty-four hours." Addison took a steadying breath. "We can do this." Her eyes locked with mine.

"We have to do this," I replied.

***

Addison worked a minor miracle on me. The woman staring back in the mirror looked nothing like me. My eyes had heavy makeup around them, making me look exotic. She'd piled my hair in a mass of curls on top of my head that cascaded around my shoulders. My outfit was deep golden tones with a tight-fitted bodice adorned with carefully selected crystals to amplify my powers. A long flowing skirt had slits up to my waist to allow me to kick if needed.

We'd planned everything with military precision. Wyverns were already in place within the forest, forming a magical network. Addison had enthralled many of the blood concubines so Ophelia couldn't control their minds. Aunt Agatha was cloaked in Raegel's elven magic. He'd become incredibly protective of her, making my aunt roll her eyes at him behind his back.

The feast was in full flow when I finally made an appearance. Ezekiel's blood had taken my headache away and calmed the baby. I sensed their distress through our magical link. They needed access to their father's blood the same as they needed a connection to my magic. Addison insisted our baby was a boy, and Aunt Agatha was firmly in the girl camp. Me? I just needed to find a way to be with their father.

Vampires were feeding from blood concubines; incubi were starting to leave or engage in sex with some of the vampires and concubines. The air was heavily scented with blood and sex.

Isodora pawed over Ezekiel at the top table, her red nails dragging up and down his arm, her tongue delicately running over her lips. She leant over to whisper in his ear, pressing her breasts against him in the process. My gaze narrowed at her in anger.

My stomach churned when a blood concubine straddled Ezekiel's hips, running her hands through his hair the way mine itched to. I knew he wasn't feeding, but that didn't stop the jealousy piercing through me.

I could do this. For the sake of our future I had to.

My eyes flicked to the clock. It was almost midnight. Ophelia knew that as soon as that clock struck the hour that Ezekiel was outside her control for twenty-four hours. She wouldn't want him to feed because she needed him weakened.

"Look at you, sweetheart. Couldn't stay away?" I stiffened at the sound of Remiel's voice. He wasn't at his table where he was supposed to be. His hand traced from my shoulder, down my back, to my ass. "No one will notice if we slip away." His breath fanned my cheek since he was standing so close to me.

I shrugged his hand off. We didn't have time for his interruptions.

His hand clamped on the back of my neck. "You've teased me enough, vampire. You are here to fulfil my every wish. Valek would not be happy if I complained about you." He pressed himself against my ass and I felt his erection rub my lower back.

My mind swirled in panic. Magic pulsed under my skin, ready to attack.

"You will submit to me, and I will gorge myself on your flesh."

I was born a witch but trained a warrior. There was only so much any woman could take. My body bowed and I twisted, grabbing his arm and flipping behind him, forcing him to the floor.

"You are a disgusting sex pest. I would rather masturbate than have intercourse with you. If you touch me again, I will personally cut your dick off and shove it up your ass. Are we clear?"

Silence descended around me like a curtain falling as every eye on the room turned in our direction. I kicked him forward onto the ground. There was a line that should never be crossed. Remiel had destroyed that line and any decency associated with it.

"Sorry, but no means no." I fluffed my hair up and sauntered away from Remiel and further into the room. Gabriel headed in the direction of the delinquent sex pest to deal with him.

Addison sat from her vantage point watching the room, her head shaking slightly when I turned my attention to her, indicating that she hadn't spotted Ophelia.

I sensed her magic polluting the air, snaking through the crowd, nauseating me with its dark energy.

Aunt Agatha had included some metal rods infused with an enchantment to mask my magic from Ophelia. They formed part of the structure of my bodice. Everything adorning my body had a purpose tonight.

I needed to risk using magic to find her. If I was hiding in plain sight, then she could be as well. I rubbed my thumb and ring finger together on my left hand, muttering a spell to reveal a lost item. Technically, Ophelia was lost to us right at this moment. I merely added her name to the spell instead of the object.

My eyes widened when I realised she was the woman currently gyrating on my mate's lap. He stared off into the distance as if in a trance.

Hairs stood to attention all the way up my back and my fangs descended in anger.

I frantically nodded to Addison and she stood abruptly when she noticed who was trying to seduce Ezekiel.

The trap was set. I just never imagined her being so close to Ezekiel when we sprung it.

***

Chapter Forty-Four

Ezekiel

I was going to fucking kill him.

Remiel had really done it this time.

The young female vampire left him lying on the floor after she kicked his ass. He deserved it. Gabriel stood and made his way through the developing orgy toward my brother. Only a few minutes remained until the equinox arrived and we could deal with Remiel.

He'd shamelessly flirted with Ilana earlier and it killed me when she smiled at him and agreed to a date tomorrow. That was never happening. I didn't care if I had to kill him to stop him meeting her.

I tried to push the blood concubine from my knee. I'd only let her climb on me to deter the advances of Isodora. That vampire was worse than a sexual predator. She was an undulating mass of hormones that was constantly trying to seduce me. At times it felt like she had eight arms because she was constantly touching me and trying to unzip my trousers.

"Excuse me." I peeled the concubine's hand from my arm to help Gabriel retrieve my wayward brother.

Her nails dug into me and I pushed her back by the hips.

"Are you not hungry?" she whispered in my ear, her tongue tracing a path from the back of my ear down my throat.

My stomach clenched, and not in the good way when having a female straddling your hips.

"Not tonight," I insisted, trying unsuccessfully to remove her as her knees clamped on either side of my waist. What was wrong with these women?

"I can make your every desire come true." Her hands tried to open the button of my trousers.

"No thanks." I removed her hands and clasped them together in my grip. I was sick of people touching me without my permission. First Isodora, and now a blood concubine. My dick was refusing to work for anyone but Ilana.

The concubine rubbed her hand over my groin like she was frantically trying to summon a genie from a lamp. This lamp was defective, and she needed to try her luck somewhere else.

Her head jolted back when someone dragged her back by her hair with their fist.

"You really need to get your hands off my mate." My eyes shot up to find Ilana standing there. The same woman who'd assaulted Remiel a few minutes ago. I recognised her eyes, but heavy make-up camouflaged her from prying eyes.

The concubine squeaked, trying to grab hold of me to keep her in place. Isodora went to move forward, but Ilana pointed at her. "I wouldn't touch him if I were you."

She dragged the squealing concubine across the floor. I stared in disbelief as she morphed into Ophelia.

What the fuck was going on?

The Blood Queen stood gracefully, brushing imaginary dust from her clothing. "I was informed that you no longer remember Ezekiel."

"You need better informants," Ilana retorted, her eyes briefly met mine. "I know exactly who he is."

My heart nearly leapt from my chest. She remembered me?

"You are a silly little girl. At least Agatha is a worthy adversary," Ophelia drawled in a haughty tone. "Ezekiel needs a real woman to satisfy his urges."

For the first time ever, I saw a malicious grin spread over Ilana's features. "He doesn't want you. Do you think he's been playing hard to get for two hundred years? Did what happened with Lucas not teach you anything?"

Ophelia's hand clenched at her side. "Where did you hear that name?"

Ilana smirked. "I know so much more than his name. I know your love killed him." She deliberately kept moving until she stood between me and Ophelia.

"This ends today," Ilana said with complete conviction. "If I have to drag your hold from him one finger at a time, I will. I love you, Ezekiel."

I didn't realise how much I missed those words until they washed over me, giving me strength and something even more precious—hope.

"Love you more, baby."

Ophelia studied Ilana. "How did you stop the curse affecting you?" she asked, her tone genuinely curious. It was a question I wanted the answer to as well.

Ilana shrugged. "Maybe you're not as powerful as you think. You've twisted magic until it no longer resembles its original form. There are places it still exists in the pure form it was created in. That will always combat your dark, twisted perception of magic."

Ophelia's hands were clasped so tight that her knuckles were white. Sparks of black magic emerged from them as her temper built.

Did she honestly think that I would let her fight the psychotic witch? I grabbed Ilana's hips, dragging her to me. "What are you doing, baby?"

Her body swayed into me instinctively. "Killing the witch to have our happily ever after."

My hand splayed across her stomach to hold her in place. A small pulse of power rippled against my fingers and my knees threatened to give way. I'd heard that we could sense our children growing inside our pregnant mate. That was how Father knew Mother was pregnant with me before anyone else. I sought him out from inside her womb. I kicked myself for not realising sooner that the reason she'd needed my blood was because she carried my child.

Her hand gripped mine over her stomach for a split second in confirmation.

I heard Ilana muttering and found myself at the opposite end of the room, watching in horror as my mate and The Blood Queen attacked at the same time. Magic clashed and hissed high into the air above them.

Without thinking, I started to run toward them.

Remiel struggled against Gabriel, launching himself at me and bringing us tumbling to the floor. My head came up to see his smirking face.

I was fucking done with his shit.

***

Chapter Forty-Five

Ilana

The Autumnal equinox, or mabon, was when the Earth realm's equator passes through the centre of the sun. There were twelve hours of day and twelve hours of night, reminding us that everything in nature has an equal and an opposite. Ezekiel was that to me—my equal and opposite, the kindle to my flame. He made me want a better future.

Ophelia's hands rose and sparks emanated from them. I gathered every piece of energy and knowledge that I had, activating the tattvas on my left hand, all of them together, and sent my own attack to counter hers.

Magic evolved long ago when the Earth was created in the big bang. It lay dormant, deep within the core as the overlapping realms were created. The first witch discovered magic pulsing in a crystal. Her sister demanded half of it when she brought it home, grabbing the crystal and throwing it to the ground. It fractured, forming light and dark magic. The sisters formed the two strands of the magical community. My mother was the queen of the light covens.

Every witch contained a connection to both light and dark magic since they were created from the same source. Ophelia had spent so long practicing and wielding dark magic that she forgot to protect herself using both. Aunt Agatha taught me to envelop myself in layers of protection from both sides of the one whole—equal and opposite, just like this equinox.

Sparks flashed through the air around us as the elements met and clashed. I knew going into this that I could never defeat Ophelia. Her life force was linked to all four princes through her curse. Agatha had been studying Raegel for months and was convinced Ophelia had created a soul connection. My aim tonight was to break her connection to Ezekiel.

A commotion broke out below us, and out of the corner of my eye, I saw Ezekiel and Remiel fighting in hand-to-hand combat.

I returned my focus to Ophelia, searching for the golden cord in her aura that connected her to Ezekiel. There were too many flowing from her in all directions. She had linked herself to the princes, her coven, the wyverns. All of them continuously sent power to her.

Please, please, please. I silently chanted in my head. This was our only chance.

I hit Ophelia with another blast of light magic, followed by a hit of dark, and followed my instinctual pull to Ezekiel.

Remiel's arm hung at a strange angle, and his face was swelling and covered in red marks. Gabriel kicked Remiel's knee, bringing him to the floor. I guessed everyone had had enough of the playboy prince.

Ezekiel's gaze met mine, his hair falling over his eyes. He arched an eyebrow in question.

"Kiss me," I said quickly.

Surprise registered on his face as I grabbed his black shirt and hauled him toward me, breathing golden energy into him. It would strengthen him and allow me to track his connection to Ophelia.

"Love you," I said into his mouth and turned to face Ophelia, who was storming down the room toward us, with literally a storm behind her.

A golden cord from her etheric body pulsed brighter than the rest. Bingo!

Ezekiel's hand latched onto my wrist and spun me to face him. "Be careful." His lips crushed against mine in a hard, brief kiss. "We do this together."

Side by side we faced the wrath of Ophelia. Ezekiel may not have been able to attack her directly because of the curse, but every incubus and succubus in that room was under his control. He and Addison worked together to drain powers from their court, strengthening me through our bond.

Izzy was my connection to the wyverns that formed a web around us. I'd spent time in the forest with them. Every wyvern sang a particular note that, when added to the rest, formed a melody that intensified the power of magic. No one could force them to sing, as Ophelia had discovered over the years. You could possess the body of a wyvern, but you could never control their soul because they were created from elemental magic.

One by one they began to sing. I felt it deep in my chest as a cacophony emerged of magic's beautiful song of creation. Ophelia's eyes widened as she realised what I'd done with all the beasts we'd freed from her grasp. Her gaze clouded with anger, the storm clouds flashing lightning that surrounded her, power coalescing in her body.

Her jaw tightened as she raised her hands, harnessing the force of her magical storm. Thunder rolled throughout the room, lightning striking her body repeatedly. Her voice rose in a chant that made terror claw its way up my back. She was summoning dark souls, I felt them crawl their way toward us.

This needed to end before they got here because we didn't have enough witches to face them. We would need all of Mum's coven.

I hit her with a blast of light magic, drawing every piece of strength from inside me. I felt our baby fully connect with me, adding her magic to mine. Our daughter.

Ophelia screeched in anger, her gaze moving from me to Ezekiel, who was pulling extra energy to share with me through our mating bond. I knew the moment she decided that to stop me she had to remove the one player from the board she wanted to possess with every beat of her heart. She'd tried to stop me and failed, so instead, she moved her attention to Ezekiel.

She wore her heart in her eyes as she stared at him for a moment too long.

The elemental storm tore through her body, accumulating destructive power as it passed through her and emerged from her hands. I closed my eyes and concentrated on that golden cord that connected her to Ezekiel.

May the great goddess protect us.

I leapt in front of the body of the man I loved, the force of her attack throwing me through the air and projecting me into the wall at the bottom of the room.

Ezekiel screamed my name, but I refused to let the pain that soared into me divert me from this one moment. The golden cord pulsed in my hands.

Lust was the deadly sin that was a corruption of the basic need to reproduce. The moment our daughter was conceived through our love, the curse on Ezekiel began to unravel. I summoned the power of my ancestors, the women who practiced the craft throughout time.

I call upon my guides and guardians, the ancestors whose footsteps I walk in…

Raw magic pulsed in my hands, my tattvas burning into the ethereal cord.

It throbbed and vibrated in my hand until cracks formed.

"Now!" I shouted.

Aunt Agatha and Addison controlled the force of the wyverns' song and turned it into an attack that ricocheted into Ophelia, sending her stumbling back several paces. Izzy flew from her hiding place in the chandelier, her talons dragging down Ophelia's back.

"Ilana." Ezekiel fell to his knees beside me. "Fuck, baby."

"Remiel," I gasped.

I felt Ezekiel's incubus thrall building beside me before rippling away. "That should keep him quiet."

Ezekiel dragged me against him, my head tucked under his chin.

Ophelia screeched in tormented rage, her anger radiating through the room in a terrifying embrace before silence descended.

"She's gone," Ezekiel whispered into my hair.

I sunk into his arms, allowing myself the luxury of his strength. Izzy nuzzled me with her snout, her tongue licking my face.

I closed my eyes and submitted to the darkness that was tempting me.

It was done.

Ezekiel was free.

***

Chapter Forty-Six

Ezekiel

I was beyond fucked off. My emotions were sharper than they'd been in a long time, the constant pressure inside me finally gone.

She'd achieved the impossible. Ilana had broken Ophelia's curse.

I'd sacrificed myself for Ilana, nearly dying—only, she'd saved me. Our baby changed our future and reversed the effects of Ophelia's curse. Tonight, Ilana sacrificed herself to save me, dragging the curse from me.

The Blood Queen had taken my wayward brother with her. She was welcome to the traitor. His fate had been sealed the moment I saw the pictures of him and Ophelia together in the folder from the base. He was never walking back into our castle alive. She'd prevented me committing the sin of fratricide.

We were sitting in my suite, Ilana sleeping against my chest. I didn't care how many times Agatha assured me she was fine. Until she opened those green eyes, I was going to panic. She was hurt and exhausted, no one knowing what a baby derived from a witch-vampire hybrid and incubus would do to the mother.

Our story had never been one of rainbows and laughter. We met in the middle of war and fell in love without realising what that actually meant. The fact that Agatha deliberately sent us to the Earth realm with the hope I'd impregnate Ilana blew my mind. She might not have conceived in a month.

"Seriously?" Agatha taunted me. "You two were probably at it like horny bunny rabbits from the minute you realised Ophelia's curse didn't extend to there."

I glared at her. "And if she didn't get pregnant?" I demanded.

Agatha shrugged. “It was the only chance I could see in the crystals to break the curse. There had to be an unknown factor that Ophelia couldn’t account for. Incubus babies are notorious for linking to their father during pregnancy. Vampire babies need their father’s blood. It would draw both of you together no matter what was happening. Throw in the blood from Ilana’s strong magical lineage and you have an enchantment more powerful than a curse.”

Addison’s brow furrowed. “How does that affect the others?” She nodded to where Raegel, Valek, and Lycidas sat watching storm Agatha.

“We will have to evaluate each curse separately,” Agatha replied.

“Do we all have to get a witch pregnant?” Valek asked.

“No.” Agatha shook her head. “Each curse is different. We will have to determine what Ophelia infused into each of you. We took a chance she would come for Ezekiel before he could feed on the equinox. She wanted him weak and hungry.”

My attention flew to the other princes she’d cursed.

“She never wanted us in the same way she wanted you,” Lycidas replied to my unasked question. “She demanded power from us, but she wanted your willing body.”

A shudder rippled down my back. Thoughts of her touching me in my dream state taunted me. Ilana’s grip on my shirt tightened and I stroked her hair to calm her. I couldn’t imagine being with anyone else but Ilana.

Thank fuck it would never happen again.

“She really is a sick bitch,” Lycidas barked out. “Someone needs to buy her a phallus so she can go fuck herself.”

“What about Remiel?” Gabriel asked.

A grin twitched my lips. “Just before she took him, I hit him with an energy blast. If she’s been using Remiel as a lover, he’s just become redundant. Remiel is currently impotent."

Lycidas threw his head back and laughed. "Bad luck, Ophelia. He always was a useless prick."

Ilana roused in my arms, her huge green eyes blinking several times. "What did I miss?"

"Not as much as I did, considering you got your memories back a few days ago," I scolded her.

She smiled a tired smile before yawning. "Couldn't risk Ophelia sensing your emotions." Ilana kissed my neck and settled herself on me again.

My arms tightened around her protectively.

"How did you work out how to break the curse?" I asked Agatha.

Ilana answered, "Only a witch could break her spell, one directly involved in it. She cursed me when you fed from me. Only our baby intercepted what she took, I would never have gotten my memories back. Ophelia acquired memories and senses from those women because it allowed her to experience sexual release the same time as you. She never got to see my memories, because they were kept safe magically."

I took a shuddering breath, feeling violated all over again.

"Right," Agatha said, standing. "Everyone out. Ilana needs to rest. She was very ill without Ezekiel at the beginning. The baby needed its father and took from her to sustain itself. We're lucky they both survived."

Ilana was where she belonged now. If I needed to handcuff her to our bed, she was never leaving my side again.

When everyone left, I settled her in my bed. "You need to feed and build up your strength," I muttered as her hands moved up my chest.

Ilana wrapped herself around me, hauling me against her. "So do you."

I drew her mouth to my neck, my thumb coaxing her fangs out. A hiss escaped me when they pierced my flesh, sending a wave of pleasure throbbing through me with every tug of her lips on my throat.

"You've been donating your blood to me to keep me strong through all of this." Her lips kissed up my neck. "I couldn't keep anything down until Dad arrived home with your blood."

"Fuck, I've missed you." My lips met hers in a desperate embrace. We clung to each other and my heart beat wildly in my chest. I needed Ilana more than I needed air to breathe. She consumed me, igniting a fire deep in my soul.

I knew I had no right to ask, especially when she couldn't remember me at the time, but the image of her with those other men clawed at me. "What about the blood concubines?"

"You taught me the art of pretending, Ezekiel." Her hand cupped my cheek. "I suppressed them with magic and pretended to feed, releasing them to go to their rooms when we left the hall." Ilana reached up to press a kiss to my lips. "You know I can feed from no one but you."

Our hands were frantic as they got rid of the remainder of our clothes, and our eyes locked together as I pushed into her velvet warmth. She was tighter than I remembered because we'd spent over a month apart. I went to pull out, but her hands grabbed my ass, her legs clamping around mine. Ilana coaxed me deeper into her core until I was balls deep and completely intoxicated. We needed this connection to reassure ourselves that we were both safe.

Ilana and I lost ourselves in the give and take of our bodies moving to the rhythm of the ancient dance of life. Every thrust added to the energy, every moan or groan painted a new note into our melody. Our foreheads pressed together, our eyelashes tangling as we stared at each other.

A few hours ago, I wanted the pain to end. I'd even considered going to Ophelia and telling her that she'd won, as I couldn't take any more. Now, Ilana was back in my arms and the nightmare that had gripped me for six weeks was finally over.

Her body arched as she screamed, pleasure trickling down my spine and my balls tightening. Her fangs dug deep into my neck again, sending a shot of erotic pleasure directly to my dick. I growled as her energy flooded me, nourishing my body and soul.

I collapsed into the cradle of her body and felt the presence of my baby deep in her womb.

Our little miracle made my heart swell with love.

I never realised that you could love someone without ever meeting them. Now I knew differently. Our daughter was a culmination of our love for one another.

I stared into her wide green eyes. "I love you, Ilana. If you ever do anything like you did tonight again, I'm going to spank you and tie you to our bed. Understand?"

Her teeth sank into her bottom lip, her pupils dilating in desire. "Promise?"

"Absolutely. Now get that gorgeous ass in the air, I'm not finished with you yet."

Ilana wrapped her arms around my neck, her body clinging to mine. "I love you, Ezekiel." She nipped my bottom lip with her fangs. "I can't wait to be tied to our bed."

We were grinning so much we could barely kiss. I would never understand how I was lucky enough to find this goddess in the middle of a war. One fact remained true—I would never let her go.

I spent two hundred years hating magic, only to find a woman who wielded it was my redemption. Together, we would spend an eternity loving each other.

***

Epilogue

Ilana – ten years later

"Mom!" Our daughter flew in through the window of the castle on the back of a dark purple wyvern—Izzy's mate Ivan. He'd been rescued from Ophelia's castle at the end of the great battle. Iona was her father's daughter, throwing caution to the wind and living life at full speed. Ezekiel gave her everything her heart desired, spoiling her with affection and love.

Our firstborn child had her father's black hair and my green eyes. Every day she grew into her beauty. Ezekiel would be a nightmare the day she first took an interest in boys.

"Grandmamma is nearly here." Iona jumped from Ivan's back and raced across the room. Ezekiel had taken an entire wing of the castle for us when we were finally allowed back above ground after the great battle. Iona seemed to have developed an aversion to doors and tended to use the large windows designed for wyverns to perch on.

Our son stared at her for several moments from his book before rolling his eyes at her in a characteristic he'd adopted from his father. Eoghan was a miniature version of Ezekiel in every way, and no one would ever doubt his parentage. The first male witch ever born, he wielded the elements with a familiarity that required no tutelage. Mum declared him the dawn of a new era of magic in our world.

Ezekiel and I spent our time between Purgatory and the Earth realm, hence the reason I was currently waddling around heavily pregnant with our third child. He loved the sunlight after spending his life in this constant twilight. Iona and Ezekiel spent countless hours staring at the stars, while I recanted mythological stories of the constellations in the night sky.

Remiel never returned. There were some souls too dark to be redeemed. His was one of them, and Ezekiel would never have forgiven his treachery or the losses we suffered because of him.

The summer solstice ball was tonight, and this year it was hosted in the incubus realm. Mum and Dad were attending, along with some of the witch council. The other dark princes were already here, ready to celebrate the festivities with their mates.

"He's driving me in-fucking-sane," Ezekiel raged, stomping into the room, trailing his fingers through his hair.

"Language," Eoghan chirped from his seat. He was an old man in the body of an eight-year-old.

Ezekiel stared at our son for a heartbeat and rolled his eyes, mimicking Eoghan's expression from earlier.

"Who's upsetting you now?" I asked, wrapping my arms around his waist. I was too big to get close to him. I missed being able to see my toes, but I missed the way our bodies used to fit snuggly together more, my head under his chin.

"Raegel! Agatha is not the first woman to be pregnant in Purgatory. You'd think he invented something new. He is driving me crazy with his endless list of demands. What the f—." He glanced at Eoghan. "What is a pregnancy pillow? And why can a normal pillow not suffice?"

"Maybe I should be more demanding when carrying your children," I mused.

His hands spanned my stomach, a smirk dancing on his lips. For a man who'd managed to avoid fatherhood for over four hundred years, he revelled in it now.

"Love you." He pressed a soft kiss on my lips, tilting my head with his fingers.

I heard the protests from our children as they moved out of the room, complaining that no one else's parents acted like us. I didn't care.

"I can't hug you properly," I complained, my bump getting in the way.

Ezekiel spun me until my spine fitted along his tight stomach muscles, his arms holding me against him, his head on my shoulder.

"Hmmm," I sighed in contentment.

A tiny wyvern plodded down the hall with Iona behind it. Izzy and Ivan's three young lived in our wing of the castle, much to our daughter's delight. She carried them around like dolls.

New life blossomed around us after so much pain and death under Ophelia's reign.

Addison and Gabriel had two sets of twins, Ezekiel joking that my magic had put everyone into a breeding frenzy.

There was a new dragon in the dragonry, Magnus' son Marius. Eoghan and the small bundle of fire and temper bonded from the first time they met. I often found Marius asleep on Eoghan's bed. Ezekiel said Magnus used to do the same with him.

Every day I thanked the great goddess for the blessings in my life.

Ten years ago, I was a vampire who couldn't feed and was unable to endure a man's touch. Now, I was a witch, a wife, and a mother. Ezekiel changed my life the moment he pinned me against the wall by my throat. The fantasy was a pale reflection of the reality.

"What are you thinking?" Ezekiel whispered in my ear.

"I was just remembering the first time you pinned me against the wall. You told me that you knew exactly how to asphyxiate someone for pleasure."

"I still do." He kissed a trail down my neck.

Ezekiel's hand moved my head to give him access to my mouth. His kiss heated my soul, his lips soft yet bruising in their intensity.

“I love you,” I muttered.

“Love you more, baby.”

I closed my eyes and lost myself in his embrace. It was the safest place in all the realms.

***

Curse of Darkness continues the adventures of the Dark Princes of Purgatory and is Raegel and Agatha's story.

https://geni.us/CurseOfDarkness

If you enjoyed Ezekiel and Ilana's story, please consider leaving a review, and keep in touch!

Website – www.crrobertson.com
Email – crrobertson-author@hotmail.com
Mailing List – https://geni.us/CRRobertsonmailinglist
Facebook Group - https://geni.us/RobertsonsOtherworld
BookBub - https://www.bookbub.com/authors/cr-robertson

Other Paranormal Romance series available by CR Robertson:

The Otherworld Chronicles

Elements of Flames is FREE to start reading today.

https://geni.us/ElementsFlames

The Gaian Otherworld

Dragons of Destiny starts the adventure.

https://geni.us/DESTINY

Printed in Great Britain
by Amazon